SANTA MONICA

SANTA MONICA

a novel

Cassidy Lucas

HARPER PERENNIAL

NEW YORK • LONDON • TORONTO • SYDNEY • NEW DELHI • AUCKLAND

HARPER PERENNIAL

HarperCollins books may be purchased for educational, business, or sales promotional use. For information, please email the Special Markets Department at SPsales@harpercollins.com.

FIRST EDITION

Designed by Jamie Lynn Kerner

Library of Congress Cataloging-in-Publication Data has been applied for.

ISBN 978-0-06-301844-0 (pbk.)

20 21 22 23 24   LSC   10 9 8 7 6 5 4 3 2 1

For Julia and Caeli

Populus felix in urbe felici
Translation: "Fortunate People in a Prosperous Land"

—SANTA MONICA CITY MOTTO,

APPEARED ON THE INLAY OF CITY HALL IN 1938

SANTA MONICA

SUNDAY, MARCH 24, 2019

PROLOGUE

LETICIA

HER BROTHER LAY ON THE GYM FLOOR. A STRETCHY BLUE BAND WRAPPED around his neck. The kind, Lettie knew, that the people who came here to exercise looped around their legs or arms when they hopped and squatted to music so loud it hurt Lettie's ears.

Her brother's skin was as pale as the marbled kitchen countertops Lettie wiped down, week after week, in the homes of wealthy Santa Monica families. With his face turned toward the wall of mirrors—sea-green eyes open; thick lashes unblinking—it seemed to Lettie that he was admiring himself.

She had often teased Zacarias, her half-white, half-Mexican, *delincuente* of a half-brother, about his love for his own reflection. *There he is*, she'd say, when she caught him staring at himself in the window of a car, in the door of a microwave, anywhere that offered him a view of his own handsome face and full head of wavy hair, the same coffee color as her own. *Your favorite person.*

"Zacarias," she whispered now, nudging his bare leg with the toe of her sneaker, making the muscles in his thigh jiggle. She swallowed a giggle—her brother loved to make jokes. Even out in public. A risk, Lettie knew, no brown-skinned man would take these days. But Zacarias lived as a white man, free from fear. Lettie was an illegal full-blooded Mexican; Zacarias a handsome mestizo, an American citizen thanks to his rich Floridian papa. They were both bastards but Zacarias wore the ultimate disguise, that of a white man with a perfect Southern California tan. All the doors, and borders, opened for him.

Lettie and Zacarias shared a mother, and the *accident*, which is what Zacarias insisted on calling the mistake he had made that almost killed Lettie's son, six-year-old Andres. It bound Zacarias to Lettie like a shared scar, raised and grizzled. She knew he felt guilt for it—the *accident*—why else would he spend so much time with Andres and Lettie, take them to Mass on Sundays, picnics afterward, to the grocery store, to Andres's endless doctor appointments? For which Zacarias paid. Since the accident, he'd begun giving Lettie money before she'd even asked him for it, little stacks of bills on his paydays, which Lettie stashed under a loose floorboard of her apartment. She knew it was shame that drove him to pay her, but she did not care. It was the least he could do.

"Game over, Zacarias," Lettie said, fighting a yawn. "Enough, *por favor*." She was too tired for childish play tonight.

But there was no Zacarias jumping to his feet and yelling *Surprise!*—always the joker, always the clown.

Louder: "Zack!" The American name he'd insisted she use, especially when they were around the rich white people who put food in Lettie's and Andres's mouths, roofs over their heads. The bosses who did not know her brother was a bastard with a Mexican mother.

"You stop this playing *right now*, Zacarias." Firmly—this is how her bosses spoke when they sent their spoiled children to a timeout. Many of these same rich white women stayed thin and hard by exercising at this gym. How amused they would be, Lettie thought, to see their handsome trainer—*Coach Zack*—acting so silly.

One of her brother's hands was stretched out, and just past his fingertips was that damn prayer book he carried everywhere, often tucking it in the waistband of his shorts when he lifted weights, that showoff—wanting the world to believe he was as pious as a monk. How many times had Lettie called his name—*Zacarias!*—before he lifted his face from the smudged pages, blinking at her, dazed. How he loved his lady saints. Almost as much, Lettie thought, as the many ladies he'd loved in the flesh.

She counted to ten, waiting to see his wide muscled chest fill with breath.

Nothing.

Something was wrong. A loosening spread low in her belly.

She knelt on the spongy floor of the gym and placed a hand on her brother's chest. Waited. Prayed his chest would rise and fall, just as she had the first night her Andres had returned from the hospital, after the *accident*. She had slept on the floor by her son's bed, startling herself awake to check he was breathing, thanking the Virgin when his tiny chest trembled like a baby bird's.

Lettie pounded on the place where she guessed her brother's heart might lie, using both her fists, begging him to breathe, wake up, rise, move. She shouted prayers to the saints he had loved. *Oh, Santa Teresita del Niño Jesús, por favor. Por favor! Please! Please!* How could they abandon him—abandon her—now?

Frantic, she rolled him onto his side. A puddle seeped out from his gym shorts. She smelled the stink. He had shit himself.

The cheeseburger she'd eaten at lunch rose in her stomach.

She made it to the bathroom just in time. She heaved long after her stomach was empty, losing control of her bladder. Her pant legs were heavy with warm piss.

So many messes to clean now.

Her own face in the bathroom mirror was pale like her brother's. As frightened as a child's. Reminding her of Andres, who, at that moment, was sound asleep in her car parked in front of Color Theory Fitness. Only a few steps away from where his beloved *Tío* Zacarias lay on the floor of the gym, the blue band looped around his neck.

Lettie knew what she had to do. There were no choices for people like her. No open doors. Only deportation. She had just three more days before the immigration police took her to the "facility," where she would be forced to stay until they shipped her back to

Mexico. Leaving Andres behind, without a mother. And now, without Zacarias. That Andres would still have his uncle had been Lettie's only consolation.

She ran to the gym's front door and bolted it. Pulled down the blackout shades that covered the storefront window. Locked the second door that led from the reception desk to the exercise studio.

She found the container of powdered bleach in the bucket of cleaning supplies she used to wipe away the sweat left on the foam mats, weights, and treadmills after all-day back-to-back classes. She tugged on the yellow gloves she wore to clean the gym toilets. The thick rubber refused to slide over her sweaty skin—she pulled until she felt the hairs on her arm rip away. She bent to her knees, sponge in hand, and cleaned. The sponge turned heavy. No matter how many times she wrung it out in the bathroom sink, the water that ran smelled foul.

Kneeling over Zacarias's body, gently wiping the spots where she'd touched him—his cold cheek, his unmoving chest—holding her breath so as not to smell his death, she thought of how sad the ladies her brother trained would be to see him like this. The many beautiful Santa Monica women who raced on the treadmills—so fast Lettie had often wondered what they imagined chasing them, as she waited, always waiting, for them to finish so she could wipe down the gray mats where they'd done sit-ups until they moaned. She knew pain was also a pleasure for these women whose lives seemed so free from suffering.

Her brother had sought out pain, too. She stopped herself from checking his sneaker for the stone he tucked in one shoe during his jogs. He'd proudly shown her the stupid rock once, as if she'd pat him on the back, congratulate him. These fools—the women, her employers, her half-brother who wasted his born luck and his pale skin, all the rich white people of Santa Monica—wasting their fortune. Failing to enjoy their good lives. Making problems out of the air.

Poof.

Her half-brother may have been a selfish fool, but he loved his nephew like a son. He would have done his best with Andres. And in the end, everything she, and Zacarias, had sacrificed, and the lies they had told, all to stop Lettie from being deported, was not enough. Not to save Lettie and Andres. Or Zacarias.

He was free from his burden now, lying there so still. The man who had, in life, never stopped moving—who'd grab Lettie and twirl her around her tiny apartment when a Tejano song came on the radio, drop to the ground and do push-ups until Andres grew bored with counting, throw a back flip on the beach to make Andres squeal and, Lettie thought, smiling now, her eyes turning wet, to steal looks from pretty girls.

There was no time for memories now. Only work. And work, as she'd told Andres again and again, was why she was here, in America. *My people*, she'd told her broken boy who would always walk with a limp, *we come to this country to work. So you can have everything you want.* A life like that of Zacarias. A life that is not all work but also some play. A life so comfortable Zacarias whined the few days a year the sun hid behind clouds. A life so free of problems that not getting a new car or an acting role in a hot dog commercial had felt like tragedy to him.

For Andres, Lettie understood, it was probably too late. He would not have the luxury of inventing his own problems, not with his limp and his scars and his endless pain from the *accident*. The thought made Lettie want to grab the blue band around her brother's neck and twist and tighten, make that beautiful face swollen and ugly, add more mess.

When the firemen had lifted the car off little Andres, the skin on his legs sheared away, his foot dangling from his ankle, Zacarias had looked right into Lettie's eyes and whispered, his voice strangled but certain: *It was an accident.* The same man who lay in front of her now, still at last, eyes open, soft curls like a halo.

Zack, *el ángel*.

A sob pushed its way up Lettie's throat.

There were no *accidents*. Only mistakes. And no matter how hard you tried to fix a mistake—scrub, bleach, polish—a stain remained. Always.

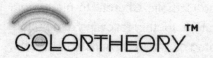

COLORTHEORY™

March 26, 2019 7:31am

TO: all@colortheorygymSM.com

FROM: jensen.davis@colortheorygymSM.com

Dearest Fit Fam,

As most of you have heard, a tragic event occurred at Color Theory Fitness, Santa Monica, on the evening of March 24. We lost our beloved coach, Zack Doheny. I'd be lying if I said I even had words for what happened. I don't. Like you, I am shocked. Like you, I am confused. I am grieving.

In his fourteen months working for CT, Zack had become like a nephew to me. If you had the fortune of training with him, I know he had a special place in your hearts, too. Zack let us get close—he was that kind of guy, the kind who let you IN. Who was not afraid to GO THERE.

The fact is, we never know what is going on inside another person.

I know this news hurts. Maybe more than anything you've felt before. But as Zack was fond of saying when he taught class: "Pain is beauty and vice versa."

Sometimes we have to push through the hurt to find out how tough we really are.

Zack Doheny was not only a dedicated, disciplined athlete and coach; he was also a spiritual man and committed member of the Roman Catholic Church. In his honor, please consider donating to the following charitable causes you can find listed on www.showupforzack.com.

While Zack's family has opted to keep funeral services private, I would like to propose a memorial to be held on June 30 on the bluffs at Palisades Park. A short, "Zack-themed" workout will be followed by an informal sharing of our best memories of our dear coach and friend.

Hope to see each and every one of you there.

With compassion and gratitude,

Jensen Davis

Owner & Founder, Color Theory Fitness

We are franchising!

PS: Due to the circumstances, and in compliance with routine police investigation, Color Theory Santa Monica will be closed until further notice. However, our Culver City, Marina del Rey, and Westwood locations will remain open as per usual.

FIVE MONTHS EARLIER

SATURDAY, OCTOBER 13, 2018

1

ZACK

SHORTLY AFTER DAWN ON A SATURDAY, ZACK DOHENY SNAPPED AWAKE IN an unfamiliar bedroom overlooking the western edge of Los Angeles. His naked body felt clammy with sweat beneath the crisp white duvet and his heart galloped as if he'd just surfaced from a nightmare, though he hadn't been dreaming at all. He sat up and blinked at the window, trying to work air into his lungs and steady his pulse while blotting his damp palms on the sheets.

Outside, he could see the mellow green peaks of the Santa Monica Mountains and, in the distance, a choppy gray swath of the Pacific Ocean shrouded in the morning marine layer. A multimillion-dollar view. Zack had been in LA long enough to know that a million dollars was not nearly enough to buy a house with a glimpse of the ocean. In Santa Monica, where he rented a one-bedroom on a grimy block of Pico Boulevard practically underneath the I-10 freeway, it was not enough to buy a house at all.

His fingers flew to the rosary at his throat and he was relieved to find it there, the delicate rosewood beads intact. The woman had gone at him with an animal fervor last night, clawing off his gym clothes and raking her nails into his scalp as she kissed him while sitting on the island of her gleaming kitchen, her lean muscled legs clamped around his waist.

How easily she might have ripped the beads from his neck, sent them skittering over the polished Mexican tiles of the kitchen floor, into the dark space beneath the stainless-steel double fridge. He could almost hear her careless laugh, see her slender hand cupping her puffy, glossed lips in mock-horror. So often in Los Angeles, Zack had learned, middle-aged women spoke and gestured like teenagers, stretching out their vowels and jabbing the air with painted nails, as if imitating their daughters could make them younger.

He rolled a bead of the rosary between his thumb and forefinger. It felt smooth and cool in contrast to the hot, thrumming pulse in his neck.

Exhaling slowly, he forced his eyes from the window to the opposite side of the bed.

The woman lay curled on her side facing him, gold-brown hair splayed across the pillow, her slender flank slowly rising and falling. Her ample breasts flared from the sheets, on full display. *Au naturel, my friend!* she'd said last night, pulling up her tank top in the middle of her luxury kitchen to show him, then doing a little striptease that had gotten him instantly hard. Soon he'd been cupping one *au naturel* in each hand, eyes fixed on the bare curve of her back as he pummeled into her. In the kitchen, and again in the garden, where huge succulents rose around them like green sea creatures, and later yet again here, on her massive bed.

Last night, Zack had not been able to get enough. Even after she'd fallen asleep, the acrid-sweet smell of pinot grigio wafting from her pores (as usual, Zack had not touched a drop—the sex itself supplied its own mind-altering effects), he'd found himself hard all over again and had jerked off beside her as she snored.

This was how his problem worked: a ravenous flame, followed by cold ash. *The typical pattern of any dependency,* he'd read in *Overcoming Sex Addiction*, which he'd skimmed in the library but had been too ashamed to check out. Zack gritted his teeth, wincing as the familiar feeling began to take hold inside him: a hollow, gut-scraping disgust that set in every time he slipped.

The disgust was not for the woman who'd brought him home last night—Joanna? Deanna?—he couldn't remember her name. It wasn't her fault. She was just a lonely divorcée out for a sunset run up and down the Stairs, the famous outdoor path that started on Adelaide Drive, where she lived in this big house, and dropped steeply down into Santa Monica Canyon. Zack had been on the Stairs too, a sharp rock wedged into one of his sneakers, one of his variations on daily penance. The pain helped him stay focused as he exercised, reminded him to push himself harder, toward the person he wanted to be.

But yesterday, the rock hadn't been enough. He'd nearly collided with the woman on one of the landings, accidentally, her cheeks flushed and ponytail swinging, and their awkward apologies had morphed into flirtation. Soon they were jogging together up the stairs and back onto Adelaide Drive, toward her house, the woman, who was probably in her mid-forties, giggling playfully. She'd asked him to give her a piggyback ride for the last half block of the walk to her giant house on a corner lot, and he had, her knees jammed into his ribs, her sculpted arms roped around his neck.

Zack steered his gaze back to the window, blinking, hard and fast, to stop the memory of last night from bearing down on him. It was a tactic he'd been using lately, blinking furiously to ward off unwanted thoughts, and found it actually helped. He wanted to forget all of it: the beachy smell of her skin, the slick feel of her thighs as she bounced on top of him, saying *goddamn* over and over, a word he hated so much it had made him want to shove her to the floor.

Except that he hadn't.

Blink blink.

Outside, sunlight was beginning to throw citrusy hues over the canyon.

Zack needed to get out of this house. *Now.* Before Joanna/Deanna woke up. He had a group workout to teach at nine A.M., in the backyard of another lavish Santa Monica home, this one just north of tony Montana Avenue, owned by a woman named Melissa Goldberg, whom Zack had never met. The event—a morning of "intense exercise and healthful delights"—was the brainchild of Zack's fitness client and sort-of business partner, Regina Wolfe. It was essentially a sales pitch for Zack's personal training services: he'd teach a free, invitation-only group workout to twenty women, each handselected by Regina (including the hostess, Melissa Goldberg) based on their levels of vanity and disposable income. After the workout, Regina reasoned, the women would feel so exhilarated, so high on endorphins and Zack's training methodology (he'd been told he had *a gift*), that they'd enroll, on the spot, in an individual eight-week training program with him.

Regina had named the program, which cost $5,000, Version Two You!

She and Zack would split the profits. It was a clean, fast, honest way to make money. Far preferable to their current business venture, which was fast, but far from honest or clean. Sometimes, when he forced himself to face the hard facts of the "solution" (Regina's word) he'd gotten involved in, he was shocked by the truth of it: that he was engaging in a crime that technically qualified as *felony embezzlement*, an offense punishable, according to the Wikipedia page he'd read with rising panic, by up to three years in a jail, plus a fine of around ten grand.

Regina never uttered any of the scary legal terms. No, when she'd pitched him the idea, one chilly night as they'd walked on the bluffs in Palisades Park, her arm managing to press against his, no matter how much distance Zack tried to keep between them, she'd made the plan sound like a minor administrative adjustment. Just a bit of temporary "shallow skimming," as she put it, off the top of the Color Theory gym franchise's vast reserves of corporate wealth. All Zack had to do, Regina had explained, was process a few of her phony invoices while he worked his usual part-time gig in the gym's back office—just a few keystrokes, a click of the mouse—and *ta-da!*, they'd have some of the extra cash each of them so desperately needed.

Of course they'd replace the money, Regina had assured him that night on the bluffs, her breath shooting in cottony puffs. It was a short-term solution. Imagine how good it would feel, she'd said, to take the pressure off, *just like that.* She'd snapped her fingers for emphasis, a sharp sound that nearly made him jump, and he'd heard himself say, *Okay. I'm in.*

That was five months ago. The "solution" no longer felt temporary. Now, both he and Regina wanted a change, to find projects that would allow them to sleep better at night and Version Two You!, if it worked, would be a step in the right direction.

Zack knew Regina would kill him if he was late. Most of the Santa Monica women he trained were type A. Regina was type A–plus.

He scanned the bedroom for his clothes; his gym shorts and dry-mesh T-shirt were nowhere. Only his red-and-black-plaid boxers lay crumpled on an armchair on the far side of the big room.

As quietly as possible, Zack eased off the bed and onto his feet. He took a small, cautious step in the direction of his boxers. The sheets rustled and the woman began to stir, stretching her bent arm over her head before turning away from him and resettling on her opposite side. Zack hopped off the bed to the armchair and snatched his underwear. He tugged them on and scanned the room for his possessions, but there was nothing on the gleaming dark wood floor or the brightly patterned area rug or the surfaces of the woman's expansive dresser, which was suspiciously free of clutter—surely the work of a housekeeper. Zack knew, from his half-sister Lettie, who cleaned houses all over Santa Monica, that wealthy women were the biggest slobs.

The woman was moving again, making mewling sounds, coming to life. Shit. He'd have to bolt and risk leaving behind something essential he'd have to return for later. He'd rather deal with that than speak to the woman now. On the balls of his feet, stepping lightly as possible, he hurried across the room to the door, holding his breath, asking God for the small favor of keeping the woman asleep, just for a few more minutes. He reached for the doorknob and turned it softly. As he crossed into the hallway, a light snapped on, and he recalled her telling him last night that since her husband had moved out, she'd had "smart lighting" installed all over the house. *You never know just how chickenshit you are until you live alone in four thousand square feet*, she'd said to him, her voice bitter-bright.

Zack had not mentioned that, actually, he lived alone in about four hundred square feet, and was perfectly aware of just how chickenshit he was. Instead, he'd jammed three fingers between the woman's taut thighs and caught her earlobe between his teeth, losing himself in her wet heat.

No. No. He blinked over and over, the smart light of the hallway stuttering in and out of his vision as he moved toward the staircase.

"Wait." The woman's voice reached him just as he'd set foot on the top step. His breath caught in his throat; he'd lingered a few critical seconds too long.

He stood still but did not answer.

"Zack. Come here." There was a command beneath her childish whine.

He turned and stepped back onto the landing. "I gotta run," he called to her. "I have an important class to teach."

He began to descend the stairs.

"Hey, you. Where do you think you're going?"

Zack turned to see the mystery woman standing above him at the top of the stairs. She was entirely naked, breasts fixed on him, hair wild over her shoulders. Her bare face, which he'd found pretty last night, now appeared unnaturally whittled by "work": too severe at the jawline, the skin over-smoothed with Botox, lips over-plumped by a needle. If Zack had to guess, he'd put her at forty-six. It was the older women he found hardest to resist.

"Sorry to bail." He gripped the banister, keeping his eyes away from her breasts, and summoned what he hoped was an apologetic smile. "It's just that I have to—"

"Zack," she purred. "Get back up here."

What could he do? Every muscle in his body resisting, he trudged back up the stairs, gripping the banister. On the landing, she stepped forward and wrapped her arms around his bare torso, sidling against him. He looped his arms around her in return, but loosely. The woman began to gyrate against him, her pointy hipbones driving into his crotch. Any other man—any *normal* man— would have instantly responded, Zack knew, would have lifted her off her feet and carried her back into the bedroom and consumed her body, which she was now offering him with gusto.

But he was not normal. He was a slimy, weak fuck.

If only he could pry her off and disappear. He pulled back slightly and caught sight of the thin gold necklace she wore around her neck, displaying the name *Arianna* in cursive. Arianna! At least he could use her name. Leave her with some modicum of respectfulness.

"Just come back to bed," Arianna murmured. "It's Saturday."

"I have to work."

"Call in sick. I'll make it worth your while." She slipped a hand into his boxers and pressed it against his dick. Her fingers were freezing. "I'm sore from last night," she whispered. "And I don't mean from running the stairs." She kissed his neck, just above his collarbone. "God, you're so hot."

He cleared his throat and, gently as he could, pulled her hand out of his underwear by the wrist. "Look. Arianna."

Her face snapped up toward his, crossed with anger.

"*Arianna?*" she hissed, releasing him from her grasp completely.

His body chilled with the knowledge of some unacceptable error.

"I'm sorry—" he fumbled.

"Arianna," she said, her delicate nostrils flaring. "Is my *fourteen-year-old daughter.*"

She crossed her slender arms over her breasts and narrowed her eyes at him, defiant, demanding a response. Zack turned and ran down the stairs, nearly howling with relief when he spotted his car keys on a sideboard by the front door, then burst out into the chilly, clean morning air, wearing nothing but boxers, barefoot and shaky, tears burning behind his eyes.

2

MEL

THE DOORBELL'S DIGITAL PULSE CAME JUST AS MELISSA GOLDBERG WAS losing a battle with her new leggings in the upstairs master bedroom of her five-bedroom Tudor on Georgina Avenue.

A year and a half into her new life in Santa Monica, Mel still hadn't grown accustomed to such a large space; back in Brooklyn, she and her husband, Adam, and their ten-year-old daughter, Sloane, had lived in an apartment so small they could practically hear each other breathing. A claustrophobic but happy home.

Now, three thousand miles and a spiritual galaxy away from Brooklyn, Mel's new house was so big, she'd joked to Adam that she could probably be murdered in one of the upstairs bedrooms, and no one downstairs would hear her screaming. *Don't let your mind go to such a morbid place*, Adam had responded, without cracking a smile. *It's not healthy.* This was the new, California Adam: earnest, health-obsessed, disciplined with a whiff of New-Agey judgment in his voice. Since they'd moved, he'd shed every ounce of fat on his body, and along with it, Mel thought, his sense of humor. Brooklyn Adam would have grinned at her murder joke and mentioned their excellent life insurance policy.

"Lettie!" Mel called out, breathlessly, in the direction of her bedroom door. "Sorry, but can you get the front door? I'm . . . busy with something." Mel bent over, wincing at the popping sound in her knees—she was only forty-two, wasn't it a little early for all the involuntary sounds her body had started to make?—and yanked at the waistband of the skintight Lycra pants stuck just below her dimpled knees.

The leggings did not budge.

The doorbell trilled again.

"Kill me now," Mel muttered. Then she called at a cheerful volume, "Lettie! Sorry, but are you able to get the door?"

Mel knew Leticia, her housekeeper-turned-friend (at least Mel hoped the feeling was mutual), was somewhere downstairs in Mel's large house, likely immersed in some ridiculous task assigned by Mel's friend, Regina Wolfe. This morning, Regina was hosting some sort of "fitness party" in Mel's yard, an arrangement Regina had proposed just days ago, after declaring her own backyard too small for the event. Mel had only a vague understanding of the nature and purpose of the party, beyond the fact that twenty women would soon be arriving for a "high-intensity workout" on her property, and she was expected to wear these evil leggings, currently gripping her legs like a boa constrictor.

The leggings were a gift from Regina, to thank Mel for hosting the event, which Regina was calling Version Two You! a name that made Mel cringe, though she'd complimented Regina on its cleverness. *It's good, right?* Regina had responded, with a knowing smile.

This was the obsession in Los Angeles, Mel had learned. Everyone, it seemed, no matter what their age or level of success, was on some quest for transformation. No one's Version One was good enough.

Even her own husband had joined the quest. Adam had once been an unknown indie filmmaker in Brooklyn who considered bodega coffee and a bagel a perfectly fine breakfast, and the five-block walk from their apartment to the F train "exercise." Then, two years ago, *Rewriting the Stars*, the low-budget feature he'd written and directed, became a sleeper megahit, earning over a hundred million at the box office and a Best Picture nomination from the Academy. Mel still had trouble believing that a single movie—a quirky time-travel romance that bounced between World War I and the near future—had changed their lives so profoundly. Adam had become an A-list Hollywood darling, one of the most sought-after film directors in the business. Once a man who hated to fly, Adam began to travel between New York and LA frequently, where studio execs clamored to take him to lunch, desperate to know what blockbuster ideas might be kicking around in his head. After nearly a year of "commuting" between the East and West coasts, Adam had convinced Mel to move to Los Angeles, luring her with the promise of an actual house (no more cramped apartments!) and real outdoor space (front *and* back yards!), instead of the one sad balcony she'd lined with mismatched flower pots in Brooklyn. No more winter!

Shortly after they'd moved, Adam, a man who hadn't stepped into a gym since college, became a person who "trained" at a jiujitsu academy four days a week, and ran frantically up and down steep flights of stairs at the beach. He'd renounced all "white foods"—no more toxic bagels!—and restricted his alcohol consumption to a single drink in "social settings only." He'd also adopted a new style involving shirts with whimsical patterns—hearts, skulls, horseshoes—purchased at boutiques in Venice, plus black-framed glasses and sneakers that belonged, Mel thought, on a high school skateboarder.

Where had her Adam gone—the same version who had practically worshipped Mel for almost two decades? A measly eighteen months in the California sunshine couldn't change that. Could it? Surely, beneath his newly chiseled muscles and condescending suggestions, he was still the sensitive, creative, evolved man she'd fallen in love with.

Wasn't he?

Lately, Adam's favorite topics of conversation, to Mel's annoyance, were how well he was eating and the stats reported by his Fitbit. Just that morning, he'd waved the lit-up strap in her face, triumphant over the news of his resting heart rate (Or was it his blood pressure? Mel's brain switched to *Off* when Adam assailed her with health-talk), and offered yet again to buy her a Fitbit, adding, *It's important to start watching these things. Positive role-modeling for Sloane.*

Thanks, but I can already see that I'm fat, Mel had replied, with false merriment. *No purchase necessary!*

Adam had sighed, tying his sneakers with a sharp yank to the laces. *All I'm saying is that you might want to consider a little more self-care—*

Before Adam could finish, she'd beelined into the bathroom and shut the door hard before starting to cry.

Mel missed her old life in Brooklyn, where she could hardly walk a few blocks in their artsy, bohemian neighborhood without bumping into someone she knew. There, she'd run a popular letterpress store-and-workspace, Dogwood Designs, known for its unique, handmade wedding invitations, greeting cards, and birth announcements. Her best friend from college, Jo, a curator at the Guggenheim, lived just a few subway stops away, in the shabby but artfully decorated brownstone Mel visited frequently for lethally strong coffee and interesting conversation.

In Brooklyn, where the Version One of Mel had felt like plenty, she and her friends had agreed that cresting forty felt like entering a new phase of self-acceptance, a time to settle into the person you'd already spent decades becoming. An era of new freedom.

Isn't it nice, Jo had mused, *to be old enough to stop giving so many fucks?*

Amen. Mel had nodded vigorously.

But Santa Monica had begun to erode Mel's middle-aged brio. First, there had been her failure to transplant her business to Santa Monica. Dogwood Designs West, despite its primo location on Montana Avenue, the city's swankiest retail street, never got off the ground. Three months after she'd opened, sales were nonexistent, the daily count of walk-in customers routinely in the single digits. Still Mel had continued to work alone in the empty store five days a week, in a state of disbelieving paralysis. Finally, at the end of the opt-out window on Mel's staggeringly expensive lease, she forfeited the space and shuttered Dogwood Designs West.

I forbid you to view this as a failure, Adam had coached her, his voice teeming with new LA-positivity. *It's just a different demographic here, babe. You couldn't have known.*

Maybe he was right. Perhaps Santa Monicans were incapable of appreciating Mel's work. Still, it didn't stop her from feeling like a failure. All people noticed about her in California, she'd declared weepily to her therapist, Janet, was the extra twenty-five (okay, thirty) pounds she carried, and her tendency to speak her mind. So what if she blurted out her opinions, unedited, or struck up debates with strangers? So what if she liked to "overshare," as Regina put it, her voice tinged with disapproval?

In Brooklyn, Mel had been considered interesting and out-spoken.

In LA, it seemed, she was just considered messy.

And that's how she'd begun to view herself: as a messy nobody. Invisible among the willowy women of Santa Monica who con-sumed bowls of kale with gusto, as if it were ice cream, and consid-ered Instagramming about "school campus beautification day" a valid form of volunteer work.

Help, Mel had moaned to Jo on the phone. *I'm surrounded by vain, malnourished thoroughbreds.*

Find something real to do, advised Jo, who was preparing to spend a year at the University of Nairobi, where she'd won a fellowship to study contemporary African painting. *You'll find your people.*

So, Mel had made a foray into *real* volunteer work. She'd joined an all-women's political canvassing group (WOMEN WHO WILL!) she'd seen on Facebook. The group was focused on electing a few up-and-coming young Democrats to Congress in the midterms, and Mel had set out on her first door-to-door assignment full of jittery excitement over the prospect of making even the smallest dent in

Trump's malignant regime. She'd been instructed to meet the other members of her "squad" at a Starbucks in their assigned neighborhood of Santa Clarita at "nine A.M. sharp" on a Monday morning, and had made sure to check the Waze app on her phone the night before, to learn that Santa Clarita was approximately thirty miles northeast of Santa Monica, and would require a reasonable forty-five-minute drive on the I-10 and I-405 freeways.

Buoyed with purpose, Mel had climbed into her Mini Cooper at eight A.M. on Monday morning ready to meet other smart, like-minded women who loathed the Big Cheeto and feared the demise of their country as much as she did. But when she entered her destination address into Waze the app informed her that her drive time to Santa Clarita was now *two hours and eighteen minutes.*

She'd texted her squad leader, a brisk woman named Wendy, apologizing profusely for her tardiness and asking if she could intercept the canvassers out in the field.

Wendy had replied by text: Welcome to LA traffic! Sorry you're having trouble, but we're on a really tight schedule and can't accommodate changes this late in the game. Hope to see you next time. Drive safe!

Humiliated, Mel had deleted herself from WOMEN WHO WILL on Facebook, and resolved to find another volunteer job, closer to home. Then she'd emailed the coach of Sloane's soccer team and offered to serve as team manager. Not exactly political activism, she knew, but Mel had read about the empowering impact of soccer on young girls, and frankly, the games had become her favorite part of the week. It was almost embarrassing how it thrilled her to hear the crowd cheer at top volume for Sloane, her little ankle-breaker, half the size and twice as fast as the other girls on the field.

Coach Crystal had emailed back immediately, granting Mel the job.

Okay, so she wasn't fighting to bring down the Big Cheeto. She would get to that, she swore to herself. Right after soccer season ended. After she'd figured out how to *be* in this too-happy, too-sunny place.

Mel gave her leggings another mighty tug, and finally they snapped into place, cinching her waist like a corset. A faint rapping came from downstairs. The person at the front door had switched to knocking. She suddenly remembered she had a "smart door" that synced with her phone, giving her a view on her screen of whomever was standing on the front steps, ostensibly for added security. Adam had insisted on the feature, which struck Mel as utterly ridiculous: what sort of intruder marched right up to the front door?

She grabbed her phone from the bureau, noticing Adam had already texted her a half-dozen pictures from Sloane's soccer game, which was currently happening at a park on the other side of town. Mel blanched with the guilt of missing the game (*So a bunch of rando ladies are more important than me, I guess?* Sloane had guilt-tripped Mel that morning) and tapped open the Ring app on her phone.

Standing beneath the stone archway of her front door was a tall man with wavy brown hair in a sleeveless gray T-shirt that read *Eat Pure, Train Filthy.* What did that *mean?* Mel wondered. His sunglasses and red baseball cap (Jesus, it wasn't one of *those* hats, was it?) obscured his face, but she could see the muscles in his long arms. They were . . . prominent.

She cleared her throat and tapped the *Talk* icon on her app.

"Hi! You must be here for the workout . . . um, thing. I'll be right down."

"Whoa, hey there!" he said. "I haven't gotten used to these robot doors." On her screen, she could see him grinning. His teeth were very white. "But yes, I'm Zack Doheny, here to coach your workout *thing.* Regina Wolfe told me to come to the front door and ask for Melissa. But I can just swing around to the back if you're busy."

"No, no," said Mel. "I'm . . . her. Melissa. Mel. I'll be right there."

"Take your time," said Zack. "I'm early."

Mel tossed her phone onto the bed, silently cursing Regina, feeling her heart rate skip up. Great. Now she had to make small talk with a fucking *personal trainer*, who was probably also an actor, and who would immediately disapprove of Mel's obvious lack of fitness.

She smoothed her black tank top over the skintight pants, straightened her glasses (*Maybe wear contacts for the actual workout?* Regina had said), and patted her fringe of dark bangs. The new leggings *were* sort of flattering, even if they were probably damaging her internal organs.

Her arms might resemble fat mackerels, but all in all, she didn't look terrible.

It was, as she'd heard Regina say, *go-time*.

Mel hurried out of her bedroom and down the polished red oak stairs. She speed-walked through the living room to the arched wooden doorway and pulled it open.

"Sorry to keep you waiting!" she blurted to Zack Doheny, who stood on her stone steps in the dappled morning sunshine, a large duffel bag on either side of him.

"Don't be sorry," said Zack, smiling down at her, floppy curls falling over his forehead. "I'm enjoying this gorgeous front yard."

"Okay, I'm . . . not sorry then," said Mel, fumbling. "And thank you." Zack removed his sunglasses and hung them on the neck of his T-shirt, so Mel could see the blue-green color of his eyes and the tan skin of his unlined face.

"So, it's Mel, right?" He extended a hand. Mel paused before taking it, conscious of her short, bitten-down nails, and the large diamond on her finger. "Lady of the house?"

"Um." Mel cringed. "I've never heard it put quite that way but, yes, I am, uh, *female*. And I do live here."

"I'm sticking with *lady of the house*. Old school." Zack grinned at her. His nose was straight and his chin square: a face of clean, strong angles. His features pure symmetry. He looked like a sample headshot, Mel thought.

"How charming." Mel said, making sure to sound thoroughly un-charmed. "So, you're the guy Regina brought here to torture us?"

"That's one way of looking at it. Ready for your best workout of the year?"

"Are you fucking kidding me?"

"Excuse me?"

"This will be my *only* workout of the year."

"Well, then, I'm honored." He reached down and picked up one duffel in each hand, holding eye contact with her.

"Don't be," said Mel.

"Too late." He smiled. "Not only am I honored, but I'm now making it my mission to *guarantee* you'll want to start taking my classes after today."

Mel felt her cheeks turn warm. Normally, the beautiful young creatures of Los Angeles barely registered with her: they were everywhere, floating through the city. They saw right through Mel, took no notice. She was irrelevant to them. Zack Doheny, however, seemed to be taking her *in*. Fully absorbing her with his sea-green eyes. Were colored contact lenses still a thing? she wondered.

He'd probably never seen someone so fat in Santa Monica, Mel decided.

"To be clear," she said. "I'm just doing a favor for Regina. She needed a backyard. I said she could use mine. I wasn't even planning to stick around for the 'event.' But then somehow"—she flung her hands upward—"Regina talked me into participating. And I'm not a . . ." She searched for the words. "A worker-outer. A work-outer. Or what the fuck *ever*. You get the idea."

"Hey, deep breath. No need to stress about a little circuit training. You're here. You showed up. Just relax and leave the rest to me, okay?"

"I didn't *show up*. I live here."

"Details," Zack said. "Keep an open mind. It's all I ask."

"You don't want my mind to open. I'm much more likable when it's closed."

"You're pretty likable so far," said Zack, "in an angry sort of way." He flashed his toothpaste-commercial smile.

Jesus, was he *flirting*? Mel reminded herself that fitness trainers/actors flirted with everyone; it was basically how they made a living.

"Well, you have about two dozen ultra-perky, non-angry women—I mean, *ladies*—waiting for you in the backyard." She spun on the heel of her brand-new sneaker back into the house. "Follow me."

"I'm not a huge fan of perky, actually," Zack called out behind her.

Sure, Mel thought. Still, she couldn't stop herself from smiling.

Inside, she led him past the stairs and through the kitchen, which gleamed with the steel appliances and marble countertops Adam loved so much (for years in Brooklyn, he'd been content with preparing gourmet meals on the mini-range of their tiny kitchen with the one burner that never worked; now, he acted as if the palatial kitchen were essential to his lifeblood), then into the den arranged with taut, geometric couches Mel had gingerly selected from a store on Montana Avenue.

God, why was getting rich so embarrassing?

Beside one of the sleek couches, on the floor, was a large cage made from black plastic gridding and colorful tubes. It was filled with shredded paper and, Mel knew, hamster shit.

"Sorry for the stench," she said quickly to Zack, as the manure-like scent hit her nostrils. "My husband brought some hamsters home and now refuses to clean the cage."

"Hamsters are great!" said Zack, a bit too cheerfully.

"Give me a break. They're rodents."

She hurried out of the smelly den and into the hallway that led to the back door, which was covered with family photos she'd spent a week selecting, framing, and hanging. "Hold on," Zack called from behind her. "I gotta take a look at some of these."

Mel sighed and turned around. Zack had turned his red base-ball cap backward and was studying the picture wall.

"Don't judge me for the jiu-jitsu photos. I had nothing to do with those. I'm a pacifist."

Recently, Adam had added a few photos of himself in full fighter mode to the wall, shots from a tournament he'd fought in last month. In one, he stood on a podium wearing a thick white *gi* and his brown belt, holding a trophy aloft. In another, he was shirtless and charging toward another man, wearing the expression of an attack-ing warrior, his delts and lats as defined as the glazed apple slices on the tarts Mel loved at Sweet Lady Jane on Montana Avenue, and then hated herself for eating.

"My husband Adam's obsessed with jiu-jitsu," she said to Zack. "I know what you're thinking. How can someone married to *me* be so fit? It's only happened since we moved to LA. It's like he caught a disease that makes him insanely healthy. While I'm still . . . you know. Brooklyn-ish." Instantly, her face tinged with heat.

"I wasn't thinking that at all. And I'm not sure what Brooklyn-ish is, but I'm pretty sure I like it."

"Um." Mel was confused; had he just complimented her looks? Surely, she'd misunderstood. "Thanks?"

Zack moved closer to a photo of Sloane in action on the field. "Your little soccer player's adorable. She looks like a firecracker."

"And then some," said Mel.

Finally, they reached the double-paneled doors at the back of the house and paused together, looking out at the clusters of leggy women in skintight workout gear like Mel's—except, she thought, any one of them could have been modeling the clothes for a catalogue. All over her yard, shiny ponytails bobbed in the sunshine. She spot-ted Lettie, holding an armful of towels and nodding at Regina, who appeared to be telling her something very urgent. Mel felt a wave of comfort at the sight of her housecleaner. Lettie was her only true ally here.

"You go on out," said Zack. "I'm going to hang back for a minute and review my routine one more time." He tapped a finger to his forehead.

"Ugh. I don't know if I can. It looks like some kind of sporty Miss Universe pageant is about to begin. Plus, the sun is brutal and it's not even noon. I hate sweating."

"You're wearing a lot of black," he said. "For someone who hates sweating."

"I'm a New Yorker. We wear black."

"And I'm from the swamplands of Florida. We don't wear shirts. But look"—he ran his hand down the front of his tank top with flourish, brushing his arm ever so slightly against hers—"I've adapted." Mel felt suddenly buzzy, as if she'd had too much caffeine.

"Maybe I don't want to adapt," she managed.

"So, don't adapt. But you got to get your sweat on. Sweat is the great equalizer. Makes everything else fall away. You'll see. Once I get everyone into the red zone—"

"Into the what?"

"Sorry. The red zone is what we call the top level of exertion, where you're maxing out your heart rate. When you're giving a workout absolutely everything you've got."

"Sounds horrendous," said Mel. "Like coronary arrest, but on purpose." She was becoming more fearful of the workout by the second, but somehow, also wanting to show him—this cute Millennial fitness coach she'd just met—that she could do it.

Zack laughed. "Seriously, though. The red is where the magic happens. When a bunch of people are in it together, all their petty shit—I mean, *stuff*—just dissolves."

"Please don't tell me you just corrected *shit* to *stuff* on my behalf. Because shit is my second favorite word. Next to fuck." She felt her face go hot. "I mean . . . I didn't mean—oh God, just kill me now. Self-control isn't my strong suit."

"I noticed," he said, and winked at her.

"Please don't tell me you just winked."

"Self-control can be learned, you know. Working out helps a ton with that. It's actually more about emotional discipline than physical."

Mel groaned. "Gee, thanks. But I think I'm familiar with the mind-body connection."

He laughed. "Okay, okay, I'm sorry. That was very coach-y of me. Anyway. Maybe you should just ease up on yourself a little? You're allowed to curse as much as you want. It's just that I'm personally trying to quit profanity. I'm Catholic." He cleared his throat. "Roman Catholic."

Mel tried to keep a straight face. "Are you serious?"

"Absolutely," he said, lifting a string of beads from under the neckline of his T-shirt. "See?"

"Is that a rosary? I thought you were just supposed to carry them. Like, in your pocket?"

Zack shrugged. "I feel closer to God if I keep it right here."

"You are going to hate my guts," said Mel. Then she forced a deep breath and pushed the door open, blinking as she stepped into the clear morning sunshine.

"I doubt that, darlin'," she heard him say as the door closed behind her.

3

REGINA

THE MORNING WAS HOT, EVEN FOR MID-OCTOBER, AND REGINA WOLFE felt twin pools of sweat gathering in the cups of her sports bra. She should have worn a lighter-weight top—she had exercise clothes for every season, in a wide array of styles and cuts, so many that she often hid new gym-wear from her husband, Gordon. Not that he'd notice. Probably, she thought, on days she was feeling more honest, she was hiding the stuff from *herself.* Normal people in Regina's financial situation did not purchase $200 leggings from Carbon38 or Sweaty Betty or any of the numerous "wellness boutiques" that showed up on her Instagram feed.

Then again, lately, Regina was beginning to feel she was not normal. Or at least, she'd begun to feel there was an abnormal discrepancy between the way she appeared to the unsuspecting eye—a fortyish (okay, forty-four) woman who could pass for thirty-seven (thirty-five, even, if she'd had a recent facial), living a life that most people would envy: a beautiful house situated a mile from the Pacific Ocean, and a beautiful family to match. Her own business that allowed her to set her own hours; friends who were generous with lending their desert houses in Palm Springs, lake houses in Tahoe, and ski lodges in Mammoth. Regina was in excellent health—five foot eight, one hundred and twenty pounds.

At a glance, how many women over forty wouldn't want to *be* Regina? Especially if they could see her at this very moment, standing in the middle of a lavish backyard, a quarter-acre lot so full of greenery you might forget you were, technically, in a city—giant white poppies, their paper-thin petals like parasols; fruit trees circled by knee-high lavender, and a stone wall draped in star jasmine. Its scent reminded Regina of buttered toast. She imagined her own family—she, Gordon, and their daughters, twelve-year-old Mia and almost-eleven Kaden—eating a Sunday breakfast at Mel's teak outdoor table, the pergola above with climbing purple wisteria and passionfruit blooms.

Plus, the Goldberg home had what Regina considered the most enviable amenity of all: a pool. Both of Regina's daughters were avid swimmers, with passes to the aquatic center at Santa Monica College. Regina had dangled the idea of a backyard pool to them a few years ago, when it seemed her marketing business, Big Rad Wolfe, was really going to explode, and they'd freaked out, giggling and squealing. Of course, Kaden had told Gordon that night at dinner—*Mom says we're getting a pool next year!* And Gordon had raised his eyebrows at Regina behind his glasses and said, "Oh?" in that noncommittal way that drove her crazy.

That was three years ago. The pool had not turned up.

It was *never* going to turn up.

Regina looked away from Mel's pool, toward the handsome rear façade of the house: one of many Tudors built in the 1920s revival to create an illusion of old money in nouveaux riches on the west side of Los Angeles. The steeply pitched roof and decorative timbers reminded Regina of a fairy-tale cottage, but ten times as grand. The diamond-paned lead windows looked so authentic she half expected Snow White to throw one open and greet the twenty women who'd shown up (thankfully) right at nine A.M. for the Version Two You! event she and her trainer, Zack Doheny, had organized. The women stood in small clusters, clad in spandex and sneakers, sipping kombucha from champagne flutes, bright and chirpy as jungle birds.

Some were Regina's friends, some total strangers who'd responded to her email and social media campaign, and all of them had the money to pay top dollar for Zack's personal training program. The crowd also seemed impressed by Mel's yard. The pool glinting in the morning sunshine. The garden beds circling the lush grass, resplendent with juniper and sage.

Today, Regina thought. *Today.*

Perhaps today would mark the beginning of a new chapter for her, and the end of the one in which she'd been miserably stuck for the past year, her anxiety increasing by the day, weight dropping from her already lean form, and her sleep—when it finally came—fitful and shallow. She'd never intended to let her financial arrangement with Zack stretch on for so long. Version Two You! was a step in the direction of putting it to a stop. Of replacing it with something respectable and aboveboard. A business endeavor they could be proud of. One that would allow her to get some goddamn sleep, without recurrent dreams of her daughters sobbing as a cop handcuffed Regina and escorted her into a cruiser.

Regina had been planning to host V2Y! in her own yard, which was a quarter the size of Mel's, but then she'd had a bad day—another IRS notice had turned up at her office, this one marked by the ominous bright green of certified mail: RESPONSE WITHIN THIRTY DAYS REQUIRED. Then Fernando, their gardener of ten years, had called to say her last check had bounced. She cursed him under her breath for not having Venmo or PayPal or anything that would have allowed her to squeeze his payment off a credit card. She'd told Fernando they were out of town, to take the week off, and that she'd pay him when they returned. Of course, they hadn't been out of town, and without Fernando, the yard looked too dry and unkempt to host the event. So, she'd roped Mel into hosting. Mel, a newish mom-friend from John Wayne Elementary, where Kaden, and Mel's daughter, Sloane, were in fifth grade together.

Now that Regina was actually in Mel's yard, the thought of using her own was embarrassing.

"Guess how much they spent on landscaping when they moved into this place?" Lindsey Leyner's throaty whisper filled Regina's ear.

Regina turned to face Lindsey, a fellow Color Theory devotee and John Wayne Elementary mom (Landon, also fifth grade) whom Regina had been working out with for years, and whose smarmy husband, Trey, had once patted Regina on the bottom at a PTA fund-raiser cookout—on school property! As usual, Lindsey wore her curly brunette hair in two low pigtails that bounced in corkscrews around her shoulders, and had painted her nails an aggressively bright color (this week, canary yellow); her standard workout look. Regina wanted to tell Lindsey to lose the pigtails, that a *nod* to youth was good, but a full embrace just made you look old and desperate. But they were gym-friends first and mom-friends second, and really not *friend-friends* at all, so she kept her mouth shut.

"I wouldn't have a clue how much Mel spends on anything," said Regina. "Nor do I care."

Lindsey slung her arm around Regina's shoulder. "Quick double selfie, 'kay? For posterity." Before Regina could protest, Lindsey shot out her arm and snapped a photo with paparazzi-like speed.

"Do *not* post that," said Regina. Lindsey was a relentless Instagrammer.

"Relax," said Lindsey. "I already did a story. Now I'm just documenting." She opened her arms toward the sky. "I mean, this *day*, this *house*, it's just epic, don't you think? I heard Melissa's husband personally pocketed ten million from his movie, which, by the way"—she lowered her voice confidentially—"I thought was just so-so."

"Awesome," said Regina flatly. Lindsey compulsively talked about money—estimating the cost of anything in her line of vision. The personal finance of others, Regina thought, was Lindsey's third-favorite hobby, right behind fitness and the endless regimen of cosmetic services she referred to as her "wellness routine" or "me-time."

"Come on," Lindsey said, "just give me a wild guess on the landscaping number."

"One hundred million dollars," said Regina.

"Ha!" Lindsey slapped the taut skin under her cropped T-shirt that read *Eat Pure, Train Filthy*. The sight of the phrase gave Regina an instant knot of dread in her stomach, and made Lindsey even more unbearable. Regina's firm, Big Rad Wolfe, had coined the slogan for Color Theory, a phrase that had triggered the biggest merchandise sales in the gym franchise's history. The tagline also represented a "before" period in Regina's life, when contracts like that one had seemed a smallish retainer to Regina at the time, around nine grand a month. How had she taken business like that for granted? Assumed the clients and contracts and hefty retainers, deposited into Big Rad Wolfe's coffers like clockwork, would just keep coming and coming, plentiful as the Santa Monica sunshine? That Regina could spend and lend and borrow money freely, saying yes to everything from custom-designed Halloween costumes for her kids to spring break on Kauai?

How had she allowed—no, *encouraged*—her husband, Gordon, to take a "sabbatical" from his TV writing work with its steady paychecks so that he could devote himself full time to the screenplay he'd always wanted to write?

Regina averted her eyes from the lettering on Lindsey's shirt.

"I'll give you my guess," said Lindsey, ignoring Regina's lack of enthusiasm and holding up six lacquered nails. "*This* many digits, starting with a three."

"Lindsey," said Regina coolly. "I'm here for a workout. Not a property appraisal. And for the record, I seriously doubt the Goldbergs spent three hundred grand on this yard. I think Mel did a lot of it herself, actually. She's plant-crazy."

"Bullshit," said Lindsey merrily. "You don't buy a three-point-eight-million-dollar house and then DIY the landscaping. I saw this property before they bought it and back here was like a dying *savanna*."

Lindsey worked as a Realtor, which, Regina supposed, was similar to working in finance, but required far less education and a fraction of the weekly hours. As a rule, Regina did not care for Realtors. They reminded her of mortgages, which reminded her of banks and foreclosures and her ever-multiplying debt, which gave her the same knot in her gut as the slogan on Lindsey's T-shirt. Sometimes, it seemed the world was conspiring to give her a panic attack with visual cues.

"Oh, hey." Lindsey pointed to the house. "There's your bestie." Regina turned to see Mel stepping out the back door, wearing the new gear Regina had given her that morning and an expression that was equal parts anxious and funereal.

"I've never seen Mel in workout clothes," Lindsey went on. "I didn't know she was into . . . physical activity."

"Back in a second," said Regina to Lindsey, though she had no intention of returning, and broke into a jog across the springy grass toward Mel, calling out *hellos* to the clusters of guests as she weaved around them.

"Hey, lady," she said, stopping short in front of Mel, who was holding a champagne glass at arm's length, as if it were poison. "Can you lose the frown? This is a party. Not a wake."

Mel sighed. "Please don't *lady* me. This isn't some *Sex and the City* reboot."

"Very funny," said Regina. "Can you please lighten up?"

"You sound like Adam," said Mel. "Next, you'll be telling me to *just breathe* and install a meditation app."

"It's not terrible advice."

Mel ignored her. "I cannot *believe* you talked me into this. I must have been drugged. I'm thirty pounds heavier than every woman here, minimum. I thought you said it was a party for people who wanted to get fit."

"I said *upgrade* their fitness level. And don't be ridiculous. You look amazing."

"Can someone please put a ban on women telling each other they look *amazing*? It's the world's most meaningless phrase. Next to *it's all good*, that is."

"Do you have to be so negative?"

"Yes, I do. You'd feel the same way if you had this many boob jobs in your own backyard."

"But they're tasteful boob jobs," said Regina, giggling. Snarky, neurotic Mel, with her yin-yang of brassy confidence and immobilizing self-doubt, was a refreshing change from Regina's usual friends. "This is Santa Monica. Not Beverly Hills."

Mel rolled her eyes. "Another page from the Book of Adam. He seems to think Santa Monica is some precious, authentic sanctuary, exempt from all LA bullshit."

"I wouldn't go that far," said Regina. "But he's not entirely wrong."

Mel, Regina had noticed, seemed to have a blind spot when it came to the nuances of Los Angeles. She simply lumped the entire sprawling urban metropolis into the contemptible category of *Not New York*. Her bitterness was hard for Regina to fathom: Mel got to live *here*, on this jaw-dropping property north of Montana Avenue, with her head-turningly handsome husband and adorable soccer-star daughter. What on earth did she have to be sour about? Regina herself had a number of major problems at the moment—many more than Mel, she was quite sure—and yet *she* was still managing to smile. Would it kill Mel to do the same?

Suddenly, as if reading Regina's thoughts, Mel's expression brightened. "Oh! There's Leticia. I have to go talk to her."

"Make it quick," said Regina, inwardly rolling her eyes at Mel's carefully accented pronunciation of Lettie's full name. "We're start-ing in two minutes."

"Okay!" said Mel, her mood shifted by the mere sight of Lettie. It was odd, Regina thought, that of all the things in Mel's life worth appreciating, their shared housekeeper seemed to make Mel hap-piest.

"Seriously, as soon as Zack walks out of the house, it's go-time."

"Understood, Sergeant," said Mel, with a mock-salute. Regina watched her hurry off in the direction of the large magnolia in the center of the yard, where Lettie was busily stacking mats and laying out the dumbbells, jump ropes, and rubber resistance bands to be used during the workout.

As if on cue, Zack stepped out of the house, wearing his highest-watt smile and the T-shirt Regina had designed, just snug enough to reveal a hint of his chest muscles. He looked exuberant yet relaxed; nothing on his tanned, smiling face betrayed any of the stress Re-gina knew he was under right now. Zack was the one, after all, who actually clicked the *Approve Deposit* button every week, while sitting in the back office of Color Theory, doing the part-time bookkeeping work that supplemented his measly pay as an instructor. All Regina had to do was wait for the money to appear in the corporate account of her own business. Which was plenty stressful, yes, but not quite the same as Zack's position. Sometimes, she felt guilty over letting him incur the bigger risk, but then again, *she* was the one with the husband and kids, plus a mortgage and endless other expenses, while Zack lived alone in a tiny rented apartment off Pico, so close to I-10 Regina imagined he could smell exhaust from his bedroom.

She'd never actually been to his place, of course, but she liked to think about it. Especially in bed at night, with Gordon's snores sawing through her earplugs.

Anyway, Zack had less to lose than she did. And he was profiting handsomely from the arrangement. It was okay, for now. But even-tually, someone would catch on. An eagle-eyed accountant combing the minutiae of Color Theory's profit-and-loss statements, or perhaps the gym's ultra-tanned, ultra-wealthy owner himself, Jensen Davis. Schemes like hers and Zack's, Regina knew, always had an expiration date. Even the infamous cafeteria ladies who'd skimmed mere cents off students' lunch money had gotten busted after a couple of years (she'd recently made the mistake of listening to a podcast about the scheme while stuck in traffic, causing her such anxiety she feared she might have a heart attack right there on the 405).

Today's party *needed* to work. The guests needed to fall in love with Zack, on the spot, and then pull out their checkbooks or tap the payment apps on their phones to secure more time with him. If he could just score five new clients from this group, it would mean a gross profit of forty grand. Sixteen of which would go into Regina's pocket. Not much, but enough to suspend their illicit transfers for a couple of weeks, give their consciences a break. Enough to give Regina the headspace to focus on what to do next.

As Zack moved through the yard, Regina watched the guests' heads swivel instinctively toward him; he had the sort of presence that emitted a charge. The mere sight of him always lifted Regina's spirits. Gave her a sense of possibility, an instant hit of happiness. It was silly, she knew, that a thirty-two-year-old kid with a red-state twang made her feel this way, but he did. She tried to catch his eye, but he'd broken into a loping jog toward the base of the magnolia tree, effortlessly swinging an equipment duffel bag in each hand.

"Hey, hey, happy Saturday!" he called out to the crowd. "It's time to ditch those drinks and congregate over here." He set the duffels down and beckoned toward the women. They shuffled into a semicircle around him under the tree. Regina hung toward the back of the group, keeping a clear sight line to Zack. She saw Mel walking toward her, eyes fixed on the grass, as if determined to shut out the scene around her.

"Now the real fun begins," Regina whispered cheerfully as Mel stopped beside her, appearing slightly winded from her walk across the yard.

"I really should've gotten stoned first," said Mel.

"Wait, *who's* getting stoned without me?" Lindsey Leyner installed herself on the other side of Regina.

"Nobody," said Regina curtly, and shot Mel a disapproving look. Was it really necessary to mention drugs just before the start of a workout?

Zack's voice rose over the crowd. "Howdy, and welcome to the first ever Version Two You! event! First off, I want to thank Melissa Goldberg for generously offering the use of her mind-blowing backyard. Shout out to Miz Mel, please!"

The crowd whooped and clapped.

Mel lifted her hand in a weak wave. Regina fought the urge to jab some enthusiasm into her.

Zack went on. "Second, I want to thank all of *you*"—he panned his hand toward the group—"for coming out here today to start your transformations. I'm honored to see such a great turnout. Hashtag *blessed*, right?"

"Kill me now," muttered Mel.

"*Shhhh*," said Regina, though she wished Zack wouldn't use that stupid phrase.

"Anyway, I'm Zack Doheny, certified personal torturer—I mean, *trainer*"—the crowd tittered weakly—"here to launch you into the fitness stratosphere. I'm going to push you to places you never thought possible—and then some. And you're going to thank me for it. My program, Version Two You!, is designed to transform your body—and, let's be honest—your *mind* too, because one is nothing without the other. All in just eight weeks! Regardless of your current fitness level, whether you work out five days a week or haven't worked out in five years."

"What if it's ten?" Mel whispered to Regina.

"I promise, if you stick with my program, you will see dramatic changes in your endurance, your strength, your muscle tone, and the overall topography of your body."

Regina heard Mel snort softly. She tried not to care. Regina had come up with that phrase for Zack—*topography of your body*—and she was proud of it.

"Today is designed to give you a preview of what you'd experience if you decide to commit to Version Two You! Of course, this is a group class, and the program is one-on-one, custom-tailored to every client's individual goals. But today you'll get a taste of my general methodology."

"Yum!" Lindsey called out. Regina elbowed her in the side.

"*Ouch*," Lindsey hissed.

"No catcalling," Regina hissed back.

"It's very simple," Zack went on, clasping his hands together in the center of his chest. Then, with dramatic flair, he lifted them into the air and tipped his face to the sky. Regina had to smile. She'd seen him do this in the classes he taught at Color Theory.

"You build it up!" he said, raising his voice to a cheerful war cry. "And thennnnn"—slowly, he began to lower his arms, hands in prayer position—"you bring it down. Translation: we spike your heart rates, we slow your heart rates. We burn out your muscles, we rest your muscles. All in the span of a few minutes. Then we repeat the cycle again. For one hour. Just one. Measly. Hour. Which, at first, will feel like a year. But not only will you adjust—you'll come back begging for more."

For the first time, Zack looked directly at Regina. His eyes locked with hers and gave her the feeling he was speaking to her privately. The familiar current zipped through her body, boosting her heart rate and shortening her breath. And the workout hadn't even begun.

"At the end of today's session, which we call *HIIT*, for High-Intensity Interval Training," Zack continued, "if you're still alive, that is—JOKING!—you'll have a limited time to register for my solo program at a one-time, heavily discounted rate. Just see that lovely senorita with the clipboard over there." He angled a hand toward Lettie, who, to Regina's annoyance, shrunk back at the recognition. "And she'll give you a simple form to fill out. It'll take just a few secs and you'll be on your way to a better you!"

Regina was proud of Zack. He was sailing through the introduction she'd coached him on. The lie she'd told Gordon ("last-minute client meeting") in order to get out of the house to rehearse with Zack had been worth it.

"Now, without further ado," said Zack, "let's get this party started."

"Dear God," Mel mumbled.

"No commentary," Regina whispered.

"Repeat after me, everyone," said Zack. He pressed his palms together again and lifted them into the air. "Build it up!"

"Build it up," repeated a few of the women.

"I can't hear you!" said Zack. "Let's try that again. Repeat after me. Build it up!"

"Build it up!" said the group, louder.

"Use your hands!" said Zack.

Regina clasped her hands together and began to raise them into the air. Mel hadn't moved her hands from her hips.

"Come *on*," said Regina.

"No way in hell," said Mel.

"Bring it down!" said the crowd.

"Better!" said Zack. "One more time."

"BUILD IT UP!" Now the women were screaming; nineteen pairs of prayer hands rose like shark fins toward the magnolia leaves.

"I LIKE IT!" yelled Zack. "BRING IT DOWN!"

Regina could hear Lindsey Leyner's screech above the other voices, rabid with excitement. She'd make sure Lettie brought the clipboard straight to Lindsey after the workout.

"I made a special playlist just for y'all!" said Zack, and Rihanna's "SOS" blared over the yard's invisible sound system. Regina smiled to herself, feeling her mood lift as her adrenaline began to pump. Zack knew Rihanna was her favorite way to begin a workout.

"Let's do this thing!" said Zack, beelining his gaze to Regina and giving her a wink so fast it was almost imperceptible. Instantly she felt strong and light. The most powerful woman in the yard. In all of Santa Monica.

"Down on the ground for mountain climbers!" said Zack. "Regina, show 'em how it's done."

He pointed at Regina and the yard full of highlighted heads turned to look at her. She dropped to a push-up position and began scurrying in place, thrusting her knee to her elbow and back again. Sweat sprang to her forehead and she yelled "YEAH!" into the blaring music, crawling in place, furiously, with impeccable form, as if her life depended on it.

4

LETICIA

"THE WOLFE IS READY TO ATTACK!" YELLED LETTIE'S HALF-BROTHER Zacarias, pointing toward Regina, who was bouncing from one foot to the other, lifting each knee so high it almost hit her chin. "That's what we call perfect form, people!"

From her spot at the edge of the exercise area in Miss Melissa's big yard, Lettie shifted the stack of towels she'd just spritzed with lavender oil from one arm to the other and watched Regina's lips pinch together to keep from smiling. This was the effect Lettie's dopey half-brother had on all the ladies he coached, though it seemed to Lettie that Regina fell for Zacarias's stupid flirting most of all. It made Lettie want to grab Regina—her first boss here in Santa Monica, the one who'd introduced her to all the *other* bosses Lettie now cleaned house for, many of whom were also here in this yard—by her pointy shoulder and tell her to STOP, that Zacarias was a man-whore who did not deserve her giggles.

"Forty mountain climbers!" Zacarias shouted. "Knees to elbows every time, GO!"

Lettie watched the twenty women drop to the ground, as if they'd been stung by a whip. Her *medio hermano*, she knew—delinquent as he was—had total control over these women, who in turn had total control over whether Lettie and her six-year-old son, Andres, starved.

"I *said*, knees to elbows, ladies!" Her brother wove through the rows of panting women. "I need to see contact or I'm gonna keep counting!"

"Slave driver!" called out Lindsey Leyner from the ground. Lettie would recognize her least-favorite boss's shrill voice anywhere. It followed her around every Tuesday when Lettie cleaned the Leyners' giant glass-and-steel house, reminding her to dust the tops of the ceiling fans, to use only baking soda and vinegar in the kitchen, to use scented detergent for her exercise clothes *only*.

Lindsey Leyner delighted in giving orders. Yet here, under the spell of Zacarias, Lettie saw, the whip-thin, loudmouthed woman wanted only to please him, to twist her body and strain her muscles any way he commanded.

Lettie envied Zacarias's power. And his luck—him born to a rich gringo American daddy while her father was some lazy Oaxacan *puto* who had vanished before she was born. Sure, Zacarias was a bastard like her, but his father, a real estate bossman in Florida, had, unlike almost every other piece-of-shit man (including Manuel, Andres's father), done the right thing and adopted Zacarias when he was a baby. He'd even paid Zacarias's mother, Gloria, enough to keep her liquor cabinet full and food on the table for her children: Lettie and the three others, each of whom Gloria made with a different man. Zack's white papa had also made Gloria sign a contract promising she'd never come after the boy, who would be raised like a prince in America. Not that Gloria would go to that much trouble for any of her children, Lettie knew.

In America, her half-brother was no longer *Zacarias* but *Zack*, and corrected Lettie angrily when she used his proper Mexican name.

She thought *Zack* sounded ugly, like a bad cough or a person choking on a chicken bone.

"Jumping jacks!" her brother boomed. "No one stops 'til I say stop!"

Before Andres's *accident*, as her brother called it, as if he weren't responsible, Lettie had been more agreeable about his nickname, but as the medical bills kept arriving, *PAST DUE* stamped across them in blood-red ink, and her brother failed to pay them off, she stopped calling him by his precious American name. *No favors for Senor Zack, nuh-uh.*

"One-minute breather!" he called to the women, quieting the music. "Not a second more!" This *breather* was Lettie's cue, Regina had instructed earlier, to offer the guests towels for wiping their sweat. Lettie hurried to the group and threaded her way through the rows of pink-faced women, handing each a flower-scented cloth.

"Thank *God*!" said Lindsey Leyner, snatching a towel, the giant diamond on her finger flashing in the sun. "I'm drenched."

"You're the *best*, Letts," said Regina, pressing a towel to her bright cheek.

Lettie was careful not to trip as she wove among the women's long legs and slender arms, sticking out in all directions as they stretched their muscles.

"Back at it!" said Zacarias, with an ear-piercing whistle. The loud music started again, and Lettie watched the women toss the towels she'd carefully sprayed and folded right onto the ground as they charged back into their exercise.

"Toy soldiers!" yelled Zacarias.

The women pumped their arms and kicked their legs high.

A hungry army, Lettie thought, *marching nowhere.*

She left the workout area to straighten the stacks of postcards on one of the tables by the back door of Melissa's house, relieved to be free of the women's wild dance.

It was a kind of torture they craved, the wealthy American women. They took pride in denying themselves basic comforts. Most of the women she worked for had banned one kind of food or another from their households. No meat. No wheat. No dairy. No sugar. No salt. No nuts (every Mexican cleaning lady knew the white moms were at war with peanuts). An endless list of no-no's that trapped

Lettie in a web of fear. What if she made a mistake when buying the long lists of groceries her bosses texted her, accidentally poisoning one of the families in her care?

What *were* these women punishing themselves for? Why did they insist on never-ending penance? Even the monks in Oaxaca, Lettie remembered her *abuela* telling her with a cackle, hid tamales in the folds of their brown robes to eat when they thought no one could see.

Zacarias had tried to explain it to Lettie, how by exercising themselves into pain, the women he trained became better people. *You should try it sometime*, he'd told her. *You'll be glad you did.* It was in these moments, when her half-brother spoke of exercise as if it were a type of magic, that she felt he would never understand her. That he did not care enough to try. That the only thing they had in common was their mother's blood.

His voice sailed across the yard. "You call those burpees? Because I sure don't! Come on, ladies—show me what you've really got!"

"Hell yeah!" screamed Lindsey Leyner. Lettie watched her least-favorite boss leap off the ground and fling her arms toward the sky, muscles jutting from her scrawny arms.

Zacarias had told Lettie how these women were strong enough to lift a small car. Twice as strong as their husbands. Did they have the strength, Lettie couldn't help wondering, to choke those men with their own hands? Lettie knew she had wanted to strangle Manuel, Andres's father, a few times—had even watched him sleep, drunk and snoring, her cheek where he'd punched her throbbing, wondering if her hands could fit around his thick neck.

Would *she* have been strong enough to do it?

"Let's hit those abs!" Zacarias shouted, slowing down the music. "Regina, show 'em how a plank is done. Sixty seconds starts . . . now!"

Lettie's first boss hovered over the soft green grass, her strong arms supporting her body without a tremble. If any woman could overpower their husband, it would be Regina, who seemed to be made of steel compared to Gordon, Regina's sweet and doughy husband.

"Thirty seconds to go, Reg. You got this," Zacarias said. "Don't clench your teeth."

Lettie imagined Regina instantly relaxing her jaw. She was a *teacher's pet*, as little Andres would say.

"Fifteen, fourteen, thirteen," Zacarias counted down. "Say it with me, ladies." The crowd chanted.

He'd done it, Lettie thought. Put them under his spell.

"Four, three, two . . ."

Lettie wanted to cover her ears. She'd heard enough. Instead, she forced a smile, reminding herself that Regina was paying her five hundred dollars to work this event—money Lettie would hand straight to Ms. Ochoa, her immigration lawyer. Whatever was left— if there was anything—would go to Andres's overdue medical bills. Just yesterday, Lettie had received the second notice demanding she pay her lawyer's bill in the next three weeks or lose her chance to have Ms. Ochoa fight for her in court. Without that money, she was certain to be deported, and what would come of Andres then?

"Aaaaaand—ONE!" yelled Zacarias. "Shout out for Regina, y'all, our planking queen!"

Regina hopped back to her feet and waved a fist in the air. The women cheered, and again, Lettie could see that Regina, who usually wore a face as serious as a nun, was happy.

"That's strength," Zacarias crowed. "The *real deal*. Now everyone. Do as the Wolfe just did. Plank position!"

The women dropped to the ground, imitating Regina. Lettie wanted to laugh: Did they know how silly they looked? Like the hyper, purebred dogs who jumped up on Lettie at many of her bosses' houses, desperate for attention.

She felt her phone vibrate in the back pocket of her jeans.

"Wind sprints!" Zacarias commanded, and when Regina shot toward the back of the yard, away from Lettie, Lettie plucked out her phone and glanced at the screen.

It was a message from Andres, sent from the phone of her *tía* Corrina—*ReeRee*, as Andres called her—who was watching him until Lettie finished work.

can I do screens, ReeRee say no.

Yes its OK love you, Lettie typed back, adding a kiss-blowing face before returning the phone to her pocket—quickly, so that Regina would not notice and wonder if Lettie was *really* working. A pang of missing Andres cut through Lettie's chest. She was away from her son so much—working, always working, leaving him in aftercare (which was free, thanks to some forms her favorite boss, Melissa, had filled out) at John Wayne Elementary until it closed at six P.M., or with Corrina in the garage Corrina's rich boss had fixed up for her to live in, or (when Lettie was desperate) at Zacarias's apartment.

Lettie had not always felt guilt when leaving Andres while she worked. It was why she had come to the United States in the first place, after all. To work and work, so her son would have a decent life. So he might have a chance at *not* working all the time. This goal had once guided her like a reassuring light, keeping her from feeling sad when she had to pry little Andres from her hip in order to go scrub some rich family's floors, or fold their mountains of laundry, or disinfect the stinky gray mats at the gym where Zacarias worked and had gotten her a night job cleaning—one of the few reasons she still had to appreciate him.

Then, she'd made the mistake that changed everything. That had changed *work* from the thing she was doing for Andres's future to the never-ending punishment for one stupid, thoughtless sin.

"Grab a partner!" commanded Zacarias. "Don't think about it, just pair up with the person next to you." Lettie watched the women clutch hands and link elbows, like girls in a schoolyard.

Her phone buzzed again, but now Lettie was afraid to check it; Regina was in clear view, hopping from one foot to the other while punching the air like it was her worst enemy. Next to Regina, Mel seemed to be barely moving, her face the color of a fever. (Was she *okay*? Lettie wondered.)

Lettie calculated the number of hours until she would pick Andres up from Corrina's; at least two hours to clean up after the party, then she had to stop by Color Theory to wipe down the exercise machines before driving an hour across the city to her aunt's apartment, where Andres would be waiting, restless and grumpy.

At least five hours until she was with her boy.

The guilt curled thick and stubborn in her gut, like bad food.

Nearly a year ago, around Thanksgiving, just before Andres's sixth birthday, Lettie had made a mistake—she would not let herself call it an *accident*. She had been caught taking three packs of Pokémon cards at Cosmic Cove Comics. Andres's classmates traded the cards at lunchtime, marveling over the make-believe creatures that were both cute and ugly, competing for the best collection. The animals reminded Lettie of her *abuela*'s stories about the half-man, half-animal beasts that roamed the desert at night. A warning, Lettie understood now, meant to keep children from wandering into the wasteland and dying from thirst and sun.

In the store, she'd slipped the cards into the buttery leather purse her boss Melissa had given her, so Andres could trade with the other boys—most of them white boys who Lettie knew had piles and boxes and crates of cards.

She'd only wanted Andres to be proud, to be able to impress the little gringo boys.

Still, how could she have been such a fool?

Seconds after Lettie had tucked the cards into Melissa's old purse, she'd felt the clamp of the store owner's hand on her shoulder.

And now, because she'd stolen eleven dollars' worth of cards with silly creatures on them, Andres might lose her—the only person who would sacrifice everything to keep him safe in this unforgiving country. Lettie's hearing was scheduled to take place in less than six months. Then, ICE would probably send her—an *illegal*—straight from the courtroom jail back to Mexico. As if her seven years of work here, on American soil, work that had kept her body sore, her hands calloused, counted for nothing. As if she did not deserve to call this place home. Santa Monica, a city named after a saint tucked beside a city named after angels—shouldn't it show her more mercy?

What was a home but a place where you are needed? And so, it was here, in Santa Monica, that she had found her home. These rich ladies needed her—much more than they needed Zacarias, a "real" American. Lettie was the one who carried their secrets on her back.

Who else but Lettie knew that Antoinette Wexler's bedside drawer contained not only a purple vibrator—no big deal, lots of her bosses had those—but also a stack of dirty magazines: women doing things to other women with bright pink tongues. That the giant bathroom of Lindsey Leyner (who hadn't given Lettie a raise in three years) had a secret cabinet stuffed with bottles of pills. That tall, thin former supermodel Sukie Reinhardt's toilet was often splattered with diarrhea from the laxatives she swallowed with her no-dairy, no-sugar frappuccino. Lettie knew which women had the starving kind of eating problem, and who had the throwing-up kind, who "froze" their fat off and who had a doctor vacuum it out from under their skin. Whose breasts were fake, and whose face had the most "work," a word she'd heard her bosses use with a winking kind of smile, never imagining this word, one that meant survival for Lettie and Andres, could have such a different meaning for her bosses.

"Feel the NEW YOU awakening!" Zacarias yelled from the yard, as the women lay on their backs with their legs curled up, hands clasped behind their heads, flexing their chests up and down. "This is *our* happy hour!"

It was Lettie, not Zacarias, who made these women's messes vanish—empty bottles of alcohol the color of gems, sheets stained with the seed of a man who was not their husband. She wiped their children's snotty noses, and, on occasion, their behinds. She had seen their teenagers' bad report cards, the balances of their credit cards, and the curse-filled texts they sent their husbands and ex-husbands and lovers and so-called BFFs. She had pulled nests of long blond hair from their clogged bathroom drains and found precious diamond earrings alongside vape pens under sofa cushions. She had comforted these women as they cried. About real problems—cheating husbands, miscarriages, bankruptcies. And make-believe—five pounds gained over the holidays, not receiving an invitation to their neighbor the movie producer's party. But was their need for Lettie big enough to make them help her when—*if* was no longer a possibility—she asked for money, a terrifying task that seemed more inevitable with every medical bill and court summons that arrived in the mail?

Finally, Zacarias released the women. "You did it! You rock! You're all a better YOU right now!"

The women's groans were replaced by laughter as they pushed sweaty strands of hair from their faces. They looked so happy now, their heads tilted up at Zacarias adoringly. Like flowers drinking in the sun.

"Towels, Lettie, more towels!" Regina called, then added, "Please!" as Lettie hurried to the patio.

She handed out the towels to one woman after another, each parroting, "Thank you, Lettie," in sugary voices. She was spinning inside the circle of women, all taller than she—a wall closing in. The women smelled clean, like oranges and fancy shampoo, even after all that sweating.

Lindsey Leyner stepped forward and snatched another towel from Lettie's arms.

"Thanks for all your help today," she purred. "You're the *best*."

That skinny bitch was acting like they'd never met. Lettie wanted to kick her least favorite boss in her no-cushion ass.

"Good exercising, Mrs. Leyner," she mumbled.

Arms emptied of towels, Lettie ducked out of the circle of women and back into the sunlight, where she spotted Regina by the refreshments table on the patio talking to Zacarias, flushed in the face and giggling like a schoolgirl. That brother of hers was as much of a slut as their mother. How many of the squawking birds in that backyard had Zacarias seduced? Not that Lettie cared. But she did care about Regina, who had opened the door to a new life for her and Andres. Regina, who frowned so often her forehead had a deep wrinkle. She'd told Lettie, proudly, that she refused to have the Botox shots. *To set a good example for my daughters.*

Regina had been the first to give Lettie work in Santa Monica. It was Regina who first noticed the bruises circling Lettie's upper arms; who had, in the middle of a spring night last year, answered Lettie's frantic call, picked up Lettie and Andres in her big fancy car, their belongings stuffed in black trash bags, and driven them to a motel, later insisting on loaning Lettie the money for a security deposit— all so she and Andres could leave Manuel and his cruel hands.

Lettie had yet to pay her back.

"*Where* is Lettie?" Regina called, and Lettie rushed across the yard to the patio, where her boss stood beside Zacarias.

"I am here," she said, tapping Regina's shoulder, panting a little from her short jog.

"Oh, thank God!" Regina said. "Can you help with all this? Clear everything away and fold down the table?" She motioned to the mess of lipstick-stained champagne glasses, protein bar wrappers, paper drink umbrellas, and orange rinds strewn across the tables Lettie had set up so carefully just hours ago.

"Yes, of course," said Lettie, reaching for a tray.

"Thanks for your assistance," Zacarias said to her, in the stiff, polite way Lettie knew was meant to suggest he'd never laid eyes on her in his life.

"Oh, I'm sorry!" said Regina. "Zack, this is Lettie. She's been helping me for years."

Helping, thought Lettie, as if bleaching toilet bowls was something she just happened to enjoy.

"Much appreciated." Her half-brother reached out a hand to Lettie. "I'm Zack."

Lettie stared at him. No way was she shaking his hand. They had agreed they would not even speak to each other out in the real world. The white world. His world.

"Lettie!" Regina exclaimed, closing her hand around Lettie's forearm. "What's up with you?" Then, to Zacarias, "She's really quite friendly, I swear."

"I've been known to make some women, well, speechless," Zack said. He winked at Lettie. *That dirty rooster*, Lettie imagined her *abuela* would say. "I think I've seen you before."

"Yes?" Lettie said, shifting into the I-don't-know-or-understand mode she used often in America, where it was safer to play dumb.

"Sure," Zack said. "Ah, I know, at the gym!" Maybe, Lettie thought, her brother wasn't as rotten an actor as she'd guessed. "Color Theory. You clean there."

"Yes," Lettie said when what she wanted to say was *No shit*. She wasn't at the gym to exercise. "I'm sorry. Bad memory."

"No worries." He flashed a smile.

Lettie knew his American parents must've spent a fortune on his teeth.

"Lettie's an absolute godsend," Regina went on. "This event could not have happened without her."

"I'm sure," Zacarias said. "But you masterminded the whole thing, Reg. And it was killer." He slid Regina a wink. As if, Lettie thought, he was an old-fashioned movie star—the hero in one of the westerns Manuel had watched on Saturdays before he stood in line on Colorado Avenue, hoping to be picked for garden work in the Valley, Orange County, places Lettie knew by name but had never visited. Now, with the ICE raids, she was more scared than ever to leave Santa Monica.

"No, no," Regina said, slapping at Zacarias's muscled chest, letting her hand rest there. "It was teamwork." She drew an invisible triangle between the three of them.

"If you can excuse me," said Lettie, "I'll do the table now."

"Thanks!" Regina said, and she and Zack returned to their chatter, so rapid Lettie could not make sense of it. She was invisible again, magically making messes disappear while the women relaxed in the sunny yard and nibbled little balls made of egg white and broccoli that Lettie had shaped with Regina at dawn that morning. As she cleared glasses and gathered soiled napkins for the trash, a new, biting anger at Zacarias seeped through her body. Why had he gone on in front of Regina about having recognized Lettie—was it some sort of joke? Later, would he claim they'd played the women like a herd of stupid cows—as if they'd been in it *together*?

She knew he was not to be trusted. And yet, she needed him: his money he gave her in drips and drops, never enough; and his love for Andres, which was so fierce she had to hope he would protect her son—if she was sent back to Mexico.

She folded up the newly stained tablecloth she'd steamed to perfection just hours before. Then she arranged the dirty champagne glasses onto two big trays.

When Zacarias had shown up in her Facebook messages, claiming to be her brother, asking to meet (*Family is family!*) she'd been sure it was a scam. She used the website only once every few months, to spy on ex-boyfriends and to check in on her mother, who posted fat-filled recipes and inappropriate joke photos, most involving short mustachioed men and big-breasted women. She'd opened a few suspicious messages from men, most in military uniform, asking How are you, gorgeous? And Want to chat? Not that she'd ever; especially now that she feared every strange man—the UPS driver, a new neighbor—was an immigration agent working undercover.

She had remained cautious, cold, in their first Facebook chats, even as her dropped-from-the-heavens brother's excitement had ballooned and he seemed more like a child waiting for Christmas gifts than a grown man begging her to meet in person.

She'd given in. Reluctantly sending him the address of the studio apartment she shared with Andres—Manuel having taken off weeks earlier after a fight that had ended with her on her knees, begging him to stop, fearing the neighbors would call the police. *Deportation*, she'd gurgled through a bloody lip. *Andres*. Both she and Manuel had uncles and cousins who'd been deported after arrests for domestic abuse.

When Zacarias had arrived at her front door, all doubts about their relationship flew away: he had her mother's angular face (much better on a man), all straight, clean lines, and Gloria's thick brown curls. Lettie had been embarrassed at the swell of pride she'd felt— she, a nobody with a plain brown face and thick body, was the sister of a man as handsome as one of the superheroes in the movies Andres loved.

Soon after, when she and her brother discovered they both worked for rich white people in Santa Monica, perhaps some of the same people (though only *his* job existed in the eyes of the law), Zacarias had said to Lettie, with little Andres snuggled in his lap, "It's probably best if we keep this situation on the down-low, then, yeah? Santa Monica's basically a small town."

She'd had to ask him what *down-low* meant.

His explanation stung. She didn't understand why he needed to keep her a secret—making her promise that, if they bumped into each other in public, they'd pretend not to know each other. Never mind that they were related by blood. And after the fuss he'd made about meeting Lettie. But he had seemed to think the agreement was important to their safety, or their incomes, or *something*—Lettie was not sure. Maybe it had to do with *el presidente* Trump? Or her brown skin?

"Let me help you, senorita," said Zacarias, appearing beside Lettie and lifting a half-empty tray of champagne glasses. He angled an elbow toward Melissa's big house. "Lead the way to the kitchen."

"I don't need help, but thank you," Lettie said politely. With so many of her bosses near, it was best to be on good behavior. She shouldn't have let her anger at Zacarias show, as she had in front of Regina. But it was like he was trying to poke her, test her, with that stupid comment about "recognizing" her from the gym.

That was Zacarias: always playing, always winding people around his finger. He did it to these ladies in the yard all the time, Lettie thought; they just didn't know it. He was never *really* on anyone's side but his own.

"Lead the way," her brother said again, his voice tight. Lettie understood he was giving an order. She had no choice. Saying no to Zacarias meant risking saying no to his money.

He stood holding the tray, muscles poking from his arms, staring down at her. The late-morning sun glowed around him like a stage light. Lettie noticed the blackberries floating in the brownish liquid at the bottom of the glasses; she'd taken extra care that morning, at Regina's instruction, to wash them with special fruit soap.

"Follow me," she said to Zacarias, and stepped toward the house.

"Wait, wait, *wait!*"

Lettie turned to see Melissa hurrying over—it was the fastest Lettie had seen her favorite boss move—and, then, Melissa tried to tug the tray from Zacarias's hands.

"Put that down, Zack! You're the guest of honor. Leticia can take care of cleanup."

Lettie tried not to feel offended by her favorite boss's suggestion. Or by how cheerful Melissa's voice sounded when she spoke to Lettie's idiot brother, like a little girl who'd just gotten a new toy.

"Didn't mean to break the rules," Zacarias said to Melissa, his voice back to warm honey. "I was raised to never let a lady carry something heavy."

"Leticia is a badass *woman*," Melissa said. "She can handle it. Don't insult her."

"I can see that," said Zacarias, a grin spreading over his face as he handed the platter to Lettie.

She could have sworn she hadn't *meant* to grab the platter and jerk it so the glasses toppled over, clattering together like chimes. Her arms seemed to move on their own.

Zacarias's pretty red-lipped mouth dropped open in shock as smelly brown liquid splashed over his tight shirt, soaking, Lettie hoped, right through to the skin of his hard belly.

"I am sorry, sir!" She forced herself to sound sorry. "My big apologies!"

"Oh no!" said Melissa, grabbing a towel and dabbing at Zack's wet shirt.

"Watch it, I'm ticklish," he said, stepping away.

"Sorry for the mess," Lettie repeated as Melissa swiped at Zacarias again and they both fell into laughter like dumb teenagers.

Do not fall for it, Miss Melissa, Lettie thought. Her favorite boss was much too good for her no-good whore of a brother.

"Come." Lettie had had enough of her half-brother for one day. She reached for his thick arm and gripped it hard, so he knew she meant business. He stopped laughing. "I take Senor Zack to the bathroom so he can clean up. And Miss Melissa can enjoy the rest of the party."

"Um, okay," Melissa said, sounding disappointed. "Thanks, Leticia!"

Lettie steered Zack through Mel's house to the kitchen, where the sink was lined with the hand-painted marigold tiles Melissa had been so excited to show Lettie (*Made in your beautiful Mexico!*), and where they were too far from the yard for anyone to hear.

"What's up, *Leticia*?" Zacarias leaned back on the counter.

"Why you make fun of me, Zack?" She spat his American name.

"What are you talking about? What'd I do?" He blinked fast, again and again, his green eyes flashing like a desert lizard.

"Stop that stupid wink-winking!"

"Enlighten me then. What's with the raging?"

"Pretending you know me from the gym! In front of Miss Regina. You think that's funny? You think I'm stupid?"

"How can you be so dense? The less these people"—he jerked his thumb toward the backyard—"know about us, the better. I was being *smart*, actually. Protecting us. You're the one who's happy to jeopardize everything we've built by acting rude and defiant right in front of these women."

He used big words when they fought, not caring if she could not understand. Trapping her in that in-between place of knowing and not knowing. Powerless.

"Built! Built what? I have nothing. Just a little bit of the money you promised. You swore on our ancestors' graves, *hermano*."

"Lettie." He raised a hand. Always trying to silence her. "You promised you'd be calm. 'Member when we talked about *playing it cool*? Keeping it on the *down-low*? That's all I'm asking here."

Always speaking to her like *she* was the child.

"I'll *play it cool* when you make good on your promises. When you give me the money."

"I'm giving you money, Lettie." His voice quieted and she heard shame inside it. "Almost every week. I'm trying. The gym doesn't pay big bucks, in case you're not aware."

"There are always other ways. Try harder. I have hospital bills up to here." Lettie raised her palm to her forehead. "If I don't pay, I get deported. Period." She made a slicing motion at her neck. "And then Andres has nothing."

Her brother's face softened at the mention of Andres, just as she'd known it would. This was the only part of her brother she could trust. His love for her son.

"When I am not safe, Andres is not safe. You get it?"

"I'll take care of it," he said.

"You take care of it, and then I'll *play it cool.*"

"Do you think I *want* to be here, doing this dog-and-pony show for a bunch of rich ladies already fitter than Jillian Michaels? Do you realize I'm here sweating my ass off today for *you?*"

"Jillian who?"

"You're clueless," he mumbled, rolling his blue-green eyes all the ladies loved.

"And you are a *player.*" She might not know English as well as him, might not understand all his big words, but she knew this expression was perfect for him. She dropped her voice to a whisper. "Play with your rich ladies all you like. But do not play with me, Zacarias."

He slammed a fist on the marble counter. The tray of empty glasses shuddered. It was too easy. One word—his birth name—and he transformed into *el ogre* from a fairy tale. It felt good to make him lose control. He was nothing more than a spoiled brat.

"I told you. Do *not* call me that."

"Oh, I so sorry, Senor Zack. Senor Americano." She fluttered her lashes, raised her hands in an *I don't speak English* apology. "You are so smart. So wise. I am just a stupid illegal."

He cut her off. His voice dangerous. Like Andres's father, Manuel, before he attacked. "Stop it, Lettie. Right now."

He reached for her arm—he was always touching, squeezing, pushing, it didn't matter if it was her or one of the rich ladies, if there was a woman nearby, Zacarias's hands were on her body. Lettie pulled back. Her elbow knocked into a glass. It shattered on the polished wood floor and Lettie was certain it was over, she was finished, she would open the tall oak front doors of Miss Melissa's house and find

ICE in combat gear ready to take her away. No good-bye hug for Andres. No last inhale of his peanut-butter-and-jelly little-boy scent.

"I'm sorry," she whispered, not sure what she was apologizing for now. Something much bigger than a broken glass.

"You're freaking me out, Lettie." Zacarias was on his knees, picking up pieces of glass with his fingers. "Ow, shit!" A bead of blood rose on his thumb. "Look," he sighed. "I'm doing the best I can. All *you* have to do is play it cool, like we discussed. Got it?"

"Play it cool," she repeated, looking down at him on his knees. She knew it was her place to pick up the glass but she was frozen, her back pushed against the marble counter.

"What's going on in here? Did something break?"

Melissa stood in the arched doorway of the kitchen.

"I break a glass," Lettie said. "I have bad day. Too many mistakes. So sorry, Miss Melissa."

"Just," Melissa sighed, "just go outside and see if anyone wants another drink. Okay?"

"Okay," Lettie said, her head ducked as she exited the kitchen, fighting the urge to lift her middle finger at her brother.

She stopped in the hallway and listened.

Lettie heard Mel say, "I'm so sorry, Zack. I mean . . . she *has* had a super-tough life. Her little son, the poor guy, has a serious disability."

Lettie's chest tightened. This was the truth but, still, she hated the pity soaking Melissa's voice.

Melissa continued, "And just imagine what life is like now, for women like her, with you-know-who in the Oval Office."

Zacarias cut Melissa off, his voice suddenly cold. Just as it had been when Lettie called him by his birth name.

"Maybe she's fine," he said. "You shouldn't *assume* you know what her life is like."

Lettie felt a tingling anticipation—Melissa was about to give him hell.

Instead, her boss's voice was gentle. Respectful.

"I appreciate you calling me out like that, Zack," Melissa said. "You're right. Thanks for teaching me something. I have the tendency to, well, overgeneralize."

Melissa did not sound like herself. Or at least not like the woman Lettie had spent hours talking with (mostly listening—Melissa loved to talk-talk-talk, just like Lettie and Zacarias's mother, Gloria) every Wednesday as Lettie cleaned the Goldberg home. How could Lettie have been so stupid to think a rich white woman could be a *friend*?

"It's all good," Zacarias said. "No worries." Lettie heard the wink-wink in his voice when he said, "But I'm guessing you probably hate those SoCal phrases."

Melissa giggled, girlish.

"I have a confession," Zacarias whispered. A lover's voice, Lettie thought. "I hate them, too."

"Well, then," Melissa said, "I guess we have something in common after all, don't we?"

As much as Lettie wanted to believe Melissa could be trusted (hadn't she called Lettie her *beautiful Mexican sister* once?), and believe all her bosses needed her, she knew she could never speak to them like Zacarias just had.

Lettie kept her spot in these women's lives by never saying no. She made every accommodation they asked. Used special cleaning supplies—a bottle of vinegar and nothing else so her hands smelled like salad dressing for days. She cooked vegetarian, vegan, gluten-free, dairy-free, all organic. She kept their secrets, even when one employer asked about another in a tone so sweet Lettie could tell they were fishing for gossip. She knew how easily these women could replace her with another desperate-to-please immigrant.

Lettie headed outside to begin the cleanup, the sound of the women's chatter a shrieking now that they were energized by their exercise.

One mistake, she thought, and she was out. Like a bag of garbage.

5

MEL

A THICK LAYER OF FOG HAD ROLLED IN FROM THE OCEAN, TURNING THE night air damp and sweet-smelling. *Like vanilla cookies*, Mel thought, inhaling deeply as she hurried up the front steps of her house, the smooth slate cool under her bare feet, a brown paper bag clutched in each of her hands.

The bags were filled with $500 worth of medicinal marijuana goodies the cannabis delivery guy had just handed her in exchange for the stack of crisp twenties Mel had swiped from Adam's dresser drawer stash. The second she'd clicked *Purchase* on Greenly.com, she could almost taste the first sweet hit—the pleasant burn in her lungs, the instant grounding calm that would spread from her head to her toes like a magic cloak. She'd *earned* this relief, goddammit: first she'd endured the V2Y! (cringe) party that morning, followed by an afternoon's worth of criticism from Adam. He'd returned from Sloane's soccer game an hour after the event ended, when Mel and Lettie were plucking the last stray cocktail umbrellas and crumpled napkins from the lawn, and immediately declared the backyard *trashed*. Mel had tried not to laugh as she watched Adam stoop over to examine a patch of slightly churned grass as if it were a dead body.

Trashed? Mel had said to Adam, when Lettie was out of earshot. *Give me a break.*

Then please give me the courtesy of respecting our property. That's all I'm asking. I'm glad you threw a party, babe, and got some exercise in. But keeping up this yard isn't cheap. Just be more mindful next time, okay? Then he'd veered over to the pool, grabbed the long-handled net, and fished out the postcards of Regina's that had blown into the bright blue water along with a couple of soaked hand towels, his face tight with disapproval.

Mel wished she'd had a glass of that putrid kombucha, just then, to toss in his face. There were few words she loathed more than *mindful*, which Santa Monicans constantly peppered throughout their sentences. Adam knew she hated it. So she'd answered him, in a tone that was admittedly snarkier than necessary, *Okay, got it. Right on, and namaste!*

Adam hadn't spoken to her for the rest of the day.

Then, a few hours ago, he'd softened, and texted her a shirtless pic of himself in bed, chiseled arms flexing. An invitation for makeup sex. Which Mel knew would smooth things over and make both of them feel better—at least until their next round of the same argument, anyway.

But tonight, she needed to get stoned more than she needed Adam's restored goodwill, or her orgasm that would accompany it. (Makeup sex was always their hottest—and since moving to California, they'd had plenty of it—Adam still wanted her, even if she was the fattest woman in town, still moaned with delight over her naked body and went down on her almost every time.) At the moment, she needed a break from his constant expressions of "concern," which, lately, felt more like expressions of his disappointment in her. So, she'd responded to his text: Sorry, I love you, but not tonight, and turned off her phone so she wouldn't have to see his wounded responses. She could already imagine them: I wish you'd find a way to be less angry was one of his favorites. As if he'd had no part in her anger. Or perhaps a variation on the one he'd sent her last week: Consider ditching the weed & getting more sleep. Health affects mood. Another reminder of her lack of discipline.

Since they'd moved west, he'd begun using that awful phrase more. *You've got to take care of yourself, Mel.* On the surface, it looked like a husband caring for his partner, but Mel knew Adam was a director in every aspect of his life, on and off the set. Too bad, she thought, remembering the svelte women exercising in her backyard that morning, he'd married the only woman in Santa Monica who lacked self-control.

She didn't want to think about the (kill me now) Version Two You! party. She must've been out of her mind to let Regina talk her into hosting twenty (twenty!) women for some cultish collective sweat-a-thon.

The only bright spot in Mel's day had been Zack, the sweet, handsome trainer with the *y'all* southern charm, even if his gung-ho energy reminded Mel of a car salesman. But, damn, those eyes—okay, and that *body*—had her forgiving him for even his "hashtag blessed" comment. More importantly, he seemed to forgive her for being more than just "out of shape." It was as if he hadn't noticed her blobby form among all those gazelles. She reminded herself that Zack was an aspiring actor, a fact she'd learned from Regina, who seemed to know a great deal about him. Could *they* be having a thing? Mel wondered. Was she the only woman in this town not having an affair? Regardless, Zack's warmth and sincerity toward Mel could not be trusted, no matter how authentic it had seemed.

Stop, she told herself. This was exactly the kind of overthinking that had Santa Monica women calling Mel *funny* and *interesting*, when what she knew they meant was crazy.

Mel shook the contents of the brown bags onto the Oriental rug in the den and began sorting through the childproof tubes of vape pen cartridges and pretty glass jars of red-haired bud. She smiled, thinking of how, in just a few weeks, Sloane would count her candy at the end of Halloween night on this same rug. She plugged in both rechargeable vape pens, retrieved a black Sharpie pen from the junk drawer next to the kitchen sink, and began her ritual of labeling each of the cartridges filled with the amber-toned oil that reminded her of honey. Labeling minimized her risk of, God forbid, smoking the wrong strain at the wrong time. *I* was for indica, which she used only before sleep; *S* for sativa and its heady highs; and *H* for the more mellow hybrid, perfect for public outings to the beach and park, and, occasionally, to help Mel endure a school talent show.

Labeling complete, she unwrapped one of the slender white pens containing a strain of Indica advertised on Greenly.com as *calming* and sucked on the tip. With each long inhale, the pen vibrated, causing her lips to tingle pleasantly. *Soon, soon,* she told herself, *you'll be CALM.* After a few generous hits, she opened *Tiny Sheep,* the virtual sheep farm game app on her iPhone, and began the satisfying routine of shearing her cartoon sheep—they came in all colors, including patterns of polka dots and snowflakes—and even pairing them, male and female, in a little heart-shaped mating hut where, if she was lucky, they'd copulate and add a baby sheep to the flock.

Normally, when she played the game stoned, it numbed her mind, blotting out any bothersome thoughts the weed had failed to erase. But now, the tiny sheep couples on her screen boomeranged Adam back into her thoughts. Since moving to Santa Monica, Mel had listened to women she hardly knew, especially the school moms, plus a handful of gay men, gush over Adam. *You're so lucky. Where'd you find him? Is he for real?* As if, Mel inferred, a woman like *her,* with saddlebags and frown lines, could not possibly have landed such a man without divine intervention.

Perhaps they were right. Perhaps Adam was too good for her, or Mel not good enough for him.

Twenty years? Mel's new mom-acquaintances gasped, when she revealed how long they'd been together. If Mel was feeling looseygoosey after too much wine, she'd add, "I was the hot one back then!" Haha. But this was the truth. She was a bona fide hottie when they'd met in college—a trim chain-smoking modern dancer in her perpetual all-black uniform of patterned stockings, miniskirt, and faux leather platform boots. All types of guys had wanted her, from muscled-up soccer players wearing headbands and Umbros to hip raver boys with tongue piercings and wide-legged pants.

Then she'd met Adam at the end of her senior year at RISD. Sweet and transparent film-guy Adam. What-you-see-is-what-you-get Adam. He seemed the very opposite of the guys she'd dated, aloof bad boys who had refused to call her "girlfriend," claiming they weren't into labels. Adam had wanted the whole world to know he and Mel were a couple—insisting on holding her hand as they walked across campus, a gesture Mel had, at first, recoiled from. Gentle, earnest Adam who wrote her cheesy love poems, sent flowers to her dorm room, and called sex "making love."

He was the man who had counted her contractions for three full days when she'd been in labor with Sloane. Who'd stayed up all night to help Mel finish her first big batch of wedding invitations soon after she'd opened the press, his ink-stained fingers Twilight-blue (Pantone number 19–3938) for days after. Who insisted he loved (loved!) performing oral. Who went to the women's march after Trump won the election, wearing a T-shirt announcing, *This Is What A Feminist Looks Like*.

Adam had given her everything she'd thought she wanted. A daughter whose spunk matched Mel's own. A house so large and decadent, Mel could hardly believe it was theirs. Enough money to hire a housecleaner—a luxury she'd never imagined. Her frugal parents would have been jaw-hung with judgment if they knew about Lettie, having instilled in Mel that housekeepers were for the rich and lazy.

Technically, she had time to do the cleaning herself, especially now that Dogwood Designs was, as the message on the letterpress website declared, *On Hiatus*. It sounded better than the truth, Mel thought.

She'd been excited to introduce her letterpress work to a brand-new city where disposable incomes were sky-high and people viewed putting on lavish events as a critical life skill. She'd rented a shockingly expensive storefront on Montana Avenue and put in fifteen-hour days decorating Dogwood Designs West to understated perfection, coordinating the opening with Sloane's first week of school at John Wayne Elementary. She'd imagined the comfort in introducing herself to the throngs of leggy, taut-skinned moms as the entrepreneur and artisan behind a buzzy new store on Santa Monica's trendiest street. Slipping the business cards she'd painstakingly designed into their manicured hands.

She'd actually forced herself to hand out the cards, feeling bumbling and awkward each time she introduced herself to yet another mom waiting outside the schoolyard, clad in a skintight "athleisure" outfit and space-age sneakers. Most of them cooed appreciatively and issued vague compliments in a language Mel had come to recognize as distinctly SoCal (no self-respecting fortysomething Brooklyn mom would say *Adore this!* or *Stop it, you are amazing!*), but none of them ever showed up at Dogwood Designs West.

Nor did practically anyone else. For three months, Mel sat in near-solitude at the shop, growing increasingly despondent while bleeding money (earned entirely by Adam) into rent and advertising and social media placement. She'd even gone to such humiliating extremes as creating a few fake Yelp accounts from which she posted glowing reviews of her own store.

Finally, at the end of ninety days, when the opt-out window Adam had wisely negotiated on the store's lease was up (Had he somehow foreseen the failure? Mel wondered. Could he simply have wanted her to have something to do in those first months in LA, so that she would have less time to fixate on missing Brooklyn?), he'd convinced Mel to close Dogwood Designs West.

I forbid you to view this as a failure, he'd coached her, his voice teeming with new LA-positivity. *It's just a different demographic here, babe. It turns out LA just isn't a letterpress-shop kind of town. Different aesthetic values. Maybe your work is just too subtle and classy. This is an opportunity to do something new, go fully online, talk to Etsy. Or just give yourself a break from work, now that we can afford it. Start getting some exercise . . . Get to know the city . . .*

On Hiatus, Mel knew now, described not only her business but her life in a nutshell since they'd moved to the West Coast. Melissa Goldberg, *on hiatus*. Melissa Goldberg, her career in limbo but, on the surface, living the perfect life on the dreamy north side of Santa Monica, where the public schools were as good as any of the privates they'd been considering for Sloane in New York. A neighborhood where silent electric cars with six-figure price tags glided through magnolia-lined streets, disappearing behind the heavily secured gates of bloated Spanish revivals, stark modernist monstrosities, Tuscan villas, or faux elegant Tudors like Mel's. Thanks to Adam, this was her life: ensconced in a massive house, surrounded by all the plants and flowers and trees (Six! She owned six trees!) she could only ever have dreamt about in Brooklyn.

So why was it all so lonely? Why did she feel she was constantly letting Adam down, falling short, annoying him, even though, by her own assessment, she was the exact same Mel she'd always been? Chubby and neurotic and messy had been just fine by Adam in Brooklyn. Because she was also creative and funny and smart. Which added up to the woman he'd fallen head-over-heels in love with.

Mel Version One.

So, it was Adam who'd changed. Wasn't it?

Suddenly, she missed him, a wave of guilt welling up in her chest. Perhaps she'd take him up on his offer in the morning, rouse him from sleep with makeup sex, maybe even squeeze into one of the many pieces of lacy lingerie he'd bought her. Show him she was sorry. He was, after all, she thought as the vape pen's vibration tickled her lips, as good as a man gets.

She was in the middle of shearing a fully grown virtual sheep when her phone died. Too lazy to find a charger and still too amped to go to bed, she tiptoed into the bedroom and slipped Adam's fully charged phone from his bedside table.

She watched him for a moment. He slept like a corpse. When they'd first started dating, there were moments when she had feared him dead. Had failed to stop herself from giving in to her paranoid obsession and shaking him awake. Back then, he hadn't minded. Found it endearing, even.

Now, she was quite certain he'd call her crazy.

Mel tiptoed back downstairs to the den and settled on the cool brown leather of the couch, Adam's phone in one hand, *CALM* vape pen in the other. She scrolled through the news—op-ed after op-ed on the Big Cheeto and the inevitable death of democracy.

Then she saw the texts.

First the words: UR like

Followed by: a tongue emoji, then a flame, a vibrating pink heart, and a lipstick kiss.

Then: I'm thinking about u & how hot ur right now. We're gonna do it again soon RIGHT!?!?

Then: If peach is the emoji for ass what do I use 4 cunt?

And finally: xoxoxox goodnight sexy (if ur still awake). U better delete this before we get in trouble lolz

Mel released the smoke with a sharp cough that sent her into a spasmed hacking. She coughed until her eyes teared, whispering, "What the fuck?"

The barely literate series of texts felt like a bastardization of the cute, private exchanges Mel and Adam had in the past. The lipstick kiss was *her* emoji—the one she often sent Adam mornings after they'd had sex. A cute reminder that she was thinking of him. To which he'd send the tongue emoji. And the other idiotic line, the question about emojis, the *c-word*—oh God. What *was* this?

Reality closed in around Mel like a toxic fog: someone who was not her—not by any stretch of the imagination—was sending Adam the cartoonish kisses and tongues.

Someone who assumed they'd *do it again* soon.

So not only had Adam already cheated at least once, but he was planning to do it again.

And with someone whose brain actually considered what the emoji for—

Mel's throat dropped and her stomach lurched; she was going to throw up.

She shot up from the couch and rushed to the guest bathroom down the hall, still clutching Adam's phone. She lifted the toilet seat and knelt on the cold tiles, bile roiling in her gut.

But she could not vomit.

She eased into a cross-legged position and looked at the messages again. It was from a 310 number she couldn't identify. Later, she'd reverse-search it on Google and cross-check it with the contacts in her own phone, and come up with nothing.

She sat on the bathroom floor, unable to stop reading the messages, over and over.

Five in a row. Time-stamped 12:42 A.M., as if sent in a drunken, late-night deluge of feeling.

Mel reached for the towel hanging on a silver bar above her. She pressed her face into the soft white cotton and sobbed into it.

She tried to banish images of the possible sender from her mind, but they flashed relentlessly behind her eyes: a pigtailed teenager in booty shorts, speed-texting between hits off her Juul, or a twenty-something actress in a slinky black dress, gyrating against Adam on the dance floor of a club, while Mel and Sloane slept in their over-sized bedrooms in Santa Monica, oblivious.

Finally, she sat up, took a screenshot of the texts and sent it to her own phone, making sure to erase the screenshot from Adam's. Breath ragged, she stood unsteadily, using the bathroom wall for support. Silently, she made her way down the hall and up the stairs to her bedroom, where Adam was still snoring, and returned his phone to the bedside table and plugged it into the charger, exactly the way she'd found it.

She climbed into bed, staying on the edge of the mattress, as far from Adam as possible. The combination of the weed and weeping had left her utterly exhausted, but she could not sleep.

First thing in the morning, Mel resolved to herself, she'd confront Adam about the disgusting texts. As soon as her eyes opened—if they ever closed—she would start talking.

She hoped she'd have the strength.

WHEN MEL WOKE in the morning, having finally drifted off around dawn, Adam was in the shower; even on Sundays, he woke early and dressed in perfect weekend jeans and designer T-shirt ensembles just to take Sloane to soccer practice. California had made him a meticulous groomer and he now had more products for his hair and skin than Mel, another bit of suspicious evidence she'd overlooked, apparently.

She checked his phone, which was still sitting on his bedside table, attached to the charger, just as she'd left it.

Except the texts had disappeared.

Nothing but squeaky-clean messages from his coworkers, jiu-jitsu buddies, soccer parents. Kiss emojis from Mel, pictures of Sloane.

No trace of the filthy messages Mel had read last night.

Adam had deleted them.

He was *definitely* cheating.

Mel felt ill all over. She curled around a pillow and squeezed her eyes shut.

"Mom?"

Mel opened her eyes to see Sloane standing in the bedroom doorway, dressed in her favorite pajamas—a large gray tee that reached her knees. *BALLER* in block letters arched over a giant soccer ball. "Are you *ever* gonna get up? This is like the third time I've come in to see you."

"I had a terrible night sleep, honey. I'm going to stay in bed so I can be fresh to take you for boba tea later."

"Fresh?" Sloane asked skeptically.

"Mmmph," was all Mel could manage.

"Can I have a Pop-Tart?"

"Um. Sure," said Mel, blinking in the bright morning light.

"Yesssss."

"Have a great day, Sloanie." It took every ounce of Mel's effort to make the sentence sound remotely normal.

"As if," said Sloane, and took off for the kitchen.

Mel curled onto her other side and pulled the comforter over her head, hating herself for being a terrible mother.

But, she reminded herself, it was only because she had a terrible husband. She commanded herself to get up—get up!—and march into the bathroom, and have it out with Adam, but found she could barely move. Barely *breathe*.

She'd have to wait until later to confront him, when her head was clear.

She pretended to sleep in until Adam left to drive Sloane to her marathon Sunday soccer practice. Only after they'd gone, leaving Mel alone in her perfect house, slouched beneath the twin streams of scalding water in her spa-style shower, did she allow herself to cry: big, shuddering sobs from the pit of her belly. She grabbed the fat at her midsection as she wept and leaned her head against the cool tile of the shower wall, trapped in the wobbly walls of her flesh. Hating her body, hating Adam, and wondering how she would possibly make it through the rest of her life, now that she knew the truth of it.

Mel had always believed Adam was too self-righteous to cheat on her. A comforting side effect of his moralistic attitude, a by-product of his perfectionism.

It was a joke she'd used often in their past twenty years of marriage. *Too bad you'd never let yourself cheat on me, haha.* The joke had gathered extra mileage in Santa Monica where, it seemed to Mel, the majority of couples they met were mid-divorce—usually a result of infidelity, the soon-to-be ex-wives confided to Mel. The women referred to their wealthy, soon-to-be ex-husbands as *sociopaths* with a teeth-clenching vehemence that disarmed Mel. As if there might be a conscience-less con man hiding behind the gorgeous hibiscus bushes lining the sidewalks of Georgina Avenue. Or, worse, she thought, hiding in plain sight in her matrimonial bed.

Adam's too sanctimonious to cheat, she'd actually said to someone recently, and laughed at her own joke.

Those beautiful, sad Santa Monica moms had warned Mel and she'd waved their caution away.

Not Adam.

He simply wouldn't.

And yet, clearly, he was.

SUNDAY, OCTOBER 14, 2018

6

REGINA

REGINA PULLED A THICK MITT OVER ONE HAND AND REACHED INTO THE oven where three pans steamed with golden rounds of hot cake. She transferred them to the cooling rack and paused to admire her work: the cakes had risen perfectly, borders retracted from the sides of the pan, surfaces lightly browned and crackled. While they cooled, she'd make the raspberry filling and coconut buttercream frosting that would complete her husband Gordon's birthday cake, which she planned to serve after lunch, when the girls had returned from their Saturday night sleepover. Later, the four of them would head down to the beach, with a soccer ball for the girls and a thermos of mimosas for Gordon and her. It would be a happy, mellow family Sunday, she hoped, the perfect low-key way to celebrate her husband's forty-sixth birthday.

If only Regina *felt* happy and mellow. She'd bolted awake at three A.M. with a speeding heart and clenched jaw. She'd tried all her standard strategies for getting back to sleep—deep breathing, reading on her Kindle, attempting to recall names of kids she'd known in elementary school, even meditating.

No matter how hard Regina tried to distract herself, her mind returned to money, numbers flashing in her mind like mean little stars, a pulsing clutter of impossible dollar amounts that she needed to pay *now*. The mortgage. The IRS bill. Their health insurance, supplied by Gordon's membership in the Writers Guild, had technically been due sixteen days ago, though Regina had learned you could push it to thirty before they canceled the policy. For the past few months, she'd been paying *on* the thirtieth day.

That was how they lived now: by the skin of their teeth. (In Kaden and Mia's case, extremely straight teeth for which the Wolfes still owed their orthodontist three grand.)

Plus, there was Mia's tuition. Gordon's car loan. Kaden's fucking musical theater class. Amex and Mastercard and Discover. The list went on and on. Every item due or overdue.

She'd reminded herself that relief was on the way. The V2Y! party had been a success. Everyone—with the exception of Mel, who'd never stopped sulking—had had a blast and left exhausted, exhilarated, and thoroughly charmed by Zack. Regina had only received two Venmo payments to secure a spot in Zack's private training program: one from Lindsey Leyner, naturally, and the other from Sukie Reinhardt, who likely was buying time with Zack for the sole purpose of making her husband, an attorney to the stars who'd had multiple affairs with multiple actresses, jealous. But whatever.

Two deposits from the twenty participants was less than Regina had anticipated, but a half-dozen more women had *promised* to sign up, just as soon as they'd talked to their husbands / checked their kids' schedules / put their gym memberships on hold / etcetera. Regina planned to call and remind each and every one of them tomorrow. Which also happened to be the day she'd instructed Zack to make their monthly transfer from the Color Theory account into the Big Rad Wolfe account.

Money is coming, she'd told herself at three A.M., curling and uncurling her body beneath the soft comforter, listening to Gordon's long, slow breaths—the sound of someone deep in a heavy, peaceful sleep.

She tried not to hate him. It wasn't his fault, she reminded herself. *She* was the one who'd encouraged him to forgo the steady income from the TV writing work he'd done since grad school (and had grown to hate), and instead devote himself to his long-sidelined passion project: a screenplay about the War of 1812. The topic sounded painfully boring to Regina, but Gordon's agent smelled a hit, declaring the idea *Hamilton* meets *Band of Brothers*, and had been encouraging Gordon to write the script for years.

And so, with Regina's blessing, he'd finally begun.

That was twenty months ago. Back then, Regina's Big Rad Wolfe had been netting over $50K a month, thanks to several new clients, including Color Theory, who'd put her on a six-month retainer to work on rebranding. Nearly ten grand a month to fiddle with their stale taglines, forgettable logo, and unfashionable merchandise. Plus, she had the blockchain start-up, the e-scooter company, the pet DNA analyzer . . . Big Rad Wolfe's client list went on and on.

Business had been booming. Regina had felt invincible.

Meanwhile, Gordon was miserable spending fourteen hours a day in the writers' room, slogging through yet another season of his spy show, *The Clue*, when suddenly, Regina had realized that she had the power to make him happy.

"You know what?" she'd said to Gordon, after another exhilarating workday. "Don't bother getting staffed next season. Why don't you finally take some time to write *Eighteen Twelve*? And sell it."

He'd looked up from his screen, blinking slowly behind his glasses.

"Are you serious?"

"I'm serious."

"Can we afford it?"

"Absolutely." The word felt so good leaving her throat.

At the time—in that moment—it had been true.

Regina had always been the one to handle the family finances. As far as Gordon knew, they were simple: mortgage and car and credit card payments on auto-pay every month, the total amount coming well under budget. They made more than they spent, much more. Every few months, he eyeballed their personal accounts, and what he saw upheld this notion.

Gordon never asked to look at the Big Rad Wolfe account. Nor did he look at the corporate tax filings, or the business Amex.

He simply trusted Regina. If she said her business was raking it in, and that they could afford for him to go income-less for a while, he accepted her statement as truth.

A year and a half ago, Regina had believed her own words. The money had certainly been there, in the form of multiple clients on healthy retainers. Sure, they were short-term contracts—usually a maximum of six months—but she'd just assumed the work would keep coming. That was how business worked, wasn't it? You got the momentum rolling, won the business, did great work, and won even more business.

That had not been the case. She'd gotten the momentum and the business, yes, but her clients were not always satisfied. The mistakes were fairly small, certainly not egregious, normal for a fledgling agency like Regina's: concepts that mirrored a competitor's too closely, images that tanked in focus groups, language that was inadvertently insensitive. (Regina cringed to think of the Facebook ad they'd run for an herbal sleep-aid company—*Wake Feeling Woke!*—that had ignited a storm of indignant criticism all over social media.)

Regina and her team had simply been moving too fast. The thrill of growth had trumped attention to detail.

She got some negative client feedback. The blockchain company demanded she refund 25 percent of her fees.

There had been the glitch with her corporate tax filing.

Then the electric scooter company had gone bankrupt and stopped paying their retainer.

And then she'd gotten some negative feedback on social media, and on Built in LA, an influential business website.

And then. And then.

Individually, each issue could be explained. If she'd clued Gordon in early, he might have understood. But she hadn't. She kept thinking she'd fix it. Turn it around. That the problems were just stumbles, typical small-business growing pains.

Instead, Big Rad Wolfe plunged into a freefall. Regina had never considered failure a possibility; she was a person who played to win. And now, here she was—failing her family, failing herself. Existing in a different universe from her other Santa Monica friends, whose money worries involved the value of their investment properties and strategies for legally concealing their assets.

She'd made sure Gordon remained clueless about their situation.

Regina had finally drifted off at five A.M., and this was when Zack had joined her in bed.

Her usual recurrent dream, and, it seemed, the only distraction these days powerful enough to shift her mind away from worrying.

When he arrived, she could not see him in the darkness, but recognized the particular weight of him as he lowered on top of her. Recognized the smooth, waxed skin of his muscular legs, the feel of his weight-lifting calluses running up and down her sides beneath her T-shirt. His lips at her ear, nipping her lobes, murmuring something she could not discern, his breath minty and warm.

Zack flipped her over, flattening her nose into the pillow, and circled her waist, just below the ribs. He lifted her hips and worked her underwear off, then moved his palms in slow circles over her ass, reached forward to cup her breasts, gently tweaking her nipples in the way she forbade Gordon; ever since breastfeeding the girls, she'd hated having her nipples touched.

But in her dreams, Regina wanted Zack to touch every part of her, to smother her with his body until she could hardly move or breathe, and then, in a single motion, when he could no longer help himself—

She jerked awake to the sound of her own voice, a cry half-stuck in her throat, and one hand jammed between her legs, fingers burrowed against the fabric of her underwear, which was still in place. Zack had left too soon. Her body felt hot and tight, her scalp damp with sweat. To wake without him felt cruel, almost tragic. Weak dawn light glowed behind the bedroom curtains.

Goddammit, she'd thought, her body humming with frustration—why had she woken already—*why?*

Beside her, Gordon shifted and sighed. She turned in bed to face him and suddenly animal desire took hold, a leftover force of her dream, and she found herself pushing her husband roughly from his side onto his back and rolling on top of him, where she worked her body against his to rouse him.

What? he'd muttered, in sleepy confusion. *Reg? What time is it? Give me just a . . . I'm sorry I'm just not quite awa—*

She'd come before he'd even gotten hard. He'd sighed and rolled over, falling instantly back to sleep. He probably wouldn't even remember it had happened.

Now, hours later in her quiet, sun-filled kitchen, Regina pulled a carton of heavy cream from the fridge and blushed at the memory. What if Gordon *did* remember? Their sex life had been so dormant lately, her sudden, aggressive desire for him might have actually registered in his permanently occupied mind; these days, if he wasn't working on his screenplay, he was thinking about it, dictating notes into his phone, scrawling in the margins of fat biographies of Andrew Jackson and James Madison. In fact, he treated *Eighteen Twelve* with such worshipful fixation, Regina had begun to think of the goddamn screenplay as his mistress. How long had it been since they'd done it? She ticked off the weeks in her mind as she ran scalding water over the mixing bowls and measuring cups she'd used for the cake, landing on four and a half weeks.

Over a month! Was that normal? Didn't men—*all* men, even long-married writers—want sex with their partners frequently? Wasn't it the women, like Regina, who were supposed to be rolling their eyes in their forties, complaining that their husbands were still horndogs, whereas they had moved on to more enlightened pursuits, like Iyengar yoga or intermittent fasting?

Once a week sounded normal to Regina. Not once a month.

It wasn't just the sex she missed, but the conversation, too. As recently as six months ago, they'd debriefed with wine on the couch nearly every night before curling up to watch a show. But gradually, as Regina's business problems escalated, and Gordon's dedication to his screenplay crossed into unhealthy obsession, they talked less and less.

Every relationship is a dance, she'd read in some pop-psychology book. *Between two active and accountable parties.*

The metaphor had stayed with her. She pictured herself break-dancing furiously, throwing flips and spinning on her head, while Gordon drifted in a slow waltz. Sometimes, when she was angriest, she fantasized about asking Gordon why he was willing to let her dance so much faster, so much harder. To utter exhaustion.

Then she remembered he had no idea she was exhausted. Regina had become a professional hider. Gordon knew nothing of the stress she was under, or the truth of their financials. Yes, he looked the other way. But Regina had trained him to do so. Which was worse: Gordon's willful cluelessness, or Regina's chronic lies of omission—how she withheld the truth in order to allow her husband to remain cozily in the dark?

Probably the latter, she thought. At the core, she was a much worse person than Gordon.

Today, though, she was going to be better. They would celebrate Gordon's birthday like the stable, comfortable, enviable family they used to be not long ago.

Regina shook flaked coconut into a bowl of softened butter.

"Do I smell my all-time-favorite cake?"

Gordon stood at the kitchen island, holding a stack of paper, smiling and blinking at her in the room's bright sunlight from behind smudged glasses. His hair was still mussed from last night's sleep and his Rustic Canyon Day School T-shirt had a coffee stain.

"Hey. I didn't even hear you walk in. Yep, that's the cake." *Stable, normal*, she reminded herself, moving around the island to slip her arms around him. "Happy birthday."

"Aw, thanks, hon. You're the best." Gordon pulled her tight against him. His body felt soft and burly. So different from Zack's. "What did I do to get a wife who bakes my favorite cake *and* tries to take advantage of me while I'm sleeping?" He nuzzled her neck. Apparently, he was in a good mood, which meant, Regina knew, that he'd had a good morning of writing.

"Just born lucky, I guess."

"Seriously," Gordon murmured in her ear. "What was going on with you this morning? You were so hot. Sorry I couldn't keep up."

"Um, I'm not sure. I just woke up, and—" Regina trailed off.

"Oh, hey!" Gordon released his grip and stepped back, grinning at her. "I almost forgot. I have a surprise."

"The suspense is killing me," she said, grateful for a topic change.

He produced an envelope from the back pocket of his jeans.

"It's my birthday present. To all of us. It's no fun if I don't get to celebrate with my whole family. I know I haven't exactly been in the mix lately because of the screenplay. I miss you guys. So . . . I got us this." He handed the envelope to Regina. "Open it. Happy birthday to *us*."

Inside the envelope was a folded piece of paper. She opened it slowly, feeling Gordon's anticipatory gaze. Her heart rate shifted gears.

It was a printed certificate. For an all-inclusive, seven-day "luxury cruise" to the Mexican Riviera in March.

"A cruise?" Regina blinked at him.

"A cruise!" said Gordon happily. "To Cabo! For the four of us. Over spring break. We haven't been to Mexico in ages. I know it's a splurge, but it's been so long since we've done anything really special like that together. And I picked spring break because I'll probably be done with *Eighteen* by then, and we can really relax."

Regina stared at the paper, unable to speak, trying to will away hot tears of disbelief.

"I know what you're thinking," said Gordon. "Cruises are cheesy.

Cruises are for fat midwesterners who want to lie in chaise lounges and stuff themselves at the buffet. Normally I agree with you. But not *this* cruise, Reg. It's high-end with gorgeous cabins and a whole wellness program and tons of healthy food options."

He wrapped his arms around her and lifted her off the kitchen floor. "You won't even have to miss a workout."

"High-end?" A shot of anger replaced Regina's oncoming tears. How had he even paid for this? Either Mastercard had granted them a serious favor or he'd sent their checking account into deep, deep overdraft. "How much did you spend on this cruise?"

Gordon lowered her to her feet, looking hurt. "It's my birthday present. What's it matter?"

"I'm sorry. It's just . . . I . . ." She trailed off. "Since you're not working, I thought we'd . . . scale back a little this year."

"We *have* scaled back. We didn't take a summer trip. The kids barely went to camp. You and I haven't been going on date nights. At a certain point, you have to prioritize things other than money."

Regina could not decide whether to laugh or scream. Gordon! Giving *her* advice about priorities. As if he ever prioritized anything other than himself and his goddamn screenplay. As if he ever thought about money.

For a moment, she thought about crumpling to the floor and telling him everything. Curling up so she wouldn't have to see the look of horror on his face as she confessed all the terrifying facts of their financial life, one after the other. The sum she owed the IRS. The fact that the house they were standing in right this minute, the house they'd bought and loved and renovated and raised their children in, could easily slip into foreclosure if Regina did not do financial backflips every single month.

Meaning: if she did not keep doing the *illegal* (she could barely think the word without a shiver of panic) thing she'd convinced her thirty-two-year-old trainer to do in the back office of their gym, all would be lost.

What if she simply told Gordon everything? What would happen?

She'd imagined this before, and the relief that might come after. After he'd exploded and cried and hated her and maybe even divorced her, and who knew what else. Took Mia and Kaden away from her? Their irresponsible, deceitful fuckup of a mother.

No. Of course, she could not tell him.

Regina gave the insides of her cheeks a hard bite. *Get it together, Reg.* Then she reached for Gordon's hand and used all her might to summon a smile.

"You know," she began. "You're right. We *are* due for a family trip. Sorry for the buzzkill on your birthday."

"No worries, hon," said Gordon. "I appreciate it, actually. You're just keeping us in line." He pulled her back into his arms. "Can we have a take-two of that thing you did earlier?" he whispered. "I've been thinking about it all morning."

"The frosting," Regina mumbled. "I still have to make the fr—" Despite her anxiety, she felt an unexpected current of desire move through her. She'd become so accustomed to Gordon ignoring her—padding upstairs to bed long after she'd fallen asleep, hardly looking up when she returned from school drop-off and the gym in the morning—that his sudden attention came as a surprise.

"The cake can wait. Come with me."

He took her by the hand. Numbly, Regina let him lead her up the stairs to their bedroom.

"Gordon—" she began, as he lowered her onto the bed. She told herself he did not deserve this. After four and a half weeks, he should not get to sail into the kitchen and whisk her back to the bedroom.

Still, it felt good to be wanted.

"You're so tense, baby," he whispered, lifting her shirt over her head. "Just relax." As the fabric briefly enveloped her head, Zack's face flashed to Regina's mind—a lit-up smile and green eyes peering through floppy hair.

A moan flew from her lips, and she gave herself over.

MONDAY, OCTOBER 15, 2018

7

ZACK

IT WAS ANOTHER GORGEOUS DAY IN SANTA MONICA, THE SKY GEMSTONE-blue and the temperature hovering close to eighty, despite winter being around the corner. Zack parked a few blocks from Color Theory and walked down Bay Street toward the ocean, pausing to glance up at the spindly, graceful palm trees stretching high above him. For a time, the sheer beauty of this place—the air that smelled of flowers and sea salt, the dazzling plants spilling from yard after yard, the views of the sun-sparked Pacific—had never failed to lift his spirits. Before his life had gotten so complicated, he'd been in love with Santa Monica. Florida seemed laughable by comparison, the equivalent of a crass, boozy ex-girlfriend.

Lately, though, his feelings toward Santa Monica had changed. The splendor of his surroundings was no longer a balm; in fact, it often seemed to be taunting him. Who could possibly have real problems, in a place like this?

Zack could.

Turning onto Main Street, he nearly collided with a trio of young women riding electric scooters on the sidewalk. They were dressed for the beach, long hair fluttering behind them. One carried a foam boogie board under her arm as she steered her scooter with one hand.

"*Excuse me*," said Zack. "Scooters are supposed to be ridden in the bike lane."

The woman with the boogie board braked and hopped off.

"Sorry! We totally didn't see you. We're just learning how to ride these things."

"Consider learning with helmets," said Zack.

"Haha. You sound like my dad. Oh my God, they're *so* fun though!"

"No need to bring God into it," said Zack, knowing how curmudgeonly he sounded, not caring. "Just pay attention."

"Sheesh, dude," the woman said, adjusting her giant sunglasses. "Someone woke up on the wrong side of the cabana. Wanna come chill at the beach with us? I bet it'll put you in a better mood." She flashed an inviting grin.

Her friend, a short-haired brunette in a tank top that read *Oh, hi*, pointed toward the large backpack she was wearing. "We've got supplies. Beers, chips, and guac. Weed."

For a short, hot beat, Zack imagined saying yes. He could almost feel the word pushing its way from his mouth, like a bitter drink he could not swallow. What if he did it: turned in the opposite direction of Color Theory and followed the girls with their beer and pot down to the ocean? What if he turned off his phone and never set foot in the gym again, simply stopped showing up to teach, never logged into the accounting system installed on the computer in the back office?

What if he never made another transfer to Regina?

Would his life really be any worse for it? Would he be at any more risk than he already was?

Then he thought of Andres, the two of them tossing a ball at the beach, his nephew's bad leg dragging behind him. A line from St. Thérèse flashed to his mind—*A soul in a state of grace has nothing to fear of demons*—and he felt himself moving past the girls, stepping around their scooters and long legs and backpacks stuffed with substances, not allowing himself to look at the willowy geometries of their bodies.

"Thanks for the invite, ladies," he said over his shoulder. "Unfortunately, I've got a pesky thing called *work*. Enjoy the beach."

"We'll be at lifeguard station twenty-six until sunset!" one of them called to his back.

Zack didn't bother answering. His fingers shot to the rosary around his neck, and he took several long, slow breaths, focusing *inward*, shutting out the girls, the bell-bright sound of their voices and the sheen of their golden skin. Pretending they didn't exist.

Yes, he thought, reaching the entrance of Color Theory and trying to stay calm as he gripped the metal door handle, running away at this point *would* make everything worse. His situation was, after all, about to improve. Forty-eight hours had passed since the Version Two You! event, and so far, Regina reported, they'd already received four deposits for Zack's personal training program. Never mind that one of the deposits came from Lindsey Leyner, whom Zack detested. Or that Melissa Goldberg was, as Regina claimed, *on the fence*. Mel was the one he'd been most hopeful about. He'd found himself thinking about her more than once since their conversation at V2Y! She had a certain dark edge about her, a barely contained storminess that Zack found interesting, as if she might say something outrageous or burst into tears at any moment. So different from the polished, breezy women he spent all day training.

He'd considered texting Mel, to encourage her to sign up—her number was right there, on the list of "hot prospects" Regina had emailed him—but what would he say?

It didn't matter who the clients were, he reminded himself. Four clients meant roughly nineteen grand for Zack; a life-changing amount. Enough to give Lettie what she needed *and* pay his own bills for a couple of months.

"'Sup, man?" Zack flashed a hang-ten sign to Davit at reception, a newly slim Persian dude who'd lost one hundred pounds following the Color Theory training method, then headed through the workout studio, empty until the next class started in two hours, to the cramped back office where he performed his accounting duties. Basic payables-and-receivables work, the stuff he'd learned in his first semester at Central Florida Community College. The gym's owner, Jensen Davis, paid Zack fourteen dollars an hour to move money in and out of the corporate bank account. The skills required for the work were basic—a detail-oriented eighth grader could probably do it, Zack thought—but the trust factor was considerable. And that was where Jensen had a blind spot: he had enormous faith in his own power, and mentally slotted Zack as a minion, just one of his dozens of coaches (Jensen owned five Color Theory franchises) lucky to have steady instructing work at a trendy gym. A peon so grateful for the sixty bucks an hour he earned per class that he'd never do anything to endanger his job. Zack had worked for Jensen long enough to conclude his boss believed Zack would never have the balls to cross him.

The same way, Zack supposed, that the wealthy women who employed Lettie left their diamond jewelry and cash lying around everywhere, in plain view. They assumed Lettie would never take such a risk.

These thoughts gave Zack courage.

In the office, he locked the door behind him, flipped on the light, closed the venetian blinds, and settled at the cheap IKEA desk in the center of the room. On the desk was a MacBook with a Color Theory logo sticker on its closed top.

Designed by Regina, Zack remembered, almost appreciating the irony.

He wiped his hands on his gym shorts and ran his tongue over his teeth.

Then he opened the laptop and typed in the passcode, whispering, as always, the Lord's Prayer—*Father in heaven, forgive us our debts, as we also have forgiven our debtors*—in sync with his keyboard taps as the pulse in his neck began to throb. His throat was dry so the prayer emerged raspy and strained. He swallowed hard and opened the accounting software.

Each time he did it was more nerve-racking than the last. He reminded himself that Jensen was in Denver for a conference at the moment; there was no need for panic. Jensen had made him a long string of unkempt promises: creating a head trainer role for Zack; starting a Color Theory YouTube channel featuring Zack; making him the manager of the newest franchise location, slated for Malibu.

For the past year, Jensen had been spouting this pie-in-the-sky bullshit at Zack. Endlessly promising to transform Zack's future while continuing to pay him peanuts for working his ass off in the studio, week after week, hustling for his pathetic three bucks a head at five thirty in the morning, while Jensen snoozed in his massive Palisades compound, lifted weights in his private home gym, or swam in his own lap pool, which he was forever inviting Zack to "come check out"—as if Zack had time for such leisure activity.

Don't you see? Regina had told Zack, wringing her hands. *That's how Jensen keeps people around. Dangling carrots he'll never, ever give you. Do you not think he's promised the same exact crap to Shawn? To Bri?*

Zack had been too embarrassed to admit the thought had never occurred to him.

Don't fall for it, Regina had said. *Get your own damn carrot, Zack.*

He entered the accounting program's password (*M_A_G_A_2018*—Jensen's political leanings veered right like Zack's, and unlike most of the Santa Monicans) and braced himself for the numbers that would flash on the screen, the mind-boggling record of the cash that gushed into Jensen Davis's corporate accounts week after week, fast and steady as mountain runoff during a spring thaw.

Zack clicked on *Vendors* and selected *Big Rad Wolfe, LLC.*

He hovered the cursor over the *Pay Vendor* field, his index finger trembling over the laptop's track pad.

He thought of Jensen, how his boss's easy smile slid across his tan face and deepened the crow's feet that fanned from his eyes as he told Zack, yet again, to *just hang tight, because I've got some big plans for you, just as soon as . . .*

Then Zack pictured little Andres rushing toward him across the sand, skinny arms spread wide, left foot scraping the ground as he struggled against the pull of his flimsy, ruined leg.

He could almost hear the *ping* of a fresh text from his half-sister Lettie. The demands for money came day and night: in texts, emails, voicemails, even DMs on Facebook and Instagram until Zack had blocked her.

> I need more money.
> When you give it to me?
> MORE MONEY WHEN???

Lettie's troubles, she claimed, had gotten out of control. They were bearing down on her faster by the day, threatening to remove her from the life she'd fought so hard to make for herself and her son, here in the US. Her clock was ticking, she told Zack. It was just a matter of time until ICE found her. Her unpaid medical bills from Andres's accident, along with the court notices from her shoplifting charge, would lead them to her.

The only solution was money. Fifteen grand, minimum, to pay her past-due hospital bills and legal fees. Fifteen grand was what she needed to have even a chance of staving off deportation. She'd showed Zack the documents: first, demanding she pay fines for the Pokémon cards she'd shoplifted last year on a sudden (stupid, Zack thought) impulse to make Andres happy, the numbers multiplying at a sickening rate, then the subpoena demanding she appear in court.

On top of her fines, there were the past-due fees Lettie owed her lawyer, Ms. Ochoa, the one person Lettie believed could make ICE retreat. Ochoa's fees were modest but inflexible—when Lettie failed to pay, Ochoa seemed to stop working. Where, Zack wondered, were the bleeding-heart attorneys who would help Lettie for free? How could his sister have been stupid enough to hire Sandra Ochoa, a woman she'd found through a billboard ad on the I-10, and who, according to Zack's too-late Google research, wasn't even trained in immigration law, but personal injury.

Zack guessed Lettie had been too afraid to ask for the right kind of help. Too scared to show her face at a legal aid clinic, or to ask the rich and educated women whose houses she cleaned for advice.

It was too late now: Lettie was neck-deep in debt. Due largely to Andres's accident.

The accident for which Zack was responsible.

You are the reason he is a cripple, Lettie told him, eyes flashing with anger. *So, you will help pay for our problems. You will make it right.*

His finger hovered over the track pad. He lowered it over the *Approve Transfer* button until he heard the mouse click.

Transfer successful! flashed the green text on the screen.

Zack exhaled, selected a Florida Georgia Line song from Spotify on his phone, and cranked up the volume, eager to move on to his legitimate duties.

He'd finally settled into his work and was humming along to the music when a loud rap on the door cut though an Imagine Dragons chorus. His eyes snapped up from the screen to see Jensen striding into the office. Instantly, Zack felt his palms tingle and his sweat glands kick into gear. He removed his earbuds and forced what he hoped was an easy, welcoming smile.

"Jens! Nice surprise."

"Z-man. Glad I caught you, buddy."

Zack's airways constricted, as if he'd suddenly developed asthma. He took a pull from his smoothie and cleared his throat. "I, uh, thought you were still in Denver. At the . . ." He searched his memory. "CrossFit conference?"

What the fuck was Jensen doing here?

"Oh, I bailed a day early." Jensen looked freshly showered in his crisp white polo and pressed khakis, his salt-and-pepper hair gelled and combed to the left side. "Those CrossFit dudes are a bunch of Neanderthals."

"So I've heard," said Zack. "Welcome home."

"Got a minute?" Jensen closed the office door behind him, then took a seat in the folding metal chair on the opposite side of the desk, facing Zack, giving him an instant sense of claustrophobia. "Just need to chat with you for a sec. Sensitive topic. Won't take long. I know you're teaching the three fifteen."

Zack's stomach churned. In his mind, blinding red flares exploded against a black sky. So, this was it. Jensen knew. About the transfers. It was over. Zack would go to jail. Lettie, and maybe even Andres, back to Mexico.

Perhaps it would be something of a relief.

"Earth to Z-man?" said Jensen.

"Sorry," Zack said. "Been a busy day already. What's up?" He was seized by the urge to run. Pictured the open window directly behind him, imagined wheeling around and kicking the screen away, leaping out and running down to the beach and into the ocean. Swimming straight toward the horizon until his muscles and lungs gave out, surrendered like the tubercular-ravaged lungs of young and innocent St. Thérèse, his guiding light, who, Zack had read, died at just twenty-four.

Thérèse: *The world's thy ship and not thy home.*

Beneath the desk, he balled his hands into fists. But the rest of his body could not move. He was paralyzed, bolted to his seat.

"Don't worry, this won't take long." Jensen sighed and held up his phone. "I just need a little help managing the tattooed wildcat. She texted me ten minutes ago. Says she needs to sub out tomorrow."

Zack blinked at his boss as he struggled to process Jensen's words.

The tattooed wildcat was the nickname he and Jensen privately used for Bri Lee, a longtime Color Theory trainer whose inked-up body offended Zack as much as her foul mouth.

Jensen was not here to accuse Zack of embezzlement.

He'd come to talk about *scheduling issues*.

Under the desk, Zack's fists uncurled. Oxygen returned to his lungs, sweet and plentiful.

"What—she wants to sub out? Tomorrow? Which classes?" he asked Jensen. Bri taught the coveted early-morning weekday workouts, five through nine A.M., all of which were routinely full with a waitlist. Clients adored her. When she subbed out, they were unhappy.

"All four of them."

On the laptop, Zack pulled up the schedule. "She hasn't submitted a request." If a trainer needed a shift covered, protocol was to submit a request to Zack via the scheduling software at least twenty-four hours in advance.

"That's the problem," said Jensen. "She feels at complete liberty to bypass you and come to me. At the last minute. It's unacceptable."

"*Absolutely* unacceptable, man." Zack shook his head, feeling a surge of camaraderie toward his boss. He wasn't going to jail, not today! "I'll set her straight. She won't be bothering you with low-level stuff again. And I'll make sure she shows up to teach tomorrow. She knows better."

"That's not the worst of it," said Jensen. "Not only is she trying to bail last-minute on eighty clients that are counting on her, but get *this*." He leaned across the desk toward Zack. "Her excuse is that she decided she needs to go to a fucking *women's march* first thing in the morning."

Zack rolled his eyes. "Remind me. What even *is* a women's march?"

"Last I checked, it was something like a bunch of privileged women who have perfect lives in the greatest, freest country on earth making angry posters and then meeting up to whine about problems they invented. All because they have too much time on their hands."

"Amen," said Zack. "Since 'feminism' "—he hooked his fingers into air quotes around the word—"has absolved them of all the duties that female humans have been doing for the past, what—two hundred thousand years?—they've got nothing better to do than get together and chant."

Jensen barked a laugh. "Right? A women's march is basically a big fuck-you to history."

Zack nodded vigorously. He felt almost manic with relief, a newfound happiness washing over him, words readily available. "What does a woman like Bri have to be angry about? She's young and healthy and makes enough money to tat up her body, which ain't cheap. She lives in one of the most prosperous cities in the most prosperous nation on earth. Her workplace is two blocks from the Pacific Ocean. Cry me a river."

"Truth, my man, truth. But you know what the *deeper* problem is?" Jensen lowered his voice confidentially. "It's that Bri is almost *thirty* years old. Not that I'm allowed to ever mention an employee's age, or the Department of Labor will come a-knocking. But I'll tell you, Z-man, women her age start to get *real* restless right about now."

"One hundred percent, man." Zack nodded vigorously.

Jensen went on, "It's because this garbage culture tells them they shouldn't start having kids until they're thirty-five. Which you and I"—he jabbed his index finger toward Zack, then back at his own chest—"and any thinking human with a basic understand of biology, know is completely unnatural." Jensen clasped his hands behind his head and fanned out his elbows. "Basically, the chick needs to quit going to goddamn marches and start breeding instead."

"You're so right-on, dude." Zack felt a warm flush of kinship with his boss, his fear of just moments ago withered and gone.

"Remind me why we live in this deep-blue state full of batshit crazies?"

"The weather," said Zack. "The beaches. The tacos. Makes up for all the angry, barren women."

"Amen. Plus, I'm a sucker for a perfect avocado." Jensen grinned, showing the creases in his face. Still, Zack hoped he looked as good as Jensen when he was fifty-eight. Perhaps, after Zack's business with Regina was done, Jensen would actually become a friend. Zack had *zero* true bros in California. He was estranged from his crew back in Florida and his own father was a hotheaded asshole who enjoyed berating Zack in every way possible. God knew he could use a spiritual ally here, in this land of rich, white pseudo-yogis.

"Oh, and, Zee," said Jensen. "One more thing."

"Hit me."

Jensen touched his palm lightly to the stiff surface of his hair. "I got wind that you've been doing a little side hustling."

"Side hustling?" The paralysis returned.

"Look, I admire the entrepreneurial spirit. Hell, it's what I'm all about. It's what got me where I am today. But you can't be fishing in my well, Z-man. It's a conflict."

"What well? I'm not following, Jens." Zack felt dizzy. A stamping-out of all the good feelings he'd just been riding.

"A little bird told me you threw a party to rustle up some private training. And that most of the guests were Color Theory clients."

"Oh! Yeah, I did throw a party." Zack was confused. Again, Jensen did not seem to be referencing the transfers or threatening to call the police. "But where's the conflict? The privates are just *supplements* to group training. It's a cross-sell to Color Theory. You know these women, Jens, they're always looking to do more, not less. I would never step on your toes, man."

"Sorry, Zee. It's a violation of the non-compete you signed. Last page of your employment agreement. Explicitly prohibits you from recruiting CT clients for private coaching. I can show you a copy."

"Who ratted?" said Zack. "Who told you about my private training?"

Jensen paused. "Just between us, it was Lindsey. You know, the manic little thing with the pigtails, who's here every single day? Her last name is escaping me."

"Leyner." Zack felt anger replacing his fear. "Yes, I know who she is." Lindsey fucking Leyner, the queen of babble. *Of course.* He wished he could punch Lindsey smack in her puffy lips, silence her motormouth once and for all.

"For the record, she wasn't trying to turn you in or anything. I follow her on social media because she's great about promoting the gym, and I happened to see a bunch of posts and stories about your, ah, event on Saturday. She was really raving about it on Instagram. Bunch of great shots of you and some other CT clients. Lots of Regina Wolfe. Looking awfully good for a cougar, if I do say so myself."

At the mention of Regina's name, Zack felt himself shrink in his seat and his eyes shift to the floor. She was the last person he wanted to discuss with Jensen.

"Lindsey is . . . very intense," Zack said lamely.

Jensen laughed. "That's diplomatic of you. Anyway, I asked Lindsey to delete all her posts related to the party you guys threw. Sorry, but it's basically advertising that works against Color Theory's success. The woman's got like two thousand followers."

"I'm not one of them," said Zack.

"Good choice, my man. Though I noticed you do show up on her feed pretty regularly."

"I do?" Zack was genuinely surprised. He had never looked at Lindsey Leyner's social media. After today, he wasn't sure he'd be able to face her in class again; he might be unable to stop himself from ripping her pigtails right out of her scalp.

"Evidently she starts snapping the second every class ends," said Jensen. "The woman is a posting machine. Hashtag FitFam, hashtag TurnedUpTuesday, it never ends. Anyway, moral of the story here is that you gotta read the fine print of any contract, bro.

I don't mean to be an asshole. But business is business. I can't put mine on the line to rev up yours. Are we clear?"

"Clear." Zack's head began to throb.

"Thanks, buddy. You won't have time for privates soon, anyway. We're about to close on the Malibu location, and then you and I will talk serious business about what's next for you. I just need another week or two. You still in?"

"Sure," Zack managed.

"Rad." Jensen stood and extended a hand to Zack. "You're a keeper, Z-man."

"Thanks."

"And you'll call the tattooed wildcat, right? Make sure she gets her tatted little ass in here first thing tomorrow morning?"

"You know I will, man."

Jensen opened the door, letting in a draft of mercifully cool air, finally leaving Zack alone.

He popped some Advil, then sat fingering the rosary at his neck, thinking of what St. Thérèse might say to him now.

By humiliation alone can Saints be made.

Lindsey was a moron, but Zack's real anger was at Regina. How had she neglected to prohibit photos at V2Y!, on top of not thinking about Zack's non-compete? Wasn't she supposedly some hotshot business woman?

He reminded himself Regina was a quarter-mil in the hole. Not exactly a hotshot's situation.

He took some long, slow *prana* breaths. He would get through this. There had to be another way. He didn't need Regina. Didn't need Jensen, didn't need his dickhead father, didn't need anyone, except God.

By humiliation alone.

Zack relaxed a little, his hands unfurling under the desk. He closed his eyes and thanked Thérèse, and God, then whispered a repeated Hail Mary until an alert on his phone interrupted his prayer. Ten minutes until he had to teach a class. And he still hadn't finished yesterday's tallies. Who gave a fuck?

He tapped out a text to Regina. V2Y is dead. Jensen found out from frickin Lindsey and says it's basically illegal. Will explain more later. He added a panicked-face emoji, along with a skull.

She wrote back immediately: Explain NOW.

Zack sighed and typed out the basic details. Then he pulled up the tattooed wildcat's number, thinking, as he listened to her perky voicemail message, how nice it must be to be a person like Bri Lee, lucky enough to invent their own problems.

8

LETICIA

Lettie's bosses were in love with their electronic calendars, sending Lettie an invite every week for each of their appointments. As if she needed to know exactly when Lindsey Ratface Leyner was having the hair on her chin ripped off.

She wondered if her bosses thought her too stupid to remember. Like she'd forget to show up for the work, and the money she and Andres so desperately needed. Only a rich person needed a calendar to remember how to live. Lettie had two things to remember—work and Andres. But her bosses' days were as stuffed as their medicine cabinets, with lunches and exercise dates and parties and weekend vacations to the desert to hike and to the mountains to ski. The wealthy white people of Santa Monica hated to be still; even on vacation they were busy-busy.

Many of the appointments on her bosses' calendars had strange names Lettie could not translate—*microblading, dermaplaning, fractal laser treatment*—and took many hours, often in the middle of the day. Lettie did understand, though, that each appointment focused on perfecting a certain part of the body. Her bosses returned with thicker eyebrows, lighter hair, and long, silky lashes that Lettie would later find on her employers' pillowcases. They returned with their lips suddenly plumped, foreheads wrinkle-free, faces pink and shiny as raw chicken from being scraped and injected. Even the patch of hair that hid under their panties received special attention. It took time, being beautiful, Lettie had learned. Some of her lady bosses, like Sukie Reinhardt, who used to be on TV, wore a full face of makeup every day, even shading in parts of their cheeks and nose and forehead so their bones stood at attention. Lettie had worn that much makeup just a few times in her life, and only to special events, like her niece Chiara's quinceañera and Andres's First Communion.

Since the first notice to appear in court had arrived, Lettie had known she needed new ways to save money but also to *make* money. She took on more work, at night, in addition to days spent cleaning houses and babysitting the children who lived in those houses.

Mondays, she collected cans and bottles from the bins in Virginia Avenue Park, overflowing with weekend trash, to bring to the recycling center in exchange for cash. She waited until the park was empty but for a few homeless camped in the shadows of the leafy moonlit trees. God forbid any of the parents from Andres's school saw her gathering sticky soda cans and empty water bottles like a no-good broken-down person.

She imagined she was Blanca Flor hurrying through a winding dark forest, fleeing a terrible queen mother in love with her beautiful reflection. Of all the stories her abuela had told Lettie and her cousins back home, *Blanca Flor* was Lettie's favorite. A selfish mother, a band of friendly thieves, and a petite outcast saved by the purity of her heart (and a movie-star kiss from her handsome prince)—what was there *not* to love?

Tuesday nights, after cleaning houses all day, she worked at Color Theory gym. Zacarias, bless his *delincuente* soul for this at least, had found her work wiping down exercise machines streaked with sweat and organizing the weights and other equipment in neat rows.

She'd forced herself to ask each of her employers if they knew anyone else looking for a cleaner, a babysitter, a dogwalker—never mind her fear of dogs. Her requests had resulted in three new jobs— babysitting for a sweet three-year-old with loopy blond curls and her naughty bed-wetting twin six-year-old brothers every Wednesday night; a weekly trip each Thursday to the supermarket to purchase six-packs of Ensure, tubs of tapioca pudding, and packages of adult diapers for Marlene, Sukie Reinhardt's elderly mother; and a daily morning walk for a nervous little dog, Simon, who made Andres giggle with his funny little bark and soft-as-cotton white fur. The dog's owner claimed Simon was "famous" and had many thousands of followers on Instagram, but it seemed to Lettie that everyone in Santa Monica claimed to be "famous." She tried not to think of all the money trembling little Simon made on social media as she picked up the dog's shits that steamed in the cool early-morning air.

She was making a little more money here and there—*drip, drop*—but it was always less than she owed. There was always the need for a trip to Western Union to get money orders, then straight to the post office to mail them to her landlady and the gas company; Andres's physical therapist; her lawyer, Sandra Ochoa; and, of course, the collection agency that sent the medical bills with big red letters across the front.

Pay what you can to the hospital, Ms. Ochoa advised. *If you don't, ICE is more likely to find you before our court date.*

And then there was that, even scarier than Lettie's bills: her order to appear before the West Los Angeles Superior Court in April. If she were deported for stealing the Pokémon cards, and Andres stayed behind with Auntie Corrina or (God forbid) Zacarias, her son would need money until Lettie figured out how to return to California or (God forbid) bring him to Mexico with her. The thought of leaving Andres made Lettie's chest ache, but imagining her boy in the dusty doctor's offices and crumbling schools of Oaxaca—after all she'd done to give him this life in the USA—pained her even more.

Some nights, after work, she and Andres traveled to food banks in search of a free dinner. Lettie tried to alternate so she and Andres didn't show up at the same place too often (rich boy Zacarias had his nose in the air about Lettie and Andres "begging"—he'd even dared to use that word). There was the Mount Sion food bank in Culver City (broccoli and cheese soup on Wednesdays), and the Monte Sion Center, who handed out leftover fruit from the fancy Santa Monica open market. Oh, how she and Andres enjoyed those juicy five-dollar pears, even with their bruised skin, served on scratched plastic trays. They had tried the food closet near UCLA (with her full cheeks and long hair, she could pass as a college student, no?) but the university police in their padded vests and helmets reminded Lettie of immigration agents, making the vegetarian chili stick in her throat.

Then Lettie sat in on a special event at Andres's school—an assembly that would, she hoped now, change her and Andres's lives. The topic was climate change. *Climate change is another hysterical liberal lie!* she'd heard Zacarias complain many times. *How can climate change be real when it's so freaking cold on the East Coast with those polar vortex and Snowpocalypse things?* So, she was supposed to listen to her not-to-be-trusted brother instead of scientists? No, Lettie did not think so.

At the assembly, a pretty woman in a doctor's white coat explained the giant cleanup job heavy on the backs of Andres's generation. The doctor-lady spoke calmly and slowly. Enough that even Lettie could understand—none of those big words that made a mess of meaning like when arguing with Zacarias.

As Lettie scanned the hundreds of little heads staring up at the stage, the scientist explained how it was up to *you* (she pointed a long finger at the children) to save Earth. She spoke of melting ice and warming seas; floods and storms; and the death of polar bears and bees. Lettie spotted a little girl in blond braids crying, a teacher hunched over her, smoothing circles onto the girl's back.

The scientist spoke about recycling with a hopefulness that reminded Lettie of church.

Everything is reusable. Nothing should be thrown away. You can make a difference.

Afterward, as the children made paper sprinkled with plant seeds, Lettie and the other parent volunteers (no one spoke to her but for a quick *hello*, always a disappointment but also a relief) operated several blenders, the sharp blades grinding the soggy pieces of printer paper the children had soaked in water overnight into a pulpy mush. Then the idea came to Lettie. A revelation that felt like one of the miracles in Zacarias's Holy Saints book.

Thursdays, she spent walking the alleys behind the fanciest houses north of Montana Avenue. There was money to be made *everywhere* in Santa Monica. The things people threw in the trash—what a waste! TV sets and stereos and printers, all of which worked once Lettie lugged them home and plugged them in. Plush sofas and armchairs with stains she scrubbed away with OxiClean. Coffee tables and dressers made from beautiful heavy wood—a little paint and they were, as Lettie's employers said, "good-as-new!" All of these things, and more, Lettie sold on the site that had become her heaven on earth, her salvation—Craigslist.org. Her little apartment was so stuffed with furniture she'd found on the street that Andres was always complaining about his bruised shins. She gave thanks to God for the bedbugs that kept other people from snatching up her treasures. What were a few bugs compared to her legal problems? She'd sleep in a tub of bedbugs if it meant she could stay with Andres in America.

Lettie became a recycler. She was helping the environment, she told herself, working to stop "climate change"—a phrase she now saw in the headlines of newspaper articles, and heard on the lips of her employers, even though it was Lettie who sorted through their stinking garbage, putting aside cans and bottles she could trade in.

Most of the women she cleaned for passed on to Lettie valuable items they no longer wanted. Everything from rice cookers still in Styrofoam packing to designer shoes with scuff-free soles. Regina gave her a plastic bag stuffed with clothes every few months—thin silk button-down shirts and size-two fitted trousers, pretending Lettie was not a size ten going on twelve. It was Melissa's hand-me-downs Lettie looked forward to the most, and she had a bag ready for

Lettie nearly every week. Toys and books and video games. Designer dresses (in Lettie's size!) and handbags still wearing tags.

Her bosses also gave her an endless supply of beauty samples that arrived in pretty cardboard boxes in the mail once a month. Makeup, face creams, and masques made with chemicals whose names were so long Lettie wondered if it wasn't a big science experiment. She had spent hours cleaning wealthy women's bathrooms, making sure the sink tops were spotless, free of the bottles and tubes and tiny wands her bosses used to turn back time, transform their faces into those that belonged on much younger women.

She began selling the hand-me-down beauty products of her bosses (were they not just as vain as that evil queen in *Blanca Flor*?) at her auntie Corrina's flea market table. Placing two or three bottles in shimmery sachet bags she found at the dollar store, even offering a discount—three beauty bags for ten dollars. She sold out in one weekend, bringing home a pile of bills (eighty-seven dollars!) to add to the money she hid in her own nearly empty bathroom cabinet under her package of dollar-store maxi-pads.

Still, the money was not enough. The fines on the overdue medical bills doubled. Then tripled.

There are always other ways, Lettie had spat at spoiled Zacarias in Melissa's kitchen the day of the exercise party, and she'd meant it.

She knew she must, as she'd heard Regina say, *get creative*.

She began buying cleaning products at the dollar store on Pico—nice-smelling but not organic, as her bosses demanded. She'd been saving empty organic bottles for weeks in the trunk of her car. Products with names like Common Good, Better Life, Puracy, which were, Lettie guessed, a way for her wealthy bosses to feel as if they were the saviors of the environment the scientist lady at the school assembly had spoken of. Lettie filled the empty bottles with the dollar-store solutions and used that to clean. A few of her bosses, like Lindsey Leyner, bought their own cleaning supplies but most of Lettie's bosses, like Melissa, trusted Lettie to buy the products and then paid her back, adding the cost to her monthly check. Lettie always made sure to show them the receipts. Only Melissa waved the long pieces of paper away. *I trust you, Leticia!*

Lettie knew she should not be trusted. She mourned the good Lettie that Melissa believed in but she and Andres were in danger.

As the court date neared, she inched dangerously close to *Blanca Flor's* legendary thieves. She bought brand-new furniture on credit (thanks to Melissa, who cosigned on a Sears card), then sold the furniture on her beloved Craigslist. When she cleaned the grand houses north of Montana Avenue, she found change under the sofa cushions, behind a child's desk, even tossed in the garbage pail, and slipped the coins into her pocket. What did it matter to these people who had jars and bowls overflowing with change as if any bill smaller than a twenty was too much of a bother?

She was proud of her projects (she was an *entrepreneur*, yes?—a fancy word she heard the wealthy Santa Monicans use often). She was also ashamed. Some days, she was sure she'd be willing to sell her body; maybe even her soul had El Diablo himself knocked on her front door.

TUESDAY, OCTOBER 16, 2018

9

MEL

"Sloanie, you're going to be late for soccer!"

Adam's voice carried through the second floor of the Goldberg house as Mel, holding an armful of clean sheets, reached the top of the stairs, her sore thighs burning (damn that stupid exercise party). Adam was at the end of the hall, rapping intently on the door of Sloane's bathroom, clad in his thick black *gi*. Mel's bitterness surged at the sight of the uniform; how could she be sure he actually *went* to the jiu-jitsu class he claimed to attend on afternoons he wasn't needed on a set, or at a meeting, or in an editing room, or however the hell he spent his days?

How could she know he wasn't banging a hot young actress instead of pinning sweaty guys to the mat?

She thought of the texts and felt sick.

Sloane yelled back, "Privacy, dude! I'm constipated!"

Mel almost laughed. Instead, she called down the hall to Adam, "Give her time."

"Oh, hey, hon." Adam looked away from the door and smiled. "I didn't see you there." He tipped his head toward the bathroom. "Maybe we should still be giving her MiraLAX?"

"I heard that!" yelled Sloane.

"I thought you blamed her diet," said Mel to Adam, walking away from him toward the guest room at the far end of the hall.

She dropped the bedding on the chair in the guest room and stood still for a minute, catching her breath. She'd been racing around as she did every Tuesday afternoon, up and down the stairs, transporting piles of crap—clothes, books, and toys—to stash deep in the closets so Lettie wouldn't have to bother with them when she came to clean tomorrow. Mel thought the ritual—pre-cleaning before Lettie came to *clean-clean*—might burn off some of her rage, help her ignore Adam and Sloane who, it seemed, were taking their sweet time leaving for soccer practice and "jiu-jitsu class."

But instead, the pre-cleaning (okay, *rearranging*) was making Mel feel more worked up than ever.

Every one of Adam's belongings had taken on an ominous glow since she'd discovered those repulsive texts, and as her arms filled with her cheating husband's things, she had the wild urge to stuff all of it down the kitchen sink and flip the switch to the InSinkErator, the restaurant-grade garbage disposal Adam had been so excited about when they'd first moved in. She imagined the sound of the grinder shredding Adam's silly patterned socks (Teenage Mutant Ninja Turtles, really?), devouring the cotton man-scarf he wrapped around his muscled neck in the mild West Coast winters, the Viagra he ordered online, those pastel V-neck tees he wore now that he'd had his chest hair lasered. All solid proof he was showing off for someone, Mel thought. Maybe that new production assistant with the frayed jean shorts and tattooed mandala peeking out from between her high breasts. Miss PA had risen to the top of the list Mel had been compiling and then revising nonstop since she'd found those texts on Adam's phone. It was easy to imagine that skanky little bitch's perpetually glossed lips sliding down Adam's . . . *No!* Mel stopped herself.

In just a few days, Mel's entire view of her marriage had upended. All of Adam's goodness, his perfect-husband-and-father act, seemed a front for the double life he was apparently living. How many clues had she missed since he'd transformed from Brooklyn peon to LA mogul? How many late nights had he claimed to be working, or wining and dining some movie star or power-agent at the Sunset Room or Soho House, seducing them into his next movie?

How, Mel asked herself, as she scrolled over the vulgar texts again and again, had she been so naïve as to believe he was different than other men? That precious Adam was somehow immune to the temptations delivered by power and prestige? Hadn't he told her, more than once, that women were better than men? She had actually believed him. He was *that* good.

What sort of la-la land version of her life had she been inhabiting all these years, as her husband became hotter and richer, and Mel fatter and further removed from her past accomplishments, maintaining the delusion that Adam would *never* cheat? She'd allowed herself to drift toward obsolescence, while Adam's star kept rising, fast and bright, his net worth and pec muscles continually growing. *Duh*, of course he could now have his pick of hot, eager mistresses.

In the past three days, she'd imagined a romance novel's worth of sex scenes involving Adam and every single woman in his life. Even those on the periphery. Like the freshly divorced mom who'd moved in a few doors down and who Mel had caught flirting with Adam out on the sidewalk, leaning over to stroke Sloane's red-brown curls, the neck of the neighbor's loose tank top revealing A-plus fake boobs. Had Adam stared? Mel had been unsure. She was now unsure of *everything*, and hated herself for ever thinking otherwise. What a fool she'd been. She'd never be that gullible again. The first thing she did each morning was reach for her phone. Force herself to look at the proof of Adam's philandering, a screenshot of those texts stored in her Google Photos.

To make her loss even more cruel, Mel was losing her husband to someone who used UR *twice* in the same text thread. Someone probably born in the nineties, she thought. How many gorgeous twentysomethings had traipsed in and out of Adam's office that past year—interns and PAs and script-readers, the office manager who looked just like Jennifer Lawrence, whom Adam had claimed was a lesbian. They came fresh out of midwestern colleges, or from godforsaken places like Kissimmee and Toledo, smiles sparkling, though Mel knew lavalike ambition flowed beneath their wholesome American sweetness.

Mel had spent every morning since she'd found the texts crying her face puffy in the shower after Adam and Sloane had left for work and school. There wasn't enough eye gel in all of Santa Monica's bathroom cabinets to erase the swollen bags under her eyes.

Today, Mel had no time for a tear-filled pity party. She wanted the house to be extra ready for Lettie, who'd been complaining of pain in her heels, and who, despite Mel's urging, refused to go to the doctor. Plus, Mel was feeling extra guilty about having Lettie clean tomorrow. Early that morning, Lettie had texted, asking if she could clean Saturday instead of her usual Wednesday.

Something come up. Is ok if I clean Saturday?

The text had nearly retriggered Mel's tears. She'd been looking forward to having Lettie clean, needed her to scrub away the scent of Adam, especially the fuggy scent of his jiu-jitsu *gi*.

Mel had texted Lettie back with the extra-sad emoji face, the one with tears streaming down the emoji's fat yellow cheeks. Hoping Lettie got her not-so-subtle hint.

Oh no! I was REALLY looking forward to it. And we are having guests over both days this weekend.

This was, of course, a lie. Mel hated herself for telling it, but she hated the thought of not seeing Lettie even more.

She sent Lettie one more text. This time, going all out, including the prayer hands emoji, a kissing-face emoji, plus that cute angel-face emoji, all the while trying not to think of *those* emojis she'd seen on Adam's phone.

So sorry to be pushy but I REALLY hope you can make it tomorrow!

Usually, Lettie texted back right away. This time, twenty minutes passed. Then thirty.

The unease had morphed into a smothering dread that had Mel wanting to lock herself in her bedroom, toss back two Ambien, and call it a day. Then Lettie had texted.

Ok. I be there tomorrow. Just had to move a few appointments.

Thank you, thank you, thank you! Mel had texted back. You are a lifesaver. What would I do without you?! She made a mental note to give Lettie an extra twenty dollars to make up for the scheduling change. It was the least she could do. Who knew how difficult the life of an undocumented Mexican single mother was these days?

"Boo-boo!" Mel heard Adam call to Sloane again. "The clock's a-ticking! Daddy's going to miss his class."

"God forbid," Mel mumbled to herself as she headed back down the hallway toward the stairs.

"It's my body!" Sloane yelled to Adam, a line Mel knew her daughter had learned at the doctor's office last year. "And right now, my body is pooping!"

"Stop hovering," Mel said to Adam. "And why are you talking about yourself in the third person? You know who you sound like." Certain he'd think instantly of the Big Cheeto—they joked often about Trump's habit.

There it was—the look of surprised hurt she'd hoped her jab would accomplish. *Serves him right.*

"Um, I'm sorry," Adam began. "But why are you—"

Mel cut him off. "Not right now. I'm prepping for Lettie."

"Why are you so worked up about the cleaning situation? You're beet-red, honey. And sweating. Go take a walk. It's gorgeous outside."

"It's *always* gorgeous out," snapped Mel, thinking, *It's not the cleaning situation, you asshole. It's your slut-screwing situation.*

"I just want you to take care of yourself."

Just. She nearly snorted at the ludicrous suggestion that her care was all he wanted.

"You know I hate it when you say that."

Adam shrugged. "What did the doctor tell you at your last visit?"

She felt the momentum in her anger, like a train barreling forward.

But then—*no.* She gripped the banister tightly, forcing herself to hold back. Let him wonder.

She'd resolved to wait to confront Adam about the texts on date night / couples' therapy night, when Sloane would be off at a sleepover and Mel would have the soothing presence of Janet, there in the room for what would certainly be the worst conversation of Mel's life. In the meantime, she'd have a full three weeks of bottled rage to contain, as she and Adam had cut down to a monthly "maintenance" (ha!) session. They'd begun making an evening of it—the six P.M. appointment at Janet's home office, followed by Paprika, the vegan restaurant Adam insisted on going to even though he knew Mel loathed the cauliflower-heavy cuisine.

"Why are you so *sweaty*, Mom?"

Sloane emerged from the bathroom and stood next to Adam, crossing her arms across the chest of her white-and-black tracksuit in silent judgment. A matching headband was tugged over her bowl cut. "Like *extra* sweaty."

Mel heard the silent *ew* in her daughter's voice.

Ten going on forty! Mel joked to mom-acquaintances.

She felt the sweat—dampening the crotch of her thin black palazzo pants, trickling down her back, the side of her face, caught in the clutch of her weighty breasts, and thought suddenly of Pokémon. How, at the height of Sloane's obsession with the never-ending Japanese franchise, she'd begun calling Mel and Adam by the names of Pokémon characters. Mel had been assigned Jigglypuff, a round, pink blob of a creature. Adam got to be Xerneas, a majestic elk-like thing with antlers, while Sloane herself was Zigzagoon, a fur ball with a sweet raccoon face.

Fucking Jigglypuff, thought Mel. She'd laughed when Sloane had announced the name—they'd *all* laughed, but it had hurt.

"I'm sweaty," said Mel, hearing the tightness in her own voice, "because I'm doing some cleaning. And this is a big house." She took one step down the stairs, feeling her extra weight shimmy and roll around her.

"We do actually pay Lettie to clean," said Adam. "A lot."

"Yeah, Mom," Sloane said, her head cocked in confusion, "if maids are supposed to clean, like, why are *you* cleaning?"

Mel bolted back to the landing and strode toward her daughter. "Don't ever—*ever*—call Leticia a maid, Sloane Ruby Goldberg!"

Sloane flinched.

"Lower your voice," hissed Adam.

"But look at what you're teaching her!"

"Are you in a *mood*, Mom?" asked Sloane.

"What?" said Mel. "No! I'm just trying to get things done!"

Adam gave an exaggerated sigh. "Maybe Mommy should *rest* first," he said, hardening his eyes on Mel. "Does she need a nap? Or maybe some medicine?"

The words hit Mel like a slap, and she blinked to hold back tears of disbelief. Just last week, he'd promised he'd never say those words again, after she'd wept while explaining to him how demeaning it was to be dismissed like that. Especially in front of Sloane. *Nap time, Mommy! Medicine time, Mommy!* Meaning, Go to your room, Mel. Smoke some pot. Get lost.

Oh, no, Mel thought, he wasn't going to break her. Not today.

She summoned the biggest artificial smile she could muster.

"Actually," she said to Adam and Sloane brightly. "I'm signed up for a class. An *exercise* class."

The lie had left her lips without a thought.

"Really?" Adam asked, not trying to hide his surprise.

"For real?" Sloane's head peered out from under Adam's elbow.

"Yep!" Mel tried to imitate the endless chirpy positivity she heard from the Santa Monica moms. "And I've got to hurry if I'm going to make it to class on time. You know how Regina is—she's meeting me and probably *expecting* me to be late."

Now she was telling lies on top of lies, adding Regina into the mix.

"'Cause you *are* kinda always late," Sloane said quietly. Mel pretended not to hear.

"Wow, Mel, I'm so proud of you," Adam said. As if she was a feeble child, Mel thought. But she kept smiling.

"Way to go, Mom!" Sloane ducked under Adam's arm, raising her hand for a high five.

"Go get your cleats on and meet me in the garage," said Adam to Sloane. "Two minutes."

"Why?" Sloane arched a brow. "Because you and Mommy need to have a private talk? Are you getting a divorce?"

"No!" said Adam and Mel together.

"Sloane. Go." Adam pointed to the stairs.

Mel grabbed her daughter and planted a kiss on her cheek, letting her lips linger. "I miss you already, my super soccer star. And you haven't even left yet."

"Alrighty then," said Sloane, detangling herself and bounding for the stairs.

"Sweetheart," Adam said to Mel when Sloane was out of earshot. "We can't keep going like this."

"That's for sure," Mel mumbled.

Adam reached for her, the coarse fabric of his *gi* rubbing Mel's side. She recoiled.

"*What* is going on with you?" he whispered. "I know something's wrong. Please. Talk to me."

"Jesus," she said, "this isn't some corny scene in one of your movies."

She'd hit the mark. His hewn jaw dropped.

"I'm not ready to talk about it," she whispered, aware Sloane was all ears. "I need to wait for date night." Knowing he'd get the gist, that she'd meant *wait for therapy.* "And please stop trying to coerce me into talking before I'm ready . . . It devalues my suffering." A phrase Janet had used in their last session.

"Coerce you?" He sounded hurt. Then again, Mel wondered if there was a man on earth more skilled at feeling sorry for himself. "I thought things—between us—were good. Almost great."

"Congratulations."

"You're so confus—"

"Stop, Adam. I'm not ready. "

"I guess I won't ask *ready for what.*"

"Thank you," said Mel.

For a moviemaker, he was a terrible actor, she thought. Could he really hide an affair from her? The man could barely keep a secret, or stop himself from giving her birthday presents a few days early.

"I can be patient, Mel. It's just that"—Adam lifted an arm and let it fall back to his side—"I miss you."

His eyes went unfocused with that faraway look, the same distant stare he wore right before he climaxed. In their new life out west, Mel's desire for Adam had rekindled. It was after sex, lying in the blotted glow of dawn with her head on Adam's chest, feeling the steady rise and fall of his breath, that Mel had felt the deepest sense of optimism she'd ever known: that together, they could do anything. They were like the pioneers who had ventured west to strike gold, and wasn't that what Adam had done? She had been sure Adam felt the unlimited possibility, too.

Of course, now she knew the truth. He'd been thinking of someone else. For her, he'd felt nothing.

"I need to get to the gym," she mumbled.

He looked defeated. "What gym?"

"Um. Color . . . Theory." *What a stupid name*, she thought.

Adam nodded approvingly. "Circuit training. Nice." He leaned in quickly and brushed his lips to her cheek. "I better get Sloanie to practice."

He stepped around her toward the stairs and seconds later—*finally*—was out the door.

Mel went downstairs and grabbed her phone from the table by the front door, looked up Color Theory, and, before she could chicken out, tapped *Call*. As the phone rang, her eyes rested on the gold decal she'd stuck to the back of the front door on the day they'd moved in. It mocked her. *Happiness Lives Here!*

"Thank you for calling Color Theory!" chirped a female voice. "How can we help you?"

Where to fucking start? Mel thought.

"I'm, um, hoping to take a class today. Like, your most beginner-ish class. Do you have any openings?" She paused, then continued. "And I hear great things about one trainer specifically. Zack? Yeah, I think that's his name."

"Sad!" the voice sang. "Zack's done teaching for the day. Sorry to bum you out!"

"No problem," Mel mumbled.

"But I do know Zack would *highly* recommend Bri. He hits her 4:15 class all the time.

"Great! I'll sign up for that one." Was she too quick? Desperate-sounding?

"Lucky you! There's one spot left. Yay!"

Mere minutes after she'd booked the class at Color Theory and was searching her dresser drawers for the sports bra and leggings she'd worn at the Version Two You! party—Mel's phone pinged with a text.

> Hiya, Mel! It's Zack, your fave trainer. Thx for the epic party. Hope it was a little bit fun??? Are you ready for more . . . maybe a one-on-one?

Was this kismet? A coincidence? Or had the cheerleader-chirpy Color Theory receptionist informed Zack of Mel's call?

Mel's face flamed.

A one-on-one?

She told herself to calm down, that Zack could not possibly be flirting with her over text, and even if he somehow *was*, well, Mel was married, for God's sake.

Then again, she thought, fresh tears burning her eyes, *so was Adam.*

Suddenly, her fingers were flying over her phone.

> Not sure if I'd call it "fun" but thanks for inspiring all the ladies! I almost died but am ready for more. I think . . . Ha!

Zack texted back a few emojis. A bulging bicep. A guy lifting weights. Then a girl lifting weights. Not that she looked anything like Mel. Still, staring at the boy and girl side by side, Mel hoped there was a hidden message there.

She hesitated, then, and before she could talk herself out of it, texted: Actually . . . I'm signed up for a Color Theory class today at 4:15. GULP.

She added the cringing-face emoji and: Regina talked me into it. You know how convincing she can be. LOL.

She was lying again. Worse, Brooklyn Mel would *never* have typed *LOL*. Maybe, she thought, this was what a midlife crisis looked like.

> Rad! Regina texted me about taking the 4:15. Yes she can be quite persuasive! How fun would it be for all of us to take a CT class together? Bri is a blast.

Fun, indeed, Mel thought, forgetting how her thighs had only just recovered from the backyard sweat-a-thon.

Mel replied: I'm in! DOUBLE GULP.

See you real soon! Zack texted back, adding a flexing-bicep emoji. Studies have shown people who work out with friends, partners, and/or significant others have a higher chance of success with a workout program.

While it sounded like something he'd copied and pasted off the obesity page at WebMD, she liked his tone, as if they'd known each other much longer than just a few days.

Looking forward to it! If I can get myself there on time. Self-control isn't my strong suit. But I am still hoping to rise from the ashes as Mel 2.0. (She added the googly-eyed, tongue-hanging-out emoji to show she was joking, when, in fact, she was dead serious).

LMAO, he texted. Self-control can be overrated.

Oooh, intriguing, she thought. Maybe there were some brains under all that brawn.

10

ZACK

ZACK LAY ON HIS LIVING ROOM COUCH, UNABLE TO NAP DESPITE BEING severely sleep-deprived, listening to afternoon traffic whoosh down the I-10. He'd slept terribly the previous night, dragged himself to Color Theory to teach his early-morning classes, forced himself to take Shawn's nine A.M., then worked in the back office for a couple of hours. He'd planned to beeline home and crash all afternoon, but as soon as he'd showered and sprawled out on his too-soft second-hand couch, wearing only boxers (his tiny apartment was an oven in the daytime), he found himself unable to sleep because each time he closed his eyes, Melissa Goldberg's face flashed to his mind. Her flushed, heart-shaped face, with its dueling expressions of uncertainty and wryness. Followed by her curvy body, thick but amply proportionate, with breasts that moved like actual human flesh and fat and blood, a little floppishly, the way God had intended, instead of the rigid, bouncing cones of his surgically enhanced gym regulars.

Finally, he'd sent her a text. Just a friendly thank-you for hosting the V2Y! party, short and sweet. When she'd written back almost instantly, basically inviting him to join her at Color Theory that afternoon, he'd said yes—never mind that his quads and abs were already blasted from Shawn's class—making sure to add some coach-like lines about fitness to keep it professional.

Now, with an hour and a half before his second workout of the day, he found himself still unable to nap. The room was too warm, the traffic noises from the I-10 too grating.

And then there was the stirring in his boxers.

No. He would not taint Mel with his weakness. Would not allow his hands to push under his waistband at the thought of her. Mel was an authentic, substantial woman, with a massive house north of Montana, an adorable daughter, and a *gi*-wearing husband who resembled a young Chuck Norris.

Zack raised his palms and tucked them beneath his head, trapping them against his pillow, away from his growing erection. *Mind over matter.* Despite some of his actions of late, he was becoming a better person. Wasn't he? His mind traveled to thoughts of himself just three years ago, when he'd first arrived in LA. He'd driven his pickup from Ocala to Los Angeles in five days flat, armed with nothing more than five grand and a burning desire to leave the steaming cesspool of Florida—where he'd done nothing but fail, make messes, and live like a heathen—for good.

Almost immediately, despite his shock over landing in a blue state still enchanted by godforsaken Obama, life in California had seemed promising.

Zack had scored the gym job right away, and spent money on quality headshots, landing an agent who sent him on auditions. He moved into the chintzy little apartment on Pico and Centinela, just past the edge of Santa Monica, with the flimsy vertical blinds and the stainproof carpeting and the absence of any cross-breeze whatsoever. Sure, he was old to drop everything and move to LA. Nearly thirty. But he didn't aspire to be Leonardo DiCaprio. All he wanted was to act a little, earn his own money, and above all, become someone new. Shed the filthy, stupid old Zack and become someone better.

It was in LA that he'd discovered St. Thérèse, quoted on the back of a Sunday Mass program at St. Monica Church.

It was because of Thérèse, really, that he'd reached out to Lettie.

Thérèse had written: *I have learnt much by guiding others. All souls have more or less the same battles to fight.*

He'd had his own share of battles, after all.

But in those first golden months in Los Angeles, when things, for the first time in his life, seemed to be going *right*—something inside him had shifted. It had been one thing to deny Lettie's existence when she lived on the opposite side of the country, but another to do it when she was right there, in the same city. Contacting her fit right in with the new Zack: chaste, thoughtful, healthy, celibate. Focused on his work and on bettering himself. At night, he could almost *hear* Thérèse encouraging him to reach out to Lettie with these words: *I have at last found my vocation; it is love!*

Surely, Lettie could use some extra love. Who couldn't?

He sent her a friend request on Facebook, and she responded within the hour. Soon, they'd met in person. Lettie balancing Andres on her hip, so small that Zack had said, *How old are you little, man? About three and a half?*

Andres had been almost five. Zack had fallen, instantly, in love with his nephew.

It wasn't long before Lettie asked him to babysit. She didn't have the luxury of interviewing and vetting babysitters, of checking references. She didn't have forty bucks a month to spend on Care.com. When she couldn't get Andres to Head Start, she simply brought him to work with her. Zack was blood and that was a good enough reason to trust him to watch Andres.

Lettie had a regular gig on Wednesday afternoons, at a house in Beverly Hills. A long haul on the bus, but worth it for the $150. Andres still napped when he could—long, heavy naps that he woke from damp-haired and stunned-looking. When Zack didn't have an audition or a class to teach, Lettie began dropping Andres off at his apartment.

On that Wednesday, Zack had been feeling that, at last, his life was turning around. His agent had called to say he'd gotten a second callback for the hot dog commercial he'd auditioned for, and that the producers were *literally smitten* with him. The spot would bring him a serious chunk of cash, plus new credibility.

That afternoon, Zack played Legos with Andres, and hide-and-seek, and they blew bubbles in the courtyard. When his nephew's lids began to droop Zack asked him if he wanted some screen time. After five minutes on the couch with Zack's iPad, he was sound asleep.

Zack recalled that moment with perfect clarity: the soft afternoon light in his apartment, Andres's long lashes and eyelids quivering slightly as he sunk deeper into his nap. The sensors of the garbage truck beeping outside.

He'd only left to transfer his laundry from the washer to the dryer. Zack's apartment was on the ground floor and the laundry room was at the end of the breezeway. He planned to be gone from his apartment, where Andres was sound asleep on the couch, for under five minutes.

Except that Casey had been in the laundry room, too. Casey, the actress-slash-beauty-brand-ambassador who'd been flirting heavily with him since he'd moved in. Wearing short denim cutoffs and a tank top that didn't quite cover her stomach. She probably hadn't covered her abs since leaving Wisconsin. More than once she'd dropped by Zack's apartment with a bottle of wine dangling from her hand, asking if he *felt like hanging.*

He had not felt like hanging, ever. Casey set alarm bells off in his head. She reminded him of girls from Florida who wanted to slither all over his lap like porn stars. She represented everything he wanted to cast off.

But he'd been in an exuberant mood when he'd walked into the laundry room and seen her there, sitting atop a washer and pecking at her phone, and so he'd shared his good news of the commercial callback.

Duuude, she'd said. *That's amazing.*

She held up her hand for a high five. He accepted. Their hands latched and she pulled him into a hug. There was a lingering. He felt her breath on his cheek.

In his ear she whispered, *Why do you always avoid me? You're not famous yet, you know.*

The proverbial door opened.

She bounced her bare heels against the white metallic surface of the washer, making soft bonging sounds. Her legs were long and lean and bronzed.

A dryer buzzed, loud and harsh. Casey released him.

That's my stuff.

She opened the dryer door and its overstuffed contents spilled to the concrete floor. She shoved the pile into her laundry basket, taking her time with a pair of thong underwear. The clothes formed a mountain well above the rim of the basket.

Can I help you with that? Zack said.

Would you? My apartment's upstairs. My upper-body strength is kind of pathetic.

I could help you change that. I'm a trainer.

I hate to sweat.

This is LA. It's too dry to sweat.

He hadn't entirely forgotten about Andres—but the boy was fast receding to a faraway region of Zack's mind. This is what happened when he crossed over: everything else fell away.

Follow me.

He lifted the clothes basket and trailed her out of the laundry room and up the concrete stairs. She practically jogged, wagging her ass in his face.

It was everything he didn't want anymore. But in that moment, it was *all* he wanted. He desired nothing else.

She pushed open the door of her apartment—it was exactly like his, but better decorated, with cheerful framed posters on the wall and red throw pillows on the two couches draped in white covers, a vase of sunflowers on a coffee table—

Helll—ooooo? she called and then gave him a sly smile, catching her tongue between bleached teeth. *My roommate's not here.*

He dropped the laundry basket and the mountain of clothes tumbled to the floor.

Hey! said Casey. *That stuff is clean.*

He could not stop himself. He grabbed her and pulled her close to him, unbuttoned her denim shorts and yanked them down. Already her hands were in his shorts, her tongue in his ear, a whiff of chocolate on her breath. The moaning, the breathy *oh yeahs*. The sounds and smells that would torture him later. He fumbled with her bra and failed. He tugged at the fabric so hard it ripped.

I've wanted this since the second I met you, she said in his ear.

His perception of time dissolved. His body stamped out his mind. He was sensation and movement. She was not Casey, in particular, but a warm, breathy thing enveloping him. She was something he required. Deserved. Needed to consume.

And then the intersection of sounds: unlike anything he'd ever heard. The blare of a horn, an *ohmygod, oh Jesus* shrieked at top volume, and on top of that, another sound, a tortured soprano keening. Like a baby animal in great pain.

But Zack was already inside her—Casey, whoever she was—his body reaching, clamoring for something he needed desperately, more than anything in the world, and he could not stop. His need in the moment felt bigger than anything he'd ever encountered, bigger even than the terrible sounds leaking through the living room's half-open window. He was nothing in the face of his need.

Baby, said Casey, in a ragged whisper. Those feet that had been lazily kicking the washing machine now thrust up in the air, above his shoulders.

MAMAAAAA!!!!

Zack heaved into Casey, emptying himself inside her.

Then he snapped back into himself.

MAMAAAA!!! From downstairs, an anguished squeal.

Zack leapt to his feet, pushing Casey to the couch. Her legs flopped down, marionette-like.

What the hell! she said. *Not cool.*

Casey ceased to exist. Zack swiped his gym shorts from the floor and stepped into them without breaking stride, then bolted from her apartment and down the stairs.

A small crowd knotted in the parking lot. A man in a sanitation worker's neon-yellow vest knelt on the asphalt, talking frantically into his cell phone. A woman in a green sundress saying, *Ohmygod ohmygod ohmygod, I swear I didn't see him, I checked all my mirrors! I didn't see him!*

Lying on the ground was Andres, his leg twisted at a gruesome angle. A nub of gray-white bone poking from below his kneecap. Blood pooling beneath his lower body.

Zack had screamed, a guttural sound from the pit of his belly, more convulsion than sound, as he knelt over the broken body of his nephew.

FROM THE CARPETED floor, his phone chimed again, snapping Zack out of his half doze, back to the gathering heat of his living room. Late-afternoon sun muscled through the closed Venetians and sweat trickled down his temples as he rose to a seated position and reached for his phone.

The text was from Regina: Melissa G says u r coming to Bri at 4:15 P.M.—true? And since when are you two texty?

She'd added the chin-cupping-thinking emoji.

None of your freaking business, Zack thought with a flash of irritation, and hovered his thumb over the keypad for a beat before deciding to ignore her. Then he stood and headed to the bedroom to change into a fresh set of gym clothes.

11

MEL

"SHOW UP!" BRI, A PETITE, MULTI-PIERCED TWENTYSOMETHING COLOR Theory trainer whose favorite word was, apparently, Mel thought, *fuck*, shouted as Mel, along with Regina, Zack, and more than a dozen other sweat-drenched people, most of them far younger than Mel—all of them in better shape—raced on the side-by-side treadmills.

"This is one goddamn hour out of your day," Bri yelled even louder as House of Pain's "Jump Around" blasted from the gym's speakers. "One hour! You didn't cart your cellulite-streaked butt through hellish traffic to fail. Did you?"

A few of the runners spit out a garbled "No."

Mel didn't dare open her mouth, scared she'd lose the little breath she had left.

C & C Music Factory's "Gonna Make You Sweat" came on—Bri's class playlist was heavy on nineties music—tunes Mel had gyrated to at high school dances.

"Oh, so you *did* show up to fail!" Bri laughed maniacally, her tight blond braids swishing side to side.

Kill me now, Mel thought, guessing Bri would punish their lackluster response, and sure enough, Bri shouted. "Add point-five to those speeds! Or if you're Zack, add one-point-five!"

"Hurts so good!" Zack yelled.

Mel had told herself, right up to the minute her Lyft pulled up in front of Color Theory, that Zack probably wouldn't show up. This mild doubt had quickly turned into *what the fuck was I thinking* full-blown panic as Mel had stepped onto Main Street in her tight workout gear, the sidewalk crammed with tourists, many careening at top speed on those damn rent-a-scooters, and a bevy of shirtless men running like they were being chased by a pride of lions. The Santa Monicans *loved* to work out in public. Daily, she spotted throngs of them running up the steep wooden steps leading to the beach, in the park doing yoga under the magnolias, even dropping to the ground for push-ups at a children's playground.

She'd been ready to call another Lyft to ferry her back home, and then, there he was—Zack, waiting by the gym's front door, smiling, the afternoon sun catching the gold in his thick hair. As if, she dared think it, he'd been waiting for her. He'd opened the glass door to the gym, and for a beat, pressed his hand against her lower back to usher her gently through.

Regina was already inside the studio, jump roping at high speed. Mel waved in her direction, then stepped onto treadmill number five and punched it to a two-point-five speed. In the mirror, she could see Regina hopping manically, smacking the cord of the rope against the ground as if she were punishing it.

The woman hustled around the clock, Mel thought, whether it was shuttling her kids to activities—Mel had seen Regina at a red light recently, angled forward toward the wheel, like a race car driver—or waiting for class to start. Go-go-go, at all times. How was it that Regina, a middle-aged mother who seemed to subsist on thinkThin bars and black coffee, could have the energy of a teenager? Clearly, she was avoiding something. It was the mystery of what exactly that might be—conversation, connection?—that had sparked Mel's interest in her. Mel found herself hoping there was a messy, dark secret roiling inside Regina, something the woman could only suppress by staying in perpetual motion.

Hey, Mel! Regina had veered over to her, jump rope dangling around her neck like a pet snake. *I can't believe I'm seeing you here. Can I ask you to scoot over to tread six? I know it sounds silly, but number five is my jam. It's just right for me.*

Um, sure, said Mel, fumbling with the controls of her machine to make it stop whirring. A treadmill, *just right?* What was this, some deranged SoCal version of "Goldilocks and the Three Bears"?

"Add two-point-oh to that speed, bitches!" yelled Bri now, from the front of the room. "NOW!"

Mel added point-five. She watched Regina add three, the machine already beginning to shake with her high speed.

"Goody-two-shoes," Mel mumbled in Regina's direction.

"What?" Regina yelled. "I can't hear you!"

"Ladies, talking means you're taking it easy!" yelled Bri. Regina shot Mel a withering look. Bri went on. "Looky at Zack! That stallion's got perfect form, yo!"

Bri went on to give Zack extra attention all class, and halfway through class, Regina abruptly switched treads, giving up her precious number five to run a few machines down, on the other side of Zack. Mel breathed a sigh of relief; she hated exercising next to that greyhound of a woman, and plus, Regina had seemed vaguely angry throughout class. Not enough attention from Zack, Mel guessed. Bri was hogging him, making a big show of it.

When Bri, blessedly, gave them a ten-second "rest," during which Mel exhaled short puffs of breath to stop the bile from rising up her throat, Regina ran on. And on and on. A triumphant smile, if not a bit manic, stretched across her narrow face. Mel caught Regina looking in the wall-to-wall mirrors, not at herself but at Zack. Waiting, it seemed, for him to notice her.

Beep beep beep! Regina's treadmill sang as she punched the plus-sign. As if, Mel thought, the faster she ran the more likely she'd catch Zack's eyes.

"And the Wolfe leads the pack! Let's hear it for Regina maxing the tread the whole freaking class!" Bri let out a howl—*ow-ow-*

owhooo!—so piercing and realistic-sounding, Mel was startled enough to lose her footing for a second. She panicked, punched the emergency *Stop* button, her treadmill groaning as it ground to a halt.

"Ride 'em, Cowboy Zack. Yee-haw!" Bri let loose.

"Hell yeah!" Zack shouted back. The southern twang in his voice gave Mel a boost, as if he'd breathed air into her body.

She slapped the *Start* button and her treadmill whirred back to life. Her pace at five-point-five speed was half as fast as Regina's. Still, she told herself, she *had* shown up. And, someday, she dared to hope, Zack would be cheering her on.

"Twenty seconds, people. Don't you give up on yourself now!" Bri yelled, and Mel could sense the trainer moving up the row of humming machines, jabbing at each machine with a finger, the whir increasing.

Not me, please not me, Mel thought, rehearsing what she'd say when Bri reached her machine. Maybe she'd make a joke. *I'm the most out of shape person in here. Haha. Any more speed and my heart will give out.* Or straight-up lying. *I pulled something yesterday doing yoga. Gotta take it easy.*

Mercifully, Bri stopped two machines short of Mel to focus on the runner who was obviously in the best shape of everyone. Zack's treadmill ran so fast the thing quaked.

"Don't let me down, Zack," Bri said. "Don't disgrace your Fit Fam!"

"Yes, ma'am!" Zack shouted and when Mel saw his smile one word came to mind. *Golden.*

She lost her footing again but was able to catch herself before she rolled right off the machine. A nightmare scenario she'd imagined a hundred times in the last forty minutes. How long could three minutes take? When was the buzzer that notified the trainees to switch stations going to ring out? Mercy, please. Her hand hovered above the keyboard, desperate to slow the machine to a brisk walk. She'd rather speed-walk like a suburban grandma, but feared

Bri would call her out, embarrass her in front of the whole class. In front of Regina. Worse, in front of Zack.

She wanted, no, *needed*, to stop running. Her chest was burning. Dammit, she must stop smoking pot.

But no—*screw it*—she would not be the fat girl who stopped before everyone else.

"One more minute, my babies!" yelled Bri. "Before your last break."

They'd hit the last ten minutes of class. And a break was coming.

"Actually, ladies and Zack, I just changed my mind! We're running through the break. No break! Everyone adds another point-five. Don't think, just do it!" Bri would not be stopped.

Someone dared let out a groan and Mel knew this would only empower Bri. She ate their pain with pleasure.

"Don't give me that whiny bullshit. Don't give *them* a reason to doubt you. You know who I'm talking about. Those assholes who are waiting to see you fail. Don't prove *them* right!"

Them, Mel thought. Adam and his lover.

"They are watching. Waiting," Bri said, quietly now like she was telling a scary bedtime story. A shiver rolled down Mel's sweat-prickled arms. "Waiting for you to give up on yourself. Just so they can say."

"Fuck them!" a woman to Mel's right growled—an over-tanned woman who looked absolutely fantastic (and, Mel thought, might actually be a grandmother) and who'd squealed like a schoolgirl when Zack had entered the studio at the start of class.

A few people laughed but Mel felt the collective motivation lift, the speed increase. As if they were one entity moving in sync.

She punched the big plus-sign on her treadmill. Six-point-five. A new record. She was relieved she'd thought to put a maxi-pad on under her workout leggings—felt herself lose a drop of pee. Then another. Or was her crotch just that sweaty?

Bri let out a throaty whoop. "Booyah! Melanie is showing up!"

Mel knew, even if she had the breath, she'd never correct her. "Melanie just *showed up*, people!"

Half-hearted cheers rose from the row of machines.

"Yeah, baby!" Zack shouted.

Mel punched the plus-sign again. Seven-point-zero. She was flying. Were her feet even touching the ground?

"Forty seconds!" Bri roared. "You can do forty seconds, people. *NOT* thirty! *NOT* thirty-nine. Forty, bitches!"

Mel's lungs were aflame with the shortness of breath that had made her slow down to a speed walk in every other exercise class she'd ever taken. An arms-pumping, hips-swiveling speed walk that she knew made her look like the middle-aged suburban soccer mom she was. Not today. The lights dimmed so the massive HD screens above the treadmills bathed Mel's pumping arms in a blue light. As if, she thought, nearly delirious, they were all swimming underwater. A colony of porpoises.

"I want you to picture something you *really, really* want," Bri said, almost in a whisper now, and yet it felt to Mel as if the woman's breathy hush was all around them, drowning out the hum of the machines. "Right in front of you. You're chasing it!"

Mel imagined Adam jogging in front of her in that easy loping pace he could manage with his long muscular legs. He was looking back at her, smiling. Acting like he had no fucking clue why she was chasing him.

"Maybe it's a job. Maybe it's those last ten pounds of pudge you need to dump. Maybe it's that cute guy you want to ask you out. Hell, maybe you just want him to notice you. It don't matter. Chase it!"

Mel was catching up on Adam. That *who me?* smile. She'd slap it off his unlined face.

"Maybe it's a better version of yourself you're chasing," Bri stage-whispered, her voice softening. "A *you* you can love. 'Cause if you ain't going to love you, no one's gonna."

"Amen!" Mel shouted, surprising herself.

She looked to her right and caught Zack's eyes. He winked.

"Eyes forward, *Melanie!*" Regina called out. "Or you'll fall on your face."

Mel resented the jealousy in her friend's tone. C'mon, Mel was fat and middle-aged; Regina supremely fuckable. She probably steamed her vagina like Gwyneth Paltrow. The last time Mel had her bikini line waxed was Spring Break 1998. Regina could actually *have* Zack if she wanted. What harm was there in a little flirtation between Mel and a guy a thousand miles out of her league?

She banished Adam from her mind and, slowly, the image of his nude back, his hips thrusting into some other woman, was replaced by a new image.

A different man. With green-blue eyes and Kennedy-boy hair.

"Run!" Bri was stalking back and forth behind the treadmills, like a caged animal about to pounce, Mel thought, as she lost feeling in her legs. She was flying. Soaring. The faster she ran the less she felt. "No one ain't never, ever, going to give you what you need. You got to take it!"

The man in Mel's mind put his hand on the small of her back. She could actually feel it, the warmth of his large palm cupping her, gently holding her up, pushing her forward.

She kept running.

"I want to hear you claim it, ladies! I want to hear you say it. *Whose* is it?"

"Mine!" a few shaky voices answered, including the buxom grandma.

"You don't *sound* like you want it!"

"It's mine!" the women screamed back at Bri as she stirred them into a mania reminiscent of a scene from *The Handmaid's Tale*.

"You're catching up!" Bri screamed. "You're within reach! Run, bitches, run!"

And Mel ran on. And on. *Nevertheless*, Mel thought, *she persisted*. She ran until the end-of-class timer rang out.

12

REGINA

"Two Afterburn Smoothies with oat milk, please," said Regina to the cashier at Dogtown Delights, the cafe next door to Color Theory. Bri's class had just ended, and although Regina wasn't thrilled to be hanging out with Mel (not after the way Regina had caught Zack looking at Mel during class)—there Mel was, face aflame from exertion, waiting for Regina at a cozy corner table on the far side of the restaurant, which was decorated with large framed photos of famous surfers.

Whirs from the espresso machine mingled with soft indie rock on the stereo and muddled conversations of Santa Monicans lingering over iced drinks. Who *were* these people, Regina often wondered, relaxing over six-dollar lattes in a sun-filled cafe on a weekday, when every other adult in America was at work?

Then she remembered she was one of them.

"The Afterburn, great choice," said the cashier, a scruffy guy in his twenties. "Best smoothie on the menu. That'll be twenty-two even."

Regina handed him Mel's credit card, which she'd insisted Regina use. Glancing at the card—a "titanium elite" Visa with *Melissa Goldberg* imprinted on the front—Regina couldn't help wondering about Mel's finances. Was she as effortlessly, securely wealthy as she seemed? Did Adam know—or care—what she spent?

Mel certainly didn't seem to worry about money. Then again, Regina had read somewhere that a person was more likely to divulge details of their sexual history than their financial bottom line.

Regina leaned against the counter of the cafe to wait for the smoothies, her muscles spent from the class she and Mel had just taken. Bri had been even tougher than usual and Regina had logged one of her best workouts in months. She went hardest at the gym when she was most stressed, and Zack's text from Jensen about killing V2Y! had been center-stage in her mind since yesterday.

V2Y is dead . . . you've GOT to refund all deposits or Jensen will wig out

One text was all it took and—*bam*—all Regina's work was undone. The planning, the invitations, the food and the kombucha, the $500 she'd paid Lettie to set up and spritz the goddamn towels—all of it had been for nothing. The cash she'd been counting on netting from the deposits of the women who'd committed to the V2Y! program gone.

Which meant she and Zack were back at square one. Back to skimming money from the gym for at least a few more weeks, until Regina got caught up on bills and figured out a better plan.

When she'd spotted Zack and Mel entering Color Theory (Zack's tanned hand pressed against Mel's back fat) she'd had the urge to blow off the workout, to jump back into her car and cry in private—but she'd promised Mel she'd be there. Not that Regina had ended up feeling needed when it became clear that Zack would be giving Mel special attention all class.

Regina had thrown herself into the class with extra fervor, maxing out her treadmill and stacking extra weights on every machine, pushing past her limits to the place where her thoughts shut off and her problems, temporarily, ceased to exist.

I want every one of you to look at Regina's chart before you walk out of here, Bri had called out at the end of class, jabbing a dark purple fingernail toward the performance stats displayed on several wall-mounted flatscreens. *That's the chart of a fucking goddess. Let her be an inspo to every single one of you.*

Bri's compliment, on top of the intense workout, had elevated Regina's spirits from the gutter of Zack's bad news. She'd hardly been able to contain her smile as she eyed her own perfect digital chart on the wall, which indicated she'd spent most of the hour in the orange and red zones and burned 620 calories. For a brief moment, the disappointment of V2Y! evaporated, and she'd basked in the endorphin-soaked glow of her exemplary athletic performance.

It was embarrassing, really, how much a little flattery from a tattooed Millennial coach and a few admiring nods from a handful of fellow gym-goers meant to Regina. But she couldn't help it: she'd been a good student her entire life, driven by the validation of a job well done.

A *good student*—yes—that was a label Regina could claim. But an *inspo*? Didn't being an *inspiration* imply a certain level of good character, an intact moral fiber, the possession of many admirable qualities?

Could one be an inspiration, while also a liar and a thief?

Temporary liar, Regina reminded herself, scanning one of the free local newspapers strewn across the polished wooden counter. *Temporary thief.*

Her actions were necessary. She was shielding her husband and daughters from a great deal of worry and discomfort. Shouldering the stress herself, so that they could continue to inhabit the only lives they'd ever known. Right? Right???

"Two Afterburns!" the barista called out, setting two tall glasses filled to the brim with thick brownish liquid in front of Regina. Carefully, she carried the smoothies across the cafe to Mel, reminding herself to keep it together—to keep the bad V2Y! news out of her mood a little longer, until she was alone and could figure out what to do.

"Sorry that took so long," she said to Mel, setting the drinks down on the table. "I think the barista personally milked the oats."

"I didn't even notice," said Mel. "I'm so exhausted from that class I can barely move." She used a napkin to blot the sweat still dampening her pink cheeks. "I'm glad I did the class, though. Thanks for making me show up." She frowned at her smoothie. "God, what *is* this? Toxic sludge?"

"Ha. Just try it."

"You first."

"I'm proud of you," said Regina, settling in the seat across from Mel. "You killed it in class today." It was true; after Mel's first class, months ago, during which she'd walked at a geriatric pace on the treadmill, and skipped half the weight stations, Regina had been hesitant to invite her to another class. Color Theory regulars were generally understanding of newbies' struggles to keep up—it was a tough workout—but Mel's fitness level was lower than anyone Regina had ever observed at the gym.

"I love Bri!" said Mel. "So much moxie. And she's actually quite philosophical, if you can get past all the"—she paused—"hip-hoppy language."

"*Philosophical.*" Regina laughed. "That's awfully generous of you."

"Oh please. You're the generous one. Complimenting *me* on my old-lady workout? You were an animal in there! I saw your face when you were doing those squat hops."

"Jump squats."

"Whatever. Anyway, I swear, you looked like a soldier in the throes of battle. So intense! It was almost terrifying. But seriously, you're my shero! I don't know how you do it all—the business, the mothering, the extreme fitness. And you make it look so easy."

"All right, Goldberg, settle down," Regina said. "That's just the endorphins talking." Truly, it made Regina cringe when Mel got all effusive and complimentary—she could almost *see* the raw emotion oozing out of the sweating woman's pores.

She'd been surprised when Mel had texted her to say she was coming to today's class. Even more surprised when Mel had cranked up her treadmill to level seven and swung kettle bells with halfway decent form. As for Mel's chemistry with Zack, it was hard to tell. Zack had been in even more of a performance mode than usual, hamming it up with Bri and doling out high fives and hugs during the circuit changes to anyone in reach. He hadn't seemed particularly attentive to Mel, but then again, Regina had been so involved in her own workout, perhaps she'd missed something between them.

Zack couldn't possibly have the hots for Mel. Could he?

"I killed nothing," said Mel, sipping her smoothie and grimacing. "And for the first half of class, I was hating your guts. But then, something clicked, and I actually started to enjoy myself. It was kind of miraculous."

"I saw how much you were in the red zone," Regina nodded. "That's where the magic happens."

"Magic shouldn't require so much suffering."

"Trust me," said Regina. "Pretty soon you'll be dragging *me* to class."

"Now, *that* we both know is bullshit," said Mel. "You live for this stuff. I see your face when you're swinging that round anvil-thing. You're in heaven."

"Round anvil-thing?"

"You know," said Mel. "That super-heavy and extremely dangerous thing with the handle?"

"The kettle bell."

Mel waved a nail-bitten hand. "Whatever. You can't expect me to transform my lifestyle *and* learn a whole new vocabulary at the same time." She took another sip of her smoothie and wrinkled her nose. "This thing is gross. Oats should not be milked. Remind me why I can't have dairy again?"

"Inflammation," said Regina patiently. It really was incredible, how little Mel knew about her body and how it functioned. "Dairy is a known irritant of the gut lining and suppresses the immune system. It basically makes your insides swollen and irritated."

"Would that even matter?" Mel sighed, pinching the excess flesh of her upper arm. "I'm already swollen and irritated on the outside."

Regina laughed. "Oh, stop it." Mel had a way of poking fun at herself, of being completely open when it came to her self-doubt, offering up biting observations of everyone around her. She spoke without the filter employed by every other woman Regina knew in Santa Monica. Regina found it refreshing, though it also made her nervous. She never knew what Mel might say.

"I have to ask you something," Mel said, draining the last of her smoothie, which struck Regina as unnecessary, since Mel had pronounced it "gross."

"Ask away," said Regina.

"But you can't get mad at me."

"I won't."

"In fact, I'm just going to apologize in advance. I'm sorry for asking you a potentially offensive and invasive question."

"Oh, cut it out," said Regina. Mel's tendency to over-apologize, a sort of counter-habit to her frequent complaining, drove Regina crazy. "Just ask the damn question."

"Fine." Mel took a deep breath. "Is there something going on between you and Coach Zack?"

"Going on? Like what?"

Mel arched an eyebrow and grinned. "Don't play dumb, Wolfie."

"Zack and I are friendly acquaintances."

"Yeah, friendly acquaintances who flirt constantly. I see the way you two hug each other. It's impossible not to notice."

"It's Color Theory. Everyone hugs everyone."

"Yeah, but you and Zack do an *affair* hug. I hate to say it, but I'm not the only one who notices."

"What's that supposed to mean?"

"Just that you two give off a certain vibe that's easy to feel. Even a lobotomized squirrel like Lindsey Leyner is onto it."

"So, you and Lindsey Leyner are gossiping about me and a thirty-year-old trainer?"

"No! No one's 'gossiping' about it. No one's even said anything. But we're just all *thinking* it. And as you know, I suck at repressing my thoughts."

"You do," said Regina. "And I hate to disappoint you, but no, I am absolutely *not* having an affair with some kid-coach. I'm forty-four years old, Mel. With two kids and a husband. Zack's cute, sure, but come on. I would never do something"—she found herself fumbling for the words, suddenly flustered—"that risky."

"Okay," said Mel, lowering her voice. "But even if you did, you know it would be safe to tell me, right?"

Regina thought of her early-morning dreams, how Zack frequently turned up in her bed and smothered her body with his. She ran her fingers over the beads of condensation clinging to her smoothie cup.

"Thanks. But nothing's going on with me and Zack. He's all yours, Mel." *As if,* she added to herself.

"Ew," said Mel. "Please. I respect that you two are, uh, friendly acquaintances, but the guy's an actual Trump supporter. As much as Adam deserves for me to have an affair, it could never be with Zack. On principle."

"What? When do you and Zack talk politics? And *what* does Adam deserve?" Sometimes, the way Mel navigated a conversation—jumping from topic to topic, casually dropping bombs of information and then speeding on—made Regina's head spin.

Mel tightened her lips against her teeth. "I don't want to get into it. Let's just say Adam's been mistaking himself for some sort of fucking prince. Or sultan. The ones that have a harem."

"*Your* Adam? He seems so—"

"Please." Mel held up a palm. "Don't even think about using the P-word. As in *perfect*. No Adam worship. I might not be able to keep my smoothie down." The levity drained from her voice. "I mean it, Regina."

Regina lowered her voice. "Did he do something?"

"Jury's still out. And I'm too pissed to talk about it."

"You have to talk about it," said Regina. "It's your marriage."

"I can't. Not yet. It's too infuriating. You know, I think that's why I sort of enjoyed the gym today. It made me forget how pissed I am. I could pretend I was swinging the kettle-iron at Adam's head."

"Kettle *bell*." Regina couldn't help giggling. "Exercise is great for anger."

"Maybe I should invest in one of those things," Mel sighed. "Anyway, *you* never talk about your marriage. I barely know anything about Gordon!"

"Funny, neither do I at the moment," said Regina. "He's currently married to the War of 1812."

"Huh?"

"That's what his screenplay's about. He's taking a sabbatical from his regular TV writing job right now to work on it. It's basically all he thinks about."

"Seriously?" Mel widened her eyes.

Regina sighed. "Seriously."

Mel barked a laugh. "Sorry. But the War of 1812? That sounds like the most boring movie on the planet. I can't even remember who fought in it."

"The US and England," Regina sighed. "Gordon thinks it could be a really big movie, actually. Film's answer to *Hamilton* or whatever. Though I agree with you."

"Men." Mel rolled her eyes. "Can you imagine having that level of confidence? To just scrap your job and announce you're writing a *big movie* about the fucking War of 1812? That's what being born into cultural privilege gets you, I guess." She cupped her hand over her mouth. "Oh God, I'm sorry. I didn't mean *Gordon* specifically. I'm sure his screenplay will be . . . great. I just meant men in general are—"

"Gordon works hard," Regina cut in, feeling an urge to defend her husband. "You don't need to get into one of your white-male-privilege rants."

"Sorry, sorry." Mel pressed her hands to the still-flushed sides of her face. "I can't believe I said that. I really do need to work on the whole self-control thing. Zack actually might be right about that."

"Right about what?"

"Oh, we had a few chats at that awful party you threw at my house. He told me self-control can be learned. That physical discipline and emotional discipline go hand in hand, and that he thought the V2-whatever program would be perfect for me."

"What? He actually said that? Did you slap him?"

"I said maybe first he should try to sign the president up."

"Ha." Regina pushed her smoothie away. The way Mel pounded hers had killed Regina's appetite.

"I probably should have slapped him," Mel went on. Regina thought she detected a new amusement in her tone. "But he meant it as a joke. And even though he's kind of an idiot, he's also pretty cute, with the floppy hair and the southern drawl. Like a big dumb puppy. So, I let it slide."

"He was flirting with you!" Regina would not allow herself to be jealous of one stupid conversation between Mel and Zack. "Like he does with everyone," she added.

"It was his fat-lady flirting," said Mel with a shrug. "Which is completely different from his skinny-lady flirting. Which is not to be confused with his Regina-flirting. AKA his *affair-flirting*."

"Stop it." Regina rolled her eyes. "So, getting back to Adam."

Mel ignored her. "Zack's cute," she said thoughtfully, "but he's got to lose the *hashtag blessed* thing. Can you talk to him about that?" Mel pressed her hands into prayer position and giggled.

"Don't avoid my question," said Regina, cringing to herself. Why did Zack insist on using that inane phrase? He was much smarter than he let on.

"You know what I'd like to avoid?" Mel said. "Wasting our time talking about men. As it is, they dominate everything on the planet. We shouldn't let them rule our conversations, too."

"Fine," said Regina. "Let's talk about ladies' night. We're having one in a couple of weeks. No men. A group of moms with kids at Wayne. Some of them go to the gym, too. We've been meeting for drinks at Canyon Rustica for years now."

"*Ladies' night?*" Mel's mouth dropped open. "What is this, 1988? Is there a wet T-shirt contest, too?"

"You're impossible. We actually call it Minnow Night, a cutesy version of M-N-O, which stands for *Mom's Night Out*. I knew you'd make fun of me if I said that, so I changed it to *ladies' night*, and you're making fun of me anyway."

"Of course I am." Mel flashed a devilish grin. "And Ladies' Night, or Minnow Night, or Tittie Night all sound horrendous."

"Very funny. Put it on your calendar. November fifteenth."

"First of all, that's like *months* from now."

"Under a month, actually."

"And secondly, I'm terrible at keeping calendars. Adam's crazy for them. He's always color-coding things and assigning, um, importance levels or something."

"Then tell Adam to put it on the calendar. You're coming."

"Fine," Mel sighed. "Have you ever noticed that our friendship is mostly based on you forcing me to do things that are completely contrary to my nature? Can that possibly be healthy?" She fiddled with her sparkling wedding band. Regina's own fingers were bare; rings interfered with lifting weights. She wondered what was really going on with Mel and Adam. Frankly, Mel seemed like she'd be a difficult spouse.

"I *have* noticed," Regina said. "I've also noticed that you end up thanking me later. So, you're welcome in advance." She lifted her smoothie toward Mel, in a toast.

Mel tapped her empty glass to Regina's. "Are you even going to drink that thing? Or are you just giving me a lesson in self-control?"

Regina couldn't help smiling. "You're insane," she said, taking a long drink from the straw. "Oh my God. This is delicious."

"And *you* are absolutely delusional," said Mel. "But I kind of love you for it."

In that moment, Regina kind of loved Mel, too.

WEDNESDAY, OCTOBER 17, 2018

13

MEL

MEL WAS STUFFING TWO NEW DESIGNER HANDBAGS (STILL WRAPPED IN plastic packaging—she *must* stop shopping online while stoned) into a bin in her closet when she heard Lettie call from downstairs, "Hello?"

"*Hola*, Leticia!" Mel called back. "I'll be right down! Just taking a quick shower."

"No worries," Lettie called back. The oft-used phrase still made Mel cringe. *No worries? Really, no worries?* Mel wanted to respond when the Southern Californians uttered the ridiculous phrase. *There's, like, a million things to worry about! Don't you see that Big Cheeto in the Oval Office? And, by the way, my husband is cheating on me!* But Lettie could say anything. Lettie could do no wrong.

If only Lettie wanted to be friends with Mel the way Regina did, Mel thought, scanning her walk-in closet one last time, searching for anything that should be hidden, like clothes with the price tags still attached. She'd almost confessed the Adam situation to Regina yesterday, over those horrid oat milk smoothies, then lost her nerve. It was too embarrassing: she, the oblivious fat chick with the hot, cheating husband. A scenario that now seemed so obvious she couldn't bear to confirm its truth to anyone. And anyway, could Regina be trusted? She was the kind of woman who lied effortlessly. Small white lies, yes—the kind that all women told—but Mel had a hunch that Regina lied to herself, too. That tone she'd used when kvetching about her husband Gordon's screenplay, the one about some long-ago war—hadn't Mel heard a smoldering rage trying to break through? Was this the sort of person in whom Mel should confide her humiliating secret?

No matter what, Mel was grateful to Regina. It was Regina, after all, who'd spotted Lettie's handwritten index card on the bulletin board at the Santa Monica Food Co-op years ago, advertising "Good, Honest Cleaner" and dialed the number. Regina who'd recommended that Mel hire Lettie when Mel had asked for a housekeeping referral, Regina adding, in a protective tone, *She's undocumented. Just so you're aware.* As if Mel and Adam might have red *Make America Great Again* hats stashed in the back of their closet.

In truth, Mel was happy to employ members of the group the Big Cheeto in the Oval Office targeted most viciously. Paying Lettie to clean her house was, Mel believed, her own small act of protest. And pre-cleaning the house before Lettie arrived was an act of self-care: it helped stave off the guilt she felt over having a housecleaner at all.

Mel's favorite time of the week was right after Lettie cleaned, when Mel sat in the still and silent living room, inhaling the lemony scent of the cleaning products, gazing at the tracks the vacuum left across the velvety tan carpet like a freshly mowed lawn. For the moment, her home was immaculate. Even if Adam was a cheating bastard. Even if Mel's once sweet little girl seemed to resent her more every day. Her home was perfect. Before Sloane returned with dirty cleats and soccer socks hiding a hundred tiny pieces of turf; before Adam (that fucker), his *gi* drenched in sweat, made the house smell like a locker room.

Showered, Mel threw on her uniform—black palazzo pants, black tank top, dangly earrings, and a pom-pom-fringed silk DVF scarf.

On her way downstairs, she turned on the air-conditioning. She'd wanted to turn it on hours ago but waited until Adam and Sloane left the house. She'd heard Adam's voice in her head—who used A/C when it was seventy-two degrees and under every single day?

"I turned on the air for you," Mel white-lied to Lettie as she stepped into the kitchen, where Lettie had begun to clean, washing, Mel realized with horror, the breakfast dishes Adam had left in the sink. "I can do that," Mel said too quickly, nearly shoving Lettie out of the way.

Lettie laughed. "You are too good to me, Melissa."

"It's *Mel*. Please, Lettie. We've known each other for almost a year. You've got to call me Mel, 'kay?"

"Mel," Lettie said in that quiet way Mel admired. Her smile almost there.

"Has anyone ever told you that you have a mysterious smile?" Mel asked. She turned the tap toward *cold*. How could Lettie stand water that hot? "A Mona Lisa smile."

Lettie frowned and crossed her arms. "Mona Lisa? She ugly."

"Sorry, that was dumb!" Mel winced. Of course, Lettie wouldn't see that as a compliment. "You're far more beautiful than any Mona Lisa."

She was relieved when Lettie smiled and tossed her long thick black hair away from her face coquettishly before nudging Mel with her hip so Mel had no choice but to step away from the sink.

"Have you eaten?" Mel asked, opening the fridge door to see what Adam had cooked that morning. "There's leftover frittata in here somewhere."

"The kind Adam makes?" Lettie asked, instant admiration in her voice. "Those are delicious. Small piece only."

"It's not hard to make," said Mel (not that she'd ever tried), feeling herself blanch at the sound of her husband's name. Lettie had been so damn impressed when she learned busy *Mr. Adam* made unemployed Mel gourmet breakfasts every morning, leaving them in a covered dish on the kitchen counter for her to enjoy when she woke after sleeping in. And even more impressed that Adam was the one who carted Sloane off to school so Mel could take her mornings at a leisurely pace.

Adam. Adam. Adam. Maybe, Mel thought, they wrote that ridiculous Santa Monica city motto (fortunate people, yadda, yadda, prosperous land) with Adam in mind?

She felt suddenly queasy, the few bites of Adam's stupid frittata she'd forced down earlier churning in her stomach. She took a deep breath and opened the microwave.

"You okay, Miss . . . er, *Mel*?" Lettie's face crossed with concern.

Mel placed the frittata dish in the microwave and pressed *30 seconds.*

"I'm good," Mel said, as brightly as she could manage, then moved from the microwave to the espresso machine to make two cappuccinos exactly the way she and Lettie loved them: extra foam and sugar. Their ritual sweet indulgence (Mel could practically see Regina's disapproving frown) before Lettie began the long job of cleaning Mel's big house. But today, she feared she'd lose control when they sat down together, creamy drinks steaming in the cool A/C. The prospect of breaking down in front of Lettie, who gracefully contained the stress of her own (bigger, less-privileged) problems, mortified Mel. How could Mel cry over her rich husband's bad behavior when Lettie was a direct target of the hateful orange clown in the White House? When ICE was making random raids in sanctuary cities, like LA, where undocumented immigrants were supposed to be protected?

No, she could not confide in Lettie about the Adam situation. Mr. Good-as-a-Man-Gets had a way of impressing even women who'd endured terrible things at the hands of men, and thus had come to fear them in general. Lettie, Mel knew from Regina, was one of these women. Regina had told Mel the story of how she'd rescued bloody-faced Lettie and Andres from a raging Manuel in the middle of the night, driving them all the way to the Valley and paying for a motel where they'd be safe and impossible to find. Mel had found herself wishing she could've taken Regina's place. What she'd give to be able to make a difference in the life of a woman like Lettie, especially now when it seemed as if any American who wasn't a white cisgender male (Mel was determined to use the proper terminology, to be an *ally*) was viewed by the president and his lackeys as less than equal.

Mel foamed the sweetened milk and poured it into two mugs over shots of espresso. Then she eased a hefty square of warmed frittata onto a plate and set it all on the kitchen island.

"Come sit," she commanded Lettie, who was up to her elbows in soapy foam at the sink. They settled on barstools at the corner of the island, facing each other.

"I say *small* piece," Lettie said, eyeing her eggs, but Mel knew she was pleased by the portion; she loved to eat as much as Mel did. "You look more skinny." Lettie squinted at Mel. "Your arms got tighter. Maybe from that exercise party?" She took a big bite of frittata. Mel noticed Lettie's nails were done in cherry-red acrylic, which meant, to Mel's delight, that she'd finally used the salon certificate Mel had given her months ago.

"More, skinny, *me*?" Mel said. "God no. I'm such a whale." Instantly, she worried she'd offended Lettie, since the two of them were practically the same size, with matching soft, round bellies, a likeness that made Mel even more fond of her housecleaner.

"No, no, no," Lettie tut-tutted, "you looking good. This is a fact. I see it in your face. And here, too." Lettie reached under the table and poked Mel gently in the side.

"Honestly, I haven't noticed," said Mel, heat rising to her face. She was unaccustomed to body compliments and reluctant to share with Lettie the news that she'd been working out lately. (*Twice* in the last three days! Every part of Mel, right down to her butt cheeks, was sore.) She wouldn't want her housecleaner—her *friend*—to wonder if Mel was becoming like all the other white women Lettie cleaned for: vain, fitness-obsessed, flush with free time for sweating in the gym Lettie was surely paid next to nothing to clean.

But damn if Mel didn't feel better from that hour-long torture session at Color Theory. And, according to that heart rate monitor thing Zack had helped her strap to her wrist at the start of class, his square-tipped fingers grazing her skin, she was burning an average of six hundred calories in a single hour.

Had jogging up the stairs of her house that morning required a tad less effort? Or was it Mel's imagination?

"Well, if I've actually lost any weight, I'm sure I'll gain it right back," Mel added as Lettie swallowed the last of her frittata.

Lettie hopped off her barstool and transferred her plate to the sink. Then she turned back to Mel and leaned back theatrically against the counter, sticking out her stomach so it stretched against the bleach-stained pink T-shirt she wore to clean. "Check out *this* belly. It's good and fat." She gave a little shimmy to make her stomach wobble, grinning at Mel.

Mel barked a laugh; she'd always found Lettie to be a natural comedian, not to mention very smart. Mel had considered gifting her some kind of creative experience. An improv acting class? A humor-writing workshop? A few hours at the pottery studio on Wilshire?

Lettie went on, emboldened by Mel's amusement. "Today I take Andres early to school so I can go to the religious place where they have the free food. You know, the people who wear the dresses and sing and dance on the street? The happy people?"

"Hare Krishnas?" Mel guessed.

"Yes!" Lettie said as she rinsed their empty cappuccino mugs. "You so smart, Melissa."

"Well, they *are* pretty hard to miss."

"But," Lettie continued, "I do not like the food that much. It's all vegetarian."

Mel mirrored Lettie's look of disgust. "Yuck. I know how you love your meat."

"And the beans." Lettie lowered her voice. "They give me gas."

They laughed together, both clutching their soft stomachs, and

Mel felt happier than she had all week. For the moment, Adam and his lies did not exist.

"How's Andres?" Mel asked, eager to maintain the good feeling, to stay in Lettie's comforting presence. "Did you get him those services?"

She'd been honored when Lettie had shared with her the challenges six-year-old Andres was having at school. Delighted to complete the paperwork Lettie handed her nervously, falsely claiming Lettie worked for Mel forty hours a week, a minor lie that enabled Andres to attend the excellent John Wayne Elementary in Santa Monica, instead of the crappy LA public school for which he was zoned. At Wayne, Andres would be able to get the services and therapy he so desperately needed, for free.

"The therapist," Lettie said, looking down at the sudsy dishes, "she says Andres is depressed."

Mel heard disgust in Lettie's voice. As if the diagnosis was an insult.

"And you don't believe that?" Mel asked, treading carefully, not wanting to mess up again like she had with the Mona Lisa comparison.

"What do I know?" Lettie said. "He is six. A baby. Babies have depression?"

Mel wondered if Lettie might cry. What would she do to comfort her? What could Mel, with her designer shit and rich-people problems, say?

She wanted to tell Lettie that only she, Andres's mother, knew what was best for him. That Lettie was smart and capable and that Andres was lucky to have her.

Then she heard Regina's voice in her head: *Dial it down, Goldberg.*

"Please, Lettie," Mel said, "let me know if there is *anything* I can do to help. Anything at all. I want to help."

Lettie looked up from the sink, using the back of her hand to push a strand of dark hair from her forehead. Mel could tell there was something Lettie wanted to say but feared any prodding would make her friend retreat. Mel had noticed how Lettie averted her eyes in conversation, especially with Adam, but now Lettie was looking straight into Mel's eyes. For the first time, Mel saw the patch of green in Lettie's dark brown iris.

"You are a good person, Melissa. I tell my friends, *Melissa, she is my favorite white person*. This is a fact."

Lettie, Mel thought, couldn't know how much this meant to her. What a gift it was to hear this today of all days.

"And now," Lettie said, her voice strong and firm again, "you go." She pointed to the stairs. "I need to get to work."

"Okay," said Mel reluctantly. She wasn't yet ready for coffee time with Lettie to be over. "But I'm going to strip the beds. I'll help you."

"You are crazy." Lettie gave a deep belly laugh and slapped her hand to her forehead. "I tell you, someday, if I hire a cleaner, I won't help her clean my house. Nope and never ever."

Mel laughed, too. "No way. You'll sit back and drink cappuccino while she cleans."

Lettie thumbs-upped with her long red nail. "Now you making sense, Miss Melissa."

UPSTAIRS, MEL STRIPPED the sheets (patterned with soccer balls, naturally) from Sloane's lofted mattress, then moved on to the master bedroom, where the sight of the giant, unmade bed she shared with Adam triggered a spike of rage. She charged toward it, and yanked so hard at the fitted sheet (two-hundred-dollar Egyptian cotton—how did she live with herself?) that it ripped at the seam. "Fuck!" she said, under her breath, and gave the cherrywood bedframe a swift, impulsive kick with her bare foot.

Which, of course, hurt like hell.

"Fuck!" she wailed, at top volume this time, plopping down on the bed (Adam's side—ugh—but she was in too much pain to care) to examine her injured big toe.

"Miss Melissa?" Lettie called. "You okay up there?"

Before Mel could steady her voice enough to answer *Sorry, I'm fine!* she caught sight of a wad of Kleenex on the carpet, at the base of Adam's night stand.

Instantly, Mel burst into tears.

He couldn't even give her the respect of throwing away his used cum rags.

She snatched the stiffened ball and threw it as hard as she could. It bounced off the wall by the bathroom and back onto the floor.

Mel crawled to her side of the bed and lay on her side, sobbing as her bruised toe began to throb. The reality of what Adam had done, cheating on her after almost two decades together, was too much to bear. She could not move, or stop her tears, even when she heard Lettie's feet on the stairs, coming to check on her.

Mel opened her eyes to see Lettie kneeling.

"Melissa? You okay? What happen?"

Mel stopped crying, but could not speak. This was exactly what she *hadn't* wanted to do: confess her rich-lady problems to Lettie, who had no money, a handicapped son, and lived under the constant threat of deportation.

"Tell me," Lettie pressed. "What is wrong?"

"Everything!" Mel finally burst. To hell with it. She'd never had any self-control, anyway—probably the reason Adam cheated on her in the first place—why should now be any different? "Adam's having an affair!"

"No!"

"Yes!"

Instantly, all her rage at Adam turned to an unbearable, smothering sadness. She curled into a ball and began to weep again, though this time over the prospect of actually losing him—the same man who, just last Friday, had called her out of the blue, for no reason, to tell her he loved her. (Though in the same call, Mel remembered now, Adam had apologized in advance for needing to get home extra late that night—*Stupid drinks meeting with studio people.* Should Mel have been suspicious?)

The same man who'd told her how beautiful she looked when she'd first woken up the other morning, groggy and wild-haired. (Though he'd followed up by asking whether she was sure she hadn't lost weight.)

Adam, the man who patiently stroked her hair until she fell asleep on nights she was too anxious to sleep. (Though he also mentioned, yet again, how she might consider learning to meditate. As if.)

She didn't want to lose him. Despite the vulgar, incriminating texts she'd found. Yes, he was a cheater, and yes, their marriage had been strained this past year since moving to California—so much bickering!—but what about the nineteen happy years they'd had together? Shouldn't their relationship be salvageable, based on the math?

Then the texts flashed to mind: thinking about u & how hot ur . . . and the awful reality of Mel's situation engulfed her. Adam was lost to her. What if he had already found Mel's replacement—his Version 2.0 partner to match his Version 2.0 West Coast life?

"Ohhhh," she moaned, face-planting into the mattress, the pain of her thoughts turning physical, overriding the ache of her stubbed toe.

Then she felt Lettie stroking her hair. Finally, when her tears subsided, Mel slowly sat up, unable to meet Lettie's eyes.

"I'm sorry," Mel mumbled.

"Do not be sorry, Melissa," said Lettie gently, handing Mel a soft, damp washcloth to blot her swollen face. As Mel pressed it to her cheeks, she saw Lettie's expression harden. Her teeth clench.

"Hijo de la chingada!" Lettie hissed, eyes flashing.

Mel didn't speak Spanish, though it was on her to-do list, but she didn't have to. She knew exactly what Lettie was saying. Or, at least, the gist of it. Men are dogshit.

Lettie was enraged at *Adam.*

Lettie understood. She *cared*. She was, Mel realized, her only true friend in the state of California. The thought both comforted and saddened her.

"Thank you, Leticia," Mel said, sniffling. "You are *so* kind. I don't know what I'd do without you. Sometimes, I feel like there's just nothing, no one, here for me."

"That is not true. Many people here love you. Regina says you are a very special friend to her."

"Regina? She's not really a friend per se. More like, um . . . " She searched for a simple way to explain. "We're in the same place at the same time, and got pushed together. You know?"

"*Si.*"

"I mean," Mel said, catching a glance of her face in the mirror and loathing the sad person she saw—eyes puffy, nose and chin shiny—"look at me, and then look at her. Regina's basically perfect."

"*You* are beautiful!" Lettie said with the astonished reflex of a mother.

"Oh God, now I'm really pathetic." Mel used the bed to hoist herself to her feet. "I'm so sorry, Lettie. *This*"—Mel pointed to her own swollen face—"is not part of your job description."

"You have been hurt, Melissa. You have the right to be sad. And angry!"

"Maybe. But it's not your problem."

"You are my friend, so it is my problem, too. I want to help. And I think I have the answer. A big Band-Aid!"

Hearing Lettie call her *a friend* lifted Mel's ravaged spirits.

"What you need," Lettie went on, "is a fresh start. What is it that man, the coach—*muy guapo* coach—said at the exercise party?"

"Um. Zack?" *Muy guapo, indeed*, thought Mel, remembering his turquoise eyes, the tousles of hair, and sun-browned skin. The cords of muscles in his arms.

"Yes, Zack!" Lettie said. "What was the name of his program?"

Mel winced. "Version Two You?"

"Yes! A new you!" Lettie sounded downright excited. "My idea is, you should do the program. It will make you strong. Ready to start Melissa's *new* life. I see it like a fortune-teller. All the good things coming to you."

"That's sweet of you, Lettie, but—"

Lettie cut her off. "And with the new Melissa comes a new man. Like French fries come with a burger."

"I doubt that," Mel said. "You know what the women look like here." She waved a hand toward the windows. "They're . . ."

"No, Melissa!" Lettie practically shouted. "You are wrong. No man wants a skinny no-ass like Lindsey Leyner. The men, they like the meat." Lettie opened and closed her fingers like she was squishing a handful of dough.

Mel couldn't help giggling. "Men don't want vegetarians."

"Right." Lettie grinned. "So, I am not saying to get skinny. Only that I think you will be happy getting strong. It will help you forget"— she tapped a curved red nail to her temple—"about Mr. Adam."

Downstairs, the oven buzzed, indicating the end of its self-cleaning cycle. Lettie stepped toward the bedroom door. "I will go finish my work now. And you start thinking about the New Mel. About that program with Coach Zack. No more tears. Deal?"

"Deal."

Alone again, Mel moved to the sitting area by the picture window and watched the palm trees swaying in the light breeze, the sun lighting the thick fronds so they gleamed like plastic. Lettie was right: she *did* need a change. Something radical, in a direction Brooklyn Mel would never have considered.

Could she actually sign up for Zack's program with the terrible name? After two measly one-hour workouts, Mel's first in practically a decade, could she possibly hire a personal trainer—one who used the phrase *hashtag blessed*?

Then she closed her eyes and pictured it: flying east to New York for the weekend, stepping into her old friends' cramped living rooms dressed in some trendy new outfit four sizes down from her current one, everyone going gaga over her new svelte body. Marveling at her toned arms, her accentuated waist. The new *her.*

She opened her eyes, feeling something like hope spread through her chest. Outside, the clear blue sky blinked through the magnolia leaves.

Good-bye, double chin, she thought.

Good-bye, hump of back fat!

Good-bye, Jigglypuff!

Hello, Mel 2.0.

14

ZACK

ZACK DROVE ALONG THE BLUFFS OF OCEAN AVENUE UNTIL HE REACHED Montana Avenue, made a hard right, and gunned his truck in the direction of John Wayne Elementary, where Andres attended kindergarten. For the *second* time. In some sort of special ed class.

Special ed, the poor kid.

It was Zack's fault. *The accident.*

He punched the truck's stereo and Waylon Jennings's voice filled the air. Reflexively, he closed the truck's windows before cranking up the volume.

Zack never felt comfortable playing country music with the windows down when driving through the streets of Santa Monica, as if he everyone he passed would immediately think, *Hick, redneck, racist,* and think to blame him for the president and everything else wrong with the country right now. That was how this city made him feel: as if he were playing defense at all times, protecting his dignity from all the rich, smug liberals ready to brand him as another white guy whose privilege had been handed to him on a silver platter. He could feel it in their eyes, whenever the subject of The Donald or immigration or Me Too came up. If he didn't jump *right in* and agree with them that everyone white and male was a spoiled misogynist, that women who claimed to be victims were *always* telling the truth, that "people of color" were in a state of permanent persecution, that illegal immigrants deserved the utmost compassion and to be exempted from the rules, that the president was an evil sociopath, then Zack himself was clearly an asshole, one of the "deplorables" responsible for flushing the great U-S-of-A down the toilet.

Well, Zack thought, braking to swing onto the leafy residential street that led to Andres's school, he had news for all those frowning, judging, Prius-driving, Clinton-loving, white-male-hating people who frowned at him daily in Santa Monica: he wasn't even white. And he could guarantee them he'd personally done more to help immigrants than any of those pretty white women gazing tearfully at Instagram images of Mexican toddlers at the border. Yes, he'd made a huge mistake. But before the accident, he'd been a model uncle to Andres, and had been bleeding cash into Lettie's floorboards even before he truly owed it to her. Despite this, Lettie's texts were more and more desperate. Like her latest text, begging for a sky-high sum of money, over seven grand, claiming she needed it in the next two weeks or she'd almost definitely be deported:

Deportation ☠ ☠ ☠

Zack reached the school and parked alongside the play yard with its blue-and-yellow climbing structure and spongy reddish surface—God forbid the precious children of Santa Monica skin their knees on a regular old blacktop. But he was glad Andres got to go to John Wayne Elementary, with its cheerful yellow buildings intersected by sunny breezeways with colorful murals painted on them. He was grateful for the big, grassy field with handball courts (not that Andres would be playing sports anytime soon, but still), and the landscaping and the vegetable garden, and even the "peace wall," where the kids hung strings of concentric paper circles with sappy messages written on them.

Andres deserved all of this, Zack thought, as he showed his ID to the receptionist and signed in, feeling the eyes of the other admins seated at desks behind her assessing him.

"Room 403," said the receptionist, a woman with florid cheeks and the double chin of someone on the fast track to heart disease. "Right next to the library," she said. "I think they've already gotten started." She handed Zack his guest pass. On it she'd printed *Zacarias*. He felt a flash of anger at her, as if she were letting him know she was aligned with Lettie, even though she'd simply transcribed the name on his driver's license.

Get some exercise, he wanted to snap at her. *Have some respect for yourself.*

"Thanks," he mumbled, and slapped the name tag onto his T-shirt.

He strode down the breezeway toward the library. The door to room 403 was cracked open. Zack rapped on it and walked in without waiting to find Andres sitting in a chair in a small circle with three adults Zack vaguely recognized: a young black woman who was some sort of kids-with-problems expert; the vice principal, a guy in his thirties who was already balding with a paunch; and Andres's teacher, Ms. Redding, a hippie-ish type with long graying hair and ugly sandals. Andres adored her.

"*Tío!*" Andres called, with obvious delight, from a chair in the middle of the room, his face lighting up.

At the sight of his nephew, wearing the glasses Zack had gotten for him and a too-big Pokémon T-shirt, his hair gelled to one side with the cheap gunk Zack despised—a favorite with Mexican moms, but at least Lettie was bothering to groom him—Zack felt the negativity leave his body, replaced by a rush of love that hit him right in the back of his throat, making him feel he might tear up. He swallowed hard and grinned at the boy.

"Hey there, little man."

"Can you sit next to me?"

"You got it."

Zack squeezed his way into the circle and took the kid-sized chair next to Andres, noticing Andres's little metal cane propped against it. The good feeling in Zack's chest wilted.

The vice principal cleared his throat. "Thank you for coming,

Mr. . . . ah." He squinted at Zack's name tag. "*Zacarias*." He rolled the *R* carefully—as if to say, Zack supposed, *See, I respect your culture!*

"Just Zack."

"Sorry, Zack. I'm Lee Waldron, vice principal, and this is Ms. Gates"—he gestured to the black woman—"director of our special ed program, and of course"—he opened his hand toward Andres's teacher—"you know Ms. Redding."

"We've all met before, actually," said Zack. "Several times."

"We're running a little behind, so we'll need to do this a little more quickly than usual."

"Sorry about that. I got here as fast as I could," said Zack.

The vice principal glanced at the clock on the wall. "Not a problem. We'll chat with Andres here for a few minutes, then send him on his way, so that the four of us can discuss some options."

The black woman—Ms. Gates—jumped in. "Let me just start by saying how proud I am of Andres. He's doing an incredible job in kindergarten this year."

"Well, he ought to be, right?" said Zack. "Since it's the second time around?"

Andres's teacher gave him a withering look.

"Every child has his or her own individual pace," said Ms. Gates. "Last year at this time, Andres was challenged by participating in class activities. Now he's engaged in the classroom and communicating with his peers."

"He's a smart little guy," said Zack, ruffling Andres's crusty hair. Andres ducked but flashed Zack a grin.

"Having said that," Ms. Gates went on, "there are a number of standards that still need to be met in order for Andres to continue on his current track."

"Meaning?" asked Zack.

"It's only October," said Ms. Redding. "So, there's plenty of time for catch-up. That's why we wanted to meet with Andres's . . . family.

So that we can put measures in place to guarantee his success, and ensure there's a spot for him here at John Wayne."

"Where else would he go?" said Zack.

Ms. Redding turned to Andres. "Sweetie, you like it here at school, right?"

Andres shrugged.

"Words, please," said Ms. Redding.

Andres muttered something, pulling at his shirt.

"Clearly, please," said Ms. Redding.

"No," said Andres. "I hate school."

"You don't *hate* school, little man," said Zack.

"Of course you don't, Andres," Ms. Redding said brightly. "I see you having fun every day. What about our counting songs? What about playing with Julian and Ileana?"

Other Mexican kids, thought Zack.

"*Tío*," said Andres to Zack, ignoring his teacher. "Can we go home now?"

"No, buddy," said Zack, cringing. "It's still time to be at school."

"I want to go home."

"No." Zack tried to keep his voice gentle.

"I *want* to go home. My leg hurts," Andres whined.

"Buddy, come on."

"Take me home!" Andres writhed in his seat.

"Andres, knock it off, right now!" Rage at Lettie spread through Zack. She should be here, dealing with her son. Like any half-decent mother. Instead of slapping this meeting onto him so she could fold rich women's laundry.

"It's okay," said Ms. Redding, leaving her chair to kneel on the rug in front of Andres. She put one hand on either of his shoulders and massaged them gently. "Shhh. Sweetie, sweetie. There's no need to yell. We're all your friends here. We respect your feelings." She continued to rub his shoulders and make soothing noises.

Andres quieted, his little body relaxing back into his chair. Did

Zack detect a smug look from Redding? *See, this is how it's done.* He felt like stomping her Birkenstocked foot.

The vice principal cleared his throat. "Perhaps we can let Ms. Redding and Andres get back to class now."

"That's a good idea," said Ms. Redding. She helped Andres to his feet and helped him maneuver his cane into the proper position. Zack could hardly watch.

"I'll see you later, buddy, okay? Right after school."

Andres didn't answer. He hung his head and did not look up. Feeling desperate, Zack held out his palm for a high five. Andres stared at it for a moment, then weakly tapped his hand to Zack's.

"After school, okay, little man?"

"Okay," mumbled Andres, and let Ms. Redding usher him out of the room.

Zack swallowed hard and ran his fingers through his hair, which was damp with sweat.

When the door closed behind them, Ms. Gates turned to Zack. "I'm sorry Andres got upset," she said. "But it was actually a perfect example of why we called this meeting."

The vice principal nodded his balding head. "Andres has had a lot of outbursts lately."

"He's exhibiting frequent loss of self-control in the classroom," said Ms. Gates.

"Well, isn't that the school's job?" said Zack. "To teach him self-control."

"To an extent, yes," said Waldron.

"But our feeling is that Andres requires a good deal of additional attention, designed for his particular needs," said Ms. Gates. "That may be outside the bandwidth of the special ed resources here at John Wayne."

"Bandwidth?" said Zack.

"We don't want to make any premature moves," said Ms. Gates. "But we just wanted to put it on your radar that if Andres doesn't make significant progress in a number of areas in kindergarten this year, we'll likely recommend he transfer over to Newton next year."

"What's Newton?" said Zack.

The vice principal gave a dry cough. "It's a dedicated special-needs school right here in Santa Monica," he said. "A place that could give Andres all the support his situation requires."

His situation.

Zack felt an invisible fist punch him straight in the gut.

"And. And what"—he fought to access his own voice, to keep it together—"what if we want him to stay here, at a—a normal school?"

"We don't classify schools as 'normal' or otherwise," said Ms. Gates quickly. "Newton is simply designed to meet Andres's needs in an appropriate way that John Wayne isn't. There, he could get a whole host of therapies in the classroom." She counted with her fingers, pointing them toward Zack, as if *he* were the kindergart-ner. "Speech. Occupational. Play therapy. In addition to the physical therapy he already receives."

What kind of world were these kids growing up in, Zack thought, where a kid needs help to simply *play*?

"He doesn't need all that crap. All he needs is to strengthen his leg and keep learning. All he needs are better language skills and some confidence. Which you guys"—Zack panned his hands toward Waldron and Gates—"are clearly failing to provide him with."

"Andres has made enormous progress here at Wayne, actually." Ms. Gates said sharply, "We care a great deal about him. And it's my professional opinion that he would be much better off at New-ton. Unless you and Andres's mother are prepared to address his needs through private services, that is. Which would be very . . ." She paused. "Costly."

Oh. *Of course.* So, this was really a conversation about money. Why hadn't Zack realized it sooner? Waldron and his sidekicks had assumed that Andres's family couldn't possibly afford private services, and that they were probably too dumb to realize he needed them. Therefore, they wanted to boot him to some other school, for handicapped kids, where he'd probably learn to see himself as "different" for the rest of his life.

No way in hell would Zack let that happen. He stood up, nearly knocking his mini-chair over.

"You know what?" he said, hearing the venom in his own voice but unable to control himself. "I feel sorry for you people. You suck at your jobs."

"Oh-kay," said Waldron, sliding his eyes to his colleague. "Perhaps we can continue this conversation at another time, when Andres's mom is available to join us?"

"Good luck with that," said Zack, peeling off his name tag and crushing it into a ball. "Because I can tell you right now, Andres isn't going anywhere."

He flicked the balled-up name tag onto the table, where it bounced off the surface and into Waldron's lap.

FRIDAY, OCTOBER 19, 2018

15

MEL

MEL STOOD OUTSIDE COLOR THEORY IN THE FADING TWILIGHT, CRAFTING a text to Regina. They'd planned to meet at Zack's five P.M. class, and then go for Thai food afterward, but at 4:58, when Mel was already on treadmill number six, having set a towel and water bottle on number five to save it for Regina, Regina had texted: Last-minute family outing came up; going to have to bail on tonight. Sorry.

Mel had been genuinely surprised, and more than a little hurt. Regina never missed a workout—and *she'd* been the one to suggest dinner. It had seemed a step up from their usual smoothie date, a mark of progression in their friendship. Mel had been looking forward to it, albeit a little nervously. She'd never shared an actual meal with Regina—what would they talk about for all that time? Would the rail-thin woman actually eat? Mel had even, in the shower that morning, rehearsed how she'd tell Regina about Adam. And his dirty whore.

But then Zack had bounced into the studio, wearing a tight maroon *Train Filthy* T-shirt, and called out, "Okay, beautiful people! Time to get down on the floor and heat up that musculature!" and Mel had become too flustered to answer Regina's text.

Now, damp with sweat and bone-weary from the workout (dare she admit she was actually beginning to crave this feeling?) Mel lingered outside the gym, wondering what could have come up to cause Regina to cancel last-minute. Regina was the sort of person who kept both a Google calendar *and* a Cozi calendar (*Different interfaces*, she'd explained to Mel, who hadn't had the courage to ask what the hell that meant), which she meticulously filled months in advance. Regina was not the type to cancel exercise-and-dinner at the last minute.

Mel tried to keep her tone casual, her phrases short—Regina had mentioned more than once that she "valued brevity" in texting—finally settling on, Missed you in class! I was 43% orange zone. Hope you had a nice fam outing & that all is OK? She added a flexed-muscle emoji and hit *Send*.

She slipped her phone into the thigh pocket of her leggings and considered the empty evening ahead of her. Adam had taken Sloane to a soccer tournament in Santa Barbara; they'd be gone until tomorrow night.

She didn't want to go home to her big, empty house. Embarrassingly, her reluctance had something—just *a tiny* bit—to do with the fact that Zack was still inside the gym, straightening weights and wiping down equipment before the next class. He was slated to teach one more class, the last of the day. Knowing he was still right there, so nearby, was a strange, tingly comfort. She wished she had the strength to march back into the studio and take another class, the way Regina sometimes did.

But she'd probably die of a heart attack.

Still, she didn't want to leave the area just yet. It was stupid, she knew, and Zack would soon be immersed in the theatrics of his coaching routine and unavailable for conversation. But it wouldn't hurt to go back inside and buy a protein bar, would it? And if she happened to see him, maybe say good night?

She found herself pulling the heavy glass door open and stepping back into the cool, recycled air.

The reception area was empty but for Davit, the receptionist who sat behind the desk disinfecting the heart monitors CT clients rented and strapped to their wrists, returning them after class soaked with sweat. Wearing the loaned monitor grossed Mel out and she'd been meaning to buy one of her own. Zack would be proud of her. She was a true worker-outer now.

"Back so soon?" said Davit from behind the desk, smiling at her. "Whattup, girl?"

"Oh," said Mel, instantly flustered. "I just forgot I wanted . . . a protein bar."

"Sure thing. Salted caramel or cake batter?"

"Um. Which is less likely to induce projectile vomiting?"

Davit laughed and handed her the salted caramel. "You are *so* funny! I'll charge it to your account. How's your Friday been?"

Mel had loved the apparent friendliness of the Southern Californians when she and Adam first relocated. But she quickly realized that just because someone was asking *How are you?* did not mean they necessarily wanted to hear the details. Holding back on telling people exactly how she felt in 2018 (year two of the Big Cheeto's reign) was a challenge with a new political scandal daily. She decided not to hold back now—after all, this guy had nowhere to be.

"My Friday's been great!" she said. "Except for my friend totally blowing me off for a dinner date."

"Not cool," said Davit, returning his attention to spritzing and wiping the monitors.

Was she *that* boring? Mel tried again. "Oh, and there's the state of the country and all that."

"How do you mean?" Davit looked at her blankly.

Could he possibly be serious? Was Davit just extraordinarily dumb, or a Republican-in-hiding, like Zack?

"Hey, hey." She heard Zack's honeyed southern drawl behind her, through a swell of music from the studio as he stepped into the reception area.

Instantly, Mel forgot the clever comeback she'd been composing for Davit.

"Hey, man!" said Davit. "Aren't you supposed to be teaching now?"

"Bri subbed in," said Zack, shrugging. "Last minute. Class is practically empty, anyway. Not worth my time." He turned to Mel. "Did I interrupt some leftist propaganda going on out here?" He made a sweeping gesture with his hand and—oh God—winked at her. "Please, carry on."

Mel's just-cooled cheeks flared again—she felt like a kid who'd been caught talking smack about her schoolteacher.

"Let's just not, 'kay?" she said, hoping to sound cute. She'd avoided talking politics with Zack, knowing it would become a never-ending debate. She was proud of herself—she was friends with a bona fide Republican—and congratulated herself on her open mind. After all those years spent in the liberal bubble of New York City, she'd never imagined she could admire a man who not only voted for the Big Cheeto but who seemed like one of the president's biggest fans.

But Zack was waiting for her to respond with a smile so condescending it made her remember Trump in the last presidential debate shaking his head, lifting his brows, making ridiculous faces every time Hillary opened her mouth.

Davit continued to scrub the heart monitors but Mel could feel him waiting. Was there a hint of a smile? She felt trapped and thought of Hillary again, Trump lurking behind her on that blue-carpeted stage, ready to pounce.

"What is the topic of the day?" Zack asked. Clearly, Mel thought, enjoying himself. "The poor Dreamers? The evil Wall? Or the Supreme Court?"

Mel groaned. "Don't get me started on the Supreme Court." She turned to Davit. "What do you think?"

"Well," Davit began, slowly, "I agree with you both."

Zack let out a braying laugh. Instead of making her recoil, she felt the urge to fight back. After all, she thought, this political wrestling was as close to fucking as they'd ever get. So why not play a little?

"I would imagine," Mel said to Davit, ignoring Zack, "as a man of color . . ."

"Don't assume!" Zack interrupted. "You don't know him. He's Iranian-American."

"Armenian, actually," Davit said.

"I *said* 'imagine,' not 'assume.'" Mel's heart rate spiked—not in the red zone but on its way. "You know, that little thing called empathy—it takes imagination."

"Whatever," said Zack. "You're still generalizing."

She knew he was right, on some level. But she couldn't stand down about the topic of immigration, not when there was so much at stake. If privileged American citizens like her didn't speak out now, then the fate of America, as dark as it might be, would be her burden to carry. Worse, Sloane's.

She faced Zack. "What do *you* have at stake in all of this? A good-looking single white guy with his whole life ahead of him? You don't have to worry about your kids asking if what Trump says about women being pigs is true. Or about people of color being rapists and murderers. You're not vulnerable. You're white. And you're not a woman!"

"No," Zack said, leaning close so she could smell him—cedarwood mixed with something sweet like vanilla, plus the faintest brine of sweat—"I'm not."

"I need to get going," she said weakly, her legs suddenly jelly.

"I'll walk out with you," said Zack.

"Don't kill each other, you two," said Davit, returning to his spritzing.

"After you, Lady Melissa," said Zack, opening the door with a sweep of his arm.

Mel stepped through, abandoning her protein bar at the front desk.

Outside, Main Street smelled like flowers and salt off the ocean, two blocks away. The restaurants were packed with attractive, sun-kissed diners crowded around sidewalk tables. Mel tugged at the hem of her *Eat Pure, Train Filthy* tank top, which was too tight despite being size XL, suddenly self-conscious to be walking next to Zack in public wearing so little clothing. She tugged again at the flimsy fabric, coaxing it to cover her butt.

"Shit, my sweatshirt," she said, more to herself than to Zack. "I left it back at the gym."

"It's a balmy seventy-one degrees. Get it next time."

"Then can we walk down an alley or something? I hate wearing all this tight stretchy stuff in public. I'd feel better if we were less visible."

"Incognito. I like it." Without breaking stride, he reached into his backpack and pulled out a navy track jacket. "Here." He draped it over her shoulders. "Now you are in disguise."

She thought of protesting—she was, she thought, the kind of woman who hated to have doors held open for her, a true feminist—but when was the last time she'd felt this charge, as if an industrial-strength power cord connected from her soft and round belly to his taut abs? Maybe as far back as 1993—the junior year homecoming pep rally when Dustin Lewis, the baseball star, had let her borrow his letterman jacket that smelled of Kodiak tobacco dip and spearmint gum. She felt like a teenager again now.

"Hey," Zack said, "Sorry I lost my cool back at CT." He winced, as if genuinely ashamed. "Jensen would fire my ass if he knew I was talking politics with the clients."

"I would never say anything," she said. "Ever! Cross my heart." The skin of her chest felt hot under her fingertips and she wrapped his jacket more tightly to hide the cleavage that spilled out of her too-tight sports bra. "Let's talk about something else."

"Like?" He tossed his hair out of his eyes and she was a teen again, flirting with Dustin Lewis as the pep rally bonfire raged.

"Anything but the Big Cheeto, okay?"

He snorted. Instead of finding it gross she found it adorable.

"What?" She slapped at the hard muscle of his chest. "That's what I call him. Don't make fun."

Please, she thought, *make fun. Don't stop.*

An electric Bird scooter careened down the sidewalk, inches from running her down.

"Sorry!" a twentysomething woman in short-shorts and flip-flops called over a shoulder, a yippy dog tucked under one arm.

"Use both hands next time!" Mel shouted in full Brooklyn 'tude. "And a helmet!"

"Nice reflexes," Zack said.

"Did you see that? She almost killed me. I know I sound like an old lady—okay, I am an old lady—but I hate those things. And she had, like, Toto, tucked under an arm."

"Did you sign the petition? For the scooter ban?"

She couldn't tell if he was teasing her. That dazzling smile, all those perfect teeth, seemed to suck in the fading ocean light.

"What would you say if I *did* sign the petition?"

"I'd say"—he hooked his arm in hers, the soft hair on his arms tickling—"I signed it, too."

"I thought you'd be proud to know," she said, "I'm getting my own heart rate monitor."

"Good girl." His voice was pure honey.

She'd missed feeling this—a buzzing in her ears . . . and elsewhere.

"You know," he said, "I can get you a *free* heart monitor."

"Is that a bribe?"

"Mmm," he said, like he'd tasted something delicious. "Well, you're definitely the teacher's pet."

16

REGINA

REGINA COULD FEEL THE MEN'S GAZE BEND TO FOLLOW THE GIRL IN MIR-
rored sunglasses walking across the sand toward the ocean, a tote
bag bouncing lightly against her slim hip, gauzy white dress and
long dark hair fluttering behind her. She couldn't be more than
twenty-five, Regina thought, and her languorous-yet-purposeful
gait suggested she'd spent time on a fashion runway.

"Quit staring, guys," Regina said to Gordon and his friend-
slash-manager Bryan, who were seated in beach chairs next to Regina's blanket, eating the burritos she'd packed for their supper picnic
and swilling wine from a thermos. "You look like dirty old men."

"*Old?*" Bryan grinned and turned toward Regina, his angular
face profiled by the setting sun. "How dare you, Reg."

"Staring at what?" Gordon said, feigning innocence.

"Don't play dumb," said Regina, as the girl by the shore stepped
out of her dress, revealing a tiny metallic-gold bikini underneath.

The girl's flawlessness triggered a pang of jealousy in Regina,
and she momentarily regretted having blown off exercising with
Mel. Then she reminded herself that one more measly hour at the
gym would not restore her youth.

She couldn't have faced Color Theory this evening anyway. The
Friday evening classes were always half-full at best, which would
allow Zack plenty of time to dote on Mel. Regina couldn't make
sense of his attentiveness toward her—what was he thinking? Yes,
Mel was pretty in the way of an overfed Shetland pony, and had per-

fected her helpless-yet-pissed-off act at the gym, which was sort of cute, but surely Zack wasn't actually *attracted* to her—was he?

More likely, Regina had been telling herself, Zack was trying to make her jealous by lavishing attention on Mel during classes. Perhaps it just fed his ego—heroically assisting the out-of-breath newbie, adjusting Mel's weights and, ugh, her form. Was it Regina's imagination, or had his hands lingered on Mel's hips at the squat rack the other day?

Whatever the case, Regina didn't want to think about it. Although she was not a fan of Bryan, she'd been grateful for his last-minute idea to meet her family for an evening beach picnic so that she could justify bailing on her workout-and-Thai-food plans with Mel. Though, admittedly, she'd felt a ripple of guilt after sending Mel a purposefully vague cancellation text, knowing it would send her into a tizzy of speculation.

Over the ocean, Regina watched the sun slip down toward the horizon, painting the sky pink and red as the afternoon receded. At the shoreline, the fashion-runway girl scanned the sand, looking for something Regina could not discern, then bent to pull what looked like a silky round tablecloth from her bag, maroon with gold tassels around the border. Then she removed a leather-bound notebook from her bag, opened it, and placed it face-up on her blanket.

Regina watched Gordon's and Bryan's heads slowly swivel back in the girl's direction.

"You guys are pathetic," Regina said.

"It's just anthropology," Bryan shrugged. "We're observing a native species in her natural habitat."

"Observe elsewhere," said Regina. "This is a family picnic."

"Apologies, boss," said Bryan. "Though I'd like to point out that you're staring, too, Regina."

"A curious glance is not the same as shameless leering," said Regina.

"The lady doth exaggerate," said Bryan in a British accent.

"Don't force me to blind you, Bry," said Gordon. He reached his free hand toward Regina's leg and closed it around her ankle; a gesture of solidarity, she supposed. She considered pulling away but didn't.

"How about some basic self-control, Bryan," said Regina.

"*Burn.*" Bryan grinned. "As the kids say."

Regina checked for Mia and Kaden and saw them twenty yards up the beach, bumping a volleyball back and forth over a net. The sounds of their laughter carried on the dusky mellow air, making Regina feel, for a brief moment, that all was well in her life.

As if.

The girl in the bikini stretched out on her shiny blanket like a languorous jungle cat, her impossibly slender body offset by small, firm curves. She must have chosen her spot deliberately, Regina thought. The beach was practically empty. Clearly the girl enjoyed flaunting her youthful perfection in the presence of a few middle-aged parents, an opportunity to remind perfect strangers of how unattractive and encumbered their lives were by comparison.

The realization gave Regina an irrational surge of rage. The girl's body alone was irksome enough—Regina knew she'd never look like *that* again, no matter how many hours she logged at Color Theory or how little she ate. Young-skinny and middle-aged-skinny were entirely different. But it was the girl's air of leisure that chafed at Regina, emanating from Miss Pretty Young Thing's golden skin like sound waves. Not having a care in the world besides basking near-naked in the sunset. Regina had the irrational urge to punish the girl for being so flagrantly vain and carefree, for having the audacity to preen at the edge of her family picnic.

On cue, she heard Mel's voice in her head: *The way that girl makes you feel? That's how every middle-aged mom I've met here makes me feel. And anyway, this is Santa Monica. Everyone's vain and carefree. We should all be ashamed of ourselves.*

Fuck Mel. Who, at this very moment, was probably struggling

to lift the lightest of medicine balls, groaning adorably until Zack darted over to help her.

The thought made Regina want to scream.

Then again, she'd been wanting to scream since that morning, when she'd gotten a second voicemail from the bursar's office (what the hell was a *bursar*, anyway?) at Rustic Canyon Day School, requesting a conversation *before end of business today*—a small but menacing variation from last week's message, which offered the cushion of responding at her *earliest convenience*. Regina had ignored it. Today, she'd replied to the voicemail with an email, apologizing profusely, explaining that she was *completely and utterly slammed with a work project*, and promising to connect as soon as she *came up for air*. Her face had burned with shame as she typed, and she'd immediately deleted the message from her *Sent* folder.

No way could she have handled a Zack-and-Mel flirting session at the gym, not after the day she'd had.

"The script is just so damn good, dude," Bryan was saying to Gordon.

Their conversation had turned, of course, to Gordon's newly finished draft of *Eighteen Twelve*. *Early draft!* Gordon had emphasized to Regina. *I'll still get tons of notes*, implying he'd be returning to his day job none too soon.

Bryan went on. "Historically immersive, yet totally timely."

Gordon bobbed his head. "That was the goal."

Regina wanted to cover her ears. To hear nothing more about *Eighteen Twelve* until it had sold for seven figures. She reminded herself that this was her fault. All Gordon had done was accept her invitation to focus on his screenplay. All he'd done was trust her to be the primary breadwinner for a while. Something *he'd* managed to do, without fail, for practically two decades. How was she failing so royally at something millions of the most ordinary men did every day?

She grabbed a handful of sand and squeezed until her finger joints ached.

"*Hamilton* meets *Band of Brothers*," Bryan was saying.

Regina squeezed harder.

A few hours after her call from the bursar, Regina had gone to the mailbox (thankfully, Gordon hadn't bothered checking it in years) to find a notice from the Writers Guild declaring that their health insurance had been canceled due to non-payment of the premium. It had to be an error. Regina had been careful to mail the payment in time to arrive just before the cutoff, as she'd been doing for months. She was quite sure she could straighten out the insurance issue with one phone call. But *still*.

Regina dropped the sand and brushed her hands together. Then she eased back on the towel and closed her eyes, forcing a long breath of saline air, focusing on the raspy shush of the ocean before her and the manic screech of gulls overhead.

"I want to start shopping the script as soon as possible, man," she heard Bryan say to Gordon. "How long do you need for revisions?"

Regina's ears pricked, but she kept her eyes closed.

"It takes as long as it takes," said Gordon firmly.

Regina's eyes flew open and she shot upright, as if stung. She could not listen to this any longer.

"You okay, Reg?" said Gordon, crumpling the waxy white paper that had held his burrito. "You haven't eaten any dinner." He nodded toward her unopened brown rectangle of take-out salad.

"You know what? I think I'm going to jog home. Get the blood flowing. I have a bunch of invoicing to do tonight, and a run will help me get through it."

If only she had actual clients to invoice.

"Run home?" said Bryan. "Isn't that kind of far?"

"Not at all," said Regina, a bit curtly. "Two miles, tops."

"Have I told you my wife's practically an Olympic athlete?" said Gordon with pride.

"She looks like one," Bryan said, nodding toward Regina admiringly.

Regina hated that his validation pleased her. Bryan was semi-slimy; currently in the process of divorcing his second wife, he'd been lightly ogling Regina for over a decade, ever since he'd signed Gordon as a client. Still, the appreciation of her hard-won body felt good, even from a guy whose next wife would likely be the age of the gold-bikini-clad Millennial sunbathing by the water. Her body was the one thing Regina securely *possessed*, a thing that couldn't be taken from her, even when everything else in her life felt on the verge of slipping away.

"Don't forget the girls, Gordon, okay?"

"What girls?" said Gordon, smiling at her. "Can I get a kiss good-bye?"

The request made her feel instantly guilty. She leaned down to press her lips against his. What would Gordon do if he knew the mess she'd made of their lives, which she continued to hide with endless lies of omission? Would he ever kiss her again?

She jogged to say good-bye to the girls at the volleyball court, then sprinted up the sand to the footpath. To her right, the sun grazed the horizon, deepening the light to shades of honey and blood. Up ahead, the Ferris wheel on the Santa Monica pier turned on, shooting spikes of neon color into the fading sky.

Somehow, the sight of it gave Regina hope. She ran faster, toward the lights and the graceful curve of the coastline beyond. Her lungs began to squeeze and sweat rose at her hairline; she was beginning to feel better. Running home had been a good idea.

She had planned to take the footpath all the way to the metal staircase that led off the beach and up to the edge of her neighborhood, and run straight home. But when she reached those stairs, she found herself glancing at the smartwatch on her wrist, then cruising past her exit toward a different neighborhood on the other side of the city—toward a certain southernly block of Main Street.

The Color Theory class she'd been scheduled to take with Mel was about to let out. Maybe, Regina reasoned, she could catch Mel at the studio as she was leaving. They could have dinner together after all.

17

MEL

THE COLOR THEORY VAN WAS PARKED IN THE GYM'S LOT, WEDGED BEtween a pickup truck and a red VW bug with *Girlz Rule* and *Show Me Your Tats* bumper stickers.

Zack sighed, nodding toward the VW. "Freaking Bri and her slogans."

"I kind of love her," said Mel.

"Of course you do," said Zack, stopping in front of the black van with *Train Filthy* emblazoned across its side in yellow. He pulled a key fob out of his pocket and pressed it. The van unlocked with a chirping sound. Mel felt her pulse thrumming in her neck. What was she *doing*, standing here in a parking lot with a man so handsome he was practically edible, and young enough to qualify as a Millennial? A man who routinely attracted stares from women a hundred pounds lighter and twenty years younger than Mel?

"The monitors are in there?" she asked dumbly, as the van's door slid open.

"Duh, totes," Zack said. Mel cringed; could he *please* stop speaking like a teenager?

"You sure you're not a secret serial killer?"

"Oh," he said, smiling big (did he look like Ted Bundy, or was that just the twilight?), "it's no secret."

"Very funny."

"Seriously, you should pick out the monitor you want," he said, gesturing into the van's dim interior. "There's a bunch of different ones in there." He stepped inside and beckoned toward her. "They all have a different fit. Hop on in and try a couple."

Alarms clanged in Mel's head; clearly, she should run in the other direction, straight to her own car, and hightail it. She shook her head. "That's okay. You can just choose one for—"

He cut her off. "Now, now, don't be ungrateful. Not everyone gets the privilege of choosing their very own complimentary monitor. C'mon, m'lady." He extended his arm toward her, grinning. "I know how you love to be called that."

"It beats *ma'am*," she said, her voice wobbly as she gripped the cool metal frame of the van, bypassing Zack's proffered arm, and hoisted herself up. Once inside, she crouched awkwardly beside him in the cavernous interior, making sure to keep a few inches between their bodies.

"Atta girl," he said. "Now, look around and help me find them."

"Find what?"

He laughed. "The heart rate monitors! I know there's a stash of them in here somewhere." Mel blinked, trying to get her bearings; despite the van's interior light, she could hardly see anything but Zack's hulking form.

"Isn't this illegal?" she said. "Rummaging around in a vehicle that doesn't belong to us? I *could* just buy one. I'm happy to, you know, to support the studio. Small biz and all."

"No, ma'am, your husband and kid won't have to bail you out of jail tonight," he said—she actually liked it when he called her *ma'am* but wished he wouldn't remind her of Adam's existence, and definitely not Sloane's. "I'm embarrassed to admit that Jensen, the owner of the studio—you met him yet?—he let me sleep in here a few times when I first started training. I found a job before I had a place to live."

"It does smell a little like Old Spice in here," Mel said, then worried she might have offended him. He was sharing with her, and here she was, as always, cracking a joke, then hating herself for it.

"Hey, we can't all shop on Rodeo Drive." He sounded a little hurt.

"Fuck," she sighed. "I'm sorry."

"Don't be. I need to get me some thicker skin."

She wanted to say, *I like the skin you're wearing.* A desire to be honest welled inside her.

"Not to go all political on you again," she said. He held his hands up in mock surrender, his long arms silhouetting on the van's upholstery. "But, ever since the election—"

"The Big Cheeto?"

"Ha, yeah. Ever since the orange guy took over, well, I'm doing this thing with men. Starting arguments over nothing. And, well, everything. I try to tell myself to shut up. To keep it all in. But, as you can see"—she motioned at her body, her hands smoothing over the curves she loathed—"I don't have much self-control."

"There you go again," he said and, suddenly, his breath was warm on her neck, "being hard on yourself."

The heat of his body was so close. She wanted to touch the curve of his back, trace the humps of muscles under his thin T-shirt. She thought of how, in class earlier, he'd done a handstand, and his shirt had fallen down, exposing chiseled abs and the trail of golden-brown hair leading from his navel into his shorts.

"There they are!" Zack said, jutting his chin toward the back of the van.

"There *what* are?"

"The belts, dude," he said, shimmying toward the single bench in the far rear. "A whole pile of 'em, right here."

"Great," said Mel.

"Come on back here, so I can show you how these medieval things work."

"Medieval?" Mel said, feeling a queasy tremble in her stomach. "Aren't they just like . . . wristbands?"

Zack patted the seat beside him. "Nope. These are old-school.

They go around your upper torso. Totally easy, once you get the hang of it. Get back here and I'll show you."

Holy shit, she thought, was this really happening?

She moved to the back of the van and sat next to Zack, who was holding a belt-length strap affixed to a black square.

"Sit up straight, missus," he said. "No slouching."

His arms reached around her, and she felt the pressure of the band at her bra line, and then the click of something plastic in the center of her back. She sucked in her gut, as much as she was able. As he fumbled with the monitor, his face was close enough to rest against her cheek. She felt the rhythm of her own breath, rising and falling.

"See, it's kinda complicated. I always help clients strap it on the first time."

"That's what she said." Great, Mel thought, now she sounded like a drunk college freshman. Where had that come from? Now was not the time to go filter-less.

But Zack barked a genuine laugh. "You crack me up, Goldberg." He drew away from her, and she tried not to feel disappointed. "Your monitor's all set. Fits perfectly. Consider it yours."

"Most of the time, I don't even mean to be funny, you know," she said. Was her voice shaking? "It just comes out that way." She thought of Adam, who criticized her overuse of sarcasm, called it *emotional deflection*.

No, she told herself, *don't think of him. Be here. Be now.*

Zack sat back, engulfed by the darkness for a minute so she could see only the shape of his face. "You do that a lot," Zack said.

"Do what?"

"Say bad things about yourself."

"Oh," she said, "that. What can I say? I'm a realist."

"More like a nihilist."

What was he saying? Was this going to be some rehash of the

whole *new you* spiel? Version Two You!, blah blah blah? Or did he mean something else?

He was looking at her—really looking at her in a way she wasn't used to, not since she'd morphed into post-Sloane Melissa. Invisible, especially to men—a freedom she resented but also appreciated.

She ran her hand over the monitor in the center of her chest, suddenly paranoid that he'd actually turned it on, and would be able to see how her heart was racing, rocketing all the way up into the red.

"Can I share something with you?" he asked.

She nodded, barely able to speak.

"It's a quote I like to share with clients."

"Okay." She'd been hoping, like an idiot, to hear something only for *her.*

Zack closed his eyes and Mel swallowed a giggle.

"Your body can stand almost anything. It's your mind you have to convince."

He opened his eyes and looked straight into hers.

"Wow," she said, hoping she sounded genuine. "Oh yeah, totally."

"It's a good one, right? I can't remember who said it—sorry about that—but it really gets at the integral connection of body and mind . . ."

He kept talking. Spouting the typical shallow bullshit intended to be deep and meaningful that she'd heard every trainer at every gym she'd joined (and quit) say. *Believe in yourself. You are stronger than you know. Mindfulness* and *intentions* and *self-actualization.* She nodded, knowing she was stroking his ego—the same game she felt forced to play with most men. Telling him what he wanted to hear, knowing that later, hours or even days after, she'd hate herself for doing it. But with Zack, she felt different, didn't she? Was she hallucinating, or could she trust the part of her that believed he just might be different from those other men?

"Hold up for a sec," Mel said, lifting a hand, and silence him she did—his mouth froze mid-sentence. "I don't mean to be rude, and I know what I'm about to say *is* rude, so sorry in advance. I know you're not just some meathead gym dude." His eyebrows lifted and she cursed herself silently. "You said some *really* smart things in my backyard at the workout party. But"—she paused, realizing there was no sugarcoating the shit that was her marriage since she'd uncovered Adam's affair—"I need to be concrete. Let you know where I'm, so to speak, *at*."

"Cool." Zack nodded. "Lay it on me."

He ran his fingers through his hair, seeming suddenly nervous, which made him all the more attractive, and emboldened her.

"Look, Zack. I need to start over. Like *from scratch*."

"I get you," Zack said. "Promise."

That squint, that sheepish smile. She wanted to believe him almost as badly as she wanted to reach out and touch his hard chest, run her finger along the straight pretty line of his jaw. Then she remembered he was a *coach*. A person who made people feel good about themselves for a living. As if someone as gorgeous as he was could actually relate to her woes. *Sure*. She, a plus-sized middle-aged woman whose husband was cheating on her—a husband she'd been delusional enough to believe had actually loved her, was attracted to her, thought she looked beautiful in the lingerie she could barely squeeze into. As if!

She was a needy mess, a person so lonely she paid people—Lettie, and now Zack—to be nice to her. And then was foolish enough to hope they actually cared. She felt a surge of anger rear inside her. She was mad now, at Adam, at Zack, at this entire phony feel-good city, the whole damn *it's all good* West Coast. Best coast, her fat ass!

Mostly, she was angry at herself.

"You were saying?" Zack tipped his head at her, expectantly, eyes crinkling with something that looked like concern. "About starting over?"

"Right," she managed. "It's nice of you. To try to understand. With the pep talk and all. But it's not just my outside that needs . . . renovating." She gestured at her legs, her chest, as if she was shooing away a gnat. "It's me. Everything about me is just—ugh, I don't know. It's just not . . ." She paused and looked down, only to realize her boobs were nearly climbing out of the sports bra she'd outgrown. "I'm not *me*. Not anymore."

She hooked her thumbs under the sports bra straps and adjusted it to better cover herself. Zack looked away. Great, she thought, not only was she making a fool out of herself sounding all neurotic and corny but now she was grossing him out.

"I have to go," she said, dropping her eyes to the grimy floor of the van, but not moving. "I'm sorry."

"Hey," he said softly. She looked up to see him stone-faced, his light, actorly charm replaced with solemnity. Oh God—was he about to cry?

"I know what that feels like," he said. "I haven't been *me* since I left Florida." He sighed. "Please don't leave yet. We can just sit here. Honestly, I just don't want to be alone."

Was he for real? She glanced around, unable to shake the paranoid fear that this was all a joke. Maybe Regina put him up to this, and was about to throw open the van door and yell *Surprise!*

"Okay," she whispered.

They sat in silence. Mel stared at the shadows dancing across the dumpster lit by a streetlamp. It was full dark out now. For once, she felt no pressure to find words. Always, her impulse was to fill the quiet spaces in conversation, uncomfortable with awkward pauses—especially with someone as handsome as Zack. Better to hide behind the noise.

But not now. Now, she was only surprised by how calm she felt sitting next to him with no words to shield her. Calm and safe.

"I'm going through a thing with my husband. It's been"—she paused—"bad."

She hadn't meant to say it. But she had. Not the whole truth, but enough.

Relief washed over her.

"That sucks," he said. "I'm sorry."

She waited for him to say more, but was grateful when he did not.

"Maybe we both don't belong here," she said. She clamped a hand over her mouth. "Oh God, that was a stupid thing to say. I'm so fucking negative all the time."

He reached over and tugged her hand away from her face. His fingers were so close to her mouth she could smell his sunscreen, or whatever he put on his face, something coconutty, tropical.

"Hon, you *got* to be kinder to yourself."

Did he really just call her *hon*? She knew she should be offended—she'd reprimanded strange men in public before (mostly waiters) for calling her *sweetheart*, *babe*, even *ma'am*. But coming from Zack, she liked the way those saccharine endearments sounded, embarrassing as it was to admit to herself. Weren't they names that had belittled women for ages?

"Yep," she said. "My whole adult life men having been telling me to *relax. Smile*." She dropped into her surfer dude impersonation. "*Chill out. Take it easy*—that one's the worst, like I'm trying to attack them or something."

"Almost as bad as *It's all good*." He laughed. "I'll never get used to that BS."

"Oh God." She giggled now, too. "That one's the worst. Nothing makes me want to beeline back to Brooklyn more."

"I love talking to you," Zack said.

Really? she wanted to ask.

"Sometimes," he said, "I really—I mean *really*—want to give up. Pack my shit and go home. People come here to, I don't know, rewrite their story, you know?"

She nodded. She did know. Adam had rewritten his story and now he'd flown past her. On to bigger and better things.

"I mean, look." Zack blinked a few times—Mel wondered if it was a tic. "I've been here, what, two years, and I've seen people go from nobody to somebody with a single audition. This one chick I know"—Mel tried not to react, reminding herself he was young—"she's from deep-south Alabama . . . she's famous after one freaking YouTube video. And I don't just mean internet-famous. She's on a show now. It just got picked up by Starz."

Mel wondered if that was what he wanted—to be a "famous" star in some forgettable TV show on a B-network? Oy, he was so young.

"We—you and me included—we're all here to be a better version of ourselves," he said. "I know how cheesy that sounds, like gag-me-level cheesy. And it was Regina who came up with that dumb-ass Version Two You! name but, sometimes, the cheesy things are the truest things."

"Well, well, well," she said. "Mr. Doheny is a romantic. Maybe you *do* belong in the City of Angels after all."

He let out a big laugh. "What do I know? I'm just a meathead—you said it yourself."

"Lame joke," she said. "And I didn't mean it. Swear. I think you're . . . great." She gripped his arm for emphasis, blushing in the darkness, and felt him flex under her touch.

"*Great*, eh?" he said. "Oh, how you spoil me, sweet Melissa." She did not move her hand from his arm.

"Glad to help," she said. "In any way."

Had she really just said that?

"Who'd you see running ahead of you in Bri's class?" he asked.

"What?" She let go of his arm and tugged at the heart rate monitor, which was cutting into her flesh. This was too close. Intimate. He was doing that thing again. Reading her mind.

His fingers reached for her, found her knee, sending a tingling current up her leg. He hooked his fingers in hers.

"Zack, I should—" she began.

What was there to say? She hadn't felt *this* in almost twenty years. Since she was a Melissa she couldn't even remember.

"No, you shouldn't," he said firmly. "Not yet. Do you want to know who I was chasing?"

"Uh-huh." Her body was humming. She was sure to do something awful if she didn't get out of the van right then. She felt a throbbing between her legs, as urgent as when she was thirteen, lying on the sofa late at night watching her dad's Playboy channel, her fingers slipped into her panties, praying she'd come before her parents caught her.

"I was chasing myself. That better me," he said. "The me *you* help me to see."

Whoa, Mel wanted to say, wishing she could freeze time, have a second to figure out what exactly was happening.

"Who do you *think* I was chasing?" She heard the sadness in her voice. How pathetic. "My cheating son-of-a-bitch husband."

"Oh, Mel." He stroked her arm, sending a shiver through her body.

"Yep, I've got irrefutable proof." She held up a hand. "But I don't want to get into it now. Just trust me. It's real."

"I trust you, darlin'."

Oh, how she wanted him now.

"Then"—she paused, knowing she was taking a step forward and that there'd be no turning back—"there was *someone else* in front of me."

"And . . ." He was playing with her, she thought. He knew it was he who she wanted to chase.

"Next time," she said, desperate to change the topic, cut through the thick warm air of the van, the humming attraction, "I'm going to imagine it's Regina I'm chasing. With a knife. That skinny bitch stood me up. We were supposed to take class together, then have dinner."

"Yeah," Zack said, sounding exhausted all of a sudden, "she can be hard to deal with sometimes. Be careful with that one, okay?"

"If there *is* a next time. Seems like Regina might want nothing to do with me and my rotund fanny anymore."

"Well, I do," Zack said softly, leaning forward so his face moved into the strip of yellow cast by the streetlight. "Rotund fanny and all."

Her body went instantly hot and she stood up, slamming her head into the ceiling of the van. It hurt, and she dropped to her knees, felt the crotch of her leggings tear, heard the fabric rip.

"Ouchy," she said in between laughing. "Oops. Fuck. That was dumb."

"I've done that same thing a dozen times," Zack said, massaging the top of her head. She knew she should push him away, remind him how inappropriate this was. But she didn't want him to stop.

"Well, I bet you've never ripped a hole in your pants at the same time."

"You didn't," he said.

"I did!"

"How bad is it?"

"I'm scared to look," she said. "I should get out and see." She slid her hand across the side of the van. "Where's the goddamn door?" Then, "Sorry, I didn't mean to take the Lord's name in vain."

"Too bad," he said. "You'll just have to stay in here with me."

"Forever?"

She reached into the darkness toward him, finding his mouth, and tracing her fingers around it.

"*In aeternum*," he said, shifting his head side to side so her fingertips caught his lips.

"Forever," she translated. "You're probably not going to believe me . . . but I took Latin for two years in high school."

He palmed his chest. "A girl after my own heart, indeed. Now," he said, in his trainer voice, instructive and firm, "take my hand. And show me where this tear in your pants is."

He offered his hand and she took it, letting herself press into the hard wall of his chest. Then slowly, she guided his hands down to her inner thigh, where he began to move his fingers until he found the hole, drawing slow circles over the bare swatch of her inner-thigh skin. The crotch of her panties was wet, she knew. Thank God, she thought, and with genuine gratitude, she'd removed her maxi-pad after class.

His mouth was at her ear, nipping at her earlobe, whispering, "*In aeternum*. Eternally. Always. Endlessly."

She remembered him back at the gym reception desk, red-faced and enraged, defending the Big Cheeto, of all people, high on his arrogance, but instead of feeling repulsed by the thought, she felt her clit harden under his fingers. Her libido was as alive and kicking as a sixteen-year-old virgin's. Mel 2.0 was starting off her rebirth with a bang.

"Jesus," she moaned. Then, "Oops, sorry. I'll stop saying that. I swear."

"Don't," he whispered. "I like it."

"Okay, then," she whispered. "Jesus. Thank you, Jesus."

He was on top of her now. Both hands—she felt the calluses on his palms, thought of pressing her tongue to them—working over the hole in her leggings, and, in one quick movement, he tore the pants open with a rending that made her gasp.

18

REGINA

"Lady Wolfe!"

Regina looked up to see Jensen Davis ambling toward her on Bay Street, a block from Color Theory, waving at her and grinning. She dropped from the brisk jog she'd held since leaving the beach to a slow walk, her chest clutching at the sight of him. She leaned over and rested her hands on her knees, gulping for breath. She hadn't felt winded until just now. An animal urge to wheel in the other direction and sprint back to the beach rose inside her but Jensen was too near, closing the gap between them on the sidewalk with a brisk, scissoring stride.

She straightened and watched him approach, feeling helplessly rooted to the spot. He wore slim black jeans, a white T-shirt crossed by the strap of the messenger bag he carried, and a close-lipped smiled that reminded Regina of a reptile.

Breathe, she reminded herself. *Stay cool.*

"If it isn't my star client," Jensen said, lifting his palm for a high five. "Fancy running into you here."

"Hey, Jensen," Regina said, slapping his hand reluctantly.

"You're late for class, missy." He feigned a stern look.

"I skipped the gym today. Took a run on the beach instead."

"Nature instead of Color Theory? How granola. I take that personally." He grinned at her, unsealing his lips to reveal teeth even whiter than the typical Santa Monican (*Veneers?* Regina wondered). "Kidding. If the Lady Wolfe needs a beach run, she needs a beach run."

"Ha."

"You know what you *can* do to make it up to me?"

She wanted to tell him to fuck off, that she didn't owe him a thing, but her mouth was too dry. She reminded herself that Jensen couldn't possibly know anything about the transfers—that was why she'd installed Zack as a buffer, given him the hands-on role—but she could not quell her rising panic.

"Um," she managed. "What . . . can I do?"

"It involves your, uh, good buddy Zack. He was supposed to be at CT, in the back office, doing the number-crunching work he does for me."

Regina's stomach lurched. Maybe he *did* know.

"But the golden boy is MIA. Maybe out getting a bite to eat," Jensen said with a shrug. He shifted his messenger bag to his hip and rummaged through it. Then he extracted a small, worn paperback book and handed it to her.

She recognized the cover instantly: a black-and-white photo of a tiny nun in habit, head bowed beneath the title *The Little Way for Every Day: Thoughts from Thérèse of Lisieux*. Zack's prayer book. It felt mealy and fragile, as if it might shed pages under her touch.

"Found this on the bathroom shelf in the back office," said Jensen. "Guess Z-man likes the company of a nun at *all* times." He shrugged and arched an eyebrow. "No judgment, right? Anyway, I walked off with it by accident. And now I'm late for a thing. Do you mind popping your head in the office and giving it to him? He might not be able to say his bedtime prayers, otherwise." Jensen laughed.

"Heh. Sure, no problem."

"Thanks. And I'd better see you at the studio tomorrow. No more of this running-by-the-ocean crap." He winked. Regina tried not to blanch. "You have a good night, Lady Wolfe." And he breezed off into the evening.

Regina stood on the sidewalk, shaky with relief and adrenaline, and tried to collect herself. She was certain she'd been correct:

Jensen knew nothing of the money Zack had been skimming from him. Carefully, she opened the cover of *The Little Way for Every Day*. Zack's name and phone number were written inside, in tidy pencil. The sight of his handwriting gave her a jolt of anticipation—she was now *on assignment* to see him (maybe running into Jensen had not been so terrible)—and she broke into a jog again, crossing Main Street and turning down the alley that led to the parking lot behind Color Theory. Overhead, the last dregs of sun had drained from the sky, replaced with the soft gray of evening, the final minutes of dim light before darkness settled in. She reached the parking lot and saw Zack's truck parked there, next to the customized Color Theory van, black with ultra-dark tinted windows and the yellow gym logo emblazoned across the sides, with *Eat Pure, Train Filthy* printed underneath.

Zack's Tacoma and the van were the only vehicles parked in the lot. The sight of them side-by-side gave Regina a sudden strange feeling in her stomach. She could not have said why. Nor could she have said precisely what moved her to veer off the sidewalk and cut through the parking lot to the gym's entrance, or why, exactly, she chose a route *between* the truck and the van, instead of simply walking around them both.

Spidey sense, duh! her daughter Kaden would have said.

Regina stopped short when she noticed the van's back window. It was cracked open a few inches, the opening one might leave for a dog to breathe. She stood a few feet behind the two vehicles and kept perfectly still. The sweat from her run had dried to an invisible scrim, making the skin of her face feel tight. She stood listening to her own breathing. Overhead, a seagull cawed.

And then, from somewhere much nearer, a strained, groaning sound.

Regina stayed perfectly still.

The sound came again, this time more urgently.

From the van. Breathy sighs. Feminine. Feline.

Regina stepped forward, to the open back window, and lifted onto her tiptoes, just high enough to peer inside.

Straight at the leg of Melissa Goldberg, thick and dimpled and startlingly white, hiked up against the back of the passenger bench, her black gym pants still partially covering her, though the fabric at the crotch appeared to have been ripped, exposing her thighs, her crotch, the stubbly landscape of her vagina, which appeared to have been—oh God—*shaved*.

Between Mel's legs was Zack's head, his face obscured, but Regina would know his dark brown curls anywhere. Mel's head was tipped back, her mouth hanging open, more moaning sounds wafting from her throat. One side of her layered shirts was pushed up to expose a large breast, cupped underneath by Zack's hand. His face was hidden from Regina, nestled between Mel's legs.

"Oh fuck no." The phrase tumbled from Regina's lips. She could not move.

Mel's eyes snapped open.

"Shit!" She bolted upright, struggling to unprop her leg from the back of the seat. "Jesus fucking Christ!"

Slowly, Zack turned to face Regina. His eyes skated over her. His curls were pasted to his forehead with sweat. His tanned face, the clean slopes she knew so well, had imagined holding between her hands so many times, was fixed in a look of pleading. He blinked several times, quickly, as if willing her to disappear.

"Regina," he said, his voice sounding different than usual. Thick and muted. Dead serious. "Please go."

She did not move. Kept her eyes locked on to him.

"Now," he said and flicked his wrist. Shooing her away.

Regina's body went numb. Her mind wiped clean.

She forced herself to look at him. Then at *her*.

"I hate you both."

Regina whirled around and sprinted across the parking lot toward home, crushing *The Little Way for Every Day* in her hand.

Thursday, March 28, 2019

COMMUNITY MOURNS LOCAL COLOR THEORY COACH

A well-known local fitness coach, Zacarias Robert Doheny, known as Zack to friends and family, passed away on March 24th.

A funeral mass has been scheduled for three P.M. Friday at St. Anne Catholic Church, 2011 Colorado Ave., Santa Monica. Doheny will be buried at Woodlawn Cemetery.

News of Doheny's passing hit hard at the Color Theory gym on Main Street where Doheny was a popular trainer and administrative assistant.

Born August 27, 1987, in Ocala, Florida, Doheny attended Sacred Heart primary and secondary schools; interned at his father's real estate development firm, Doheny & Jackman; and went on to earn an associate's degree in accounting from Central Florida Community College.

A devout Catholic, Doheny spent a year at the Sacred Heart Seminary and School of Theology in Orlando, before moving to Los Angeles to pursue a career in acting and personal fitness.

"He was the real deal," Bri Lee, a fellow Color Theory coach and actor said. "Zack oozed faith, and inspired it in everyone around him."

"Zack brought so much joy," said Color Theory patron Lindsey Leyner. "He'll be remembered as pure sunshine."

WEDNESDAY, OCTOBER 31, 2018

19

LETICIA

LETTIE AND ANDRES, THE LITTLE BOY DRESSED IN HIS COWBOY COSTUME, stood on the corner of Georgina and Twenty-Second, waiting—*like always*, she thought—for Zacarias to appear.

Lines of trick-or-treaters paraded past. Superheroes, ninjas, and pirates in all shapes and sizes; too many Disney princesses to count. A gang of grown men dressed as clowns whooped as they ran down the sidewalk, each carrying a red balloon, like in that scary movie, making Andres lean into Lettie as if he wanted to crawl back into her womb.

She dug her phone out of her purse and sent a text: Where are you, Zacarias?

A noisy group of teenagers wearing rubber Trump masks rushed past, the likeness so real in the dim street light, she startled, pulled Andres into her body, his cowboy hat tumbling to the grass.

"Mommy, you pushing me!"

"I'm sorry, *cariño*. Mommies get scared too sometimes." She smoothed the lapels of the black suit jacket she'd borrowed from a friend—a size four for six-year-old Andres. His doctors at the UCLA Children's Hospital had explained how an injury, like *the accident*, could stunt a child's growth.

"How much longer 'til *Tío* gets here?"

"Soon, soon."

She rose to her toes searching the crowd, turning Andres to face the other direction as a bunch of werewolves, blood dripping from rubber snouts, crossed the street. The crowd grew more frightening as the sun fell. Damn that Zacarias. He, of all people, should think of his nephew's bad leg, making him stand on the corner like that. And after that mess he made at Andres's school meeting. Making Lettie clean up after him, like usual, not even thinking to warn her, so she'd been surprised by a call from that son-of-a-dog vice principal who combed a few pieces of hair over his head like the whole world was too stupid to know he was bald. She'd had to stop comforting poor Melissa, who'd been crying like a brokenhearted teenager over that bastard Adam, and spend twenty minutes apologizing to Vice Principal Waldron.

How many times, she wondered, did the words *I'm sorry* leave her mouth each day? Too many to count. *I'm sorry* to her bosses. *I'm sorry* to her son's teachers and therapists. *I'm sorry* to the angry white man on the bus whose lap she'd fallen into on her way to work. Anyone could be a cop, an ICE agent, a proud citizen willing to stick his nose in her business and report her for deportation, doing his part to *Make America Great Again.* Everyone had more power than she, and so she apologized.

There was just one person she did not need to apologize to—Zacarias.

The vice principal had called her half-brother many things, words Lettie did not understand, but she knew one too well. *Angry.* She hadn't bothered to text Zacarias after the call, nor had she punished him with Oaxacan curses she knew he'd have to Google translate. Instead, she had waited for tonight, even looked forward to it, imagining all the ways she would make him squirm out here in rich-people land. Zacarias's land. Maybe she'd wait until they saw one of the women they worked for and show the truth, expose him for the lying half-Mexican mutt he was. If only she didn't need his money. If only one of these palaces, their many windows lit gold against the dusky sky, were hers and Andres's. If only she were a different woman. If only, if only.

She disliked crowds and had tried to convince Andres to spend the night trick-or-treating in Sunset Park, the southern side of the city, where there would be fewer people. Not that the Sunset Park area was that much different—*rich is rich*, as Lettie's mother said—but the fancy north of Montana Avenue neighborhood where Melissa and Regina lived was filled with three- and four-story homes designed to look like the clay-shingled villas back home in Oaxaca, but one hundred times bigger, and owned by wealthy people who worked in what Lettie had heard her employers call *the industry*. That meant Hollywood. Not that she knew exactly what they did beyond make TV shows and movies. And money. Enough to hire other movie people, the worker bees—makeup artists and set designers; electricians and prop men—who, every year, a few weeks before Halloween, transformed half of the homes north of Montana Avenue into haunted houses.

Andres had insisted on going to the "movie people's houses," and she couldn't help but smile—her smart boy knew more about who made up Santa Monica's rich and poor, and everyone between, than her no-good, clueless half-brother. She had warned Andres, *It will be scary, my love.* She reminded him of last year—after only twenty minutes of going door to door, they'd come upon a scene straight out of a horror film. A front yard full of zombies, one chomping on a bloody leg like it was an Easter ham. Andres's eyes had gone so big Lettie had feared her sensitive boy might pee the pants of his Batman suit. But children, Lettie knew, forget easily, and here they were standing on a crowded corner waiting for her always-late brother, who was probably at the gym flirting with his skinny rich clients, the very women who lived in this storybook-neighborhood-turned-movie-set-hell one night of the year.

Melissa had taught her the word *sensitive*, explaining there wasn't anything wrong with Andres, like all those smarty-pants therapists and teachers at his school said, making Lettie sign paper after paper giving them permission to help Andres with his words, his body, his feelings. They had a problem ready to attach to every part of her beautiful boy.

Lettie had confessed her worries to Melissa one cleaning day. Why she'd told Melissa these shameful things, she still didn't know. There was something about Melissa that set her apart from the other women Lettie cleaned and babysat for in Santa Monica. Melissa, who was always calling her *my Mexican sister*, which Lettie didn't mind as much now. She remembered the sobs that had broken poor Melissa in two when she'd told Lettie about that sack-of-shit husband of hers. Lettie had been wrong about Adam, whom she'd imagined all muscles on the outside, sugar and cream on the inside. He was a no-good dog with a hungry penis. Melissa had been in pain—Lettie had known it as she rocked her boss in her arms, wishing the pain away, even if she had to swallow it herself. She knew how even the rich women suffered. It was this knowing that made Lettie's jobs bearable.

Melissa had helped Lettie change Andres's life for the better, signing the paperwork that said Lettie worked for her full-time, a lie that allowed Andres to attend John Wayne Elementary, where the children of her bosses attended school. *How fancy!* Auntie Corrina had crowed when Lettie shared the good news. A rich child's public school with all the special services Andres needed, and, a bonus for Lettie, a bilingual staff. *Un milagro.* Not that Lettie believed in miracles. It was hard enough to believe in God. Why would He punish her like this for one stupid mistake—threaten to take away her boy?

Lettie wrapped her arms around Andres, absorbing the elbow jabs of children in costume passing by. Not one apologizing. As if she and her son were ghosts. There were plenty of parents dressed up. Pretty blond mommies dressed like fairies and witches, sexy bunnies and cats. Melissa said adults in New York City didn't dress up as much and made a joke about people in Santa Monica refusing to grow up, and she and Lettie had laughed together. This was what Lettie liked about Melissa—unlike her other employers, skinny Regina and Caroline the music agent who had promised to ask Selena Gomez to perform at Lettie's niece Emma's quinceañera and then never mentioned it again—Melissa made sure to include Lettie in her jokes, repeating them until Lettie understood. Melissa, Lettie knew, needed to be understood even more than Lettie needed to understand.

She and Andres had stopped at Melissa's earlier that night. After Melissa had made Lettie promise to do so, telling Lettie again and again how she would be *especially* surprised by the decorations, so Lettie had felt nervous as she and Andres made their way up the long walkway to Melissa's big house. Surprised Lettie had been, when Melissa, dressed as the most famous Mexican woman, artist Frida Kahlo, had thrown open the tall oak doors. Two strips of fake fur stuck over her eyebrows. Like hairy black caterpillars.

Melissa had stretched her arms out and hugged Lettie tightly, crying, *You were my inspiration!*

It was a Día de los Muertos celebration more beautiful than Lettie could ever have imagined. Flower sculptures made of red, yellow, and white carnations formed a giant skull in the center of the front lawn. Andres plucked tangerine-sized sugar skulls from a pyramid and dropped them two at a time into his pillowcase. There were mugs of spicy hot chocolate, plates of tamales and *pan de muerto*. All the delicacies of her childhood—details Lettie had shared with Melissa only a few weeks earlier during one of their cleaning day chats.

The gates surrounding the house were strung with what seemed like thousands of marigolds. Rows of white candles burned along the high cement walls leading to the front door, where a long line of costumed children waited for a paper cup of *champurrado*. Even Lettie's *abuela* would have been impressed, she thought.

It was as if she had walked into one of the schoolbooks she and her sisters had shared back in Oaxaca, the covers so faded they had used duct tape to mend the spine. Beautiful. Then why, Lettie wondered now, searching the crowds of trick-or-treaters for Zacarias, had she wanted to run far away from Melissa's house and the candlelight and the scent of cinnamon and cocoa and flowers wilting in the October heat?

She squatted to peek under the brim of the battered black cowboy hat swallowing Andres's head. "Don't touch your face. You mess up your mustache. What kind of cowboy has no mustache?"

"I itchy, Mommy." Andres swatted her hand away. "Where is *Tío*? I want candy."

She held his cheeks with one hand and used her black eyeliner to fix the curls at the tips of his mustache.

"Be still. If your stupid uncle isn't here in ten minutes, we go."

"Mommy, you're squeezing too hard," Andres said. "And it's not nice to call *Tío* stupid."

She leaned back to get a good look, making sure both ends curled at the same angle.

"You are right, my angel. You remind Mommy to be a gooder person."

"*Better*, Mommy. You're supposed to say *better*."

"Bet-ter," she said slowly. "Senor smartpants! Now, no more touching your face, yes?"

"Do I look like Papa?" Andres asked, tilting his hat forward and grinning.

Instantly, Lettie's heart ached with the mistake she'd made of telling Andres about his father's family ranch in the Sonoran uplands. Who knew, she thought, if it still existed—if it *ever* existed? If what Andres's father, Manuel, said was true. Still, in a moment of weakness, she had shared with their son everything Manuel had told her years ago when they were newly in love, and called each other *mi amor*, and spent sticky summer nights on a mattress thrown on the floor in Auntie Corinna's cool basement. In a weak moment, she'd told her son about the magical place his father came from, and Andres believed. In the birds with chests the color of emeralds and rubies. The burbling creek and spicy scent of mesquite; the wind in the green cottonwood. And the birdsong. *Cheedle-cheedle-cheedle-chee?* Manuel had sung, looking silly and sweet, the hardness vanished, and she'd been sure she was in love. Safe. That her life would, at last, be good.

What a foolish girl she'd been to trust Manuel. He never stayed more than a few days here and there. His love like a broken faucet, drip drop. Last she'd heard, he'd gone to live with another woman (may she roast in hell) he'd had a baby with, a lazy witch with a house in Palmdale she'd inherited from her grandmother.

Lettie hadn't seen or spoken to Manuel in six months, since he'd beaten her for what she'd sworn to Zacarias was the last time—her promise the only way to stop her brother from reporting Manuel to the police, or finding her son's father and beating him bloody.

"Oh, you look like a real *charro*," Lettie said, pulling Andres into a hug. "No one will recognize you. Your *tío* Zacarias will think, 'Who is this tough Mexican cowboy?'"

"But do I look like *Papa*?"

"Yes, just like Papa," she said, careful to keep the ice from her voice. "Hold on to your pillowcase. You are going to get so much candy tonight. Your tummy will be mad at you all week."

Where is Zacarias?

She knew her brother never meant his bad behavior. He would turn up with an apology and that pretty white smile, explaining how he hadn't meant to make them wait. Just like he hadn't meant for Andres to get hurt. And Lettie would have to swallow her anger, remind herself that as selfish as Zacarias could be, she still needed his help.

He was, after all, the only person, besides Lettie's lawyer, who knew of her problems with the law. When Lettie had received the first paper telling her she had to go to court, she'd hidden it deep in a drawer. The day of the court date came and she'd hidden inside her apartment all day, texting her employers she had a bad throw-up bug as she waited for the ICE men to pound fists on her door. Nothing. This had made her hopeful. Maybe a mistake had been made,

her file lost, her stealing forgotten—didn't those things happen?—
but when she'd confessed to Zacarias about her crime, one night
after too many beers and big laughs about the silly rich people, her
brother had gone crazy. His good mood had disappeared and he'd
spent an hour looking up things on his phone, spitting words at her
she couldn't understand then, but now knew too clearly. *Arraignment.
Misdemeanor. Crimes of moral turpitude.* Zacarias had tried to comfort
her, explaining how shoplifting was a little crime. If only she wasn't
an illegal . . . He had stopped there because *if only if only*, and with
Senor Donald in the White House, even a little crime could end in
deportation.

Lettie had been ready to go to court and beg for forgiveness.
She'd bring Andres, whose limp would surely soften the judge's
heart, she explained to Zacarias. But her brother had just shaken his
head, as if Lettie were a child.

You have to get a lawyer, he'd said. *Either you find one, or I will. I can
help with the fees.*

I will, I will, Lettie had said, too proud to rely on a man she hardly
knew (just a few months, at the time) to take care of what seemed a
simple task. The next day, on her way to a cleaning job downtown,
she'd seen Ms. Ochoa's kind-looking face on a billboard over the I-10
with the comforting message, *There's Enough Room for All of Us.* Lettie
had called 1-800-797-SAFE immediately.

Ms. Ochoa said the last thing Lettie should do was plead guilty.
She had a plan, which began with contacting the owner of Cosmic
Cove Comics, a short man with a full head of silver hair. Lettie had
heard from her bosses that Santa Monica was *liberal*, a city of open
minds, and Ms. Ochoa too had been hopeful that Mr. Silver Hair
would drop the charges. But it turned out the man was one of the few
red-cap-wearing Santa Monica Republicans in love with the Wall.
Once he discovered Lettie-the-Pokémon-card-thief was without papers, he was happy to help make America great again by kicking her
out. He'd refused to drop the charges.

We will keep fighting, Ms. Ochoa had said. *I will charge you on a sliding scale.*

Lettie hadn't known what that meant. She'd said yes without bothering to ask; what choice did she have? Now, she was afraid to tell Zacarias just how much she owed her lawyer. On top of Andres's hospital bills—now with a collection agency whose fast-talking people called her every day. Her debt was a hungry monster that kept her awake at night. The money Zacarias had been giving her each month, sometimes five hundred dollars, sometimes as much as a thousand, was never enough.

Tonight, at some point, she would tell Zacarias this. For Andres's sake. No boy should lose his mother, but especially not her boy. How stupid she had been, taking the Pokémon cards. One dumb moment was all it took to ruin a life in this new America of Trump. It did not matter, Lettie understood now, how many nice, rich liberals said they were on her side. She would still be punished for her mistake.

"Boo!" A low voice hit Lettie's ear and she stumbled forward, nearly toppling Andres. It was Zacarias, finally. He was wearing a black plastic mask—the bad guy from the Star Wars movies.

"*Tío!* Trick or treat!" Andres reached for his uncle, who scooped him into a bear hug.

"Little man! So dang sorry to keep you guys waiting. I got tied up at work."

Andres lay one hand on each side of the black plastic mask. "Darth Vader! Where your light saber at, *Tío?*"

Lettie's brother lifted the mask so it sat atop his thick curls. He was still dressed in his gym clothes, and, Lettie noticed, on his skin she could smell women's perfume. On the nights she waited for the last of the clients to leave so she could clean the gym, she watched from the back office as woman after woman, all of them looking like teenagers with no boobs or butts, stood on tiptoes to give Coach Zack a hug after class. Her brother talking and talking, touching and touching, never thinking of Lettie and how badly she needed to start her work so she could finish, go home, lie next to sleeping Andres, the whisper of his snores her only peace.

"Put him down easy," she said, ignoring her brother's apology. Andres dangled happily from Zacarias's strong arms. "His foot, it bothers him a lot today. They had a big costume parade at school. Lots of walking."

"We'll go easy," said Zacarias, lowering Andres gently to the ground. "Which house you wanna hit first, cowboy?"

"That one!" Andres said, pointing to the massive stone house in front of them, set back from the street on a green lake of lawn.

"Let's do it," said Zacarias, grabbing Andres's hand and flashing his perfect smile at Lettie. "You too, Mama. Come on."

"Just a few houses, *cariño*," Lettie said to Andres. "When I say *all done*, we are all done. No whining talk."

"Oh hey, I almost forgot," said Zacarias. ""I brought you a costume, Sis. Catch!"

He tossed her a plastic mask, brown and hairy-looking.

"Mommy is Chewbacca!" Andres cheered.

Although Lettie was not happy to be the furry beast who was always the joke in *Star Wars*, while Zacarias was the dark hero, she put the mask on, happy to let it hide the frown on her face.

They moved from house to house, Zack and Andres talking and giggling like a pair of brothers, sampling candy as Andres's pillowcase sagged with the weight of his treats. Zacarias escorted Andres to each door while Lettie waited for them on the sidewalk. She didn't need to get any closer; she spent enough time inside these big houses. Lettie watched one thin, pretty woman after the next open front doors and hold out the giant bowls of candy they'd never let themselves taste (the evil calories!), too busy flirting with Zacarias, that dog, to notice the handfuls of candy Andres grabbed, enough to last him until next year.

Finally, when they'd covered the whole block, and Andres's pillowcase was heavy as a brick and Lettie's face damp with sweat under the plastic mask, she announced. "One more house. Then we go home."

"That one!" Andres said, charging up the walkway of a house that always made Lettie think of a stack of ice cubes. It was the home of her Least Favorite Boss, Lindsey Leyner. Senora Ratface lived in the ice cubes with her over-tanned husband, who reminded Lettie of a desert lizard, and her spoiled-brat son, Landon, who left notes that read *LETTIE, DO NOT TOUCH!* beside the piles of expensive junk all over his room. Signs that matched the much larger wooden one staked in the Leyners' front lawn, that one in Spanish: *POR FAVOR NO TOCAR LA FRUTA.* It was Lettie's job to collect the rotten lemons from under the tree and throw them in the outside trash can. What a waste.

Zacarias began to follow Andres up the path to the Leyners' front door, but Lettie grabbed her brother's arm, moved by a sudden courage that, she knew, had a lot to do with her hidden face.

"Stay back for a minute. I have something to tell you."

"Sure," he said, easy-breezy. "Shoot."

She lowered her voice. "I get two more bills. One from the hospital and another from Ms. Ochoa. I need more . . . help."

"Okay. But do we have to talk about it right now?"

"My apologies. The bills, they make me nervous. And you are always so busy."

"You think they don't make *me* nervous?"

"It's almost fifteen thousand, the total," she blurted. "You know that?"

"Whoa, whoa," Zacarias repeated. Lettie imagined that, under the mask, a look of real shock ruined his movie-star face. "Fifteen *grand*? How's that possible?"

"Lawyers are expensive, Zacarias. And medical bills. What happened to Andres was not cheap." She held back from saying, *What you did to Andres*, knowing it would only make him angry.

"Why don't you get a lawyer for free? This is America. Read the Constitution."

"Try the homework, *hermanito*. They give free lawyers to people who are citizens. Not to people like me. I go to the center for immigration. The lady there, an expert, says I need to pay a special lawyer, or I'll be back to Mexico like—" Lettie snapped her fingers. "Without Ms. Ochoa . . . I'm done."

"It's *do your homework*."

"What?"

"The expression is *do your homework*. Not *try the homework*." Lettie heard the sneer in his voice. No respect.

"Focus, fool brother! You need to find the money. I gave Ms. Ochoa your phone number. She is calling you tomorrow to tell you the number herself. She takes credit cards—I ask. You wait and hear it. Fifteen thousand, Zacarias."

"Dammit, Lettie." Her brother grabbed at his hair with both fists. "My name is *Zack*."

Her brother was extra angry. Her cheeks burned under the plastic mask.

From the front door of the Leyners' house came a shattering sound; something had broken.

"Andres?" Zacarias called toward the house. "Everything okay, buddy?"

"Excuse me?" a man's irritated voice cut through the night. "I have a little boy here, sans his grown-up!"

Lettie turned toward the ice cube house; the voice belonged, of course, to Trey Leyner, Senor Lizard.

"I'll go," said Zacarias.

"No, I will," snapped Lettie. She'd had enough of her brother's bossiness. "I know the people who live here."

She took big strides toward the front door. Zacarias followed her anyway. She felt a small thrill of power knowing something he didn't: that Lindsey Leyner, one of his precious gym "clients," lived in this house. Let him stammer and squirm and figure out how to explain to Senora Ratface exactly who the three of them—Lettie and Andres and Zacarias—were to each other.

Let *him* be the one who had to "play it cool."

But when Lettie reached the front door, Lindsey was nowhere in sight, only her too-tan husband with the slicked-back hair, wearing one of those Captain America costumes with the padded muscles. He was tall, her boss's husband, with wide shoulders and a gut that humped out from under his tight costume. Thick like a man who once, long ago, lifted weights to impress the girls.

Andres was bent over several large shards of broken blue glass on the stone landing, covering his face with both hands as if he were crying.

Lettie knelt down. *"Que paso?"*

"I break that," said Andres.

"Your son got a little, ah, overzealous," said Mr. Leyner to Lettie, not recognizing her in the mask, although he might have recognized her voice, she thought—Lindsey had introduced them a few times. To him, Lettie was just a body who scrubbed floors and scoured pots; her face did not stick in the mind of an important man like him.

Zacarias, still wearing his mask, reached down and coaxed Andres up from the ground. "Come here, little man." Lettie watched her boy scramble into his uncle's arms. Her anger at her brother lifted away.

"What happened, exactly?" said Zacarias to Trey Leyner.

"Your boy thought this vase here was a candy receptacle. He reached right in and it toppled over."

"An understandable mistake," said Zacarias. "It's pretty late—a lot of houses are on a self-serve system now. He was just doing what he'd done at the past few houses."

Thank you, Zacarias, Lettie thought. Her brother was fixing the problem.

"Our porch lights were on," said Mr. Leyner. "As were all our lights and decorations." He made a sweeping motion toward the fancy lights—bulbs in the shape of pumpkins—that hung from the thick branches of the magnolia tree in the center of the lawn.

Lettie imagined leaning forward and biting his hand.

"He's six," said Zacarias.

"I know he didn't break it on purpose. It's just that this was quite an expensive piece and will be difficult to replace."

Zacarias shrugged. "Total apologies, man. Things get a little crazy on Halloween. We won't take up any more of your night." Lettie expected him to turn and carry Andres back down the stone path, but instead the two men locked into a stare. Her heart began to kick like a runaway donkey.

Mr. Leyner spoke slowly, as if tasting his own words. "Typically, when property is damaged, the responsible party makes at least a *gesture* of offering some compensation."

"Come again?" said Zacarias, in his cowboy voice, and Lettie realized he was playing dumb. Making a little fun with Mr. Leyner. She hated when he did this to her, but now, it made her proud.

Mr. Leyner sighed and pointed to the broken vase. "My wife got this vase in Italy. It's one-of-a-kind Venetian artistry. I understand your son is young and disabled, but that doesn't mean his parents shouldn't take responsibility for the material loss."

Lettie braced herself for Zacarias to snap, *He's not my son!*

Instead she heard him say, "He's not *disabled*, you douchebag. He's a regular kid whose been reaching into containers for candy all night. Why *you* would leave some Italian vase on your front porch on freaking Halloween night is beyond my comprehension. Why should I take responsibility for your moronic mistake?"

Lettie flinched; a tightness had taken over her brother's voice. She thought about stepping forward, whispering to Zacarias, explaining this piece-of-garbage man was husband to one of her bosses.

Mr. Leyner barked a laugh. "Wow. Just wow. This is a first. Getting insulted by a stranger on my own front doorstep. And in a Darth Vader mask to boot."

Zacarias set Andres down and nudged him toward Lettie. She pulled the boy against her and guided him a few steps back from the door.

"Let's go," she called to her brother. The crowd moving past the house had slowed to stare. Attention was only a bad thing for a woman like her in this new America. She half expected to see an ICE van screeching down the street.

"In a sec," Zacarias said. His voice was hard. Like Manuel's when Lettie said the wrong thing.

She lifted Andres in her arms. She wanted to run, elbow her way through the mob of trick-or-treaters, hurry home and wash off his mustache, make him a cup of *champurrado*, the cinnamon-sprinkled hot chocolate her *abuela* made every year for Día de los Muertos. Hers would taste even better than the hot chocolate Mel had paid a caterer to make.

But Lettie could not leave her brother, and she could not tell him to bite his tongue with his perfect teeth. Zacarias was defending little Andres in a way she could not. Showing this man that her Andres—*their* Andres—was just as important as the Leyner boy, that pale-skinned brat.

Suddenly, it was night. The streets even more packed with zombies and vampires and witches.

"Motherfucker," Lettie heard Trey Leyner growl and turned to see Zacarias and Senor Ratface on the ground, a blur of thick arms and legs as they rolled across the green lawn, past the wooden no-picking-fruit sign meant only for people like Lettie. She could see that Mr. Leyner was losing, moving slower than her brother, a chubby brown bear to Zacarias's sleek panther. Then Zacarias was on Mr. Leyner's back, an arm around the man's thick throat—squeezing, Lettie knew, because she could see the veins in her brother's arm jumping out from his skin.

Mr. Leyner's Captain America mask slipped down, and Lettie saw his eyes were wild with fear.

Thanks to God, the Darth Vader mask still covered Zacarias's face.

Andres screamed. As loud as he had the day of the accident.

"No! Don't hurt my *tío*!"

Lettie pushed her son's face against her chest to silence him. He was shaking, a little bird.

"Stop hurting! Stop hurting!" Andres screamed, just as he had the last time Manuel had stood over Lettie as she lay on the kitchen floor, the hard toe of his work boot slamming into her side again and again.

Mr. Leyner's face was purple, his lips opening and closing like a fish out of water.

She heard voices on the sidewalk behind them. *Oh my God! Someone, do something!* Then the word she feared most of all: *Police. Call the police.*

She turned and was blinded by the light of a flashlight. Or was it a camera? A phone? She covered Andres's face with one hand, felt his hot tears on her palm.

"Ayúdame!" Lettie cried, not sure who she was asking for help. *"Ayúdame, por favor!"*

Then she saw the twisted look of disgust on the white mommies' faces. Saw them shielding their children's eyes.

Lettie turned back to the two men. "Zacarias, we must go!"

Her brother sat atop Mr. Leyner, who lay in the grass like a fat rag doll, his red costume torn at the side, a pale slice of skin showing. The big man's body shuddered with every punch Zacarias plowed into the man's face. *Thud, thud.* Like the sound of a butcher knife chopping a slab of pig meat at the *carnicería*.

"Enough!" Lettie yelled, and finally, Zacarias jumped off Mr. Leyner. He looked at Lettie and made a slicing motion with his hand, telling her to *go*. To take Andres and run. Lettie lifted Andres into her arms. The boy was shaking and whimpering. "It's okay, it's okay, you are safe," she whispered, stepping across the grass, stumbling a little under Andres's weight. She was ashamed that she'd let her boy see so much of an ugly fight. Though, in her heart, she was glad that Zacarias had pounded Senor Ratface. Let the man suffer a little, the way Lettie had for so long. *This was the only way to survive*, she thought as she moved away from the Leyner house, fast as she could under Andres's weight, rejoining the streaming crowd of ghouls and devils, her breath ragged and hot in her mask. A person had to fight.

She had been stupid that one day she'd stolen some cards she'd hoped would make her little boy happy. One day was all it took to ruin a life in this new America. She wouldn't be stupid again. She knew better than to trust anyone in Trump's country, even the rich white people who called themselves liberal, as if they were revolutionaries, even sweet Melissa who had already given her and Andres so much. Trust no one, she had told Andres as his torn body mended in the hospital. No one. Not your uncle who you love very much—where was he when you needed him? Not the white people, even those who say they want to help. Not the brown people who will stand on your head in a stampede to grab one last gasp of air.

As she ran down the sidewalk, Andres gone limp and heavy in her arms, shoving people aside (even children) with her wide hips, the sound of her ragged breath bouncing off the plastic insides of her mask, Zacarias behind her urging *run, run*, she feared the day she'd have to tell her son that she, his mama, could not be trusted either.

FRIDAY, NOVEMBER 9, 2018

20

MEL

MEL SPED HER MINI COOPER AROUND THE CURVES OF HER THERAPIST Janet's neighborhood, squinting into the air turned hazy and thick from the Woolsey Fire, blazing just fifteen miles away. She knew Adam was already waiting for her at their couples' session, which he'd had "no choice" but to push from their usual evening slot to one P.M., due to a "dinner thing" with some studio exec. An excuse Mel now assumed was code for a date with his sexting slut. But Mel hadn't batted an eye when he'd requested the time change and apologized for having to miss their usual after-therapy dinner. Let him cancel *their* date night to meet up with whoever-the-fuck-she-was. Let him complain about Mel being five minutes late for therapy, in his signature passive-aggressive style. *I know Mel doesn't think her time is more valuable than everyone else's. But then why is she always holding us hostage with her lateness?*

Today, Adam could be as holier-than-thou as he liked. Because today, in Janet's back house, which doubled as an office, Mel was going to incinerate his claim to the title of *As Good as a Man Gets*. In less than an hour, Adam's reputation, and their marriage, Mel thought with stomach-flipping finality, would be as burnt as the Malibu mansions that had been swallowed by flames.

The Woolsey Fire had sparked in the Simi Valley, Mel had read, then jumped the Ventura Freeway to devour the chaparral-covered canyons of the Santa Monica Mountains. The fire was uncontained, and now devouring countless estates belonging to the richest and most famous. As Mel stepped on the gas, the local radio station was going on and on about the Kardashians having to flee their compound. As if, Mel thought, *those* were the victims they should be most concerned about. God, sometimes she truly hated LA. She considered texting Zack—knowing he'd agree with her—and nearly reached for her phone before commanding herself, *No. Focus.* She could not allow herself to think of anything but the task ahead, on Janet's cat-hair-covered sofa. The task she'd been waiting for what felt like forever to complete.

It had been surprisingly easy to avoid Adam as she waited for their couples' therapy session to arrive. Adam was a morning person; Mel a night owl. Adam was working long hours on a new project—an adaptation of some YA novel about *blah blah blah*, which was all she heard when his mouth opened these days. She was at the gym nearly every day now, taking classes, the majority taught by Zack. Her new life, that of Mel 2.0, had been largely Adam-free, and she'd felt better than ever. Ready for the next step. The purge of Adam. The punishment of Adam. Justice for Mel, all versions. It had been exhausting to hold all that rage inside, wait for the right moment to unleash it all. She'd spent the last few weeks fantasizing about revenge. She'd considered printing out the texts and tucking them like cue cards inside Adam's wallet, so it was the first thing he saw when he paid for his espresso in the morning. *Surprise!* Or sending Sloane on a sleepover, and papering Adam's home office with a thousand copies of the texts, so many that it would take him hours to tear them down. Ha! She'd even contemplated the very worst thing, a marriage-breaker for sure—calling Adam's mother and revealing to Marti Goldberg just how repulsive her baby boy truly was.

Her phone pinged with a text, and although she'd sworn to stop looking at her phone while driving, she couldn't help herself.

Adam, of course. Right on cue.

Not okay that you are late. Again.

She stopped herself from sending the middle finger emoji.

She was still wearing her sweaty gym clothes, her thighs be-ginning to chafe in the leggings Regina had given her, though they actually fit pretty well now. She'd bought a couple other new pairs, too, and tossed the ones she'd torn in the van with Zack into a dumpster in the alley behind her house. The memory of that night—Zack's hands all over her, then his tongue between her legs—made her shift in her seat, narrowly missing a landscaper lugging a bag of soil across the road. The worker was wearing a white mask and Mel felt a jab of guilt that he had to labor in the smoky air, flakes of ash falling like black snow, while she was sealed in the clean air of her A/C-chilled car, racing to therapy, where she was prepared to accuse her husband of the very sin she too had committed.

Hypocrite was one of precocious Sloane's new favorite words and, those past few weeks, each time Mel heard her daughter use it, Mel's dedication to her cause—Mel 2.0—wavered. Then, all she had to do was think of the texts she'd found on Adam's phone. She had a print-out of the texts now, carefully folded in her purse, ready to show to both Adam and Janet. Proof.

And anyway, she told herself, the *thing* in the van had been a one-time dalliance. A redemptive whirl to reestablish balance in her and Adam's marriage. Tit for tat, Even Steven, an eye for an eye, and all that. She'd felt righteous emerging from the Color Theory van into the cool night air. Mortified that Regina had caught them, sure. But also a little triumphant. She, the fat girl, desired by the drop-dead-gorgeous younger man both she and Regina, and every other woman who'd ever lain eyes on him, had pined for. *Talk about fairness, why don't you, dear Adam?* Fair was an aesthetically forget-table woman like herself being treated like she was a bona fide Victo-ria's Secret angel.

While she knew she'd never do *it* again, each time Mel had taken one of Zack's classes those past few weeks, the way he looked at her reminded her she *could* have him again, if she wanted. Not that she did, but the option made her feel a kind of justice was being served. For all the girls hiding flab under layers of control-top tanks, compression leggings, Spanx. All the invisible middle-aged women not willing to torture themselves in gyms every single day, not willing to spend $1,000 a month on creams and injections and laser treatments to look a few years younger. Mel 2.0 was the heroine in a rom-com Hollywood would never make, because, apparently, she thought, parking in front of Janet's sprawling but unkempt Craftsman, fat women weren't allowed to fall in love, or feel desire, or have a big fat orgasm (or two) in the back of a van.

Still, Mel had a conscience (unlike Adam, she thought) and she'd been worried luring Adam into what Sloane would call a *sneak attack* via confrontation on the therapy couch was unethical. But confronting Adam in front of Janet felt like the safest choice. It was hard for a woman to feel safe these days. Of course, Mel knew she didn't have the kind of problems poor Lettie had to deal with but, still, her radar was on red alert, especially now that she was reading a dozen op-eds a week decrying the pernicious harassment of women in every industry, specifically Adam's starlet-stuffed Hollywood. Could good-as-a-man-gets Adam be one of those very same predators?

She smoothed her frizzed bangs in the rearview mirror. She was ready to rumble.

The smoke-filled air from the distant fire clawed at Mel's throat as soon as she stepped out of the car. The clouds above matched the moment: apocalyptic. Thick and heavy with deep purple and ochre and burnt orange, colors she might have once used for a dramatic wedding invitation printed on her letterpress but that now only made her think of bruises on a battered body. She marched up the cracked driveway, the thin layer of ash whispering like East Coast autumn leaves under her sneakers. She was a crusader charging into battle, ready to confront that cheating bastard on her own turf. Last week, during her individual session with Janet, Mel had briefed her on the situation (minus the Zack part), and they'd agreed Mel would confront Adam today, with Janet there to mediate.

Mel hurried through the overgrown backyard, stopping outside the half-open door of the carriage house Janet used as an office, catching the smell of potpourri incense. Mel gulped a breath and stepped inside.

Adam, as she'd correctly guessed, sat upright, perched on the edge of the sofa. Mel avoided his eyes and focused instead on the familiar objects around the room that had become a comfort. Heavy symbols that Brooklyn Mel would have disdained—long-necked African fertility statues made of smooth black stone, and bowls of crystals that Janet had once, to Mel's horror, suggested Mel hold and rub during their session.

"Melissa," Janet said cheerily from a wicker armchair in the center of the cluttered and dim-lit room, her feathered blond hair tied up in a poufy, girlish ponytail, though she was well over sixty.

"Sorry I'm late," Mel said.

"Well," Adam said dryly, "we certainly weren't expecting you any earlier."

So that's how this was going to go, Mel thought. *Oh, just you wait, Mr. Punctuality.*

She took her place next to Adam on the sofa, making sure to leave as much distance as possible, a tasseled pillow behind her so her feet reached the ground.

"Adam and I were just discussing the fires," Janet said, turning to Mel. "Devastating. Some of my former clients have had to evacuate."

"The *LA Times* videos are heartbreaking." Mel nodded.

"I'm sure you ran into traffic on the way here. It's been awful."

"Yeah. Sorry again for being late."

"That's funny," Adam said, "*I* didn't hit any traffic. And I came all the way from Burbank."

The *fight* switch in Mel flicked on.

"Seriously, Adam? You're going to criticize me—here?"

"Oh-kay," Janet said. "Shall we have a do-over?" She laughed quietly and patted the wisps of blond hair around her narrow face. "That's what I used to say when my kids were young. We *all* deserve a do-over now and then."

Mel tried not show her annoyance, knowing Adam felt the same, reminding herself how wonderful Janet was, once you got past the New Agey tchotchkes all over the room, the *You Control Your Destiny* plaque on the wall (in a machine-printed cursive that offended Mel's typography-trained eyes), and Janet's tendency to speak like a kindergarten teacher. Many of Mel's individual sessions with Janet over the past year had ended with Mel in tears over a new revelation or insight. She'd been making good progress as a human. Then Adam had (literally) fucked it all up.

"So, here we are," Janet said with a shake of her ponytail.

"Oh-kay," Mel mumbled. "Guess we're honing right in."

"Homing," Adam said. "I think you mean 'homing right in.'"

"See?" Mel looked to Janet. "Why do I bother? I can't say a sentence without him criticizing me."

Adam looked down at his hands, tucked between his knees. "Sorry."

"We've talked about criticism quite a bit in previous sessions," said Janet gently. "And we can continue talking about it now, if that's what you think is helpful, Mel. But just make sure you're not avoiding your real intention here today."

Mel felt Adam stiffen next to her—the sofa cushion slid back as he leaned forward.

"Intention?" he said. "What's going on? You two are scaring me."

The room fell silent. *Just say it*, Mel commanded herself. But she was unable to speak. Instead, she stared pleadingly at Janet.

Janet took the cue. "Why don't I help us get started? Melissa, has, unwittingly, discovered something she'd like to address with you, Adam. A very hurtful and disorienting revelation. Melissa?" She looked at Mel expectantly.

"Discovered something." Adam nodded slowly. "You mean, as in, realized something here, during one of your solo sessions?"

Mel's eyes found the once-loathsome plaque hanging on the wall behind Janet's head. *You Control Your Own Destiny.*

Now, it felt like a sign. She remembered what Bri had said in that transformative Color Theory class. *No one's going to give you what you need. You've got to take it.*

Mel sat up straight, feeling the new muscles in her arms, the strength in her core. She took the deepest breath she could manage, and then she spoke.

"I found the texts, Adam. *The* texts."

He stared at Mel dumbly, as if he hadn't heard her. Was he going to make her say it again?

"You'd think"—she looked to Janet—"a famous filmmaker would be smarter. Better at covering his tracks."

Adam cut in. "Covering tracks? What?" He was rubbing his palms up and down the thighs of his designer skinny jeans— something Mel knew he did when nervous.

"*I* have a story for *you*, Adam," Mel said, feeling bolder. "You might find it a little clichéd, but here goes." She rummaged inside her purse as she spoke. "Man marries woman. Woman gets fat. Man gets rich and successful and famous. Man cheats on woman with hot young slut. The end."

"What?" Adam shook his head rapidly, looking, Mel thought, guilty as hell. *Boo-ya!* she heard Bri yell in her mind.

"I know you cheated on me, Adam."

"This is a joke, right?" Adam looked to Janet.

"No, Adam, this is quite serious," Janet said.

Mel located the printout of the texts in her purse and thrust the folded paper at Adam.

"What . . . is this?" Gingerly, he took the paper from her and unfolded it.

"Just read it."

Adam stared at the page, his lips moving ever so slightly, glasses slipping down his nose. Mel had the passing reflex to push them up for him, and then remembered she wouldn't be touching him ever again.

Adam looked up.

"This isn't me," he said, his voice cool and tight. "I don't know what this is." He extended the printout back to Mel.

She swatted it to the floor. "Bullshit," she hissed.

"Melissa," Janet warned.

Mel ignored her. "*This*, Adam, is the story you've, clearly, been living behind my back. Behind Sloanie's sweet little back!"

Her eyes burned with tears but she refused to blink. She would not let him see her as anything but strong. Self-reliant. *IN CONTROL.*

But then she saw the look of terrified confusion on his face. Watched as he picked the paper up from the floor, almost pathetically, and scanned it again, his eyes flicking left and right across the page. She hadn't seen him scared like this, so utterly lost-looking, since his father's funeral.

"Let's all take a breath," said Janet. "Adam, take a few minutes to process."

Adam did not answer. Mel watched him press his hands to his head, elbows resting on his knees. Panic shot through her: What if she was wrong? She wanted to grab Adam by the arm and drag him out of the room, lock the two of them in her car until he finally explained. Maybe, somehow, they could fix this. Hadn't Adam always been a fixer, able to find a solution, no matter how impossible it seemed? Like when Sloane had inhaled a piece of carrot at two and Adam had picked her up, run the two blocks to the hospital, and stood in the middle of the ER waiting room, a wheezing Sloane in his arms, shouting until they let him in. As the doctors intubated

Sloane, their baby's delicate eyelids fluttering, Adam had looked Mel straight in the eyes and promised everything would be okay, and it had been. Until now.

It was too late for any of that. Mel understood that the life she'd had *before* the texts, before the *thing* in the van, was irrecoverable. Their beautiful life, as they'd known it, was over. And she'd played a role in the destruction.

A mewling came from behind the closed door. Janet stood, smoothed out her long, tie-dyed skirt, and opened it. Adam sat up as Janet's smoky-gray cat slid into the room.

"Tabitha's a people-cat," said Janet, settling back into her seat.

"Do you mind?" Adam asked, with false politeness, nodding toward Tabitha. "I'm allergic."

"This isn't *your* space, Adam," Mel snapped, feeling her anger resurface. "It's Janet's. You don't control the world. And"—she turned to Janet—"he's not allergic. He just dislikes cats."

"Melissa," Janet said, shooing the cat back outside and shutting the door. "Adam deserves more information."

"I just delivered printed evidence. What more does he need?"

"No," said Janet. "I mean information about how you *feel*. And then Adam gets to talk."

"I think he prefers to *text*," Mel said, unable to help herself.

"Those are *not* my fucking texts," Adam said, through clenched teeth.

"Getting back to my question, Mel," said Janet. "About how you're feeling?"

"I feel," Mel said, "like there is no *moving on*. As for healing . . . give me a break. I'll never trust you again."

"But I haven't done anything!" Adam shouted.

Thar she blows, Mel thought. He'd finally lost his cool-as-a-cucumber attitude. Here was the Adam who choked out two-hundred-pound men on the jiu-jitsu mat. Adam—*no worries, it's all good*, West Coast Adam—had vanished.

"You're cheating. I found proof on your phone. Proof that *you* erased. The texts were there. And then, a few hours later, while I was sleeping, they disappeared. Explain that, Adam."

"I can't explain it," said Adam, "because I had nothing to do with it." He looked to Janet and spoke quietly, as if Mel were invisible. "This might be another of Mel's episodes. She's struggled with, uh, interpreting *reality* in the past . . ."

Mel barked a laugh. "Oh, so this is my fault? I should've known you'd try to blame it on me. It's always Mel's fault. Crazy Mel. Sensitive Mel. I won't let you gaslight me, Adam."

"Lay off the hashtag-Me-Too op-eds," muttered Adam.

"Time to de-escalate, guys!" Janet cut in firmly. "This conversation can't be productive if—"

But Mel couldn't stop herself now. "You should've just killed me, Adam." She punched herself in the chest and the hollow thud startled Janet, who began to rise from her chair. "Sit, Janet!" Mel snapped, smacking the air down with her palm. Then she added, "Please."

The therapist obeyed.

"Because," Mel continued. "I'm dead now. Do you know how many times I've died?" Now her fist was clenched and pressing into her gut. "Every. Single. Time. I read those disgusting texts between you and your . . . whore!"

"I swear to God, Melissa," Adam said, his hands clasped as if in prayer, "I would never do that. I never *did*!"

Mel laughed. "I want to believe you, Adam. I want to believe you are good. Good-as-a-man-gets Goldberg!"

Adam spoke directly to Janet. "I'm *deeply concerned* about Mel's stability. It's ludicrous to even *think* I'd do that to her."

"Or Sloane?" Mel asked, wiping away her tears with the back of her hand. "We'll have to tell Sloanie, of course. Maybe"—she looked to Janet—"we can do that here? Yes, I think that's the best choice. Don't you, Janet?"

"Now wait a minute," Adam said, straightening, looking from Mel to Janet and back. "Please tell me this isn't some kind of delusional self-sabotage. Did you, Mel, type those texts yourself?"

"Don't you vomit that psychobabble nonsense all over me, Adam!"

Janet tried to break in. "Mel, Adam. I think we need to slow down a little here."

"Well, *I* think we need to speed things up," Mel said, searching her purse for her car keys. "Perhaps by getting a good divorce lawyer. Or maybe we could tell Sloane that her father penetrated another woman's vagina."

"Mel, stop it." Adam stood, his bulk suddenly filling the room. "That's sick."

Mel slung her purse over her shoulder. "No, *you* are the one that's sick."

"Janice," Adam began, looking at the therapist.

"It's *Janet!*" Mel said. "Is every woman just an object to you? I can't believe I actually used to tell Sloane that Daddy is the best guy in the world!"

"This is what I'm talking about," Adam said, pointing at Mel but looking at Janet. "She's unhinged. She'd rather ruin our daughter's life. She's determined to make Sloane hate men."

He was speaking to Janet now as if Mel were invisible. Something about her needing meds and calling her old psychiatrist back in Brooklyn.

"It's no wonder Sloane refuses to wear anything but boys' clothes," Adam went on to Janet. "When her mother is telling her how horrible men are day after day."

Mel knew she had to butt in, reclaim control. Janet was listening, nodding, her fingers tented in an upside-down V. Mel knew that gesture. She was believing him. *Him.*

"Don't trust anything he says!" Mel stood between Adam and Janet. "He's said terrible things. Once he told me to move to a lesbian commune. Can you believe that? It's like a line in a bad sitcom."

"Look, Mel." Adam's voice softened. "Can we just take a step back?"

"Oh, now you're nice," Mel said. "Now that you've got our therapist on your side." She narrowed her eyes at Janet, hearing the manic desperation in her own voice. Not caring.

"I hear that you are hurting, Melissa," said Janet.

"Mel, sweetheart," chimed in Adam.

"Don't ever, ever," Mel said, jabbing her finger at his chest, "call me *sweetheart* again."

She charged through the door of the office and out into the afternoon, ignoring Tabitha's piercing mewl from somewhere close by, and ran down Janet's driveway toward her car. The smoky air mingled with her tears, stinging her eyes and throat. As she yanked open the door of her Mini Cooper and wedged herself inside, she swore to herself she'd go to the gym every single day until she was strong enough to fight Adam, right on his goddamn jiu-jitsu mat.

Choke him unconscious.

She'd make herself hot. Starting *now*. She wouldn't stop until she was as supremely fuckable as every single woman who'd sweated at the party in her backyard. And then, she'd have her revenge. By the time she was done, Adam would be an emotional castrato. No way was he going to ruin her life after he'd convinced her to move across the country, her sacrificing everything—her business, her friends, her all-black wardrobe, her Brooklyn—so he could follow his dreams and cheat on her with trashy, illiterate women.

She was going to Manifest Destiny his ass.

Mel drove a few blocks, but her hands wouldn't stop shaking on the wheel. She pulled over and opened the *Tiny Sheep* virtual farm app on her phone. Sometimes, it was the only thing that calmed her down. She sheared a few tiny pink sheep, then dragged a male and female sheep into a "mating shack."

Her phone pinged with a text.

Adam, she thought, demanding she return to Janet's. As if.
But it was a group text. From Zack.

> Winter's coming, y'all! I love the gym as much as you do,
> but there's nothing like sweating it out under the sun.
> Let's get it while we still can! I'll be in Beast Mode at
> Muscle Beach just south of the Pier on Thursday at 4 if
> anyone wants to join. Pro bono, no exchange of dinero,
> purely for fun! Hit me up if you wanna join.

In the seconds it took to digest his message, Mel almost believed in fate with a capital F. She thought of Lettie's advice to her, on
that mortifying day in Mel's bedroom, when she'd suggested Zack's
training program.

I see it like a fortune-teller. All the good things coming to you.

Mel took a breath and closed *Tiny Sheep.* Then she responded to
Zack alone: Thursday doesn't work—are there other times this exhi-
bitionist misery is happening? She added an emoji, the ponytailed
woman grimacing under the weight of barbells, counted to ten, and
hit *Send.*

THURSDAY, NOVEMBER 15, 2018

21

REGINA

"Hon? I'm leaving in five," Regina called through the crack of Gordon's office door. From the hallway, she could hear the furious tap of his fingers on the keyboard. "It's Minnow Night."

"Hang on," he said, with an intensity Regina knew meant *do not come in*. "Don't go yet. Give me ninety seconds to finish this sentence."

"That's okay," she called back to him. "Don't let me interrupt you. My Lyft's on the way." This wasn't quite true; she hadn't called a car yet. But she'd begun giving Gordon little tests, to see who he loved more: *Eighteen Twelve*, or her.

The screenplay was winning.

Regina stepped into the bathroom across the hall to check herself in the full-length mirror. Dressing for Minnow Night always felt like a low-grade competition—who could achieve the most perfect hot-mom look without crossing over into the desperate, age-inappropriate cougar zone? Tonight, she felt especially good about her outfit: faux leather leggings that showed off her long, lean gams and thighs, a swingy white top, and red ballet flats. Makeup done just to the edge of sultry.

She could definitely pass for mid-thirties. Exceptionally *fit* mid-thirties. How the hell Zack could have chosen Mel—obviously over forty, far out of shape—over her, was incomprehensible.

At the thought of them, her entire body prickled with rage. Though she'd been getting the hang of pretending Zack no longer existed. When she struggled, she just closed her eyes and pictured Mel's pale, flabby leg propped on the back of the van seat, with Zack's head planted against her thigh.

They were traitors, Zack and Mel, and Regina hated them both.

She shut off the bathroom light and stepped back to the door of Gordon's office.

Tap tap tap.

"I'm out," she said.

"No! Come here," Gordon said from his desk. The tapping stopped. "Can I at least get a kiss good-bye?"

At least? Regina thought. As if *she* were the one perpetually withholding affection?

She stepped into his office. Gordon swiveled around from the high-tech, combined sitting/standing (he always sat) desk she'd surprised him with on his last day in the writers' room of *The Clue.*

"Wow," said Gordon to Regina. "You look amazing. Are you sure you're just going to a mom's night out? Or is there some twenty-five-year-old male model I need to kill?"

"Haha," she said. "And unfortunately, yes, it's just another Minnow Night at Canyon Rustica."

"Come here," he said, beckoning to her from his luxury ergonomic chair. (How she wished she could snap her fingers and reclaim the $2,500 she'd spent on it.)

Reluctantly (would it kill him to stand up?), she stepped forward and leaned down to kiss him. As their lips pressed together, Regina's phone rang, blaring the ringtone she'd set for Mel: "By the Sea," a little private joke, since Mel hated the beach. It was also the longest of any ringtone, the grating digital notes marching on for a full ten seconds.

"Sorry," she said to Gordon, breaking from their kiss.

What could Mel want?

"That's my Lyft," she lied. "I better run."

"Have fun," said Gordon. "Come kiss me when you get home."

"Or you could come kiss me," Regina said.

"Totally," said Gordon, already swiveling back toward his laptop. "Love you."

Back in the hallway, Regina read Mel's (typically overlong) text.

> Look, I know there is big awkward stuff btwn us now and I want you to know I hate it and I miss you. Also, you probably meant to disinvite me from the Mom's Night(mare) thing happening 2nite, but Jess Fabian cornered me at Sloane's soccer practice yesterday and basically BULLIED me into saying I'd go. So, it appears I am coming to Canyon Rustica tonight and if you don't want to talk to me I totally understand. I just thought I should tell you I was coming. I miss you.

"Unbelievable," said Regina out loud. As if stealing Zack wasn't enough; now Mel was horning in on Regina's friends, too.

"Did you say something, hon?" came Gordon's voice from the office.

"Nope," said Regina. "Good night." She blazed toward the front door, opening the Lyft app and ordering a car as she strode down the hallway, determined to beat Mel to the restaurant. The bitch was usually late, anyway.

22

MEL

"THAT DRESS IS KIND OF INAPPROPRIATE, MOM," SAID SLOANE FROM THE couch, where she was nestled on Adam's lap watching *Nailed It!*, the cooking show they loved watching together. Was it normal, Mel wondered, for a ten-year-old—even one in the *third* size percentile, like Sloane—to still sit on her father's lap?

"No offense," Sloane added. *No offense* was Sloane's latest favorite expression. She tacked it on to the end of her sentences constantly, as if, Mel thought, it made any preceding statement acceptable.

"It's not inappropriate at all, Sloanie," said Adam, glancing toward the bottom of the staircase where Mel stood, testing the pair of taupe sling-back heels that had arrived from Zappos that morning. "Mommy looks beautiful."

Mel ignored him, as had become habit in the past weeks. Adam had been sleeping in the guest room, although Mel would have preferred him sleeping in a hotel. He still hadn't given up the perfect (aka *cheating*) husband act, complimenting her excessively and leaving Post-its with a heart drawn on them beside the breakfast he prepared for her in the mornings while she was still sleeping.

As if banging a slut could be fixed with charm and egg-white omelets.

She took a careful step in her new shoes, hanging on to the banister for balance. The heels were just an inch-and-a-half high, but Mel still thought it was quite possible she'd fall and kill herself, having spent the past decade in chunky Dansko clogs.

"What do you mean by *inappropriate*, honey?" asked Mel, glancing down at the kelly-green wrap dress she'd purchased from J. Jill on Montana yesterday (size ten—the smallest she'd been since college! Color Theory was torture, but she'd dropped nine pounds—nine!—after just a month of workouts), after Jess Fabian had taken her hostage at soccer practice and forced Mel to promise she'd come to dinner with a bunch of John Wayne moms tonight—the same damn thing Regina had invited her to on their smoothie date last month.

Which seemed a lifetime ago. Since the *thing* in the van with Zack (the mere sight of a van—any van—caused rays of heat to shoot to Mel's face), Regina had not spoken to Mel in any form, save a single all-caps text: JUST STOP. Of course, she hadn't responded to the text Mel had sent her, on an impulse, ten minutes ago.

"Sloane?" Mel pressed. "Are you planning to answer me?"

"Um, yes," said Sloane. "Is it okay to use bad words when it's the best possible description for something?"

"Depends on the situation," said Adam.

"The situation is *right now*. And it's only a medium-bad word. Not super-bad, like the f-word or the c-word."

How the hell would Sloane know the c-word? Mel wondered.

"Hmmm," said Adam. "I guess I'd say yes, then, since it's just your mom and me here. But only if the bad word is absolutely necessary."

Fuck you, then! Mel shot at him, silently.

"Okay, here goes," said Sloane. "Drumroll, please!"

Adam banged imaginary drums.

"Your dress is kind of slutty, mom. Aka, skanky. No offense."

"*Excuse* me?" said Mel.

"It's too . . ." Sloane pointed to her own flat chest. "Boob-ish."

"Okay, that's enough, Sloane," said Adam.

"*Megan has nailed it!*" Mel heard a voice yell from the TV. She felt her temper rise. She tried to speak, "diplomatically," as Adam was fond of recommending. Screw him, but she didn't want to give him the satisfaction of her getting "hysterical."

"You know, Sloane, these boobs kept you alive for the first year of your life," Mel said, covering the three steps from the staircase to the front door with extreme caution. "So, you might want to thank them before you get on your moral high horse." The heels felt okay, actually. Worth every penny of the $398 she'd spent on them.

"Mom, *gross!*"

"Oh-kay," said Adam. "It's bedtime, Sloanie."

"What's a moral high horse?" said Sloane.

"It's mommy feeling sensitive to criticism," said Adam.

"Good night, you two!" said Mel as cheerily as possible, opening the door to the cool night air.

"Where are you even going?" said Sloane. "It's a school night."

"I told you already, dinner with some lady friends."

"Oooooh. Sounds juicy."

"Love you," said Mel, blowing a kiss in the direction of her husband and daughter. It took all her restraint not to add, *And only you, Sloanie.* Thankfully, Sloane hadn't asked them, again, if they were getting a divorce. Mel hoped that, for now, Sloane believed the bickering was Mel and Adam's regular routine. But hadn't Sloane seemed a bit anxious that past week? Mel had noticed her daughter gnawing on her fingernails more than once, and her usual sass had begun to tip over into outright defiance. The other night Sloane had stormed away from the dining table after Mel suggested she use a napkin to wipe her ketchup-coated lips.

"Love you," Sloane and Adam sang out in unison. Like a two-headed creature, Mel thought, as she closed the heavy front door behind her.

The air was cold enough to make gooseflesh rise on her bare arms—was this "winter"?—and smelled of night-blooming jasmine.

Her phone chimed and informed her the Lyft she'd ordered was three minutes away. She felt her chest cave; *why* was she doing this to herself? She'd always hated "girls' nights" of any kind, even in college. Groups of drunk, giddy women spilling gossip and confessions only made Mel feel sour and judgmental. Which then made her feel something must surely be wrong with her.

There was only one reason she was subjecting herself to this godforsaken "Minnow Night."

She missed Regina.

Mel gripped the handrail as she walked the three steps down to the yard, and once safely on the footpath, pulled her little white pen from her purse and took a deep, sweet hit off the vape pen advertised as Bliss. The sleek packaging promised an uplifting high with its nine-to-one THC/CBD ratio (God bless Prop 64). By the time she reached the sidewalk to wait for her Lyft, she was already feeling much better.

23

REGINA

"REGINA, OVER HERE!" JESS FABIAN WAVED FROM THE BAR OF CANYON Rustica, a dim, cavernous space lit by bare bulbs extending on pendants from the ceiling. Regina made her way past tables crowded with sleekly dressed diners toward the gleaming redwood bar, where a cluster of John Wayne moms stood holding cocktail and wine glasses. Country-tinged indie rock played in the background; Regina tried not to let it remind her of Zack. She scanned the bar area for Mel and was relieved not to see her among the group.

She'd probably chickened out, Regina thought, glad she hadn't responded to Mel's rambling text.

"Wolfie, yay!" Lindsey Leyner's sharp manicure closed around Regina's forearm. "It's about time. Our table should be ready any minute. We're getting that giant booth in the back."

"You look *amazing*, Regina," said Kylie Dupree, a tiny, aggressive woman who reminded Regina of the sort of yappy dog celebrities tucked under their arms. Kylie ran the John Wayne PTA with a blend of shrill enthusiasm and a relentlessly guilt-inducing approach to fundraising. Thus Regina, who had yet to make her first of two expected annual donations (suggested contribution per family: $2,000), strategically avoided her. "I mean, look at your body, look at your skin! Are you doing Kybella?"

"Am I doing what?" said Regina.

"Oh, come on, Regina's a purist," said Lindsey. "She doesn't do injectables. Not even Botox! Nothing but diet and exercise for the Wolfe. Old school."

"I officially hate you," said Kylie to Regina. "Do you know how much I have to spend every month?" She zigzagged her index finger through the air in front of her face. "Just to keep from looking like a basset hound?"

"Five hundred?" Lindsey guessed instantly. "No, wait. Seven-fifty?"

"Basset hounds are cute," said Regina, wishing she'd stayed home.

Jess Fabian, the improbably nice redheaded mother of two menacing redheaded fifth-grade twins, Tyler and Torrance, swiveled around from the bar and extended a highball glass with a lime on the rim to Regina.

"Here, Reg! I got you a vodka soda."

"Thanks." Regina had been planning to have no more than a single glass of white wine with dinner, but accepted the cocktail. Jess was easily offended. Perhaps this somehow fueled the entitled, greedy vibe of her ten-year-old boys, though Regina wasn't sure how. Kaden called them *the double demons*, and Mel had once referred to them as *next-gen-#METOO*.

"How are those handsome boys of yours?" Regina asked Jess.

"Oh, you know," Jess said, a bit helplessly. "Already . . . tween-ish. I'm terrified to send them to middle school next year."

"Your table's ready, ladies." A handsome male server with sculpted cheekbones and shoulder-length dark hair—hadn't Regina just seen him on some commercial?—appeared and beckoned the group toward the restaurant's main floor. "One of your friends is already waiting at the booth for you. The lady in the green dress. She looked a little lost on her way back from the restroom so I took the liberty of seating her."

Regina instantly knew he was referring to Mel. Who else would get lost between the bathroom and the bar? Mel had a terrible sense of direction and was probably stoned to boot. Regina took another sip of her vodka soda, feeling her empty stomach flutter at the prospect of seeing her ex-friend, the traitor. The drink was strong.

"Wait 'til you see how amazing Mel looks tonight!" said Jess to Regina as they followed the server toward the back of the restaurant. "She must have lost at least twenty pounds, right?"

"I wouldn't know," said Regina.

"Oh, I thought you two hung out all the time?" said Jess.

"I'd say Mel's lost eight to ten pounds," Lindsey cut in. "It shows more on short people. But still, it's definitely a step the right direction. And I see her at Color Theory all the time now."

"She does love Zack's classes," said Regina.

"Uh-oh," said Lindsey. "Is someone else after your boyfriend, Reg?"

"Shut up," said Regina. Then added a smile.

The server rounded a corner leading to another crowded dining area. Regina saw Mel sitting on the edge of an enormous U-shaped banquette, looking at her phone.

"Melissa, there you are!" screeched Lindsey. "We heard you got lost."

"Hi, guys." Mel stood up from the booth, wobbling a little on her feet.

"Regina, hi!"

Mel was not wearing her glasses, Regina noticed, and had put on a good amount of makeup, including liner applied cat-eye style and red matte lipstick.

"Good evening," said Regina, with as much cold formality as possible. Mel *did* look noticeably slimmer, and was wearing an uncharacteristically flattering wrap dress that exposed her cleavage.

In fact, she looked great. Far too heavy, still, but glammed up in a way that suited her.

The Zack effect, Regina thought darkly.

Regina drained her drink and watched the server set a stack of menus on the table. She waited to sit until the other women had arranged themselves before taking a seat on the edge of the booth, as far from Mel as possible.

"I'll let you ladies get settled," said the server, "and be right back to take your order. My name is Brandon, by the way."

Lindsey tapped a fuchsia nail to her wineglass. "Could we get another round? And a few orders of those buffalo cauliflower thingies?" Regina smiled to herself; Mel loathed cauliflower.

"Certainly!" Brandon flashed a smile. "Let's see, we've got two pinot grigios, two vodka sodas, and for you, in the green dress—?"

"The green dress will have a Coke," said Mel.

"Diet, or . . ."

"Or not," said Mel, "Just regular Coke with shitloads of corn syrup."

"You got it," said Brandon, looking perplexed.

When he was gone, Lindsey snort-laughed and jerked her thumb toward Mel, seated beside her. "How *funny* is this one?"

"Right?" said Kylie. "You're such a firecracker, Mel!"

Mel shrugged. "Sometimes men need a little extra help. Often, actually."

"Oh, do they?" said Regina, feeling suddenly loosened by the vodka. "What kind of help?" It was all she could do not to add, *Like fucking-in-the-van help?*

She did not typically drink vodka so quickly. Or at all.

"Oh, ah," Mel fumbled. Regina hoped to God she was blushing. "You know. Just basic . . . guidance."

"I was just telling Regina how smoking hot you look, Mel," said Jess. Regina could practically feel Mel cringe at the compliment.

"Smoking," Regina repeated.

"Speaking of smoke," said Kylie. "How terrible are things in Malibu right now, with the Woolsey Fire?"

Jess nodded vigorously. "It's atrocious. I watched a slideshow on the *LA Times* website earlier. Almost a hundred thousand acres burned up."

"I saw that, too," said Kylie. "Heartbreaking. I was thinking the PTA could start a donation campaign at school, for victims of the fire. We could just suggest that all families tack on a little extra to their usual spring contribution, and I'll stick it into a GoFundMe."

Was it Regina's imagination, or did Kylie shoot her a pointed look?

Fuck the PTA, she imagined blurting.

"Let's do it!" Lindsey squealed. "It's the *right thing*."

"I don't know," said Mel, "I'm not all that sorry about Whatser-face Kardashian's house burning down."

"What?" Lindsey clapped her hand to her mouth. "You can't *say* that, Mel. Just because she's rich doesn't mean—"

"She deserves to burn to death?" offered Regina. "Is that what you meant, Mel?" God, the drink had been strong. She should probably eat something.

"No!" said Mel. "Sorry, I didn't mean—"

"Don't apologize," said Kylie. "I love your honesty, Mel. And you're right. The Kardashians are not the people we need to worry about. Do you know how many domestic workers there are in Malibu? *Thousands*."

"Right?" Jess shook her head sadly. "And lots of them are undocumented. So, when their bosses' big houses burn down, they're left with nothing. Nowhere to live, no insurance, no way to make money, just"—she snapped her fingers—"*zilch*."

"Ugh," said Mel. "And that's on top of the Big Cheeto already trying to deport them and break up their families." Regina watched her lift the glass of Coke Brandon had just delivered into the air, as if waving a flag. "These people are already living in fear, hour to hour. When they've done nothing more than try to make better lives for themselves and their kids. It's sick and malicious to start a national campaign against them. My friend Leticia was just telling me—"

"You mean your *housekeeper*?" Regina cut in, unable to restrain herself. Mel, the activist! Mel, the kindhearted friend to undocumented workers! Regina had known Lettie for years before she'd introduced her to Mel. *Regina* had been the one to pick Lettie up in the middle of the night to rescue her from some violent asshole. *Regina* had co-signed for the financing on Lettie's car. *Regina* had paid for physical therapy after Andres's accident.

Mel, the selfish, stealing slut.

"Leticia is my *friend* first," said Mel, narrowing her eyes at Regina.

Regina fought the urge to extend her middle finger. Mel had stolen Lettie. Not that Regina had ever thought of Lettie as hers. But for years she'd had fond feelings and a comfortable (generous!) relationship with the timid Mexican woman, until Mel had horned in and made Regina feel guilty for the way she treated Lettie. As if Mel were the good employer, the one who truly cared, and Regina was merely someone who wrote Lettie checks, just another out-of-touch privileged white woman who didn't really want to *know* her housekeeper.

First Mel had claimed Lettie. And then she'd helped herself to Zack. Regina's head swam from the vodka, and for a moment, she let herself miss him. The feeling rippled through her, a dislocating current of sadness. She'd never *had* Zack either, but Mel had taken away Regina's vague hope of having him at some fuzzy point in the future—the only thing that had gotten her through the punishingly anxious days of the last year.

And now, thanks to Mel and her stubbled vagina (oh God), Regina's hope was gone.

Feeling woozy, Regina pressed both palms into the soft leather of the banquette to steady herself.

"Ready to order, ladies?" Brandon and his blinding smile materialized again.

The women rattled off requests for salads and grilled fish (even

Mel, usually quick to bypass a healthful meal, ordered salmon, Regina noticed); Regina said she'd already eaten.

"So, ladies!" Kylie Dupree jumped in as if calling a PTA meeting to order. "I say we make this fundraising campaign really targeted. Maybe we don't involve the PTA. Maybe we just tap all of our personal networks really hard, specifically raise money for domestic workers in Malibu displaced by the Woolsey fires. Not to sound, uh, elitist, but it's just a fact that we all know people who *know* people with, well, resources. God knows my husband could stand to give back more. He writes one check a year to the Democratic party and another to the ACLU and thinks he's some kind of philanthropist."

"I don't think my husband contributes anything to anyone," said Mel. At the mention of Adam, Regina detected a new edge in Mel's voice, as if she were more awake, firing up. "Except maybe his goddamn jiu-jitsu academy and Sloane's soccer team. Then again, we're new to this whole having-money thing."

Regina cringed. *Mel, the shameless over-sharer.*

"Ha!" said Kylie. "You're right, Linds, she *is* hilarious."

Regina was sick of everyone's endless amusement with Mel.

"Sloane is so gifted!" said Jess. "Tyler is a big fan of hers. He says she's the coolest kid in fifth grade."

"How sweet," said Mel, though Regina could imagine her preferred comeback—something like, *Aw, and Sloane says Tyler is the biggest douchebag in fifth!*

Mel *was* pretty funny.

"I do love this fundraising idea," said Jess, whose husband, Regina knew, was an executive producer of the Avengers franchise. "We could blow up a GoFundMe!"

To avoid chiming in—how could you get excited about a plan to give money when you had none?—Regina busied herself downing the fresh vodka soda she hadn't wanted and discreetly glanced into her purse to check her phone.

Then, before she could stop herself, she texted Zack: Hey.

A single word, nothing more. Still, her heart rate zoomed. She turned her phone off.

"I don't know," said Lindsey, spearing a hunk of cauliflower coated in a purplish-brown glaze. "Not that I don't have total sympathy for the immigrant situation, but I can sort of see both sides."

"Both sides of what?" said Mel.

"Well." Lindsey tipped her (third? Regina guessed, or fourth?) pinot grigio to her lips. "I'm all for doing a fundraiser for the Woolsey Fire victims. And I love Lettie, too, Melissa. She's been like family to me for years."

"Has she?" Regina asked.

Lindsey ignored her. "Also, let me state that I am one hundred percent against the Wall."

"What?" Mel looked as if she'd been stung. "I would hope so, Lindsey. I mean . . . Jesus."

"But, it doesn't mean that there isn't some risk in welcoming . . ." Lindsey paused. "Foreign workers."

"Oh, Lindsey, come on," said Kylie. "Don't get started on that Halloween incident again. It's over."

"Let me remind you that my husband was *assaulted*, Kylie." Lindsey set her empty wineglass down hard on the table. "It doesn't just become 'over.'"

Regina closed her purse and sat up straighter, glad for a change of topic. "Assaulted? What do you mean?"

"Yes!" said Lindsey. "This little Mexican boy showed up on our doorstep on Halloween. I was out trick-or-treating with the kids, but Trey was home. The boy was really young, like four or five, and Trey could tell he was handicapped. Or, challenged, or whatever. He was rooting around the front of our house all by himself. It seemed like he was trying to steal the floor vase on our front steps, you know, the giant glass one I got in Venice last summer."

Kylie nodded. "It's gorgeous."

"That vase weighs like a hundred pounds," said Mel. "Why would a kid try to lift that?"

"Like I said, he seemed to have *problems*," said Lindsey. "Anyway. Trey was very gentle with him. He just called out, like, *Did anyone lose their kid?* and when he did, the dad and mom just charged in off the street and the dad—or whoever—*attacked* Trey. Like just started shoving him and then punching him."

"That's rather extreme," said Mel. "Almost hard to believe."

"Maybe if you had seen Trey's black eye and fat lip you'd believe it," said Lindsey. "Thankfully, the guy's wife broke it up, before Trey got *killed*."

"Oh my God!" said Jess. "Did he call the police?" Regina watched Mel; one of her eyebrows had arched and her eyes were squinting, the way she did when she was getting upset.

"And get this," Lindsey added, "they were wearing Stars Wars masks. Can you believe it? My husband was brutalized by Darth-fucking-Vader and his Chewbacca wife."

"Very disturbing," said Jess.

"Sorry to interrupt the story," said Mel. "But what on earth does this have to do with undocumented workers?"

"They were Mexican illegals," said Lindsey. "Trey just knew it. And this is a man who does not have *one* racist bone in his body."

Now Regina spoke up. "How does one just *know*?"

"Thank you, Regina," said Mel. She met Regina's eyes. Regina felt herself almost smile, then looked away. *No.* She would not let Mel be her ally tonight. Not tonight, or ever again.

Lindsey sighed. "Look, I'm sorry I brought it up. The Mexican immigrant thing, it's just become a . . . a trigger for me. Trey was so beat up when I got home. I still have PTSD from the way his face looked. But no, Jess, we didn't call the cops. We didn't want to get those people in trouble, even though the guy obviously had rage issues and deserved it. We didn't want a little boy to get sent back to Mexico, to who knows *what* kind of life."

Regina glanced at Mel, who had angled herself toward Lindsey and looked pissed.

"I'm sorry Trey got hurt," Mel said. "But, Lindsey, connecting a random squabble to someone's race and country of origin is just utter, pardon my French, fucking bullshit."

Regina watched Lindsey's pointy face squinch at Mel in disbelief.

"I'm sorry that my husband's so-called squabble, aka, *trauma*, offends you, Mel," said Lindsey. "Why don't you pick a new topic? But first, I want Kylie to know that Trey and I will be the first to contribute to a fundraiser for fire victims. Regardless of their 'race' or 'country of origin.'" She hooked her painted nails into air quotes.

"Not if Adam and I beat you to it," said Mel. "Kidding!"

"Amazing!" said Kylie Dupree.

"You love that word," said Regina, draining her vodka soda.

"I'm in, too!" said Jess. "I'll even ask Larry if we can match other contributions."

"I'll *inform* Adam that we're matching," said Mel.

Now Regina wanted to scream.

Lindsey went on, "And I'll do heavy promo for it on my Insta. We just need to come up with a good hashtag. I have over three thous—"

Regina could no longer take it. "Oh-kay! Can we please move on? We've agreed we're doing a fundraiser. Yay. But we're all in our forties here—can we please leave Instagram out of it?"

"Oh, I'm *sorry*, Regina," said Lindsey. "I didn't realize you were above social media."

Mel piped up, defensively. "No, it's just that Regina has this insane self-control. Like she can just leave the Instagram app on her phone and never open it."

"Because social media is boring and stupid," Regina snapped. "They're all just big bragging platforms."

"Well, I guess the rest of us are just weak-willed *braggers*, then," said Lindsey.

"Braggarts," corrected Mel.

"Whatever," Lindsey went on, her voice tight and icy. "All *two-point-five* billion of us."

"Perhaps we should cease and desist with this topic," said Kylie.

"Wait!" said Jess, stirring the ice at the bottom of her glass with a cocktail straw. "I have one more question. Who's the hot trainer guy all over your Insta, Lindsey? Like in all your workout posts and stories. I tried to find him but his account's private."

"Oh, that's Regina's boyfriend," said Lindsey gaily. "Zack. She can tell you all about him."

Regina stood up and took an unsteady step away from the booth. "You know, I'm suddenly not feeling great." This was true; the vodka was sloshing acidly in her stomach and her knees felt unstable. "I'm going to head home."

"Sheesh, Reg, I was just joking," said Lindsey. "Can we call a truce? Sit back down."

Cautiously, Regina took another few steps, managing not to fall. Perhaps she could make it out of the restaurant, after all.

"Regina, wait!" she heard Mel call. "I'll go with you."

But Regina was already hurrying toward the restaurant's doors.

WHEN REGINA GOT home from Canyon Rustica (after a minor struggle with unlocking her front door—she was even tipsier than she thought), Gordon was sound asleep on the couch in his office, still wearing his glasses and snoring heavily, a half-full tumbler of bourbon beside the lamp on the end table. The sight of him came as a relief; Minnow Night had left her feeling achingly empty—devoid of friends, of money, of the pleasure of fantasizing about Zack—while also brimming with a hot, restless anger toward the women at Minnow Night and the luxurious cocoons of their lives. In this condition, she wasn't sure she'd have been able to say good night to Gordon without falling apart.

She covered him with the blanket draped on the back of the sofa and then, on an impulse, took a long drink of his bourbon. She hadn't been this drunk in years and was not quite ready to sober up. The bourbon almost made her gag going down, searing her throat. Once she'd absorbed the shock, she switched off the lamp and made her way out of the office in the dark. Then she went upstairs, checked on the girls, and went to her bedroom, closing the door behind her. She pulled off her top and dropped it on the floor, then sat on the edge of her bed to wriggle out of the faux leather leggings. As she pulled them off, her phone fell from the back pocket and bounced off the hardwood floor.

Down to her bra and underwear, she picked up her phone and lay in the center of the mattress, facing the wrong way, toward the mound of pillows. She tucked one arm under her head and propped her feet up on the headboard, telling herself she'd just rest for a minute, then get up and wash her face and change into her pajamas. But as she lay on her bed, a gnawing, desperate urge to make contact with Zack took hold of her, zapping her will to move. She closed her eyes and imagined him standing before her: shirtless, muscles standing to attention, hair tousled over his tanned forehead, his blue-green eyes dancing with amusement and understanding.

"Hey, Echo," she called out to the smart speaker on her nightstand. "Play Mumford and Sons."

Mumford & Sons was Zack's favorite band.

Acoustic guitar chords started.

She eased one hand beneath the lace border of her thong.

It was stupid—she knew—but she'd really believed Zack had *gotten* her. That they'd gotten each other. And that feeling of being understood by him was far sexier than his muscles or pretty face. Was the glacier that had formed between them really necessary? Yes, he had hooked up with Mel, but should that single incident erase everything Regina had built with him over the last two years? The hundreds of hours of sweating together at Color Theory, the confessional conversations, the bantering text exchanges, their business ventures?

She moved her hand down, pleased with the smooth feel of her Brazilian. Waxing was her single cosmetic indulgence, and she'd felt guilty every time she'd shelled out sixty bucks to an esthetician at Bare Bar in the last year, aware of how unjustifiable an expense it was given the state of her finances.

Still, she'd kept going, month after month.

Now, as she traced the pad of her index finger over the silky, stubble-free (take *that*, Mel Goldberg) skin between her legs, she was glad she'd kept spending the sixty dollars she didn't really have.

There was dignity in keeping yourself up. An embedded optimism. All those bikini waxes had, in a way, kept her hoping that one day, somehow, she and Zack might . . .

She pushed two fingers inside herself and stifled a groan.

Regina had been a good friend to Zack. Hell, she'd been *better* than good—she'd handed over thousands of dollars to him in cash, just for his willingness to click a few buttons on the Color Theory laptop.

She did not deserve a glacier.

Maybe Zack considered the incident with Mel a huge mistake. Perhaps she'd had a fight with Adam and thrown herself at Zack, along with a dose of her neurotic charm, and maybe Zack had just gone along with it. He was a red-blooded male, after all.

Regina flexed and unflexed her wrist, accelerating the rhythm of her fingers.

Maybe he was ashamed to have done it. Wildly embarrassed. Perhaps his shame was the reason he hadn't bothered acknowledging Regina's Hey text—or the second one she'd sent on the way home in her Lyft—So, you don't even bother saying hi back to me now? I guess Mel was all you ever needed????

Abruptly, she pulled her hand from between her legs, her mood suddenly shifting. Whatever Zack's reason for ignoring her, she needed to get to the bottom of it. With her other hand, she tapped *67, to make her number private, and then called Zack. Distantly, she was aware of her heart pounding, but the whiskey dulled her nerves.

He picked up on the third ring, sounding sleepy. "'Lo?"

"It's me. Regina."

Long sigh. "'Sup?"

"Nothing. I'm just calling to . . . say hi. We haven't said hi to each other lately."

"Yeah. It's been a minute. Did I mess up the schedule?"

"What? No. I'm not calling about business." *The schedule* was how they referred to the transfers. "I was just calling as a friend. Because we're friends, right?"

His voice softened. "Of course we're friends."

"And friends keep in touch, don't they?"

"Yes. They do."

"So, can we keep in touch? That's what I'm calling about. To ask if we can keep in touch."

"Are you moving or something?"

"Moving? No! I'm not going anywhere. I just . . . miss you. You didn't answer my text tonight."

Silence. Then: "I'm right here, Regina. And I didn't answer your texts because I was *sleeping.* I have to get up to teach the five thirty in the morning." Did he sound irritated? Regina wasn't sure.

"Are you and Mel having a thing?" she blurted.

A pause. "Are you drunk? Because you sound sort of, like, slurry."

"No! You know I hate being drunk. Just answer the question. Are you and Mel having a thing, beyond whatever the fuck that was I saw in the van? Which, by the way, totally traumatized me. And is that why—"

"Regina?" he cut in, almost gently, as if interrupting a child. "I'm going to hang up now."

"Don't hang up. Not yet. I'm playing Mumford and Sons."

He chuckled. "I thought I heard that. Love those guys. But I'm still gonna get off the phone now. I need to sleep. I'm still your friend, but I'm hanging up."

"No! We're not done yet." She knew she was being too loud, but didn't care.

"We are."

"Zack! No. Just two minutes! I need to talk to you." She couldn't remember exactly what she wanted to say; only that she felt a primal, desperate desire to keep him on the phone with her.

"Good night, Regina. Sleep off whatever's gotten into you, 'kay?"

"ZACK, DO NOT HANG UP!"

Silence.

"ZACK!" she yelled again.

But he was gone.

She dropped her phone, laid her arm over her face, and sobbed into the fold of her elbow.

It was after her tears finally subsided and she'd pushed herself up on one palm and cleared the damp strands of hair from her face that she noticed the door. It was open six inches, letting in a slice of darkness from the hallway. She blinked, feeling the mascara heavy on her lids, trying to remember whether she'd left it open.

No. She hadn't. Yes, she'd been drunk—was drunk still—but she distinctly remembered the clicking sound it made when she'd closed it.

She pulled herself into a seated position and wrapped the bedsheet around her body.

"Gordon?" she called out softly. "Honey, are you awake?"

There was no answer.

SATURDAY, NOVEMBER 17, 2018

24

ZACK

THE BEACH WAS SHROUDED IN MARINE LAYER AT SEVEN A.M. WHEN ZACK arrived at the popular outdoor workout spot adjacent to the carousel nestled against the Santa Monica Pier. Muscle Beach was an iconic SoCal spot, a swath of sand half the size of a football field—a cross, Zack thought, between an outdoor gym and a playground on steroids. When Zack had first moved to Santa Monica, he'd been smitten with the place, which attracted everyone from old-school weightlifter dudes with sun-grizzled faces and bulging biceps to professional gymnasts to homeless people having push-up contests. It was one of the few parts of Santa Monica where he didn't feel out of place.

Most days, Muscle Beach was crowded from morning until sunset, but now, on a gray and chilly November morning, it was empty but for a cluster of grandma types (still looking pretty dang good, he couldn't help but notice) doing vague stretching movements, and a few classic gym-rat guys grunting through sets of push-ups. Zack set down his bag, which contained only one large beach towel and a water bottle, and watched two cyclists shoot from the long pedestrian tunnel that ran under the pier, pedaling furiously and whooping, teeming with camaraderie. Zack felt a wave of envy; he could use some real bros.

He took a long breath of moist salt air and scanned the various exercise structures, considering which would intimidate Mel the least. The famous rings course—a series of staggered rings designed to swing across Tarzan-style—was out the question. So was the slack line, which required a strong core and steady balance, and the parallel bars, which were difficult for everyone except the gymnasts.

The trapeze, though, was a possibility, as were the climbing ropes, which would give Zack the opportunity to assist her. The thought of being able to touch her gave him butterflies. He glanced at the parking lot at the far corner of the sand, but no sign of Mel's green Mini Cooper. His phone read 7:13. He turned his gaze to the ocean, fifty yards off, where choppy gray waves slapped the shore, and told himself to be patient. Mel was rarely punctual. Out in the water, Zack could make out the shapes of a few surfers waiting for a swell. He'd been meaning to learn to surf since moving here, but hadn't found the time.

Perhaps, he thought, he and Mel could learn to surf together.

Since the *thing* with Mel in the van nearly a month ago, Zack had been feeling happier than he had in a long time. Which was unusual. Such *things* usually left Zack feeling desolate, reaching new lows each time he slipped. They required days of repentance: stones lodged in his sneakers, fasting, even the occasional shallow cuts administered to the flesh just below his hip bones with an X-Acto knife—just enough to draw little lines of blood that itched after they scabbed.

But the thing with Mel had left him with none of those self-punishing urges. And even more surprisingly, with very little shame. Instead, he'd felt galvanized from being with her, more alive, as if shot through with positive electricity. What had happened between them—even if it had been in the back of a van—seemed somehow sweet and good, almost wholesome. Their bodies had been channeling a deeper current of feeling. Something far beneath the flesh.

But also, there was her *flesh*: Mel's softness, her gentle heat, the luscious curves of her body that felt both decadent and comforting under his hands. Utterly new and yet somehow familiar, as if he'd arrived at some long-lost home.

To live in love is to sail forever. This was one of his newly discovered lines from *The Little Way for Every Day*, which he'd ordered from Amazon after he'd somehow lost his copy of the book.

How badly he wanted to be inside Mel. Not to erase himself, as was usually the case—that crude, searing need to consume, then empty himself (some girl he'd slept with a few times, years ago, her name long-forgotten, had accused Zack of having *sexual bulimia*)— but to join Mel in a place far beneath the superficial surface of their lives. Since that evening in the van, he'd dreamt twice of the two of them swimming in vast, blue water, holding hands, angling down toward an unseen ocean floor.

It was silly, he knew, that a torrid make-out session could leave him feeling so smitten. So *alive*. But it had. Since that Friday night with Mel, he'd found it hard to think about much else. Replaying every detail over and over in his mind, imagining how it might happen again.

He was still staring at the sea, imagining Mel and himself in sleek wetsuits, paddling their boards side by side out into the waves, laughing, when he heard her voice call out behind him.

"Sorry I'm late."

Zack felt his face go hot, as if she might have glimpsed the fantasy in his head. He turned to see her hurrying down the sand, wearing her usual all-black workout ensemble, her dark hair clinging damply to her face, as if she'd just showered.

For a moment, his voice stuck in his throat. He hadn't seen her alone since the *thing*—clearly, she'd been avoiding him—yet here she was, alone with him on a near-empty beach, making him feel like a nervous teenager.

"Hey," he managed, feeling glued to his spot in the sand, though everything inside him was lifting with joy. Mel closed the gap between them, her eyes concealed behind big dark sunglasses, despite the soft, silvered morning light.

She stopped a foot before she reached him and pushed her

sunglasses to the top of her head. He noticed she'd put on eye makeup. Her skin looked clean and lush; he had the overwhelming urge to touch her round cheek.

"Hey," she said, all business. "I mean, good morning. So, I was absolutely going to be on time, but then I decided to take a Lyft, and the driver kept driving in circ—"

"You took a *Lyft*? When there's no traffic and the parking lot is practically empty?"

"Yeah," said Mel. "So, what? It's a fucking miracle that I'm here at all. Let me guess." She began to speak rapid-fire and Zack realized she was nervous, too. "You *never* take Lyfts, only Ubers, because you think that *poor* Uber CEO was unjustly Me-Too'd, so you're anti-Lyft to demonstrate your support of white male billionaires to—"

Before he could stop himself, his finger flew to Mel's lips. "Shhhhh."

Mel took a small step back. "Excuse me? Am I hallucinating from sleep deprivation, or did you actually just *shush* me?"

Zack put on his best Florida drawl. "You're not hallucinating, darlin'."

"I can't believe I dragged myself out of bed to be shushed." She crossed her arms over her chest, but he saw the smile playing at the corners of her lips.

"Truly a Herculean feat," he said, letting his own smile fly. "You are one hardcore woman, Melissa Goldberg, getting out of bed before *seven* A.M."

"Oh, shut up." She lunged forward and punched him softly in the center of his chest.

Reflexively, he caught her fist and held it against him. She did not pull away. For a few long beats, they stood facing each other, her hand clasped inside his, pressed against his chest, listening to the waves. Zack fought to keep his breathing steady under her touch, hoping she could not feel the pace of his heartbeat. Overhead, gulls cawed and screeched.

Finally, Mel spoke. "So, should we start—working out or whatever?"

He detected the faintest tremor in her voice.

"No," he said, pulling her whole body to his chest and lowering his lips to hers.

She collapsed into him with a mewling sound from the back of her throat that made him woozy with desire as their tongues worked together. She tasted of licorice and mint. He was instantly hard under his gym shorts; his legs went jellied and useless.

"Can we—" Mel murmured. "Is there somewhere we can, oh Jesus, *go*?"

Zack paused, thinking as he kissed her lips, caught her earlobe ever-so-lightly between his teeth.

She groaned softly. "Like, maybe a hotel or something?"

"That'll take too long," he whispered. "I know a place. We don't even have to leave the beach."

"I . . . I can't do anything in *public*."

"Of course not, baby," he said, the *baby* flying spontaneously from his lips, surprising both of them.

"No *baby*, please," said Mel, but weakly.

"Sorry, um . . . " He cupped her chin with his hand and kissed her again. "I meant woman warrior."

"That's better." She giggled and moved her hand to his crotch; he nearly gasped at the feel of her hand closing around him. "Take me somewhere now, 'kay?"

He released her just long enough to grab his gym bag from where he'd dropped it in the sand. Earlier that morning, he'd felt himself blush when he'd packed his softest, thickest beach towel underneath his usual stash of workout props and spare clothes, reluctant to admit to himself why he was packing it.

The reason was now clear.

He grabbed Mel's hand and pulled her toward the dim tunnel beneath the pier.

LATER, AFTER MEL left the beach (flustered, having cleaned up in a public restroom on the pier, mumbling something about *guaranteed MRSA*), Zack set his phone alarm, turned on *Do Not Disturb*, and dozed by the water. The day had turned sunny and warm. He had nothing to do until two thirty, when he needed to be at CT to teach three in a row, followed by some accounting work. Today was a transfer day, which suffused him with the usual dread (especially following Regina's bizarre phone call the other night, during which she'd sounded both pathetic and deranged), followed by a tinge of relief: Lettie had a spate of past-past-*past*-due payments lurking this week, mostly from the hospital, plus another $1,200 to her greedy, exploitative chihuahua of an attorney. Lately, Zack had begun imagining Ochoa as a hungry dog with razor-sharp teeth, jumping on Lettie's legs, sinking her canines into his sister's flesh.

But he didn't want to think about Ochoa, or Lettie, or the gym, or his accounting work just yet. He wanted to savor the feeling the morning had brought him, to think of Mel while lying on the towel with the sun on his face—the towel that still smelled of *them*—and listen to the sounds of the ocean. It was a state of happiness to which he'd grown so unaccustomed, it felt strange and foreign, as if he were dreaming.

Since he'd met Mel, he couldn't remember when he'd last felt so much hope.

Although, in truth, he considered Happy Zack to be the *real him*. Mel Goldberg had awakened the pure, joyous child inside him. The one who'd been squelched, somehow, though he was never sure who to blame. There were many candidates. His parents, for starters, had been far from perfect. His dad endlessly critical, equating theater, which had called to Zack since a second-grade performance of *Winnie-the-Pooh*, with *homos* and *faggotry*, a word John-John had invented and of which he seemed particularly proud. Zack's father relished the double *Johns* of his name, a childhood nickname that had stuck, and was quick to correct anyone who addressed him in the singular, as if he were inherently superior to the non-hyphenated Johns.

Zack was sure it was not theater but Zack's Mexican-ness that his father hated. When John-John spoke of Gloria, the mother Zack and Lettie shared, his voice lost its southern ease and filled with sharp edges, as if he'd tasted poison. Zack was the result of the years in John-John's life when he'd lived at the southeast border of Texas and regularly crossed into Matamoros, Mexico, to work. Zack's mother, Gloria, had barely been out of her teens then, and according to Gloria, with whom Zack Skyped a few times a year (during which the surprisingly charming woman repeated *Muy guapo!* again and again), John-John had fallen head-over-heels in love with her.

He couldn't stay away, Gloria told Zack, her dark brown eyes huge on his monitor, her beauty still discernible beneath her lined face and tired eyes. *Year after year, he come back.*

John-John, of course, when he deigned to speak of her at all, did so with clenched teeth and rolling eyes, claiming that Gloria had been obsessed with *him*, tracking him down somehow, showing up at his work, throwing herself at him *like a bitch in heat.* This was an actual phrase Zack had heard John-John use once, when secretly listening to a fight his father and stepmother were having over John-John's former Mexican mistress. Kaye was the jealous type, Zack learned at a young age—tiresomely, relentlessly jealous—and the very fact that Zack shared a bloodline with Gloria made Kaye view him as a threat.

Okay, so his dad was a hard-ass and a loudmouth. Maybe something of a redneck. So were a lot of dads in Florida. John-John did love Zack, though, in his own way. After all, he'd chosen to bring Zack across the border and officially claim him as a son, made him an American.

There had been times—not many, but still—when Zack felt connected to his father. Shooting baskets together in the driveway, his father whistling appreciatively or saying *Damn, boy*, when Zack made swish after swish. Golf was even better, because it gave them time to talk sports and politics, topics on which they tended to agree. During the Obama years, Zack and his dad had especially savored a good joint rant against that president, whom John-John loathed, telling Zack it was up to his generation to *save this sinking ship of a country.*

Rarely did he touch Zack. A chuck under the chin, a quick ruffle of hair, and that was it. As for Kaye, well, she seemed determined to avoid touching Zack at all costs. As if his Mexican-ness were contagious. Her disdain for Zack was counterbalanced by her adoration of Vanessa, the daughter she'd had with John-John—Zack's *other* half-sister. The white one. Lily-white. From her butter-colored hair to her love of tennis, her debutante ball, her admission to Vanderbilt where she moved into a sorority house, her blue eyes the color of the Los Angeles sky, Vanessa was everything John-John and Kaye wanted in a child.

They touched Vanessa constantly. Zack remembered being little enough to watch John-John throw Vanessa up into the air, listening to her squeal of delight, and longing to be thrown in the air, too. He remembered watching Kaye sidle up behind Vanessa and begin braiding her hair, his stepmother's gleaming nails flying over the flaxen locks—imagining how it would feel to have his head touched that way, and for so long.

When Zack thought of his family, the image that came to mind was the three of them—John-John, Kaye, and Vanessa—curled around each other like puppies, full of love and contentment. The three of them were a smug little unit, complete and self-contained. There was no room for him. But elsewhere, he learned from a young age, there was plenty of room. Meaning, plenty of women not only willing to touch him but *eager* to do so. Hairdressers, drama teachers, Vanessa's friends, even their moms. They cooed over his looping brown curls, his blue-green eyes (his skin was olive-toned, not as dark as Lettie's, but dark enough so that women noticed his light eyes, straightaway), his height (he shot up at twelve, his shoulders squaring and widening at fourteen when he began lifting weights), the shape of his face (*I want your cheekbones*, he remembered some friend of Vanessa's sighing), etcetera.

It happened first when he was thirteen. An older sister of a friend on his basketball team, high from canned wine and a synthetic marijuana called Spice, working herself on top of him in a reptilian fashion. (He liked hoops okay, except that John-John used it as a bargaining chip: Zack could only take theater if he played basketball, too.) It was as if everything he'd been denied his entire childhood suddenly became accessible. The world was rife with available touch. He could not get enough. He was a starving man and women existed to feed him. In Zack's bedroom (John-John and Kaye right downstairs, oblivious), backstage after play rehearsals, in the single bathroom that locked at the gym after basketball practice. Of course, at parties. Florida, more than other places, it seemed, was teeming with parties, at parentless houses in gated subdivisions, in empty lots on the fringes of town, even in the Ocala National Forest. Cheap liquor with ominous names—Mad Dog, Crazy Horse—and the lowest-grade drugs—Spice, nutmeg rolled with tobacco, bath salts, any pills one could pilfer from a family medicine cabinet. The children of Florida scrambled their brain chemistry and took their clothes off.

Zack fucked and fucked and fucked. It was always an option, always necessary, and never enough.

And then, the TA in his econ class at Central Florida Community College. (Perhaps *this* he could blame on his father, who forced him to take finance classes to justify paying Zack's tuition).

Misty Whatever. He'd willfully forgotten her last name, which he'd heard over and over and over in court.

Ms. Whatever alleges. Ms. Whatever attests that on the night Mr. Doheny visited her apartment . . .

Misty Whatever had hair the color of crow feathers, green eyes that slid all over him during seminar. She'd even dropped a flip-flop once and rubbed a bare foot on Zack's calf. By then, he was twenty and knew all the signs of *yes*.

Misty radiated the *yeses*.

And then had the audacity to call it rape.

The court had declared her utterly bogus allegation *aggravated criminal sexual assault. Class-A misdemeanor*. Punishable by a $2,000 fine, which John-John had paid under the condition that Zack would have to pay for the rest of community college. Plus, one hundred hours of community service. Zack in an orange jumpsuit, spearing garbage off the side of US 27 alongside junkies and larcenists and dudes who'd broken their girlfriends' bones. It had been the most demoralizing year of his life.

All because he'd had the audacity to fuck Misty Whatever after they'd swilled half a fifth of vodka and smoked up. They'd *both* been wasted out of their minds. Yes, perhaps Zack had been more lucid when it came down to the moment one body (his) clamped down onto the other (hers), and yes, Misty Whatever may have uttered some mewls of protest, but it was hardly *rape*. She'd called it that, Zack believed, because he'd had the audacity to not fall in love with her. To ignore her calls and her texts and her knocks on his door.

And then she'd gone and ruined his life. He'd been unable to get back on track. Tuition at Central Florida Community College was dirt cheap, but he'd dropped out anyway. Frittered away a half-dozen years waiting tables, doing seasonal work at H&R Block (turned out even a few semesters of accounting qualified you to help people fill out their 1040s), changing oil at Jiffy Lube, and working out at 24 Hour Fitness. He'd even done a humiliating stint at his father's real estate company, showing properties at open houses on Tuesdays and Sundays. He had auditioned for community theater and catalogue modeling work, occasionally getting small parts, or a menswear shoot for JCPenney. At night he watched *Inside the Actors Studio*, *Entourage*, and *Unscripted*, and dreamt about moving to LA.

By the time he'd actually gotten the guts to move to California, he was nearly thirty. Thanks to Misty Whatever, his life had been derailed. Most of his twenties, that critical, formative decade, put on hold.

Misty destroyed him the first time.

Casey in the laundry room, a second.

Sometimes, it seemed women delighted in ruining his life.

But not Melissa Goldberg. Mel was exactly the opposite of all those women. With her, he could be the person he was meant to be: happy, virtuous, unafraid.

ZACK'S PHONE ALARM pulsed and he sat up on the beach towel, blinking against the full-blown afternoon sun. The waves had calmed and turned from gray to blue-green, but the beach was still mostly empty. He checked his phone for messages: four missed calls from an unfamiliar 310 number, one new voicemail, one text message.

The text was from Mel: Gr8 workout, thx! (flexed-muscle emoji)

The silly sentence, barely English, filled him with pleasure. Zack grinned at his phone and shot back Glad you enjoyed! LMK if you'd like to train again soon.

Then he listened to his voicemail.

The recorded voice was male and slightly nasal. *"Hey, Zack, this is Gordon Wolfe. My wife, Regina, is a devotee of your exercise classes. She told me you offer personal training, and I'm looking to get back in shape. Could we schedule a session at your earliest convenience? I'm also happy to swing by your gym on Main Street for a consultation. I'm really pumped to get started so please get back to me. Ciao for now."*

Zack's chest clenched—what? He was aware of Gordon Wolfe's existence, and little else. Regina spoke of her husband so rarely Zack sometimes forgot she was married. The few times she had mentioned him, it was in the context of her own love for exercise, and Gordon's aversion to it. She'd even used phrases like "anti-exercise" and "barely aware of his own body."

Okay, maybe the guy was having a change of heart. Maybe Regina had finally convinced him to get up from his desk (he was some sort of writer, *extremely dedicated*, Zack remembered Regina saying, with an eye roll) and move around. God knew it had to be difficult to be married to Regina, Workout Queen, without getting on board with exercise.

Still, Zack was suspicious. Why would Gordon call *him*? Surely Zack was the last trainer Regina would recommend to her husband. As far as Zack could tell, since the van incident, Regina hated his guts—and even more so now, after he'd practically hung up on her the other night when she'd drunk-dialed him. Plus, didn't she have every reason to make sure he and Gordon never met? Zack, after all, was directly involved in helping Regina solve the financial problems she'd strategically hidden from Gordon.

She'd said to Zack, over and over: *This is my mess. Gordon would never forgive me. I have to fix it first, and tell him later.*

Yes, Gordon's call was definitely fishy, Zack thought, as he stood and shook the sand from his (and *Mel's*) towel, and folded it into his gym bag. Regina must be up to something, although he couldn't work out what. There was a time when he'd viewed her with a mixture of awe and (embarrassing as it was to admit) fear. Her steely intensity, her supreme confidence, her willingness to push herself to the edge of her physical limits. How badly she wanted to *win*. All of this, combined with her teenager-like crush on him—he was her kryptonite, he'd thought once, as she'd gone from a wild-eyed beast on the gym floor to a sighing little girl when they hugged good-bye after class— had once made Regina attractive to him. When he'd started training at Color Theory, there had been a few weeks when Zack had enjoyed being around her, and let her linger a little too long against his chest when they embraced, her muscles still trembling from exertion.

But those days were over. Being with Mel had enabled him to see Regina for what she truly was: a master manipulator. All his old warm feelings for her were gone.

All that was left was a mild repulsion, and the fear.

After all, she'd convinced him to transfer (no—Zack forced himself to think the true word: *embezzle*) tens of thousands of dollars from his employer, so that she could avoid being honest with her family about the mistakes she'd made.

Who knew what else she was capable of?

As Zack jogged barefoot up the beach to his truck, hot sand flying out from under his feet, he thought of how St. Thérèse would advise him.

Do not listen to the demon, laugh at him, and go without fear to receive the Jesus of peace and love . . .

He reached his truck and tossed his gym bag in the bed. Then he climbed into the cab and sent a text to Gordon Wolfe's number: Hey Gordon, it's Zack Doheny! Got your VM and want to say I'd be honored to get you started on the path to UNSTOPPABLE! Shoot me a few times you can meet & we'll LOCK IT IN.

Then he turned the ignition and drove to Color Theory, leaving his sunglasses off and his face toward the sun.

In Loving Memory of

Zacarias Doheny

August 27, 1987 – March 25, 2019

In Aeternum

Eternal rest grant unto them, O Lord, and let perpetual
light shine upon them.
May their souls and the souls of all the faithful departed,
through the mercy of God, rest in peace.
Amen.

FRIDAY, DECEMBER 21, 2018

25

LETICIA

"How many you want?" Zacarias said, looking down at Lettie as he reached for the shelf of whipped cream, his shirt lifting to show all those muscles he had—muscles in places Lettie never knew a person could grow muscles.

The two women beside them in the brightly lit dairy aisle at Costco, both tiny Latinas like Lettie, giggled, and she knew they were admiring him. And, maybe, she thought, admiring her as well. She, a nothing-special woman like themselves, with a beautiful white American man doing exactly what she told him to do. She was *in charge*.

"Five," she said to Zacarias, fighting the urge to wink at the women who were still staring. Why should only men be allowed to do the winking?

"Correction," he said. "How many do we *need*?"

"Hmm." She made a face like she was thinking hard, deciding to give the Latinas a show. Let them watch the man who looked like a magazine model take orders from one of their own. "You decide, okay, *mi amor*?"

"How about zero?" Zacarias asked, squinting to read the label on the whipped cream. "It's just a bunch of chemicals I can't even pronounce."

"Well." She stretched out the pause, sensing the Latinas waiting. "I *love* corn starch! It is my favorite food. And Andres, he enjoys the whipped cream so much. Five it is!"

"As you wish, my love," said her half-brother, flashing his special smile, playing along. Then he dropped to one knee and took her hand, right there in the dairy aisle, and Lettie heard the Latinas titter. "For you, Leticia"—delivered with a perfect Costeño accent just like she had taught him—"I will do anything." His lips brushed the top of her hand and she squealed—she couldn't help herself.

She loved shopping with Zacarias. Even if he insisted they go to stores outside Santa Monica, where they would not see anyone they knew. What could she say but yes?—he was paying. And he goofed around the whole time, making her laugh, treating her like a queen. If it was a weekend, Andres came along. The three of them roaming the aisles of Target together, the cart full, it made Lettie feel they were a real family. By choice.

Zacarias seemed like a new man lately. Like a man who had truly found God. A man who has come out of the fire and realized how good life is. And how short. Soon after Halloween night, Lettie was sure there had been a change. His big flashy smile out all the time, even when it was just Zacarias and Lettie, Andres at school, like today. She wondered if Halloween night had woken something in him, like it had in her. If her half-brother had felt the same thrill she'd felt watching his fists thud into Mr. Leyner's swollen face. She had changed that night as well, she thought, remembering the way the crowds on the street had looked at her and Andres—their white faces staring with the look of the dumb. Like children at a zoo, scared but also enchanted by the beasts. Unable to look away. It had been right then that Lettie understood. She would never be a real American in their eyes. No matter how hard she scrubbed and how cheerful she sounded and how grateful she seemed. She could say *I'm sorry* a million times and still, she would not be one of them.

Lettie had awoken the morning after Halloween wiser, the words of her wealthy bosses' inspirational messages in her head—words hung on the walls of their big houses, printed on their T-shirts and the mesh trucker hats the Santa Monica mommies wore; on notepads and keychains and bathroom hand towels. *Let go. Be present. Choose kindness.* Lettie's favorite message—though she wasn't sure she understood its meaning—was one she'd read many times when dusting the framed posters in Sukie Reinhardt's home yoga studio, the walls painted a soothing sky blue: *Happiness cannot exist without acceptance.* Lettie had begun to whisper this to herself each time she received another past-due bill from the hospital collection agency, or from Ms. Ochoa, who had stopped returning Lettie's calls now that her payments had slowed.

Accept, Lettie told herself. *Stop fighting.*

Her next court date was in April. Lettie did not know if Mrs. Ochoa would even be there, standing at her side in front of the judge. Maybe, she hoped, they could have one last Easter together—Lettie, Andres, and Zacarias. Their little family. Maybe she'd teach Zacarias how to make their *abuela*'s fish soup with lima beans. And tamales he'd gobble up, then complain about his belly growing fat. She'd make sure there was watermelon-flavored *agua fresca* to drink, and coconut candies for dessert—as sweet as Andres himself.

Zacarias had been right about Mrs. Ochoa after all. No one could be trusted. No one could solve Lettie's problem. Not even Zacarias could save her from being deported, and he had tried, that big-hearted gringo. Her brother wasn't a *delincuente* after all—she had believed that ever since he'd fought for Andres on the Leyners' front lawn. She'd come to trust him. To forgive him, even, for *the accident*. Finally accepting that it had been an accident, knowing Zacarias would carry the guilt on his back for the rest of his life, remember his sin each time he looked at Andres's damaged leg. A never-ending penance. She had begun to accept, as well, her fate. She may have to say good-bye to her baby. Good-bye to Auntie Corrina. To Melissa and Regina. And to Zacarias. Yes, she would be sad—the very thought made her chest ache, and sometimes, she let herself cry in the bathroom, making sure to muffle the sound with a towel, so her son would not hear—but at least Andres and Zacarias would have each other.

He was a good man, Lettie thought as Zacarias pushed their shopping cart, filled with a mountain of goodies, through the crowded aisles of Costco, making choo-choo train noises (*All aboard!*) as if Andres were with them instead of at school. She was enjoying her hour alone with Zacarias the clown. He was making her forget her problems. He was in an extra-good mood that day, juggling oranges in the produce section, balancing rolls of paper towels on his head, even throwing a back flip down the empty frozen-food aisle, Lettie catching her breath, scared they'd get in trouble, looking for a security guard. Then she remembered. She was with a white man, or, at least, that's what every person in the store believed. She tried to imagine Manuel being silly, calling attention to himself, acting like a crazy person to make her laugh. He would never—too much danger.

Her brother's fun made her forget, almost, about how time was running out. That she still did not have enough dollars. The interest on Andres's medical bills kept going up, up, up, and the calls from the collection agents were coming three, four times a day now. One of them, a man with a voice like oil, had even said, *Where are you from, originally, Ms. Mendoza? Is it Mexico?* in a way that made her think ICE must be on the way to her apartment.

Lettie did not have enough dollars. Zacarias said he would give her more, soon, but when? She also did not have enough time.

She stood alone in the long line, her two carts overflowing with food, waiting for Zack to return from the produce section with the pineapples she'd forgotten. She hoped he would hurry; it was hard pushing both heavy carts forward every few minutes when the line moved. She looked back at the line of mostly white faces, all restless, checking their phones, doing the big sighs white people made when they were impatient and wanted everyone around them to know.

There were only four carts ahead of hers, and still no Zack. He had the money; if he did not return soon, they'd have to start at the end of the line again. Which would make them late to pick up Andres from aftercare at school.

Lettie stepped out of the line and walked a few customers back, standing on her tiptoes to search for Zacarias. When she returned, her carts had been pushed to the side, out of line. She'd lost her spot. Her heart began to thump. Had she done something wrong? Had ICE found her here, in her beloved Costco?

Lettie heard a grunting laugh from behind her, and when she turned, she knew it was him. The man who'd moved her carts. He was tall and blond and wore a tank top so loose it let his reddish armpit hair stick out for all to see. Across the front of the shirt was a blue swordfish and the words *Master Baiter*.

She'd show him he was no master, not of anything.

"Sir," she said. "I think you take my place." She swallowed. "By accident. I put the carts here to save my spot."

The man shrugged, his lips curling into a mean grin. "You snooze, you lose."

"It's no problem," she said, careful to keep her voice cheery.

She pushed one of her carts in front of his, careful not to touch his own, filled with boxes of beer and big bags of chips. "This was my place, okay?"

"*This*"—the man stuck his arms out to the side—"is not your place." Like he owned *Costco*, Lettie thought, furious, knowing Costco was for everyone—legal or not.

"I'm a member," she said, pulling her wallet out of her purse. "I will show you. I'm a *VIP*."

She dropped her wallet and her many plastic cards—her treasured driver's license, her library card, the EBT card her auntie Corrina let her use to get free food at stores that accepted food stamps—scattered all over the smooth floor.

The *Master—Master Asshole*, Lettie thought—laughed at her.

She squatted to pick up the cards. Her long nails, painted gold and green for Christmas, paid for with a certificate from Melissa, scraped the concrete floor. It was hard to grip the plastic cards with her new nails, and they kept slipping from her fingers. No one helped her, not even the customers standing right over Lettie. "*I'm sorry, I'm sorry,*" she mumbled, as she reached around their feet—would she have to repeat those words for the rest of her life?

When she finally had the last card, she stood. Her head spun.

The *Master* had, again, removed her carts from the line. This time, he'd pushed them farther, over to a tall tower of cereal boxes.

Lettie remembered the words on the large wooden plaque Melissa had hung over the Goldbergs' kitchen table soon after Melissa had told Lettie about Mr. Adam's cheating:

You Control Your Own Destiny

Destino. Lettie hadn't needed any translation to recognize that magical word.

She gripped the cart's handles and pushed it in front of Master of Nothing's cart, the metal clanging.

"Oops!" she said, using her pretend dumb immigrant voice, "I see you made a mistake. I will just put my carts back in line. Thank you!"

"I made no mistake," the man said, looking straight at her. He had ocean-colored eyes like Zacarias and a skull tattoo on one shoulder. "I *said*, you got no place here. Not here." He pointed to the floor. "Not anywhere in my country."

She wanted to tell him it was her country, too. Explain how she paid taxes. How she'd filled out all the forms (with Regina's help) for the Department of Homeland Security so she could get an ID. Her son was born here—a true American. She wanted to tell him she loved her country as much as he did. Maybe more—for if she had to leave, she could not return.

The man towered over her, his big finger in her face as he yelled, his spit spraying her cheek, about the Wall and illegals and terrorists and welfare and how it was women like her, squeezing out baby after baby, stealing his money.

From the back of the line, Lettie heard a woman (a white woman, she could tell from the boldness in the woman's voice) shout, "Hey, you! Stop harassing her or I'll call security!" The woman held an iPhone high above the many heads in line. "I'm filming! You're live on Instagram, mister."

Lettie was not sure if she was grateful for the woman, or terrified—she did not want a video on the Internet, where millions of people, including ICE, would see it. Would see *her*.

The Master Baiter was still giving his speech, his hand chopping at the air next to Lettie's face as he made point after point. "Cali used to be the best state in the country! Until your people ruined it!"

"Don't talk to her like that," came a man's voice, loud and clear.

It was Zacarias. An angel appearing just in time to save her.

Master Baiter looked at Zacarias, confused. Lettie knew he was wondering why this handsome white man was sticking up for a no-good illegal.

"She assaulted me," Master Baiter said. "She slammed her cart into mine."

"Sure," Zacarias said slowly. "This little Mexican woman looks like a real threat to you, buddy."

A few people in line laughed.

How quickly a white man could change everything, Lettie thought, her mouth so dry she could not swallow.

Master Baiter did not like being laughed at, Lettie saw. He took a big step toward Zacarias. He was taller than her brother but then Zacarias let his unzipped sweatshirt slip off his freckled shoulders, and said, "I'm Mexican, too. But bigger," his muscles on muscles shining in the bright overhead lights, the two men staring each other down, chins lifted, nostrils flared.

Master Baiter took a step back.

But Lettie needed to be able to take care of herself. She did not want this to be another Halloween night—she cowering, Zacarias saving the day like one of Andres's beloved superheroes.

"Excuse me," she said, laying a palm on Zacarias's chest and gently pushing him away, then whispering, "*I* got this."

In a flash, she reached out and snatched the Costco card from the blond man's beefy fingers. Then, quick as lightning, she snapped a photo of the card with her phone.

"Hey," he said, but stood frozen, his mouth falling open in shock.

"Mr. Robert Waters," Lettie announced to the line of people, all staring now. "You hear that?" Louder now: "This man's name is Robert Waters."

"Loud and clear, sister!" the white woman yelled from the middle of the line, lifting her phone higher.

"This . . ." Mr. Waters stuttered, "this is harassment!"

"Don't be silly, Roberto," Lettie said with a smile as she handed the man his Costco card. "Nothing bad is happening. Not *yet*." She nodded toward the white lady, still filming, in line. "I know you are not a racist, Roberto. But when this video goes on the Facebook, the Twitter, there are so many places for it to go—maybe even CNN!—the world *will* call you a racist."

The man pulled his cart out of the line and shoved it away, hard. As he stomped toward the store's front doors, the cart slammed into a tall pyramid-shaped display of chocolate bars, so it seemed, to Lettie, for one glorious moment, to be raining candy.

"You good?" Zacarias whispered. His arm was around her shoulders, and only then did she realize she was shaking.

Instead of wiggling free as usual, she let his arm stay.

She nodded. "It's all good."

IN THE CAR, while Zacarias loaded the many boxes and bags of food, Lettie used the hand wipes she kept in her purse to cool the back of her neck. Her chest felt tight; her stomach rolled like the waves at the beach. She would not let that bastard Master Baiter ruin her day.

She took deep breaths, just like Zacarias had showed Andres when the little boy cried so hard he could not stop hiccupping. *In, out. In, out.* This America was too dangerous for a little brown boy to survive alone. She knew there was only one choice. She'd give Andres to Zacarias to raise as his own. Just until she'd raised enough money to get back across the border, back into America.

"Zacarias," she began before he'd even buckled his seat belt. "Zack. My heart. It runs like a wild horse." She patted her chest.

"Aw, no worries, Sis. That's just the adrenaline pumping. You were a serious badass in there!" She could see he was impressed. "That guy was a major dick. Did you see the look on his face? How about we go get some fried chicken wings? Your fave. We've still got enough time before we need to get Andres. You earned it. And I could use some comfort food."

"I have something to tell you, *hermano*."

His smile faded. "I think you mean *medio hermano*." A sad little laugh. He gripped the steering wheel. Sighed. "Okay, lay it on me. What's the problem now?"

"No problem," she said. "You are my *hermano*. Total. My brother. And what I have to tell you is good."

"Oh yeah, hey, I got good news, too!" he said. "Jensen, at the gym, he wants to make me a partner. Give me my own gym! Well, not *give* it to me exactly, but, Lettie, if he comes through on this, it will be huge. It could mean a ton of money. Pretty soon!"

"You'll be the best boss, Zack."

"It's going to be okay, Lettie. For all of us. For Andres."

How she wanted to believe him.

"This is what I want to tell you, Zack." She met his eyes. "I want you to be Andres's daddy. So, you can take care of him while I'm away." She made it sound like a vacation. "Just until I get back. Will you do this for me? For our Andres?"

He was crying. His strong hands covering his mouth. Through his fingers, he whispered, "Bless you, Lettie. Yes. Yes. I'll love him like he's my own son."

SATURDAY, DECEMBER 29, 2018

26

MEL

It had been a month of sex.

Sex in her Mini Cooper. Sex in his Tacoma.

Sex at practically every hotel outside Santa Monica's limits. The Waldorf Astoria in Beverly Hills. The Charlie in West Hollywood. The Langham in Pasadena, far enough from home for Mel to feel safe holding Zack's hand as they strolled the magnificent gardens where roses of every color buzzed with honey bees, where she pointed out the plants she'd read about in her *Guide to the Flora of Los Angeles* book. She enjoyed teaching him, and learning from him, too—about exercise and food, topics she'd once found threatening—and even, gasp, the history of Catholicism, on which he liked to deliver mini-lectures, his big hands swooping the air with excitement as he spoke.

It was, Mel thought, utterly adorable, how he got so worked up—even if he still said outrageous nonsense about the Wall and Crooked Hillary. He'd spew an opinion, then look at her with those ocean eyes, asking forgiveness, saying sorry, then lowering his mouth between her thighs. Zack's conversational filter, it turned out, was as weak as Mel's. So different from Adam's controlled, well-considered sentences.

The similarity made the sex even hotter. They'd have a debate about the papacy, Zack's handsome face growing indignant as Mel argued for female priests and popes, then softening as he reached to undo the buttons on her shirt, lift her DVF wrap dress (now *two* sizes smaller) over her head, before flipping her over and yanking her underwear down in a single fluid motion.

For the first time in her life, Mel was acting first, thinking second. Leading with her body, allowing her mind to take a break, to simply come along for the ride. Living in a way she'd once believed applied only to the most superficial, self-centered sort of people. To people who lived in California.

Except that nothing about being with Zack felt superficial.

They were becoming their Version Two selves. Together.

He's mine, Mel thought, as tourists gaped at Zack's chiseled, shirtless torso beside the pool at the Hotel Shangri-La. *All mine.* She reveled in the thought of the women at Color Theory, all so much thinner and younger and prettier; and Mel, the winner. How many times had she given Sloane and the soccer girls the speech about good sportsmanship, about not gloating after a win, not celebrating *too* much? And here Mel was, doing a victory dance every other day at a different hotel. Showing off her spoils. His abs. That ass. Those eyes. Every single part of him was, dare she say it, *perfect*. And not in an *awww, what a guy, Adam* kind of way.

Zack was perfect in a *someone, catch me before I swoon* kind of way.

They had sex at the Mountain Mermaid up in Topanga Canyon. Zack had rented that one—a room called The Lover's Nest with a view of the canyon, and a four-poster bed on the patio. We can you-know-what under the stars! Zack had texted her, like a virginal teenager (*you-know-what*) scoring an empty house on prom night. And so, they had. Fucked in the cool night air as coyotes howled in the canyon below. Woke in the morning sun, the bed surrounded by hummingbirds darting at the sugar water feeders hung by each of the four bedposts.

Mel hadn't completely let her guard down. She made sure to erase their texts immediately after receiving and sending—who knows when Sloane would grab her phone to catch some creatures in the *Pokémon Go* app. She covered all Zack-related expenses on the

Amex prepaid cards she purchased at Walgreens and Ralphs, hands trembling each time she reloaded them.

Adam couldn't find out. Not just yet. She was going to leave him, yes, but not until she'd revived her letterpress business. With a new West Coast style. She already had her first batch of limited-series hand-pressed Christmas cards in mind. It had been nearly impossible to find any Christmas cards that actually looked like a SoCal Christmas. Who wanted a card with an idyllic New England winter setting, white glittery snow and sleighs? Her new letterpress Christmas cards would be decked with palm trees and surf boards. Zack had loved the idea and wanted to help. How sweet was that?

She had noticed a sense of paranoia creeping in on their fun, her pausing a few times while going down on Zack in his crappy truck, peering out the steamed-up windows, wondering what Adam would do if she were caught. Reminding herself, what did it matter when Adam was having his own affair? To each his own.

The occasional feeling of impending doom snuck in and ruined one of her orgasms. Like what if an earthquake—the *Big One* for which Sloane had to do "Shakeout Drills" at school—hit while Mel and Zack were mid-bang and she was stranded, away from home? Away from Sloane? Even, Mel worried, away from Adam, who always seemed to know exactly what to do in an emergency. She knew Janet would say that was Mel's guilt surfacing. *No shit, Janet*, she imagined rebutting, but she had quit Janet soon after the disaster of a session with Adam. What need was there for talk therapy when there was sex therapy? Mel didn't need Janet telling her what she and Zack did was wrong when it felt oh so right.

She knew she had joined the ranks of the women she'd once judged. The women—many school moms—she had, upon first arriving in Santa Monica, endured canyon hikes and beach walks and even a few excruciating SoulCycle classes with, the conversation veering toward the women's grievances with their ex-husbands. Mel silently judging them as she pretended sympathy. Women who seemed to thrive on anger and cardio alone. She had felt simultaneously envious—what she would give to have these sad women's thigh gaps and poreless skin—and guilty. Yes, these women had escaped selfish and controlling husbands and pocketed healthy divorce settlements thanks to California's fifty-fifty law, and, yes, some of them now had hot younger boyfriends who seemed to adore their children with uncanny paternal instinct. But Mel had *had* Adam.

Or so she had believed.

Mel and Zack had sex in the back office at Color Theory. Sex in the CT van for old times' sake. Sex on the turf fields at SaMo High late one night after the overhead lights had gone dark. A favorite spot was the beach—a blanket draped over their laps, Zack's fingers tucked into her panties, Mel climaxing in front of who knows how many tourists strolling at sunset.

It was the sex she didn't have in high school, she told herself. Or in college—she'd met Adam so young. She was making up for lost time. She was having the best midlife crisis a woman could dream of. Zack gave her orgasms, one right after another, like the ripples in a lake, one climax ending only for another to begin. She had to beg him to stop. *Enough, please, enough.*

Adam, thankfully, was busy with a new film. For which he was being paid nearly five thousand dollars *a day*. A big-studio adaptation of a sci-fi novel about a pill that transformed reproduction, shortening human gestation from nine months to nine weeks. *A true feminist story,* he'd told Mel, and she'd struggled not to scratch his eyes out. Him talking about feminism—ha! She fucked Zack with extra gusto that night, gyrating on top until he'd come with a gasping *Oh Jesus!*

With Zack, Mel did things she'd only ever fantasized about, and pre-Zack, always with a cringe of shame. But with him, she felt no shame. They watched porn on her phone; their favorite categories were Teacher's Pet and Sex in Uniform. They'd even discovered a super-hot clip set at a gym, a burly guy with a giant dick (*That just cannot be real*, Mel had whispered, making Zack laugh mid-kiss) going down on a big-boobed woman sitting on "quadzilla," that weight machine Mel loathed.

Today, she'd driven Zack to the Malibu Beach Inn, a place she'd read was a favorite among celebrities. They tangled the soft-as-silk sheets as the gas fireplace blazed. They devoured the eighteen-dollar Dean & DeLuca truffle-coated pretzels and hand-dipped chocolates. Calories be damned. If Zack wanted her body, which *was* twenty pounds lighter, but still a bit Jigglypuff—and oh God, he did—why should she deny herself?

Now, she was stretched out on the thick soft carpet of their hotel room on her elbows, in plank position, naked but for a tank top, as she was still too self-conscious about her body to let her belly roam free. It had been her idea—she'd surprised herself again and again with Zack—to re-create a scene from the gym porno, having him count her planking time, then make her beg for more.

He knelt over her. She felt his cock on her lower back, firm and ready.

"Five, four—" he whispered into her ear.

"Arrgh," she grunted, her body trembling with exertion and desire.

"And—one. Now. Tell me how badly you want me to fuck you."

Mel dropped to her belly, out of breath, arms shaking. "So bad."

"Ass in the air."

Mel lifted into child's pose. He spoke again, his voice gentle now, earnest.

"Okay to do what we did last time?"

"Um." She felt herself smile as her face went hot. *Last time*, she'd let him touch a part of her she'd always considered *off limits* and had an orgasm so shattering she was certain her very essence had been altered irreversibly.

"Yes." She exhaled. "Please. Like last time."

She pressed her nose into the soft carpet and closed her eyes, pushing her backside higher into the air.

Yes. She wanted him to touch her there. One of his hands stirring her in the front, the other stirring her behind. Forget Mel 2.0. Forget Mel the soccer mom. This new Mel was on fire, she thought, as she gave herself over to him.

THURSDAY, JANUARY 3, 2019

27

REGINA

"In closing, I'd like to leave you with a final thought," said Regina, stepping away from the whiteboard to face the founding team of BeastMode Wellness (current slogan: *Your body, solved!*—though Regina planned to change that, if she got the account)—three Millennial hipsters and a fortysomething dad-type wearing a Joe Rogan T-shirt—"I'm well-aware of the vast number of choices you have in the search for a perfect marketing partner. Here in LA, there's no shortage of slick, polished agencies with mile-long lists of buzzy clients in the wellness sector and beyond. Big Rad Wolfe isn't one of those agencies. We're young, we're scrappy, and we don't serve kombucha on tap at our office."

"Thank God," said the dad-type, whose name was Dustin.

Regina smiled at him. "Our client list isn't long, because we're extremely picky about who we decide to work with. Because we have something called the *passion requirement*. Which means we don't engage with a company unless its mission truly resonates with our core values. Does this mean pouring our heart and soul into the projects we do accept, and working our asses off for our small number of clients, as if they were our very own lifeblood?" She paused for dramatic effect; four pairs of eyes were latched on her. "Hell, yes, it does. BeastMode is one of the few companies I've met that has left me feeling ready to go *level ten and beyond* to ensure it becomes a smash-hit healthy-living brand. You've already set the foundation in place—the app, the on-demand virtual courses, the accountability plans—now you just need the right exposure to blow all the other imitators out of the water."

"Right on," said one of the Millennials, a woman in a camo jumpsuit.

"Should you choose to partner with Big Rad Wolfe," Regina went on, "the success of our campaigns comes with a no-strings guarantee. We hit our goals, or you get your money back."

Dustin cleared his throat. "Can you go over your pricing structure again?"

Regina took a deep, silent breath. "Certainly. For the sort of omnichannel digital campaign you need, in addition to the supplemental offline channels, we'd require an upfront retainer of—" She met Dustin's eyes and quoted an outrageously high number.

"Competitively priced," said Dustin, nodding and tapping a few keystrokes on his laptop. Regina allowed herself to relax. She let her gaze drift out the window of the eighteenth floor, where the offices of BeastMode Wellness, situated in a high-rise on the Wilshire Corridor near UCLA, looked out over the sprawl of West Los Angeles, all the way to the ocean.

If she squinted, Regina could see Santa Monica.

"Killer pitch," said a guy with a scruffy beard.

"Thank you," said Regina. "I'm so grateful for the opportunity to have met you guys and learn about BeastMode. Just when I thought *disruption* was played out in the wellness space, you guys have gone and changed my mind. Nice work."

Dustin looked up from his laptop. "We'll be in touch with a final decision tomorrow. But just to stay out in front of the process, would you mind sending over a term sheet later today?"

"You'll have it within the hour," said Regina. "And whatever the outcome, this has been a true pleasure." But she knew she'd gotten the job.

BACK IN HER car, Regina swung onto the southbound I-405 into standstill rush-hour traffic. She voice-texted a message to Gordon, who was in Hollywood with Bryan today, pitching *Eighteen Twelve* to a production company.

> Killed it at BeastMode. Tell you all about it later. GOOD LUCK IN THE ROOM! Xoxo.

Then she selected the *Happy Day Sunshine* playlist from Spotify, and, as Bob Marley's voice filled her car, she felt better than she had in months. She'd woken the morning after Minnow Night with her worst hangover since college, her recall of the previous evening hazy but for the crystalline memory of exactly how cold and cruel Zack had been on the phone. As humiliating as her drunk-dialing him was, she was glad she did it, because it had left her with a clear vision of exactly what she needed to do to fix her life:

1. Cut Zack out of it—truly and completely
2. Get a real goddamn job

She'd realized, as she'd washed down ibuprofen with black coffee, her head throbbing (*Too much fun on girls' night, huh?* Gordon had asked, smiling and rubbing her shoulders), that making Zack her "business partner" had little to do with her inability to get new Big Rad Wolfe clients and everything to do with her desire to be close to him.

Which, she'd finally admitted to herself, was no longer an option. Because, somehow, he'd fallen for Melissa Goldberg. Two of her so-called best friends. Rolling around naked together.

The thought made Regina's stomach turn.

But she would keep moving. She would never let him know how much he'd hurt her. Instead, she'd simply begun withholding Zack's

3o percent cut of the Color Theory transfers. She always delivered his payment in person, in cash—it was the only safe option—every two weeks, but now, since he'd gone gaga for Mel-fucking-Goldberg and her double chin, Regina simply began delaying their handoff meetings, via a host of creative texted excuses:

> Completely tied up with the kids on break from school, can't get away

> Gordon slammed with flu and I'm on nurse duty

> In Santa Barbara for a few days (that one was an out-right lie)

Eventually, Zack began to demand his money, always in the carefully coded language Regina had taught him, so their texts could never be used as evidence should the shit hit the fan. Zack's loyalty to her rules—You've been late for class too many times!!!!!, he wrote, followed by angry-face emojis—almost made her proud. Regina had anticipated and prepared for his requests. She addressed them with another careful text:

> Hang in there a little longer! Otherwise I'm happy 2 let Adam Goldberg know you're coaching his wife. ☺

She was almost ashamed at the pleasure it brought her to wield such power over him. But then she remembered his face between Mel's legs in the gym van, and her shame evaporated.

Regina's stalling methods worked. Zack kept doing his job. Of course, each deposit refreshed the risk of getting caught, but Jensen had been off skiing in Vail and attending a wedding in Maui, Regina had learned from his Instagram feed—leaving his minions to manage his studios, which were booming more than ever. Color Theory

Malibu was set to open in March, and Regina had heard through the grapevine that a Santa Barbara location was next.

No, Jensen would not be missing nine grand a month anytime soon. Certainly not before Regina no longer needed it. Of this she was becoming more confident by the day. In addition to Beast-Mode, she had four more pitches scheduled in the coming weeks. And who knew—maybe a production company would love *Eighteen Twelve* as much as Gordon did, and throw some real Hollywood money at it.

Soon, Regina was certain, she would no longer need Zack's services—or Jensen's money.

In the meantime, Zack's 30 percent had given her a little breathing room. For starters, it had allowed her to pay for Christmas, which wasn't too demanding this year—Kaden and Mia were in an "anti-consumer" phase, thanks to some eco-conscious theater troupe that had visited both their schools. The extra cash also had helped Regina scrape together minimum required payments on her scariest debts—the IRS, the mortgage, tuition for Rustic Canyon Day School.

When are we meeting? Zack kept texting. **You can't do this to me.**

She'd kept him blocked for a while, letting him sweat, then responded to a slew of his desperate texts, all demanding his money, with an actual phone call.

Cut the shit, Regina, he'd said, by way of greeting. *You owe me. This is serious.*

Banging someone else's wife is serious, Zack, she'd said, cucumber-cool. *Tooling with your employer's accounting software is serious.*

Are you threatening me?

Of course not, she'd said brightly. *I'm just taking my time. It's in your best interest to keep things moving.*

You're threatening me. His voice went flat.

Just keep things moving, she'd repeated. *Good-bye, Zack. And tell Mel I said hello.*

It was amazing, how life worked, Regina thought, humming to "Peaceful Easy Feeling" as she exited the 405 for the westbound I-10 that led into Santa Monica: the obstacles were all in your head. All you had to do was change your thinking, set some honest intentions, and *poof*—they began to disappear.

SATURDAY, JANUARY 12, 2019

28

LETICIA

Dear ~~Zacarias~~ Zack,

Gracias, my hermano (no medio, all-the-way-brother). I know Andres will be well loved by his tío Zack.

Here is a list of Andres's favorite things.

For school lunch, Andres loves macaroni and cheese or peanut butter sandwiches with crusts cut off. Don't tell the lunch ladies because they will throw it away since the white mommies made a rule for no peanuts.

His favorite stuffed animal is Miguel the penguin. The lucky penguin gets to take a bath with Andres once a month and this is how he keeps clean.

Use the nail brush on his nails, the blue one, until there is NO dirt.

When he wakes from nightmares he gets warm milk in microwave with pinch of cinnamon in the Pokémon mug. Works every time!

Bathroom light ALWAYS stays on at night.

I will leave a list of all the special teachers at school. Make sure he gets his therapy so he can grow up big and strong and smart like his tío Zack.

Teach our Andres to tie his shoes. Say his prayers. How beautiful he will look in the altar boy robes on Christmas Eve.

Teach him better English please but never stop speaking to him in Spanish. Make him proud to be American plus MEXICAN.

Skype with Mommy a few times a week. I will do my best to put on a happy face.

Thank you, my brother Zack. You did what you always are telling the workout people in your classes. You SHOWED UP. You saved us.

Love, your sister,
Leticia Mendoza

WEDNESDAY, JANUARY 16, 2019

29

MEL

MEL COULD SMELL ZACK ON HER SKIN AS SHE SPED TOWARD JOHN WAYNE Elementary, her hands slicking the steering wheel with sweat, heart rabbiting in her chest.

The text from Adam had come at the most inopportune time. Meaning, when several of Zack's fingers had been deep inside her, and another around her . . . bottom. Hole of her bottom. Bottom hole. *Ugh*. She couldn't find a word for it that didn't make her feel like a raging slut—but the thing he did in that place drove her crazy. The text tone she'd recently assigned to Adam, a clip from "Eye of the Tiger" by Survivor, a song he'd once claimed to loathe more than any song ever made, had started at precisely the same time as her orgasm, and she'd grabbed for the phone practically before she'd finished, reading Adam's words just as Zack's fingers were slipping out of her.

> Sloane's principal called. Wants us both to meet with her at school ASAP. I have no idea why so don't ask. Sloane is fine tho, I made sure of that. No panicking please. I'm on my way. Meet me there stat.

Of course, Mel *had* panicked. Bolted from the hotel room, leaving Zack naked on the bed watching *House Hunters International*, smiling with concern, gorgeous as hell.

"You coming back?" he'd asked, sticking out his bottom lip in a pout.

"If my daughter's still alive," said Mel. "But don't count on it."

At a red light, she checked her face in the rearview mirror and smeared gloss on her lips. Did she look disheveled? Suspicious? Sex-dazed? Would Adam even notice, or care if he did?

Of course not, she reminded herself, pulling into the faculty lot of Sloane's school. Adam was too busy fucking the next Scarlett Johansson. She parked in a spot marked *Staff Only* and turned off the ignition. Let them tow her.

Mel smoothed her shirt over her jeans, hoping it wasn't too wrinkled from its time crumpled on the hotel floor, and speed-walked to the front office, where she dropped her voice to a discreet volume to tell the receptionist she was there to see the principal.

Oh Christ, she thought, as the receptionist led her to Principal Burke's office. *What could it be?*

Adam and Sloane were already inside, seated in two of five chairs arranged in a semicircle facing Principal Burke's desk. Sloane slouched on the adult-sized chair, feet dangling above the floor.

"Mom!" said Sloane. She looked like she'd been crying. Mel's heart clenched.

"Honey," said Mel, kissing Sloane's cheek.

"That took you a while," said Adam, impeccably dressed in an olive-green button-down and the dark blue Bonobos pants Mel had bought him after she'd read online they were the "most perfect men's pants ever made."

Perfect pants for a perfect man.

Ha.

"Traffic," Mel said to Adam, taking the seat beside him. He patted her knee. She moved it away from his hand.

"Melissa, glad you're here," said the principal, whose curt manner matched her name—Liz Burke. She reminded Mel of Jamie Lee Curtis. "Now we're just waiting for the other . . . family."

On cue, the door opened and Jess Fabian walked in, followed by her son Tyler, whose red hair matched his mother's.

As soon as Mel recognized the boy she knew it was bad news.

"Jessica and Tyler," said Principal Burke. "Welcome."

"My husband couldn't make it," said Jessica. "Sorry." Then she turned to Mel. "Melissa!" said Jessica. "How funny to see you here."

"It is," said Mel. "Funny."

She hadn't seen Jessica since Minnow Night at Canyon Rustica.

Jessica and Tyler sat in the remaining chairs in the room, Tyler assuming a slumped position similar to Sloane's. The two children did not look at each other, Mel noticed.

"Now that we're all here," said Liz Burke, "I want to start by saying this room is an entirely safe space. For you, Sloane, and you, Tyler. Is that clear?"

Sloane and Tyler mumbled *yeses*.

"Good," said Liz. "Now, kids, your parents don't know why I called them in here today. So, I'd like one of you to tell them."

The room was silent.

"Sloanie," said Adam gently. "Can you do it? Tell us why we're here? You're not in trouble."

Sloane put her hands over her face and began to cry. Mel wanted to gather her in her arms, but Adam beat Mel to it, rubbing the small girl's back and whispering reassurances in her ear.

Finally, Sloane sat up and dropped her hands. She took a deep breath and looked to Adam, as if for courage.

But then Tyler Fabian spoke up.

"We sent each other dirty texts."

Mel had the sense of the yellowish office walls closing in around her.

"You *what*?" said Jessica Fabian.

Tyler shrugged. "It was a game, kinda. We were just messing around."

"We didn't mean it!" Sloane finally found her voice. "I don't even like him!"

"They exchanged a series of text messages," said Principal

Burke, "which came to our attention when our aftercare director caught sight of them on Tyler's phone."

"This is a mistake," said Mel. "Sloane wouldn't even know how to write . . ." She paused. "So-called dirty texts. She's *years* away from puberty!"

"Mom!" Sloane burst.

"Melissa," warned Adam. "It's okay, baby," he said, rubbing Sloane's shoulder. "You can tell us."

Mel wondered if Adam and Sloane were conspiring against her; if perhaps, in all those secret, giggling moments together, he'd convinced their daughter to help him hide his affair. Then she looked at Tyler Fabian, his mouth hanging half-open, and felt ashamed for betraying her sweet Sloane by thinking something so insane, even if just for one paranoid second.

"We were just having a . . . a contest," said Sloane, her voice quavering. "Me and Tyler. To see who could write the grossest thing we found on gross websites. "

"We were pretending we were boyfriend-girlfriend," said Tyler.

"We're not!" cried Sloane miserably. "I'm too young for a boyfriend!"

"You sure are," said Mel, fearing she might throw up. This was not happening.

"A *contest*?" said Adam, turning to Tyler.

"Yeah," mumbled Tyler. "Or, like, just a stupid game. We were just bored at aftercare."

"Mommy never picks me up on time!" burst Sloane.

Tyler nodded. "We're always, like, the last kids there."

"I doubt that," said Jess Fabian, sounding weary.

It was as if Mel had been punched in the gut. "Honey," she said to Sloane weakly. "I'm always . . . there to get you. And half the time you're at soccer."

Adam narrowed his eyes at her. "I thought we agreed you'd get her by four thirty on the no-soccer days."

"So, this is my fault?" Mel's cheeks blazed. How was Adam still siding with Sloane? She faced her daughter.

"It's Tyler's fault!" Sloane began to cry in earnest. "I hate him!"

"You do?" Tyler said, sounding hurt.

"It's okay, sweetheart." Adam massaged Sloane's head.

"The messages were very explicit," said the principal. "Well beyond, er, PG-13. Which is why I felt I needed to bring them to your attention immediately."

"Seriously, Tyler?" said Jess. "I give you a phone for your eleventh birthday and *this* is how you thank me?"

"Sloane doesn't even have a phone!" said Mel. "This is impossible."

"I used Daddy's," Sloane whispered.

"Jesus," said Adam.

"How explicit?" said Mel, the realization rising and coalescing inside her, suffusing her body with dread. "How explicit were the messages?"

Liz Burke sighed. "I have screenshots printed out."

"But I erased the messages!" cried Sloane. "Every time."

Mel jolted with a memory: Sloane standing at her bedroom door, the morning after Mel had found the texts.

Mom? Are you ever gonna get up? This is like the third time I've come in to see you.

Adam's phone lying on the nightstand, undisturbed.

Unless Sloane had picked it up while Mel was sleeping, erased the messages, and returned it to the same position.

It could not be.

Burke picked up two stapled documents from her desk, each folded in half, and handed one to Mel and the other to Jess. "See for yourself."

Mel slowly unfolded the paper, Adam breathing over her shoulder. She made herself look at the top sheet.

The room began to wheel.

Distantly, Mel heard Jess Fabian's voice: "Well, Tyler, you can kiss *Fortnite* good-bye for the rest of your life."

I'm thinking about u & how hot ur right now, the printout read.

And: If peach is the emoji for ass what do I use 4 cunt?

The sentences had not been written by a half-naked starlet lusting for Adam as Mel had feared. They'd been written by Tyler Fabian and Mel's very own daughter.

TUESDAY, JANUARY 22, 2019

3o

ZACK

AT TEN P.M. ON TUESDAY, ZACK FINISHED THE LAST OF HIS CLOSING DU-
ties at Color Theory—organizing the dumbbells from lightest to
heaviest, re-racking the weights, disinfecting the water station—
then hurried to the back office, where he locked the door behind
him and closed all the blinds before sending a one-word text to Mel:
Now!—signaling her to jump in a Lyft and come see him.

Sloane still awake, she wrote back. Give me 10 min & I'll get a car.

Zack jumped into the office's tiny shower, buzzy with anticipation.

He hadn't touched her in almost a week, since a text from Adam
had interrupted them, and Mel had bolted from the hotel room to
deal with some emergency at their daughter's school. In the days
since, Zack's need to see her had grown hot and gnawing, almost un-
containable. She'd been texting frequently, apologizing, explaining
she'd been *swallowed up by family stuff*, that she was a *slave to youth
soccer*, that Adam was *ultra-present*, always followed by sad-face or
eye-rolling or thumbs-down emojis.

This week, though, the stars had shifted in their favor: Adam—
Mister Jiu-Jitsu, King Hamster—was gone on a business trip for
three glorious nights, and Jensen was on a trip, to Colorado and
then Hawaii, which meant the back office of Color Theory was a safe
haven for them to meet after hours. Zack had been surprised—and
thrilled—when Mel offered, over text, to ask Lettie to babysit Sloane,
freeing Mel to come see him at work.

For a moment, Zack had felt guilty at the image of Lettie parked on Mel's enormous couch, watching her nighttime soaps on Telemundo while she fretted about money and getting deported, Andres's sleeping head cradled in her lap. Then he reminded himself how much more comfortable Mel's couch was than Lettie's own. Andres was probably thrilled to be chilling inside the Goldbergs' mini-mansion.

Zack could not think about Lettie and her problems now. First, he needed to see Mel. Desperately. She would clear his head.

He was toweling off in the cramped bathroom when he heard his phone ring. His heart jumped; perhaps she'd arrived early. Towel wrapped around his waist, he bounded out of the bathroom and snatched his phone from the desk.

The call was coming from Jensen Davis.

"Yo, Jens," Zack said. "How's vacay?"

"Z-man! I'm actually back in LA for twelve hours. I fly out to Maui first thing in the morning. Vail was unbelievable. All fresh pow. We seriously have to ski together some time."

"I'm from Florida, bro. I only waterski."

"Unacceptable. Hey, where are you at right now?"

"Right now?" Zack's chest tightened. He reminded himself he was *supposed* to be at work right now—he'd taught the eight thirty class. "Just wrapping up at CT. I taught the late one."

"Sweet. I was hoping I'd catch you there. Don't leave just yet, I'm gonna swing by."

Zack swallowed hard. "Swing by? As in, now?"

"Yeah, I'm ten minutes out. I just want to show you something real quick. It's a surprise. I was gonna wait until after I got back from Hawaii, but I just don't have enough self-control."

"Wow, dude. I'm officially curious." Zack's heart started to hammer. "Can't wait."

"See you in ten."

Zack scrambled into his clothes and texted Mel: HOLD UP. Have a small issue over here. Don't call a car until I say it's clear, OK?

She wrote back instantly: You're making me nervous but OK.

He responded with a heart, then opened the blinds and unlocked the office door.

What the hell was Jensen's *surprise*? And what could be so important that he had to show Zack during a twelve-hour layover?

Zack paced back and forth across the office, replenishing the coat of sweat he'd just showered off. Could Jensen have suddenly caught on to the transfers? Zack monitored log-ins to the Color Theory account constantly; the only visits to the site, for months on end, had been his own. He changed the password frequently. There was no way Jensen could have logged in lately—unless he'd spent a good deal of time on the phone with the bank, which, given that he'd been skiing "fresh pow" in Colorado for the past week, seemed unlikely.

Still, Zack could not stop pacing, fear roiling inside him.

If Jensen had somehow found out, and was coming to the gym now to "surprise" Zack with a confrontation, well, Zack decided, Regina was going down *with* him. If his worst fears came true, and he was about to stare down the barrel of jail time for embezzlement (*Jesus, what would become of Andres?* Zack thought, tears rising in his throat), well, he wouldn't do it alone. That bitch owed him three installments of his 30 percent cut, and seemed to have no intention of paying him. She was crazy, truly loony, he'd decided. Zack was now pretty sure she'd put her dweeby husband up to leaving that bogus voicemail about wanting personal training—just to scare him, to fuck with him. It was the only explanation; he'd never heard from Gordon again. Or, hell, maybe Regina had put some *other* guy up to calling Zack, pretending to be Gordon. Who knew; the sky was truly the limit when it came to the creativity of Regina Wolfe's manipulations.

She was insane. And dangerous. Still, for now, Zack needed her money.

He stopped pacing and tried all the other calming techniques he knew: five short, huffy breaths, followed by three long ones. Contracting every muscle in his body as hard as he could for a count of ten, then letting go. Holding a plank until his abs quaked.

Nothing worked. Finally, he reached into his gym bag and pulled out *The Little Way for Every Day.* He stared at the fuzzy image of the little black-and-white-clad nun on the cover. Then he closed his eyes, pressed the book to his heart, and asked St. Thérèse to help him.

31

REGINA

REGINA WAS DRIFTING OFF ON THE COUCH TO AN OLD EPISODE OF *SHARK Tank* when she heard Gordon's key turn in the door. She sat up quickly and reached for the remote to shut off the TV.

"You're awake," said Gordon, shutting the door behind him and stepping out of the new hip leather sneakers Regina had bought him to wear to his *Eighteen Twelve* pitches. This afternoon's meeting, his biggest yet, with a production company attached to Spielberg, had gone so well, Gordon had explained in a breathless phone call to Regina earlier, that some of the "heavy hitters" from the meeting had invited him and Bryan to dinner. "I can't believe you stayed up so late."

"I was dying to hear how it went," she said, patting the space beside her on the couch. "Come sit and tell me all about it."

"Oh, you know." Gordon shrugged, untucking his shirt from his jeans. "It was mostly a lot of hot air."

She tried her best to hide her disappointment, knowing it had been foolish to hope for anything but rejection—Gordon had been working in Hollywood long enough that she should really know better. She reminded herself of all the new business she'd scored for Big Rad Wolfe. Maybe it would be enough.

"Really? Just hot air, all this time? You've been gone for seven hours."

He crossed the room and sat beside her on the couch. She leaned over and kissed him on the cheek, detecting the sweet-sharp scent of bourbon.

"Well," he spoke slowly. "It was mostly hot air, yeah. You know how Hollywood people are. So many words, so little substance. But I guess they did say one thing of interest."

"What's that?"

He took her hand in his and squeezed it. "That they'd buy it."

"What?" She was sure she'd heard him wrong.

"Correction. They bought it in the room."

"What?" Was something good finally, actually happening?

"You heard me."

"They bought your screenplay? You're not joking?"

"I'm not joking. They bought it. On the spot. In the room. For a lot of money. Then they took me and Bryan out to celebrate. I wanted to wait to tell you in person." He smiled, though not as happily as Regina would've expected. She stopped herself from asking exactly what *a lot of money* meant. Later—now wasn't the time.

"Oh my God! Gordon! That's incredible." Then why, she wondered, did the air between them feel so still and silent? Where was the celebratory hum? "Why don't you sound more excited?"

"I guess I'm sort of in shock."

"Babe! This is amazing. I'm so proud of you!" She threw her arms around him and hugged him tightly. He leaned against her but did not squeeze back. He'd sworn the good news was true, so why was he acting so *meh*?

"Stay right here," Regina said, suddenly eager to leave the room. She needed a moment to process the news, and will herself into believing everything really would be okay. "I'm getting champagne. Even if we don't drink it, we have to at least pop the cork! This is a huge day. I almost want to wake the girls. Be right back."

"Regina." Gordon's voice at her back sounded weary.

Something *was* wrong.

She turned back toward the couch, fighting her instinct, which was to keep walking—maybe run—into the kitchen. "What?"

"I've been wanting to ask you something for weeks. But I kept chickening out. Because I'm scared to hear the answer. But I promised myself that if I sold my screenplay, I'd make myself do it. And now I've sold it. So here goes."

Regina felt her stomach twist and cave. He knew. About the money she'd stolen from Color Theory. Somehow, her husband of fourteen years, who had always believed in her, been her champion, knew she was a fraud. Their life was a fraud. This wasn't just a sharing-good-news moment, it was an intervention.

Gordon exhaled. "Regina, are you cheating on me?"

"What? Cheating on you? Jesus, Gordon. No!"

He tipped forward on the couch and reached behind him to pull something from the back pocket of his jeans: a small, worn paperback book.

She recognized it instantly: *The Little Way for Every Day*. Zack's book.

"Oh, Gordon. Oh God." She almost laughed aloud with relief. "Now I understand what you're thinking. It makes sense, but it's a total and complete misunderstanding. I promise you." She returned to the couch and sat down, eyes burning with grateful tears. He didn't know what a rotten person she was, or, at least, not the *right* kind of rotten.

Gordon, sweet harmless Gordon, scooted a few inches away from her. Like he was scared of her, she thought, and who could blame him?

"You think I was doing something with . . ." She dropped her voice to a whisper, feeling queasy. "Zack."

"Believe me, I didn't want to think it," said Gordon. "But you've given me too many reasons."

"Like what?"

Take your pick, she thought, realizing how stupid she'd been to believe Gordon too stupid to notice her flailing around these past few months. It was she who was the walking midlife crisis!

"Let's see. First, we go on a family beach picnic, and you run away from us in the middle of it. Literally, you just start running, like you couldn't stand to stay with us one more minute."

"Family beach picnic?" Regina's voice shook with righteous anger. "You mean that night you and Bryan were in the bro-zone, drooling over some girl half your age in a bikini?"

"That's an interesting take. What I remember is sitting on the beach at sunset with my wife and my friend and my daughters, enjoying a picnic and the sunset, when suddenly my wife announces she's leaving, and sprints away like she's being chased."

"You know me—I'm a card-carrying gym rat." She faked a laugh. "Sometimes, I take two classes in one day! And the way Bryan was *leering* at that girl made my skin—"

Gordon held up a finger, silencing her.

"Then, when I see my wife at home, later, she's all red-eyed and preoccupied. A million miles away. She hardly talks to me, she goes to bed early, and later, when I go to take the trash out, I flip open the lid to see Kaden's dumped a bunch of plastic in the wrong bin again." Regina fought the urge to roll her eyes—Gordon, savior of the earth. "So, I transfer it to the recycling, and what do I find sitting under a yogurt container?" He waved the book at her.

She nodded, making sure her brows were furrowed so she seemed extra attentive. As in, *Hmmm, tell me more*, hoping to seem just as perplexed as Gordon, as if she too were unraveling this mystery. All the while, searching her brain, slaloming back and forth—to tell the truth or not to tell the truth . . .

"*This* weird little book," Gordon continued. "Which piques my curiosity, since last I checked, my wife was not a practicing Catholic. Yet there's a discarded prayer book in my garbage."

She remembered coming home in a rage and shoving Zack's

book, which Jensen had given her, several layers under the top of the trash. Dammit, she should've noticed the misplaced recycling—one of Gordon's pet peeves! Could she pin the book on one of the school moms? Santa Monicans in their forties—the age at risk for midlife meltdowns—were always trying on various *communities* and *programs* that were one step shy of religious cult status.

"I can explain," she began, knowing well she had no explanation ready. Knowing that Gordon, slow talker that he was, hated to be interrupted and that he was sure to make her wait until he was finished.

"Let me finish," he said, just as she'd expected. "So, I open it, out of sheer curiosity, find some dude's name written in the front, and somehow it's familiar. I can't say why—let's chalk it up to my *Spidey sense*, as Kaden would say—but I impulsively google the guy's name. It takes me about two seconds on the Internet to find pictures of you with this guy—Zack Doheny—all over your friend's Instagram, cozy and cuddly, and—"

"You mean Lindsey Leyner? She's not my friend!" Regina had to stand her ground on this. Yes, Regina was a liar and a thief; yes, she had lusted after another man; but no way was she going to be lumped in with Lindsey-fucking-Leyner. "She's just this maniac mom I know from Color Theory who's appointed herself the social media director of the gym, along with every other organization she's associated with. And plus, *everyone* hugs *everyone* after a workout. It's means nothing. It's like a high five."

"Which is exactly what I told myself. I decided it was nothing, and that I'd let it go. I truly did. But then a few weeks later, you go out, supposedly to your Minnow Night, and I fall asleep in my office, and when I wake up a few hours later and go upstairs, I find you lying in our bed almost naked, yelling the name *Zack*."

Regina thought of Mel's favorite phrase. *Kill me now.*

Gordon sighed heavily and tossed Zack's book onto the coffee table. "Now you can talk. But no bullshit, Regina. I mean it."

"Okay." Regina curled forward and pressed the heels of her hands over her eyes. "Okay."

"Just come clean, Regina. It's the only place to start."

She breathed into her palms and imagined screaming the truth. *It's not an affair! It's not an affair! It's just a stupid harmless crush I developed because it helps me cope with the fact that I fucked up our finances and was too scared to tell you.*

Had this been the whole truth, she might have had the courage to tell him. But the rest of it—that her "stupid harmless crush" was also her partner in an embezzlement scheme she had not yet stopped—kept her curled into her own lap, rocking back and forth.

No, she could not tell him the truth, even partially. It was too risky. Especially now, when they were so close to making honest money—both of them—and she could put the bullshit with Zack to bed, once and for all.

"Regina." Gordon's voice was softer. "Talk to me."

Slowly, she straightened on the couch, her mind reaching for the solution, any solution. Regina was, as she and Gordon had joked in the early years of Big Rad Wolfe, when she was winning 50K retainers from Silicon Beach start-ups, beating out well-known agencies in the process, *the closer*. Gordon had even had a T-shirt custom-made with *THE CLOSER* in big block letters stenciled across the back, gifting it to Regina on the fifth anniversary of her business.

She just had to close this shit down.

She took a deep breath and looked square into her husband's eyes.

"Gordon. I swear on my life—on Kaden's and Mia's lives—that I am not having an affair. I'm absolutely mortified that you think I ever would. But the truth of the matter is, I do know Zack Doheny. He's a coach at my gym. And he's . . ." She let her voice quaver and trail. "Kind of obsessed with me."

"Kind of obsessed?"

"Yes. It started out as an annoyance. A trainer giving his client extra attention." As she spoke the words, they felt true. Zack *had* given her extra attention. "I'm pretty intense at the gym, so sometimes the coaches single me out. Ask me to give demos, motivate the other clients, blah blah."

Gordon nodded. "No surprise there."

"But with Zack, it escalated into something . . . different. His attention turned into something more. Doting, then needy. Then kind of . . . stalker-ish. Sort of watching my every move. Making sure he taught the classes I signed up for." That one was such a lie that she almost burst into laughter.

"God," Gordon said, his face scrunched in disgust. "That's creepy."

"He started texting me, messaging me on social media."

"What? How did he have your number?"

"Easy. He does office work for the gym, and I'm in the database, along with my contact info. He gave me that weird nun book as a"—she air-quoted—"*present*, because he fancies himself some kind of Catholic. As you know, I promptly threw it in the trash."

"And why were you talking to him on the phone? In your bra and underwear, after Minnow Night?"

"Oh God." Regina winced. "It's pretty sad, actually. And I know I shouldn't have felt sorry for him." Jesus, she thought, if Zack's Hell were real, she was surely headed there. "He gets drunk sometimes and calls me. Over and over. I've blocked his number, but he'll just call me from someone else's phone." The lies were coming effortlessly now—she was amazed at her own creativity. Maybe *she* should be the writer in the family. "That night, he'd been calling and texting over and over. Drunk and blubbering, saying he loved me. Finally, I got fed up. I yelled at him. Threatened to get a restraining order."

"So, why didn't you? This is totally insane!"

She worried she might've gone overboard—that part about Zack confessing his love for her. But it was too late now. There was no way out but forward.

"Because, honestly, he's harmless. Pathetic, actually. A lost puppy. He came to LA to be an actor, and has failed at that and practically everything else. This is the sort of stuff he shares with his workout classes, if you can believe it." She paused, and for a moment, thought she might break into tears. Not for the lies she was telling the only man who had ever truly loved her. But for her betrayal of Zack. "I feel sorry for him. *Everyone* does. He's just a messed-up Millennial kid. He hasn't really done anything to me. Just a lot of desperate over-communicating. And with all the hashtag-Me-Too hysteria, reporting it could really ruin his life. He's hanging by a thread as it is." She took a slow steadying breath, unsure if she should barrel ahead.

"Seriously, Regina? You're trying to make me sympathetic toward this asshole?"

"No, I'm not." *Quit now*, she told herself. *You're digging a hole, Regina.*

"I need a better reason. For why you haven't done anything about this. Why you've been keeping it from me."

"Because." She fumbled. "Because." Inside her, she felt the lie she was telling converge with a deeper truth. It gathered and rose, pushing up into her throat, and before she could swallow it down, she heard herself blurt, "I like the attention!"

"You what?"

"The *attention*, Gordon. Pathetic as it sounds. I don't want to have an affair with my stupid, juvenile trainer. But when your husband ignores you for months on end, you start to feel a little crazy. A little . . ." Her voice caught in her throat. "Starved."

She felt a tear leak from her eye and fall down her cheek. Gordon watched her, his expression softening.

"But nothing," she went on, her voice strained, "and I mean *nothing*, has ever happened between me and Zack."

Gordon was silent. Then he reached for her hand.

"Okay," he said, barely above a whisper.

"Wh-what do you mean, okay?" Was he really going to forgive her? Did he truly believe her monstrous lies?

Now the tears were streaming; she could not stop them, nor did she understand why they were flowing so freely, but feared they had to do with the most terrible truth: she did not deserve Gordon.

His hand tightened around hers.

"I mean," he said, "that I believe you. About this trainer situation."

"You do?" She blinked at him through her tears.

"Yes."

"I'm sorry," she said. "I'm so sorry to have made you think that I was . . . Ugh. I'll quit the gym. I'll change my num—"

"I've been pushing you away because of the screenplay. It's made me completely obsessive. I'm so deep in my own goddamn head all day that I've lost touch with the real world. I feel borderline insane sometimes. I think it's why I got so worked up about this trainer guy. But I'm done being paranoid, and I'm done being distant. Together, we'll get back on track. Okay?"

"Okay," she murmured, collapsing against him, her body shuddering with guilt.

And relief.

Yes, she thought, she was a monster. But even monsters deserved love, right?

32

ZACK

By the time Jensen arrived at Color Theory, Zack had collected himself enough to appear calm and relaxed. He'd blotted his sweat, propped open the door of the office, and settled at the desk with the latest issue of *Men's Health* to wait for his boss and the "surprise." He was pretending to read an article about best alt-protein sources when he heard "Z-man!" and looked up to see Jensen approaching with a huge grin. Like a kid about to open presents on Christmas morning—not the face, Zack thought, of a man about to accuse his employee of a crime.

"Hey, Jens!" Zack stood and offered his hand. "Long time no see."

"Thanks for sticking around, bro," said Jensen, pumping Zack's hand, then reaching into the pocket of his khakis to remove a set of keys. "I know it's late to be stuck at work. But I just had to show you something real quick." He tossed the keys from one hand to the other. "Let's take a walk."

Zack's nerves crackled. Where were they going? A tremor of fear rolled over him—Jensen was the kind of unpredictable dude whose rage simmered just under the surface of that pearly smile. Had Regina told him about the transfers? Was he about to bust Zack's head open on the dirty asphalt of the gym's parking lot? Zack stood and followed Jensen out the back door to the lot. They passed the Color Theory van (the sight always gave Zack a flush of warmth, remembering the first time with Mel) and continued to the far side, where a small white car was parked under the glow of a streetlight.

Jensen broke ahead of Zack into an exuberant jog. When he reached the edge of the lot, he stopped and whirled around toward Zack. "Check it out!" he called, gesturing toward the white car with dramatic flair, the sinewy muscles in his forearm flexing.

As Zack drew closer, he saw it was a brand-new Porsche 911.

"Ta-da!" said Jensen giddily. "Can you believe this bitch? How gorgeous is she?"

"Incredible," said Zack, still trying to process the situation. Was it possible that Jensen wanted nothing more than to show off his luxury vehicle? "When . . . when did you buy it?"

"Placed the order a few weeks ago. But I just picked her up from the dealer tonight. Little present to myself for officially closing on the new location. Color Theory Malibu opens one month from yesterday! And guess who's gonna be the manager and head coach?"

"Um," said Zack. "Who?" He wanted to believe the voice in his head crowing, *You, Zack! It's you!* But past experience with Jensen—all those promises that had never materialized—had taught Zack to remain cautiously optimistic.

"You, Z-man! If you accept the offer, that is. It'll be our sweetest studio yet, by far. Two thousand square feet, all brand-new, state-of-the-art equipment. All I need is a badass trainer to run the show and make it our most successful location ever."

"Wow," said Zack. "I'm speechless, Jens." When, in fact, he had so many questions. *Is this for real?* Could Jensen, who Mel had once called a snake-oil salesman, be trusted? "That sounds like an amazing offer. I really hope it comes through."

"Dude," Jensen said, the corners of his mouth drooping in exaggerated hurt, reminding Zack of his dad, another silver-haired charmer who could not be trusted. "That stings, man."

Jensen stepped forward and clutched Zack's shoulder. Hard.

Jesus, the old guy had freakin' Wolverine hands, Zack thought. "Have I ever steered you wrong?"

Zack wanted to be honest, explain that, yes, in fact, Jensen had made empty promises before. Of a raise, a new title, even back-pedaling from small assurances—like not giving Zack the coveted always-full morning classes Bri Lee taught. But he knew it was a mistake to be transparent with Jensen, who had enough money and power to coerce, even if gently, his employees to give him only the answers he wanted to hear.

"Never, man," Zack said. "As if! You're always there for me, Jens. And"—Zack placed his hands in yogi prayer at the center of his chest, even added a little head bow for full effect—"I'm grateful. Always." Eager to change the topic, hoping it would make Jensen release his grip on Zack's shoulder, he waved at the new Porsche. "And this car is freaking sweet!"

"Isn't she, though? Want to go for a quick spin?"

Zack hesitated. The last thing he wanted to do now, when Mel was waiting to jump into a Lyft and come to him, finally *be* with him, was get in a car with Jensen. Even if he was his boss, even if he did just offer Zack his dream job.

"You know, bro, I'm super-fried from teaching tonight. Three back-to-back full classes. I'm dying to get home and crash. Can I take a raincheck?" He knew this was not the answer Jensen wanted, even before Jensen stepped back, let his hand drop from Zack's shoulder (finally). Jensen looked at him with the same squinty disappoint-ment Zack had seen on his dad's face so many times, especially after Misty Whatever had made her BS charge and John-John had to bail Zack out of jail.

"Aw, come on, buddy. Why you gotta be like that?" Jensen put on a sad face. "I'm leaving for another week in the morning. You're not looking to crush this epic good-news buzz, are you?"

"Um, it's not that I don't *want* to . . ." John-John also had this same gift—the ability to push and push, transform a subtle threat into an accusation of hurt. *How could you?*

"Trust me, you don't want to wait that long to experience acceleration like this. All you have to do is sit back and relax! I'll have you back here in fifteen minutes. You'll be glad you did it." His voice was so hopeful—almost pleading—that Zack didn't have the heart to say no. Even if he did not trust Jensen. Even if it almost killed him to delay Mel's arrival even further. He consoled himself by remembering she was a night owl, often staying up until two and three in the morning. And he couldn't wait to tell her about his new job!

"Okay, dude. I'm in," he said to Jensen. "Let me just send a quick text."

"Yesssss!" said Jensen, opening the driver's-side door.

Zack typed a text to Mel as quickly as he could. So so sorry but Jensen just dropped into gym and I need another 15 min or so. He's leaving really soon then you can come, I'll even come pick u up if that's better, just hang tight and I'll text u as soon as coast is clear sorry can't wait xoxoxo

Five minutes later, Zack couldn't stop himself from whooping as Jensen drove way too fast down the PCH, accelerating into the curves that lined the bluffs as the Porsche blazed north along the ocean. Jensen cracked the windows so the night air swirled into the car, and Zack tasted the brine rolling off the sea mingled with exhaust. Bruce Springsteen blasted out from the luxury sound system, and for a moment, Zack lost himself, singing along with Jensen to "Born to Run," riding an unexpected wave of happiness.

He closed his eyes, inhaled the tang of new leather, and pretended it was *his* new car. Mel in the passenger seat dancing with abandon, making him laugh with her fist pumps, all the while looking sexy as hell, the tops of her breasts jiggling in a low-cut tank top.

He sang loud enough to make his throat ache.

Maybe, Zack hoped, this was the start of a new life, not just for him but for the two of them. Malibu, though less than twenty miles from Santa Monica, was its own cozy community. A playground for rich celebrities, sure, but also a secluded haven for aging surfers and bohemians. Mel would love it there. He imagined them in a little bungalow above the beach, the metal shutters rusted by salt air. A welcome mat at the front door. *Zack + Mel.*

Jensen interrupted Zack's fantasy, shouting through the whir of the wind whipping in through the open windows, "Screw going back to the gym, Z! You can clean up tomorrow. I got some cigars and a bottle of twenty-year-old single malt back home. I know you're a teetotaler like me but, hey, let's celebrate properly. You down?"

"No, man," Zack said, a bit more harshly than he'd intended. "I mean, maybe another night. I'm beat."

"What the hey," Jensen said, switching lanes at the last minute, darting in front of a truck, Zack clutching the side of the passenger door. "You'd think my number-one employee, who just got a hella big promotion, would be down for a quick drink with his boss."

Zack's good-news high deflated. What was the deal with this guy who refused to accept *no*? He heard Mel's voice. *White man privilege, simple as that.*

"You got a piece waiting for you tonight? Is that the real story, you dirty dawg?" Jensen slugged him in the chest. Zack stopped himself from wincing, and from telling Jensen to keep both hands on the wheel of the speeding car.

"No, man. I wouldn't lie to you. You know I wouldn't—as you said—fish where I swim."

Jensen let out a bark of a laugh.

"Not that this stops the CT ladies from falling all over themselves," Zack added, giving Jensen what he assumed he wanted to hear—bro-talk. "Begging me to show them *proper form* for lifting, if you know what I mean."

"Oh, indeed I do," Jensen said. "Bitches they be begging! It's cool if you hit that shit."

"What? No!" Zack steadied his voice. "I mean, that's just *totally* not my thing, man." Could Jensen know about Mel? And if he did, so what?

"Sure, it's not," Jensen said, drawing out the *Sure*. "Let's head to my place, where you can tell me all about the women you are in no way banging."

Zack wouldn't be swayed into doing something he did not want to do, and the way Jensen was weaving in and out of lanes without using his signal was starting to freak him out. Not to mention, the lewdness—what kind of employer used that language? (*Monstrously offensive language*, he heard Mel say.) Sure, they'd bonded through a few politically incorrect rants in the gym's back office, but Jensen grilling Zack about his sex life was just gross. He wanted out of this car. He wanted Mel—the warmth of her soft flesh scented by the oil she dabbed between her breasts.

"I want to go back," Zack said, trying to sound stern. "Take me back, man."

"Have it your way," Jensen grumbled and made a sharp last-minute exit onto Topanga that tossed Zack into the side door. Zack swallowed a *What the fuck*. Jensen flipped a tight U-turn (the car *was* epic, Zack had to admit), and gunned back toward Santa Monica.

Zack turned up the stereo's volume to fill the silence of the return trip, fifteen minutes that felt like an eternity. Were things tense now? Had he screwed up enough that Jensen might renege the Malibu offer?

"Nothing better than Bruce!" Zack shouted as he tapped "Born to Run" on the car's display screen. "He deserves a freakin' encore."

"Right on!" Jensen said, pumping a fist in the air. Zack was relieved to see that wide smile back on his boss's face, Jensen's bleached teeth twilight-blue in the seaside night. "The Boss is a true patriot!"

As the car raced back down the PCH toward the Santa Monica Pier, the neon lights on the Ferris wheel spokes flashed the color of flames—yellow, red, orange. A beacon, Zack thought, calling him home. To Mel. A sign from the Heavenly Father above, St. Thérèse might claim.

At last I have found my vocation. My vocation is love . . . I will be love, and then I will be all things.

Finally, Jensen turned back into the lot of Color Theory and braked hard, two inches from the dumpster, then pulled Zack into an awkward hug across the gear shift.

"Thanks for indulging me, Z-man. You're the best. Get home to bed and I'll have a contract ready for you to review just as soon as I'm back from Maui."

"Can't wait, Jens," said Zack, opening the passenger door. "I'm pumped. And thanks for the ride. This car is sick."

"We'll get you one too, before long," said Jensen. "Soon as you kill it in Malibu."

As soon as Jensen's taillights disappeared from the parking lot, Zack texted Mel. He was shaky with adrenaline—from the ride and the anticipation of finally, *finally*, getting to touch her.

Okay!!!! all clear NOW! pls hurry or lmk if you want me to pick you up. Otherwise I'll be waiting in the back of CT. He added the emoji with hearts for eyes and hurried back into the office.

He locked the door, shut the blinds, and tried to read an article— "Mark Wahlberg's Core-Blasting Workout"—in *Men's Health* while he waited for Mel to respond.

Five minutes passed, then ten. It was after eleven now; could she have fallen asleep?

He told himself to be patient. Mel was prone to distraction and losing track of time; perhaps she'd gotten into a conversation with Lettie, who, he reminded himself, was there to babysit; or maybe Sloane had woken up and needed her mom.

When fifteen minutes had passed, Zack closed the magazine and sent another text: U okay???

Almost instantaneously, she replied. Yes & no. I'm sososo sorry, but I'm not coming. I can't get into it now, but we have to stop. I know telling you over text is lame/cowardly. I swear I was going to do it in person tonight but now it's late and I just can't. I know I should SHOW UP and OWN IT etc. But you know I suck at those things. I'm really really sorry but please respect my decision and trust me that it's necessary. Thank you for everything & take good care.

He read the words again and again, not fully comprehending—actually wondering, for a moment, if they might have been written for someone else.

Surely, Mel could not mean this. The text could not have come from the same person, who, just a week ago, was draped naked on top of Zack in a hotel room, begging him to do things she claimed she'd *never done with another man.*

Breath quickening, he texted her back. No. I'm not accepting this. We have to talk. In person. Now. Please come to the gym. Just for a minute. Please Melissa.

When he hit *Send*, the message did not behave as it usually did. Instead of transforming to a white bubble on his screen with *delivered* at the bottom, it turned green.

She had blocked his number. Zack jumped up from the desk, grabbed his phone, and with all his might, pitched it straight into the wall.

SATURDAY, FEBRUARY 2, 2019

33

MEL

"Pressure, Sloanie, pressure!" Mel shouted as Sloane fought for the ball only a few feet away from the opponent's goal. *Pressure* was code for *fight*—a word, Mel had learned after being reprimanded by Coach Crystal herself, considered too combative for a ten-year-old-girls' soccer game.

Sloane, at least four inches shorter than every girl in the pack closing in on her, took a flailing kick (no, Mel thought, not the left foot) and the ball bounced off the goalpost.

Awww, the spectators on the Santa Monica side groaned.

"Do it again!" Mel shouted through cupped hands. "You got this, Tsunamis!"

She watched Adam, who was subbing for a side ref who hadn't shown, hustle down the field in his bumble-bee-yellow referee shirt and black shorts, long black regulation socks pulled up to his knees.

There was a time she'd actually found those socks sexy. Now, he looked ridiculous. Even though she'd accepted Adam had never cheated on her, something between them still felt broken, despite the fact that he was trying harder than ever to restore their marriage. He'd dialed back the criticism. Had stopped telling her to "find ways to relax" or "take better care of herself." He'd been on his best behavior. Not once, since the session in Janet's "office" had he suggested "Mommy needs her medicine." Was that really something to be grateful for? Mel wondered. Was it enough to save a marriage?

She still felt hurt. Rattled. As if she had PTSD from his imaginary cheating.

Also, she missed Zack.

She missed Regina, too. It was no wonder the woman looked the way she did, Mel understood now: Regina's willpower was hard as diamonds. No matter how many texts Mel sent, pleading for forgiveness, Regina continued to act as if Mel didn't exist.

Mel watched a throng of girls race down the field, their ponytails leaping off their backs. The striker on the other team, a gazelle of a girl wearing two tight French braids, elbowed Sloane in the ribs. The center ref, a dad with a ponytail of his own, did not issue a call.

"Come on, ref!" Mel screamed. "That's a foul!"

"Shhh, Mom," said Coach Crystal. It was when she was most irritated, Mel knew, that Coach C referred to the soccer parents, whose names she knew well, as *Mom* or *Dad*.

Mel wished she could text Zack. She pulled out her phone and stared at the screen, imagining what she'd write.

At the soccer game watching my special snowflake. Coach could learn a thing or two from you. #winningIS everything.

But that was the only place Zack could live—in her imagination. A week after that horrific meeting at Sloane's school, she'd cut all ties. Blocked his number on her phone. Deleted every single one of her social media accounts. But Zack was still with her—his voice in her head, his scent on her clothes, in her car. The memory of his hands, his tongue, on her skin. But she was, as therapist Janet might say, in *healing mode*.

"Earth to Mel!"

She looked up to see Adam standing in front of her, swigging Gatorade, sweat coating his handsome face.

"Oh! Hey!"

"Sloanie and I have been trying to get your attention. Put down the phone, babe."

"Sorry."

A whistle screamed and Adam darted back onto the field.

Dammit, she thought, dropping her phone back into her purse. She needed to be more present. More thoughtful, more *engaged.* All the things she'd promised in the two therapy sessions she and Adam had had with Janet since . . . well, since the shit hit the fan, Mel thought. She'd had to email Janet and apologize for going MIA those two Zack-filled months. In Janet's incense-scented back house, Mel had flagellated herself again and again in front of Adam, coming clean about her anger, and the hurtful mistakes she'd made— the abusive comments made to Adam (in front of Sloane, twice as bad), the mood swings that disrupted their family's life, the late-night medical marijuana deliveries, the bingeing on Sloane's school snacks until she had to stick a finger down her throat.

Mel had come clean about everything. *Except* Zack.

No one, not even Janet, knew about Zack. Certainly not Adam, with his die-hard moral center. They'd both been unforgiving of close friends who'd turned out to be cheating spouses. There was no way Adam would forgive her. As Adam himself had told her more than once, sometimes honesty was too much.

The whistle blew. Only one quarter left. The thought of the game ending, of having to go back to her house, back to her life, made Mel feel hollow. If there was one part of her life that had its shit together, maybe the only part, it was her soccer-momhood.

Why couldn't this be enough? Why couldn't she just be a soccer mom, with a star player for a daughter and a star filmmaker for a husband?

"Mom!" Sloane appeared, panting for breath, gulping air between gulps of water.

"Spray me!"

Mel picked up a blue water pump from the grass and sprayed a fine mist around Sloane's head.

"Aaah," Sloane sighed. "More, more!"

The spray caught the sunlight, and Mel watched a rainbow arch over her daughter's goggled face.

This, Mel thought. *This right here. Right now. This is enough.*

"You're kicking butt out there, baby," she said, leaning in to peck Sloane's cheek. "Just make sure you're first to the ball, 'kay? You're faster than those big girls."

"Mom," Sloane groaned, "Coach C is my coach. She says *she* is the only person who should be doing any coaching. *Not* the parents."

"Oh, did she?"

But Sloane had already run off.

Mel tried to get back in the game. To lose herself in the back and forth of the girls' passing. Pass, pass, pass, lulling her into a trance until, *bam*, one girl broke away with the ball—*her* girl!—Sloane zigzagging up the field toward the goal, faking out one, two, three girls, almost close enough to shoot, almost, and then a beast of a girl, number twelve, rammed a shoulder into the side of Sloanie's head, throwing her to the ground.

"Oh my God." Mel gasped into her hand, ready to run on the field and carry her baby off if she had to. But, as usual, Adam was there first, bending over Sloane so Mel could only see their daughter's short legs, her blue-and-gold-striped socks.

Both sides of the field erupted in applause as Sloane got to her feet and waved her fist in the air.

"Woo-hoo!" Mel screamed, eyes watering. "That's my fierce girl! Shake it off! Way to go, Sloane!"

"Melissa, *shhhh*," hissed Coach Crystal. "Give her a moment to recover. Did you see my email about not overreacting when players are down?"

"There are so many soccer emails," Mel said. "I'm sure I got it, but . . ."

"I'll resend it to you," interrupted Coach C.

Mel wanted to reach out and swipe Coach's *Tsunami* visor off her head—one of twelve Melissa had paid to have custom-made for every member of the team. How dare Coach C speak to her that way? After everything Mel had done for the Tsunamis?

Keep it together, she imagined Adam telling her. *For Sloane.*

"So sorry about that, Coach C. I'll be more on top of things from here on out."

"Good," the coach said with a curt nod.

Mel forced a smiled and turned away from the game. She needed a break from the nonstop cheering, from Coach C's judgment. She drifted away from the chaos of the field, until she found a shady patch of grass under a peeling eucalyptus tree, the ground covered with thin rolls of bark like holiday wrapping paper. She eased down into the grass and sat with her back against the tree, cross-legged, and forced herself to count slow breaths, the way Janet had taught her, claiming it *soothed the parasympathetic nervous system* and *eased the need to consume.*

One. Exhale. Two.

The need to consume. Would Mel ever defeat it? Would she ever become stronger than the tug of food, of TV, of her stupid virtual sheep farm app, of marijuana? Of any distraction she could find that blotted out the unnamable dread throbbing deep inside her?

Exhale. Three.

She imagined herself empty inside. Hollow and clean. A vessel ready, as Bri liked to say, to FILL WITH LIGHT.

Four. Exhale. Five.

Mel imagined herself filling with LIGHT.

She was LIGHT.

"Mel," a voice whispered softly. So softly she was sure it had come from her own mind.

Then she felt the hand on her shoulder. She opened her eyes to see Zack crouching beside her, under the tree. Mel bolted to her feet, using the tree for balance, and took a step back.

It was really him. His hair longer, his cheeks and chin stubbled. A look of earnest pain on his face.

"What are you doing here?" she hissed. "Jesus fucking Christ."

"Whoa." Zack raised his hands, palms facing her. "Come on now. Don't get *Him* involved." He chuckled weakly, but Mel didn't crack a smile.

"You can't be here, Zack." Her voice already trembling. "You need to go. *Now*."

He grabbed her hand. She yanked it away, but not before a buzzy heat shot up her arm and into her chest. "Is it Adam? Is *he* making you do this? Push me away?"

"No, Zack," she said. "It's me. *I* made a mistake. With you."

His face went dark, like a terrible understanding had rolled over him.

The muscle in his jaw wriggled. "Was it Lettie, then? What did she tell you about me?"

"Lettie? What are you talking about?"

"I'm a good guy, Mel," he said, voice pleading. "I would never hurt you."

"Hurt me?" She felt woozy with confusion.

The whistle blew long and high behind them and Mel remembered that Zack was standing beside her in full view of her family— Adam and Sloane were less than a hundred feet away, on the soccer field. Not to mention Coach C, and Assistant Coach Hazel, along with Mel's entire soccer community.

"You have to go." She raised her palm and took another step away from him. "Please. My family's right over there. I can't lose them."

"I need to talk to you."

She turned to face the field. She would not look at him again.

"I'm leaving," she said. "Please walk the other way."

Back at the field, Mel saw two rows of girls, one wearing blue and gold, the other red and black, high-fiving each other. The game was over, and, Mel could see from the slumped shoulders of Sloane and her teammates, the Tsunamis had lost.

Goddammit.

She felt Zack's hand on her back.

"Melissa. I miss you. I miss us."

"Don't touch me," she said through clenched teeth, sidestepping away. "My husband is *right there*."

Guilt rippled through her as she spoke the words, and she ached for Zack. Wished she could allow his fingers to keep playing over her back. That he could lead her by the arm to his dumpy truck where she would bury her face in his neck and breathe in his scent, feel his mouth hot and wet over hers.

"I'm walking away now, Zack," she said, but didn't.

"Two minutes. Please."

She scanned the soccer field for Adam; he was huddled in the center of the field with the other refs, filling out end-of-game forms. Only Sloane, standing alone with a soccer ball tucked under her arm, seemed aware of her mother's whereabouts. She appeared to be staring straight at Mel and Zack. Much too far away for Mel to read her features, but Mel imagined disgust warping her daughter's angelic face.

"Zack," Mel said. "It's over."

"I'm not giving up on us."

"Please do."

She started down the long grassy slope leading away from the soccer field toward the tennis courts, unsure of where she was going, only that she had to get *away*.

"Mel. Wait." Zack was begging.

Her willpower vanished and she looked back at him. He stood as solid as marble, one muscled hip jutting forward, his arms outstretched in disbelief. All she had to do was blink to remember him

naked. Her resolve melted and she yearned to touch him. He sensed
the shift and the smallest smile crossed his face. Her mind flashed
to their last few hours together, under the crisp white sheets at the
Malibu Beach Inn, the fireplace roaring, the feel of their bodies
glued together, moving in furtive sync with the Pacific waves pounding the shore right outside their window.

"Look. I don't need a version two you, Mel. I . . . I love the *you*—
the you that you already are. There, I said it."

She closed her eyes and shook her head, trying to contain the
joy his words sparked inside her. To push it down and stomp on it.
To remind him—both of them—that they would never be together.
Not in this life. This life was for Adam and Sloane.

Perhaps in another, she told herself.

"No," she said softly.

He stared at the ground, holding the back of his neck in his
palm. When he finally looked up at her, she saw he was giving up.

Then he held up his hand for a high five.

"You've got to be kidding me," said Mel.

"Please," Zack said. "Just a high five. I just need to touch you one
last time. Nobody's paying attention. And even if they are, it's a high
five. At a kid's soccer game. Everyone's high-fiving."

She lifted her palm to his and their hands clasped together in
the air, fingers tangled, locking together with urgency.

From the field, she heard the winning team shout, "We are
proud of you! So very proud of you!" She snatched her hand away
from Zack's and backed away from him.

"Don't ever show up like this again," she warned. "Or you'll be
sorry."

Then she turned and ran to the soccer field, to her family, her
life.

MONDAY, FEBRUARY 11, 2019

34

REGINA

THE MESSAGE WAS WAITING FOR REGINA WHEN SHE SETTLED IN FRONT OF her laptop at six thirty in the morning to check email while she sipped her coffee. At the top of her inbox was Lindsey Leyner's name, and when Regina clicked on the message, she found it was addressed to all the women who'd gone to Minnow Night, plus a dozen others.

> Subject: WOOLSEY FIRE WORKOUT BENEFIT [please read!!!]
>
> Hey guys! As some of us were discussing at the last Minnow Night, it's in our power to do something to HELP the most powerless victims of the Woolsey Fire: DOMESTIC WORKERS. (Read this great article if you haven't yet!—www.DisplacedDomestics.com) I'm writing to let you know that I will be organizing a benefit to raise money for this cause in the form of a donation-based, super-fun group fitness event, co-sponsored by none other than the BEST gym in all of Los Angeles, COLOR THEORY. I've secured a date—March 2—and a group of coaches to lead us. But I still need a VENUE, as my own home is being re-landscaped over the next month. Anyone out there have a space they might volunteer for an AMAZING cause? Please let me know ASAP & we'll SPREAD THE WORD. Let's pool our resources to do the right thing!!!!
>
> Xoxoxo LINDSEY

Regina stared at the screen in disbelief. As low as her opinion of Lindsey was, she still was shocked that Lindsey so blatantly, unapologetically repurposed Version Two You! Could her pea-sized brain truly not have come up with something more original?

Regina hit *Reply All* and sipped her coffee as she tried to come up with the perfect response. She wanted to let the group know Lindsey was ripping her off but also to support the cause, duh.

But before she could think what to write, a response to the message appeared in her inbox.

FROM: Melissa Goldberg

SUBJ: re: WOOLSEY FIRE WORKOUT BENEFIT [please read!!!]

Hi, all! Lindsey, I love this idea. It's a cause close to my heart. I would be more than happy to host the Woolsey Fire Benefit at my home on March 2nd.

Warmly, Mel

Regina set her mug down so hard that coffee sloshed onto her keyboard. She wiped it away with her sleeve and slapped the laptop shut. She hadn't been to Color Theory in almost a month, taking advantage of the free-first-week trials offered by the countless other gyms in Santa Monica. Nor had she had any contact with Zack since her first payment from BeastMode Wellness had come in last week, and she'd instructed him to stop the transfers. She still owed him around $3,500, which she *did* plan to give him—she wasn't an asshole—just as soon as she got around to it.

As for Mel and Lindsey Leyner—Regina hadn't communicated with either of them since Minnow Night.

But she'd be damned if she let them all come together for a workout without her. Hadn't it been Regina who introduced each of these women to Color Theory? Hadn't every one of these women called her some version of *Workout Queen*? Plus, not showing up would make her look worse than Lindsey Leyner, that callous . . . Regina would find a way to show up, to claim what rightfully belonged to her, and, most importantly, save face.

She was, after all, trying to fix her mistakes. On her way to becoming a better person. Regina 2.0.

THURSDAY, FEBRUARY 14, 2019

35

ZACK

IN THE ENTRYWAY OF HIS APARTMENT BUILDING, ZACK TURNED HIS KEY IN the lock of his mailbox and pulled open the flimsy metal door. Sometimes he went days, an entire week, even, without checking his mail, but the adoption agency had told him to expect a decision in mid-February and today was the fourteenth.

Valentine's Day.

A day for lovers. A silly holiday of course, but still, today more than ever, he'd been unable to stop thinking of Mel. Whom he had not seen or heard from in almost two weeks. This morning, he'd taught four in a row at Color Theory, his usual upbeat cheer nearly impossible to summon, much less make the dumb little Valentine's jokes he usually cracked. Irrationally, he'd hoped—okay, *prayed*, even—that Mel might show up for a class. Even though she hadn't been at the gym in weeks. His sole consolation was the upcoming Woolsey Fire Benefit, the workout-for-charity event in which Jensen insisted every Color Theory staffer participate. The fundraiser was slated to take place in none other than Melissa Goldberg's backyard.

Zack's narrow mailbox was stuffed with paper, much of it crumpled and crushed to the bottom of the tight space. He pulled them out, a fat clog of envelopes, promotional postcards, Trader Joe's newsletters, and fitness magazines.

And then there it was: a manila envelope with the adoption agency's logo in the upper corner.

It was thinner than he'd expected.

He ripped it open and began to read the document on top.

> *Dear Mr. Doheny,*
> *Thank you for your application to attain legal guardian-*
> *ship of Andres Manuel Mendoza. We regret to inform you that*
> *we could not grant approval, due to your prior Class-A Mis-*
> *demeanor for Aggravated Criminal Sexual Assault Conviction*
> *issued in the State of Florida on October 11, 2010. Enclosed you*
> *will find supporting documentation for this final decision . . .*

Nausea shot through him. He leaned on the wall for support. His breath shortened, his legs wobbled.

Misty Whatever. Back to haunt him.

Her and all the others. Forever haunting him, conspiring, it seemed, to bring him down. Why *him*? They hated him: all the girls from his youth in Florida, Misty Whatever and Casey from the laundry room, not-Arianna-on-Adelaide Drive, Regina and Lettie. And now, Mel. Each, in her own way, had made him choke, falter, fall on his sword. Made him learn to hate himself.

Thérèse: One must have passed through the tunnel to understand how black its darkness is.

An accumulation of angry women, turning his life to shit.

Bringing him to where he was now, at this moment, forehead pressed to the wall of his decrepit, overpriced apartment building on Pico, his tears falling on the scuffed, peeling surface.

He could not adopt Andres. If Lettie were deported, as she assured him she would be, any day now, her son would be placed in foster care—who knew where—and Zack might not see the sweet, limping little boy ever again.

It was too much. He already had nothing. No acting career, no real friends, no money, no Mel. And now, no Andres. His life was destined to sink further and further into its negative balance.

He swatted his tears away and ripped the documents from the adoption agency into quarters. The desire to see Mel gripped him with such force, he felt powerless against it.

Just to see her. She didn't need to know. Just a glimpse of her would comfort him. She and Andres were all he had left.

And soon, Zack would not have Andres either.

He dropped all of his mail, including the adoption documents he'd just torn, into the wastebasket by the front door of his building and stepped back outside into yet another brilliantly clear and sunny afternoon. He climbed into his Tacoma and started the engine, but before he accelerated in the direction of Georgina Avenue, he pulled out his phone. Dialed *67 to block his number, then called Banc of California corporate customer service. A woman picked up on the second ring and introduced herself as Natalie.

Zack introduced himself as Jensen Davis. Calling from Color Theory gym to start the process for filing a fraud claim against a former corporate customer. A marketing firm called Big Rad Wolfe, LLC.

"Absolutely, sir," said Natalie. "I'd be happy to get that process started for you. I'll need to start by asking you a few questions . . ."

Zack answered the questions as he drove in the direction of Mel's house, never hesitating or stumbling over his words, delivering a compelling, airtight story—the way, he thought to himself, only a halfway-decent actor could. When Natalie finished her questions, she assured him ("Mr. Davis") that she'd filed an inquiry with the bank's fraud prevention team, making note of his particular concern regarding Big Rad Wolfe, LLC, and that he could expect a response from them within thirty days.

Zack's hands shook as he thanked Natalie and ended the call. He knew he was taking a major risk. Knew that in reporting Regina, he was essentially turning himself in, too. But he was prepared to use the skills he'd learned from her—Regina, the consummate liar, his mentor in crime—to defend himself. Yes, the actual computer transfers might be traced to him—it wouldn't be hard to piece to-gether the laptop's IP address and Zack's log-in times—but he was prepared to play dumb. To insist, with utter wide-eyed conviction, that he'd made an honest mistake—perhaps reprocessed old in-voices, or confused her with another vendor, or something. He'd figure it out. What mattered was that Regina, thanks to her insis-tence on paying him in cash—had no proof that she'd paid Zack to help her. And since Zack had simply handed the money over to Let-tie (minus the $3,500 Regina had stiffed him—his rage over it had since turned to relief—the less of her dirty money he'd touched, the better), there was no proof he'd ever had it in the first place.

Still: calling the bank to rat out Regina had been a questionable impulse, indulged, Zack admitted to himself, in a burst of raw emo-tion. But it was too late now. What was done was done. And anyway, since he'd lost both Mel and the prospect of adopting Andres, the risk he'd incurred seemed less menacing. He was pretty confident in his ability to convince authorities—if it came down to it—that he'd simply been a sloppy bookkeeper, a meathead fitness coach armed with nothing but an AA degree from a shitty community college, clearly unqualified to manage the vast and complicated finances of Color Theory. He'd summon fake tears to his eyes and blink with confusion, knowing how the sight of a man like him, strong and handsome, in the throes of emotional distress tended to move peo-ple. His looks had always been his superpower, and he would not hesitate to use it.

In the end, he told himself, as he cruised down Wilshire with Macklemore blasting on the truck stereo, the only hard proof in the case was that Regina had kept a large sum of money erroneously transferred to her account. She had not notified Color Theory of the error, or returned the funds, as any ethical business owner would have done.

Well, thought Zack, drumming his fingers on the steering wheel, just let Regina Wolfe *try* to take him out. He would not back down, would never confess to having been her partner in crime. He'd rather die first.

He thought of Thérèse: *My whole strength lies in prayer and sacrifice, these are my invincible arms; they can move hearts far better than words.*

The words gave him fresh hope as he drove north across town, toward the grand houses lining Georgina Avenue.

36

MEL

"I love Minimum Days," said Sloane, expertly spearing a piece of salmon sashimi with her chopsticks. In the middle of the afternoon on Valentine's Day, she sat between Adam and Mel at the breakfast nook in the kitchen window, the three of them sharing a platter of take-out sushi.

"You can say that again," said Adam, pouring miso soup into the pretty Japanese stone bowls Mel had gotten him for his birthday last year.

"I love Minimum Days," Sloane repeated, giggling.

"Me too," said Mel, trying to sound convincing, though she resented the many ordinary school days declared "Minimums" by John Wayne Elementary, meaning that school ended at one thirty instead of three o'clock, always for some utterly inessential reason. Today, for example, the PTA (Mel made the "strongly recommended" contribution of two grand to join, but had never attended a single meeting) needed to decorate for that evening's Friendship Fiesta, their careful euphemism for a Valentine's Day Dance, as if any direct reference to the romantic holiday would cause the children to instantly rip their clothes off.

Then again, given the texts—ugh, *sexts*—Sloane had been swapping with Tyler Fabian, Mel didn't mind the name of the dance quite as much as she normally would. Although Sloane had been on her best behavior since the meeting with the principal, accepting without protest her full month of No Screen Time of Any Kind, and dialing back her snarkiness, Mel still couldn't see her daughter in quite the same way as she had. A certain innocence had been lost, the door to puberty's menace flung wide open.

More than anything, Mel couldn't stop wondering if she'd been responsible for her daughter's troubling behavior. Yes, the sexts had happened before Mel had climbed into the van with Zack, but could Sloane somehow have sensed the terrible, family-wrecking choices her mother was going to make? Could the sexts have been some sort of preemptive cry for help, Sloane's subconscious attempt to throw Mel off her disastrous course? Sloane was noticeably happier since her parents had reinstated kindness in their marriage—the kindness Mel had derailed in the first place.

What sort of mother left her daughter in aftercare an extra hour so that she might tear off the clothes of a thirty-two-year-old gym coach who had voted for Trump?

Stop it, Mel commanded herself, taking a sip of miso soup. Since she'd ended things with Zack and recommitted to her (noncheating, exceptionally handsome) husband, her self-loathing had ratcheted up higher than ever.

"You okay, Mom?" Sloane asked. "You're doing a weird resting face." She tipped her head and peered at Mel curiously, eyes wide.

"I'm fine, honey. I was just . . ." Mel's voice caught in her throat. How had she let herself risk hurting her sensitive, quirky, brilliant little girl by having—she forced herself to think the accurate description—an *affair*?

"Meditating?" guessed Sloane.

"Something like that," said Mel.

"How lucky am I," Adam said, clearly sensing Mel's mood and hoping to lighten it, "to be having lunch with both my girls today?"

"*Women*," corrected Sloane. "Right, Mom?"

"Sorry," said Adam quickly. "Women." Mel knew he was trying;

normally, he would have responded with some sarcastic, barely cloaked criticism of her—*Well, Mommy is the word police*, she could almost hear him saying.

Instead, Adam was being *nice* to her. So why wasn't she feeling more grateful? After all, she'd been wrong about him. Dead wrong. And those fawning Santa Monica mothers, the ones who'd batted their lash extensions at Adam during soccer games, the ones Mel had privately labeled *ditzes*, had been right: Adam was a good man. The best, really. And somehow, he still belonged to Mel. Her life was full again.

So why did she feel so empty?

Adam lifted his ceramic teacup. "A toast, please. To my favorite *women*."

"Hashtag cheesy!" said Sloane, but clinked her cup to Adam's with a grin, and Mel could hear the delight in her daughter's voice. She willed herself to focus on this—her happy family, sitting in their beautiful kitchen, winter sunshine pouring through the leaves of the magnolia in their front yard—and ignore the fact that Sloane's *hashtag* comment had caused Zack's face to appear in her mind, his aqua eyes and brown curls as clear and vivid as a photo.

Mel wasn't completely sure he'd be attending the Woolsey Fire Benefit, which she'd impulsively offered to host, but a part of her hoped, desperately, that he would.

No. Zack was the past. Mel now lived in the present, just as everyone in Southern California had been suggesting for the past two years. Facing forward.

Who was she becoming? Was it possible she was losing her inner Brooklyn? Had leaving New York made her not only a shitty, lust-crazed wife and negligent mother, but also shallow, just another California mom floating from school drop-off to the gym to Whole Foods and kids' soccer games on the beach?

Sloane abruptly dropped her chopsticks onto the table and

leaned forward, toward the large window facing the front yard and Georgina Avenue and beyond, as if suddenly hypnotized by something outside.

"What is it, honey?" said Mel.

Sloane extended her arm and pointed toward the street.

"Look," she said. "Someone's spying on us."

Mel and Adam looked.

Idling on the curb directly in front of their house was a rusted maroon pickup truck.

Mel felt the miso soup and seaweed salad she'd just eaten rise. Zack was sitting right there, in broad daylight, with the window rolled down, his elbow propped casually on the frame.

"Hey," said Sloane. "I know that guy!"

"You do?" said Adam, sounding genuinely curious.

Mel was sure she was going to throw up. Maybe this was it: the punishment for her sins. The premature arrival of the hell she'd been so certain didn't exist. You didn't get to do what she'd done—fuck a guy who wasn't your husband in half the hotels of Los Angeles County—and get away with it.

"Yeah," said Sloane. "That's the guy mom was holding hands with at my soccer game."

"Oh," said Adam. "Is it?"

Mel snapped into survival mode. "Holding hands? *What?*" She tried her best to sound incredulous. She might be a terrible, weak person, but she didn't deserve to lose her family *now*, in one fell swoop.

Did she?

"And why were you holding his hand, Mel?" said Adam calmly.

"Holding hands? Ha! Not at all. Though I can see why you thought that, Sloanie. That's just some . . . trainer guy from my old gym. I bumped into him at Clover Park a few weeks ago and he gave me a high five. He's always giving everyone high fives! He's, like, famous for it. It's a . . . like a tic. He's kind of an . . . idiot." She heard her-self stumbling over her words, saying *like* too much, as if she were a teenager caught breaking curfew.

In short, acting guilty.

Shit shit shit.

"Is he also 'kind of' a stalker?" said Adam, hooking his fingers into air quotes. "Because showing up at the home of a client from the gym strikes me as odd behavior."

Out of nowhere, Regina flashed to her mind. Mel could almost hear her saying, *You got this, Goldberg*, in her firm, imperturbable way.

What would Regina do in this very moment?

Breathe, Mel commanded herself.

Then she turned to Adam and forced what she hoped was a con-fident smile. A Regina smile. "You know what? I bet I know why he's here. You remember how I'm hosting that community fitness event thingy next week? The fundraiser for the Woolsey Fire victims? I'm sure I told you, but maybe I—"

"I remember," Adam interrupted. "What's it got to do with any-thing?"

"That trainer." She gestured to the window. "He's . . . involved with the event. He's probably just scoping out the location. The event is kind of high-pressure. And he's kind of an idiot."

"You mentioned that already," said Adam, ice-cold. "Call me crazy, but I don't like idiots loitering outside my house."

"I can go—talk to him," she managed, through her nausea, feel-ing her heart accelerate to what felt like a hazardous pace. Surely, she was in the red zone. "I'll go tell him to leave."

Her attempt to conjure cool and capable Regina had failed.

"That won't be necessary," said Adam, rising from the table, still holding his chopsticks, the "hand-sharpened" ones made of cherry bark that Mel had purchased from the Brentwood Country Mart at a whopping price. *You could literally stab someone with these*, the dippy cashier had said with a laugh as he rang her up. "I'll go have a word with him."

"Careful, Dad!" said Sloane. "I saw that guy's muscles at the park. They're huge."

"So are mine," said Adam, and before Mel could stop him, he blazed out the front door.

BURN FOR MALIBU!!!
MARCH 2ND 9 AM-11 AM

COLOR THEORY IS SPONSORING A COMMUNITY EVENT TO
BENEFIT DOMESTIC WORKERS AFFECTED BY THE WOOL-
SEY FIRE. COME SWEAT IT OUT FOR THE FOLKS WHO
NEED IT MOST! LOCATION TO BE DISCLOSED UPON RSVP
AND MINIMUM DONATION PLEDGE. SEE YOU THERE!

SATURDAY, MARCH 2, 2019

37

ZACK

THE MORNING OF THE BURN FOR MALIBU! FUNDRAISER WAS ESPECIALLY dazzling, even for Santa Monica, where Zack had grown numb to the endless perfect weather. But the first weekend of March followed several days of rare spring rain, and when Zack stepped from his apartment at eight A.M., he was startled by the beauty of the sky, a cornflower-blue dome painted with fat cumulus clouds. The air tasted clean, rinsed of its usual trace of exhaust, and was so clear he could see threads of snow on the San Gabriel Mountains, sixty miles to the east.

Could anything bad possibly happen on a day like this? he wondered, climbing into his Tacoma and heading west on Pico toward the heart of Santa Monica, his adrenaline suddenly kicking in as he cut north toward Georgina Avenue, recalling the menacing look on Adam Goldberg's face on Valentine's Day as he'd strode from his house toward Zack's truck idling at the end of the driveway. Zack had peeled from the curb before Adam reached him—a cowardly move, Zack knew, but what was the alternative? A screaming match? A fight on the sidewalk, with Mister Jiu-Jitsu himself? Zack had already been lucky once, in escaping the scuffle with that pudgy Captain America back at Halloween. As much as he relished the thought of pulverizing Adam Goldberg, of smashing his chiseled jaw, Zack knew he would not be so lucky again.

What had he been thinking, showing up at the Goldberg house? That was the problem: he hadn't been thinking at all.

He'd simply been weak. He missed Mel. Combined with the news that he would not be able to adopt Andres, the thought of losing his nephew to a foster family—or a dead-end life back in Mexico—was too much for Zack to bear.

He would remain stoic this morning, he reminded himself. At least for the next several hours, during which he'd be co-leading another group workout in Mel's backyard. He'd thought of bailing, of inventing some airtight excuse for why he couldn't participate, but Jensen had insisted, reminding Zack that his new job as the head coach of Color Theory Malibu required him to *think of yourself as the face of our brand*. Which had struck Zack as a little threatening, but the bottom line was, Zack desperately wanted the management job, which was a clear step forward, an actual mark of progress in his otherwise lame-ass "career."

So, he'd agreed to show up in Mel's backyard today, telling himself he'd simply teach the class and go home. If possible, he'd talk to no one. That seemed easier than specifically avoiding Mel.

Then yesterday, he'd received Regina's text: Hey, I know it's been a while but I've been dealing with some stuff. Sorry. I did finally find that laptop of yours and will bring it to the Malibu event at Mel's tomorrow. Promise. C U there.

He'd stared at the text, shocked. *Laptop* was her code for cash. She was bringing him the cash she still owed him—just over three grand. To Mel's house.

He'd considered texting back: Don't bother, fuck you very much!

But it was a lot of money. Lettie claimed it could not save her from her legal troubles, but what if she was wrong? Practical matters were not her forte—look at how naïve she'd been in hiring that greedy, sketchy attorney off a dang billboard. Surely one more chunk of cash could help her in *some* way, especially since Zack could not make good on his offer to adopt Andres.

Which Lettie did not yet know. He'd not had the heart to tell her. Honestly, he'd rather die than tell her, he'd thought more than once since he'd crumpled up the awful adoption refusal letter and tossed it in the trash.

He'd take the money Regina owed him, Zack decided, and hand it right over to Lettie. Perhaps it would ease the bad news about Andres.

OK, he'd responded.

How had he become such a loser? Zack wondered, as he turned onto Mel's block of Georgina, already clogged with parked cars. Wasn't LA where you came to reinvent yourself, to shed your old skin for something shiny and new?

The letter from the adoption agency had reminded him that his old skin was still in place, closed in around him like a straightjacket. How foolish he'd been to think that Mel Goldberg had transformed him, that they might actually be headed toward a brand-new life together. That he'd actually let himself picture it—the bungalow in Malibu with the rusty shutters, the lazy nights together by the sea— made him seethe with embarrassment now.

He finally found a spot to park, a good block and a half from the Goldbergs' Tudor. Carrying his gym duffel, he trailed a giggling cluster of twentysomething women clad in crop tops and micro-shorts, clearly headed to the workout event. Zack steered his eyes away from their high, round bottoms and smooth, tanned legs gleaming in the sunshine. Perhaps he was still a loser, but he would not go back to his old, sinful ways with women. Never. Mel had shown him there was a better way. She had made him a better person.

He was going to see her. Any minute now.

"ALOHA, FOLKS!" JENSEN shouted at the large spandex-and-Lycra-clad crowd of about fifty or sixty—mostly women, many of whom Zack recognized from Color Theory—arranged into rows across the lush grass of Mel's backyard. "I'm truly humbled by this turnout!"

Zack stood at the front of the group between Bri and Shawn and scanned the sea of faces: Lindsey Leyner was there, of course, jogging in place in the second row, clad in head-to-toe fuchsia. He winced at the sight of Regina, who was uncharacteristically situated in the far corner of the back row, next to Sukie Reinhardt, stretching her arms over her head. Looking at her in her skin-tight mesh-paneled workout clothes, he noticed with petty satisfaction that Regina had put on a few pounds. A few months without Zack training her and she was falling apart.

"What an amazing way to kick off our Burn for Malibu! benefit," Jensen shouted to the crowd. "As one of our favorite trainers might say, hashtag blessed."

"Yeah, Zaaaaack!" yelled Bri, and a few people in the crowd whooped.

Zack cringed inwardly as he flashed a thumbs-up at Jensen. He knew Mel considered the phrase detestable, which meant that this very moment, she might be silently laughing at him. He stole a glance at her huddled with Lettie at the long refreshment table on the patio. Seeing her now in her usual all-black clothes, pushing her bangs off her forehead as she rested her palm on Lettie's shoulder—clearly, they'd become even closer—felt like a blade to Zack's gut. So much for stoicism; seeing her was torture. Pure want and need.

"The fires of last November were devastating," Jensen was saying. "Nature unleashing her wrath. But, *man*"—he pumped his fist in the air and Zack noticed the guy's arm was as hairless as a newborn—"with discipline and with faith, man can prevail over nature."

"You mean over *climate change*," someone said from the patio, just loud enough for Zack to recognize Mel's voice. His entire body bristled at the sound.

"Which is what brings us together today," Jensen continued.

Zack felt a tap on his shoulder and turned to see Adam Goldberg, dressed not in workout clothes but in some sort of metrosexual outfit—skinny jeans and a tight, pec-revealing T-shirt—like he'd just stepped out *Esquire*.

Adam lowered his face—the dude had a few inches on Zack—and spoke into Zack's ear as Jensen continued to warm up the crowd.

"Can I have a word with you?"

Stoic, Zack told himself. *You are stone.* He checked quickly for Mel, who had disappeared from the refreshment table, leaving only Lettie, who was pouring boxes of coconut water into a large glass dispenser.

"Um, sure," Zack said, realizing, immediately, that he sounded like a pussy. Where was the hot adrenaline that had been pumping through him that morning when he'd fantasized about pummeling Adam's handsome face into mush? Maybe this was his chance to show Mel his devotion, or simply prove to himself he wasn't as much of a loser as he feared.

He followed Adam around the side of the house, trying to stay calm. Surely the dude wasn't going to grapple with him right here, under the noses of fifty people in his own backyard? And if Adam did go full-blown MMA on Zack's ass, Zack hoped it would only make Adam look like an unhinged brute; Zack the victim. Would *that* be enough for Mel to return her love to him?

Adam stopped beside a tree heavy with avocados and crossed his thick arms over his chest.

"Look, buddy," he said, "I understand you're at my house today to work. So, I just wanted to remind you to do your 'work'"—Adam air-quoted—"and then get the hell out of here."

Zack thought back to the day at the park, the soccer game. Adam must've seen Zack pleading with Mel. The humiliation made Zack want to grab an avocado and stuff it whole into Adam's smug mouth.

"And without further ado," Jensen's voice boomed from the yard, "I'm proud to introduce three senior members of my staff at Color Theory Fitness. Together, they'll lead you beautiful people in an hour of intensive exercise that'll make your heart rates go crazy! Up here I've got Bri Lee, everyone's favorite early-morning drill sergeant!"

"Look, man," Zack said, "I don't know *what*—"

Adam interrupted, raising his voice to be heard above the cheers of the crowd. "No chitchatting, no lingering, no hanging out near the goddamn coconut water, and above all, no high-fiving my wife."

Zack imagined swinging at Adam, throwing punches without aim, knocking the taller, richer, more fortunate man to the ground.

"I don't know what you were doing here the other day," Adam said, "but I'm going to give you a pass. That pass expires if I see you anywhere near Melissa. You touch my wife again and I will kill you. And I don't mean figuratively speaking. Do you know what *figuratively speaking* means?"

Jensen's booming voice reminded Zack of the announcer at a pro wrestling match. "Shawn Carruthers, aka King of Quads. Let's hear it for Shawn!"

Zack took a chance—what did he have to lose, now that he'd lost everything?—and took a step toward Adam, leading with his chest, his foot landing close to Adam's designer sneakers. Just as Zack had hoped, Adam flinched, took a step backward, and stumbled on an overripe avocado split open on the ground.

Zack almost laughed. Then he heard Jensen call his name.

"And last but not least, ladies and gents," Jensen said, his excitement ratcheting up like a drumroll, "the new head trainer for Color Theory's Malibu location, coming in June! The one and only Zzzack Doheny!"

While the crowd clapped and cheered, Zack lifted his chin to Adam and spoke. "As it happens, I do know what *figuratively* means." He stepped closer still. "It's the opposite of *literally*. As in, *I literally screwed your wife*."

"Where has the Z-man gotten to?" Jensen called over the mic.

"Let's get this party started, yo!" yelled Bri.

"Thanks for the chat," Zack said to Adam. "I gotta get to, you know, *work* now. My fans are calling for me, bro." He stepped around a jaw-hung Adam and jogged around the corner of the house, back into the yard, past Bri and Shawn, toward the front of the crowd, his heart rate already up in the red zone. He noticed Mel had reappeared next to Lettie on the patio and was talking to her urgently, her hands cutting through the air as she spoke.

"Yeah, Zack attack!" he heard Lindsey Leyner scream as he reached the front of the group. The opening notes of Flo Rida's "Good Feeling" blasted over the sound system.

Zack hopped in place, beaming at the crowd.

"Hey hey, happy Saturday, y'all!" he began, launching into yet another version of the spiel he'd done hundreds of times. "My name's Zack and the first thing we're gonna do is get those hearts pumping, so everyone, give me some high knees! Forty seconds, on the clock, in three-two-one . . ."

"Get after it, people!" screamed Bri, the Tattooed Wildcat, raising her knees high enough to touch her chin.

Zack was pumped after his showdown with Adam, filled with a surge of hope. He was doing what he loved—making the world a better place by helping each of the people below bobbing up and down at his feet like worshippers feeling the Spirit of God take one step forward on their journey to a better self.

Zack counted to forty as the crowd rose and fell. He was down to five seconds when he saw the side gate to the yard open and a hulking figure step inside the yard, a heavyset man dressed in spandex biker shorts and a neon-yellow tank top. He stood just inside the gate and seemed to be studying the pulsing crowd, looking for someone.

Zack suddenly recognized the man: it was Trey Leyner. Lindsey's husband. Captain America. The guy whose nose he'd almost broken on Halloween.

"Zack, dude, switch it up!" came Shawn's voice. "They've been doing high knees for over a minute."

"Toy soldiers!" Zack called out. "Bring your toes to your fingertips, but keep those legs *straight*. Like this!" He demonstrated the kicks while keeping his eye on Trey Leyner, who was now approaching the group. Surely the guy wouldn't recognize him—Zack had been wearing a Darth Vader mask, after all. Still, he didn't like having the racist meathead in the same yard.

"Zack, wake the fuck up!" hissed Bri.

"Sorry," muttered Zack, and then into his mic, "Okay, everybody, up to your feet! See those blue resistance bands on the ground? There's one for each and every one of you. Grab one and hike it up around your thighs. Then find a partner . . ."

"Trey, there you are!" yelled Lindsey Leyner. "Finally! Come be my partner, baby!" Zack watched Trey lumber toward his wife. As he waited for the crowd to pair off for the partner exercises, Zack glanced toward the patio and saw Mel leading Lettie into the house, gripping her by the arm.

"Oh, oh, oh, oh, oh, sometimes I get a good feeling," sang Flo Rida.

Zack forced himself to focus on the class, on working the crowd, casting them under his spell. But his magic felt inaccessible today. Time usually sped up when he taught, but with Trey Leyner huffing and puffing ten feet away from him, the workout seemed to crawl by.

After twenty very long minutes, Zack switched to his downtempo playlist.

"Okay, y'all, time for a commercial break! But don't get excited, 'cause you'll be working straight through it. We're gonna do two full minutes of planking, which is basically a big present to your abs."

"Booyah!" Bri screamed, raising a fist in the air—her cropped *Eat Pure, Train Filthy* tank lifting so it gave the crowd a view of her six-pack.

"Well," Zack said, "we know *someone* is a fan of planking. As Bri's rock-hard abs will attest!"

The crowd whooped, but a bit meekly, Zack noticed. Did they seem more fatigued than they should be only halfway through the workout?

"Alrighty, folks!" he cheered, adding a bit of oomph to his voice, hoping to keep the vibe from deflating. "We'll start in the classic forearm position. Everybody, check out longtime Color Theory vet Regina in the back, who'll demonstrate how it's done."

He'd called on Regina partly from habit, partly because he wanted to remind her of her promise to bring his money. Seeing her there, that familiar look of flinty resolve on her sweat-dripping face, had made him decide he *did* want "the laptop."

Hell, he deserved it.

Without looking at him, Regina dropped into a perfect plank as Adele's lush voice spilled over the yard.

"Everyone down on their forearms now," said Zack. "And don't move until I tell you to, ya hear?"

The first notes of Adele's "Send My Love" blared over the sound system.

Fifty bodies dropped and hovered parallel to the ground, clearing Zack's view between the yard and the back of Mel's house. Only Adam stood on the patio, staring at his phone. Why was the guy even here, Zack wondered, if he wasn't working out? Just to keep a hostile eye on Zack? Where had Melissa and Lettie gone? It was unlike Lettie to disappear during an event like this—usually she was scurrying around, working nonstop, anticipating her employer's every need.

Zack stared hard at the back door while keeping count of the group's plank time, as if he could will Mel and Lettie to appear, return to the yard. Who knew how long he'd have to wait to be near Mel again after today?

And then, with forty seconds of planking to go, the back door actually did open. Zack almost gasped into the mic when he saw Andres walk out. *His nephew.* Zack was even more shocked when Adam looked up from his phone to put a hand on Andres's shoulder, almost tenderly.

What the hell? Zack thought.

What was Andres doing in Mel's house? Lettie never brought him to events attended by Zack, since it would be a surefire way to expose their siblinghood, as Andres could never hold back from yelling *Tío!* and leaping into Zack's arms.

Then Zack saw the boy was crying. And Adam, that douchebag, was comforting *his* nephew.

Zack moved over to Bri, who was crouched beside the half-naked group of twentysomething friends she'd brought with her, imploring them not to let their shaking knees touch the ground. "You got this, bitches!"

"Yo, Bri," he said. "Can you take over for a minute? I need to deal with something important."

"Right on," said Bri, bolting up.

Zack stepped away from the crowd, still suspended in their planks, some panting and groaning, a few mumbling curses under ragged breath, and made his way quickly toward the house.

Instantly, as if sensing his uncle's approach, Andres looked up, right at Zack, flinging arrows of pure joy that slammed deep into Zack's chest.

"*Tío!*" Andres yelled and bolted off the patio toward Zack, limping as fast as he could across the long wooden deck. "Hey, *Tío* Zack!"

"Aaaaand, child's pose!" said Bri. "That was a full-freaking-two-minute plank, you animals! You showed up today like mofo gangsters! Breathe easy for a minute and then we'll crank it up again."

The group broke their planks and lifted their heads, just as Andres leapt into Zack's arms sobbing and sniffling so Zack could barely understand his nephew's jumbled words. "*Tío*, help! Someone is here in the house trying to take Mommy away. Miss Melissa is trying to stop them but I'm scared. Come help!"

"That's him!" bellowed Trey Leyner, and Zack, clutching Andres's trembling body, saw Trey Leyner's beefy finger pointing. "That's the kid who tried to burgle us! And you." He jabbed the air toward Zack. "You're that psycho who attacked me. Lindsey, it's *him*! I knew there were illegals living here! I was right. I was *right*!"

"Not now!" hissed Lindsey.

"Why not?" said Trey. "How is it that this low-class gym rat should get away with breaking my goddamn nose? We deserve justice, Linds!"

"Shut up, Trey!" said Lindsey, her voice cracking. "And he didn't break it."

The crowd began to murmur with discomfort. Zack tightened his arms around Andres and ran toward the house, holding on to the boy for dear life. Promising he would never let go, whispering into his nephew's wet cheek, "I got you, little man. Your *tío* won't let anyone hurt you. Or your mommy." Hoping he wasn't giving the boy yet another empty promise.

He reached the patio and shot past Adam, pulling open the back door with Andres still in his arms.

"Oh-kay!" yelled Bri. "Let's take this party to the next level! You came here to burn for Malibu, people, and we about to TURN UP THE HEAT!"

"Don't you dare step inside my house!" yelled Adam, but Zack was already inside, blazing down the long hallway lined with pictures.

"The front door," Andres said, his voice small and scared. "They're at the front door."

Zack tore through house, nearly tripping over the giant hamster cage, until he reached the foyer, where Mel stood with her arms round Lettie, holding a piece of bright yellow paper, both of them swaying slightly on their feet.

"What's going on?" Zack panted.

"Is everything okay?" came a voice from behind him, and he turned to see Regina had followed them into the house, face flushed with sweat.

Lettie untangled herself from Mel and they both turned to face him. It was the first time he'd seen his sister cry and the tears made her deep brown eyes shine. Mel's round cheeks were red, like she'd just finished a Color Theory class or, he let himself remember for a second, like she'd just finished climaxing in his arms.

"Oh, thank God, you have Andres," said Mel to Zack, as if he were a stranger who'd found a lost child in the mall. The hopelessness swallowed him once again. "Thanks for bringing him in. You can go back outside now. I know you have a class to teach."

Was Mel really going to turn him away like he was a stray dog who'd slipped in the back door? Mel, the woman who, as they'd lain naked on how many hotel balconies gazing at the stars, listened so attentively as he'd shared stories of his lonely childhood, and of all the destructive choices he'd made one after another in his desperate search for love?

"No, let him see," said Lettie. She took the paper from Mel's hands and extended it to Zack. He set Andres down.

"ICE come," Lettie said softly, her voice quaking. "They find me here, just now. They want to take me away but Miss Melissa convince them not to. They give me this."

Zack read the text on the page:

> This Notice to Appear ("NTA") has been issued to inform you the initiation of removal proceedings against you has begun. You ("LETICIA MENDOZA") are scheduled for transport to a designated holding facility within 7 days, and will be detained there until the Courts have determined your Eligibility for Deportation to the country where you possess legal citizenship ("MEXICO"). Any minors in your custody ("ANDRES MANUEL MENDOZA" and any others in your legal guardianship) will be placed in the care of an approved guardian until . . .

Zack stopped reading. "No. Lettie. No, this won't happen. I won't let them take you. Or let them take Andres away from you. I prom—"

"I don't want to go away!" Andres wailed.

"Wait, how are *you* involved?" Regina piped up. She turned to Lettie. "I'll take care of Andres, Lettie. Don't worry. He knows our family. He'll be just fine until we can get this sorted out."

Over my dead body, Zack thought. No way would he allow his nephew to sleep a single night under that monster's roof. Zack wished he could pick Regina up, hoist her over his shoulder, and fling her out the back door.

"If it happens, it happens," Lettie whispered, pulling Andres to her. "Shh, *caro*. You are not going anywhere. Mommy swears it. Pinky swear, yes?" She offered her finger to Andres, and Zack was relieved to see his nephew link his pinky to hers with a small smile, calming down. Lettie looked to Mel, then to Regina, and, finally, at Zack. "Just promise me you will take care of this boy."

"We'll help, too," said Mel. "Andres is comfortable here. He's been staying with us for weeks. And it's been so much fun, hasn't it, Andres?"

"He has?" said Zack.

Mel put a hand on Andres's shoulder. The boy ducked away and howled, "No! I wanna stay with *Tío*! *Please* can I stay with *Tío* Zack?"

Zack gathered his nephew into his arms again, his lips pressed to the boy's gel-stiff hair. Mel flicked her eyes up at Zack, holding his gaze for a beat, and his heart boggled in his chest. Lettie had lowered her face into her hands, and was rocking back and forth in place as Regina slipped an arm around his sister's trembling back.

"What?" Mel blinked in confusion. "*Tío*? Andres, how do you know this guy? How do you know Coach Zack?"

"What in the hell is going on here?"

Zack turned to see Adam marching toward them, followed by Trey Leyner, sweat darkening his bright yellow shirt.

Zack considered running out the tall oak front doors, Andres in his arms. Never looking back.

"Adam," said Mel. "Can you give us a minute? We're dealing with something here."

"Oh, are you?" said Adam. *Like a sassy little bitch*, Zack thought, knowing that if the guy stepped to him now, Zack might actually murder him. "Because we're dealing with something, too. Namely that your friend Mr. Muscles here assaulted *my* friend Trey a few months ago. Attacked him on the front steps of his own home. So . . . the situation is, I'd like to ask *Coach Zack*"—he added a sneer—"to vacate the premises. I don't care if the workout isn't over yet. I want him off my property. *Now*. Or I'm calling the police."

"Give me a break, Adam," said Mel. Saving him, Zack thought, wanting to believe it was motivated by love. "Zack didn't assault anyone. Stop puffing your chest and marking your territory. We've got an actual crisis going on here."

"No, Melissa." Zack's sister stood up straight and spoke, Lettie's voice strong and clear. "Mr. Adam is right. Mr. Leyner did get attacked. By me and my brother. But he was being a bad person and so he deserved it."

Zack did not move. He felt Andres breathing against him. Felt the eyes of Trey Leyner and Adam Goldberg boring into him.

"What?" said Regina. "Lettie, you're confusing us. What brother?"

"This man." Lettie pointed to Zack. "Zacarias. He is my brother."

The words of St. Thérèse, Little Flower of Jesus, came to Zack now: *What a comfort it is, this way of love!*

"What?" Mel blinked. "Lettie, your brother is *Zack*? How is that possible?"

Thérèse to Zack: . . . *you may stumble on love, you may fail to correspond with grace given* . . .

"Wow, Mel," said Regina. "Your best friend is related to your boyfriend! What a trip."

"Excuse me?" said Adam. "What did you just say, Regina?"

"She's a professional liar," Mel cut in. "Don't listen to her, Adam."

Thérèse to Zack: . . . *but whatever offends our Lord is burnt up in its fire* . . .

"I don't care if they're married, or brother and sister, or brother and sister who're fucking," said Trey Leyner. "They're a pair of violent hoodlums who should go back to Mexico."

"You're a pig, Trey," said Regina. "Just like your wife."

"How dare you," said Trey. "I'll tell Lindsey you said that. You're like a sister to her, Regina."

Thérèse to Zack: . . . *nothing is left but a humble, absorbing peace deep down in the heart.*

"Get out of my house," said Adam, jerking his hand toward Zack. "I don't care what sort of big revelation is happening right now. I want you out."

Lettie looked at Zack and spoke the most beautiful words Zack had ever heard—more beautiful than those by his beloved Saint Thérèse. "Zacarias," Lettie said. "I mean to say *Zack*. He is adopting Andres. Making him his son."

Zack kissed Andres's damp forehead and set him down on the shiny wood floor. He leaned toward Lettie and kissed her on the cheek. Right in front of everyone.

"I love you, Sis," he said. "We're going to fix this."

Then he flung open the front door and dashed into the front yard and down the path toward the street. He'd just reached the sidewalk when he heard Regina call his name.

"Wait, Zack! Hang on. Don't you want your laptop?" She rushed down the walkway toward him, ponytail springing in the sunlight.

"Burn in hell, Regina," he said and bolted away from her, into the sparkling morning.

38

LETICIA

THE ARMY OF HUNGRY SOLDIERS HAD RETURNED TO HER FAVORITE BOSS Melissa's backyard.

Lettie had made the same preparations for Zacarias's Version Two You! party, which now seemed so long ago. A time of innocence Lettie longed for, when she had believed she might be able to fix her problems. Or be saved, like Blanca Flor, when all hope was lost and the woodsman's sharp axe lifted above the princess's pale neck.

But Lettie was no princess. Melissa's house no enchanted fairy-tale cottage, though Lettie had enjoyed living there those past few weeks, sharing the guest bedroom, which was bigger than their entire apartment, with Andres. And, sadly, Melissa's big house with its iron gates and stone walls and alarm system whose many buttons glowed red and green in the dark house at night had not been enough to keep Lettie safe. ICE had found her there. The immigration police in their bulletproof vests and ICE jackets had come for her in the middle of the party, pounded angry fists on the front door, shoving the notice of deportation at Lettie like she had done something to hurt them—they looked *that* angry. How could this be when Lettie had never once laid eyes on these strange men?

Happiness can only exist in acceptance, she told herself as her family made a wall around her in the Goldbergs' house, keeping her safe. Melissa and Regina; Zacarias and Andres. A family as mixed-up as the menudo soup her *abuela* made with the pig parts, intestines and feet, which most people tossed in the garbage.

In Zacarias's arms, Andres tightened himself around her brother's body, gripping even with his ruined leg, as if he would never let go, and Lettie wished she could live in this moment forever. Her son protected by his uncle's strong arms—she so close she could smell Andres's little-boy scent: hair gel and peanut butter and sweat. The scent of innocence. Of a life unspoiled.

"Zacarias," she began. "I mean to say *Zack*." Her brother looked up at her, his white smile as bright as the California sun. "He is adopting Andres. Making him his son."

The past was the past. There was only life moving forward, and Lettie would enjoy every minute of the twenty-seven days she had left with Andres, with her family, before the American government shipped her back to Mexico.

As a little girl, she'd watched the women around her work. Their bodies absorbed blow after blow. Her mother, her *abuela*, all her aunties and older cousins. Oh, the pain those bodies endured. From the agony of childbirth to their husband's clenched fists. The back-breaking work that kept a little food on the table and shoes on their children's feet. She had once watched her mother end a pregnancy, the sharpened tip of a coat hanger dripping blood. Women's work, she'd learned, was the hardest work there was, and work was what the women she knew did best. Their *superpower*, as Andres might say, Lettie thought, as she watched her son hug his dear *tío* Zacarias. Right in front of all her bosses.

In Melissa's hallway, surrounded by the two women who had helped her make a better life in America—women now at war with each other, she knew—Lettie had finally been seen.

In America, her mother, Gloria, had repeated again and again that year Lettie had readied herself to cross the border, saving every penny she made cleaning the hotel rooms of wealthy tourists visiting Oaxaca. *In America*, her mother had said, *no one goes hungry*.

In America, every child learns to read.

In America, every person has a chance to be king or queen.

My America, Lettie thought, *began with Andres.* The little boy whose future, she still believed, overflowed with possibility. Who knew, maybe there was a President Andres Manuel Mendoza in America's future.

Her body was strong. She'd taken the blows. From Manuel, from the silver-haired comic book store owner, from the judge in court. Even from the Big Cheeto.

And also, from those she had adored—Regina, Mel, and even Zacarias, whose broken promises, though only made of words, had once stung as much as Manuel's slaps.

She would return someday and start her American story anew. What was Zacarias always yelling at his students at the gym? *Your body can stand almost anything! It's your mind you have to convince!*

She'd go back to Mexico and make her mind strong again. And when she was sure her heart was as hard as stone, the heart of a woman who would not dare believe in promises again, she'd cross the desert, a second time, and be with her boy. Forever.

FROM *THE COLLECTED WRITINGS OF SAINT THÉRÈSE*

I understood that every flower created by Him is beautiful, that the brilliance of the rose and the whiteness of the lily do not lessen the perfume of the violet or the sweet simplicity of the daisy. I understood that if all the lowly flowers wished to be roses, nature would no longer be enameled with lovely hues. And so, it is in the world of souls, Our Lord's living garden.

SUNDAY, MARCH 24, 2019

39

ZACK

Zack's Sunday had been long and unpleasant.

Usually, he looked forward to the end of the weekend. He never worked on Sunday mornings, so that he could take Andres and Lettie to mass at St. Monica's, then across the street to Reed Park for a picnic, usually tamales Lettie had made the day before and wrapped in foil. Reed Park had been one of the few public places Zack felt comfortable appearing with his half-sister and nephew, due to its popularity with the local homeless population and other riffraff. The park's grunginess virtually guaranteed they'd never run into any of Zack's clients or Lettie's employers. Not that it mattered anymore. They all knew who Lettie was to him now.

Which was a huge relief. And made him regret hiding their relationship in the first place.

Those picnics at the park he'd shared with Lettie and Andres were often the most relaxed hour of Zack's week, lazing in the grass, under the sunshine, getting up periodically to toss a ball with Andres (who was just starting to get the hang of it), or kick into handstands, while Andres counted by Mississippis. The boy went giddy with excitement when Zack broke his own handstand records, squealing *Yay, Tío!* and pumping his skinny arm in the air.

But this Sunday, Zack had gone to Mass alone and straight home right after, skipping Reed Park. Now Lettie was days away from her move to a detention facility, an hour south in Santa Ana, a fact he still couldn't quite accept. When she left, Andres would continue to stay with Mel and Adam—Zack tried not to burn with envy and self-disgust over this, reminding himself that Andres probably felt like a prince in the Goldberg castle.

He'd thought going to Mass might help, that he'd lose himself in the sweet, holy voices of the choir, in the wisdom of the sermon, but the service had done him no good. In pew after pew, it seemed, Zack caught sight of some child or another who bore a small resemblance to his Andres. A boy with gel-stiff hair. A girl hiding a Pokémon toy in her lap. It was torture.

Mass had not helped, nor had the barbecued cauliflower burger from Paprika, which he'd Postmated to his house and eaten on his sagging couch while trying to read Saint Thérèse, sipping water straight from a gallon jug because all of his glasses were dirty. He'd barely done dishes or laundry since that terrible morning at Burn for Malibu!

At some point in the afternoon, he switched from reading Thérèse to watching TV, though nothing appealed to him and he ended up wasting an hour sampling garbage on Netflix.

Then he'd fallen into a black, dreamless sleep.

When he woke, it was dark. His phone read 10:32 P.M. He'd slept for four or five hours. His mouth was fuggy from the sandwich he'd eaten, its sauce-streaked wrapper lying on the floor by the couch. Zack sat up and rubbed his eyes, instantly disgusted with himself. His apartment was filthy, complete with trash on the floor; he'd slept through the day, and hadn't exercised in nearly a week. It'd been all he could do to show up and teach at Color Theory, never mind putting in extra hours for his own workouts. His body felt sluggish and soft, unrecognizable.

He stood up and went to his bedroom and took off the rumpled white button-down and black pants he'd worn to church and napped in. From one of the many piles of dirty clothes scattering the floor, he found gym shorts and sniffed at several T-shirts before settling on one with a tolerable smell. It was one of his many that read *Eat Pure, Train Filthy.*

He needed to exercise. To clear his mind by running until his lungs screamed, by lifting iron plates so that his muscles burned and throbbed. To push himself to limits where there was no room for thinking. No room for Andres, or Lettie, or the fact that Zack had failed them both, or for Melissa Goldberg, whom he could not stop thinking about in bed at night, no matter how many months had passed since he'd touched her.

No room for anything but the pain. Which was also beauty.

A real cross is the martyrdom of the heart, the interior suffering of the soul, Thérèse had written.

On Sundays, Color Theory's last class ended at six P.M. The studio had been closed for hours. Zack was sure to have the gym to himself. Jensen encouraged his staffers to help themselves to the equipment after-hours, as long as they cleaned up.

In his truck, Zack drove with the windows down, taking the long route along the beach so he could breathe the briny air, energize himself before his first workout in a week. He blasted Waylon and sang along.

Then he turned onto Main Street and parked in the lot of Color Theory. It was empty but for one other car: a white Porsche, gleaming in the glow of the dim streetlight.

"Z-MAN?" JENSEN RELEASED the fly press with a clang and flashed a double thumbs-up. "No shit!"

"Dude!" said Zack, faking enthusiasm. He'd assumed he'd have the gym to himself. Jensen was the last person he wanted to train with—except maybe Regina. But Zack's cravings to feel his muscles burn, his lungs ache, to sweat out the shitty feelings of despair, trumped his disappointment at not having the gym to himself. And, in the weeks since Zack had stopped the transfers to Big Rad Wolfe, he'd gradually gotten comfortable around Jensen again, who was chummier with Zack than ever. Color Theory Malibu was set to open at the beginning of June, and, true to his word, Jensen had officially hired Zack as head trainer. The compensation hadn't been as much as Zack hoped, but it was quite a bit more than he was earning now, plus benefits.

Regina had been right—Jensen had not noticed the money they'd moved. He was far too wealthy to miss a measly fifty grand. Still, Zack avoided his boss. He no longer had the energy for Jensen's incessant bro-banter. He'd been weirded out by Jensen's pushy vibe during the Porsche drive his boss had practically forced on him. He hadn't realized just how needy Jensen was until that terrible night Mel had dumped him, and while he felt sorry for the guy—Zack knew how crushing loneliness could be—he was in no shape to be someone else's savior, *no, siree.*

Plus, Mel had hated Jensen, called him a douche and a bigot, among other unflattering things, and although Zack didn't really agree, her opinion had worn off on him.

As had so many things about Mel.

God, he missed her.

"Perfect timing, bro," said Jensen. "I've only done one set. Wanna hit a circuit with me? Keep each other honest?"

"Actually, I was gonna keep it short," said Zack. "Maybe just lift. I've got . . . stuff to do tonight."

"It's eleven P.M. on Sunday," said Jensen. "How much more can you do with your night? Other than take a shower and jerk off in bed?"

"Ha," said Zack flatly.

"Joke, man. Joke," said Jensen, lifting his hands in mock surrender. "Seriously, at least stick around to spot me for a few sets? I'll return the favor. Let me just put on some tunes." He tapped his phone and Bruno Mars's silky voice started on the sound system.

"Um. Okay." Zack had the intense urge to turn and walk out the gym's front door. Instead he followed Jensen to the bench. Jensen loaded his plates—the same weight Zack benched—and lay down on the padded platform. Then he gripped the barbell and hoisted it off the stopper. Zack stood behind him, counting as Jensen lifted. After three sets, Zack saw veins jumping out from his boss's temples and sweat pushing up from his scalp into his salt-and-pepper buzz-cut. He thought of his father, who'd set up a bench in the family garage in Florida, and liked to scream profanities as he lifted weights early in the morning, so that his vulgar outbursts were often the first thing Zack heard when he woke, sending him into instant low-grade panic.

Midway through the fourth set, Jensen began to struggle, and Zack pressed his palms under the barbell to help him.

"No, man, no," Jensen panted. "I'm good. Not yet."

He groaned and winced through the rest of the set, his biceps and delts puffing with exertion.

Finally, he finished eight sets and sat up on the bench, breathing hard.

"Nice job, dude," said Zack.

"Your turn."

Impulsively, Zack added a twenty-five-pound plate to each side.

"You always go that heavy?" said Jensen.

"Yup," Zack lied, and lowered onto the bench.

Halfway through his first set, he realized he'd made a mistake. The barbell was too much. His muscles were already on fire. Jensen noticed and tried to spot him.

"No," said Zack, his voice strained. "Don't."

If he was going to cut his workout short, he at least wanted to make sure it hurt.

He made it through the set, and started on the next.

"Six, seven, eight. Atta boy," said Jensen.

"Argh," moaned Zack, resting for a minute, his delts hot and pulsing. Then he lifted the barbell again. And again. And again. As his muscles protested and pain seared through them, down into his bones, Zack closed his eyes. He pictured Andres, eyes lit behind his crooked glasses, his ruined leg dragging as he ran to catch the ball his *tío* Zack had tossed high above the green grass at Reed Park.

"Two, three, four," counted Jensen, as Zack swung into his sixth set. "You're killing it, Z-man."

Six sets, with an extra fifty! And Jensen had not even touched him yet. Zack continued to pump, letting his mind rove from Andres to Mel—how she squinted one eye at him when she was embarrassed, or tugged at her bangs as if she could lower them over her sweet, rosy face—finding strength.

But then, midway through his seventh set, his arms quit. The weight was too heavy. Jensen reached out to support the barbell, and Zack let him. With Jensen assisting him, he made it through his eighth set. His tenth rep nearly shattered him. He lowered the weight back onto the stopper, then found he was too spent to move. Could not even sit up on the bench. So he continued to lie there, back flat on the padding, feet resting on the floor.

At last, Zack's mind was blank. A whiteboard and black screen at once. Sweat streamed from his face into his hair. The muscles of his arms were utterly shot. He could not move them.

This is what he'd come for. To wreck himself, in order to find peace.

"Uh, Z-man?"

Zack opened his eyes. Jensen was still standing behind the bench, but had leaned over, so his tanned, creased face was nearly touching Zack's.

"Yeah?"

"That was a heroic set."

"I might've overdone it a little," said Zack. "Haven't lifted in a week."

"You looked fucking intense," said Jensen. Zack could feel his boss's breath on his cheek. He scooted out from under the barbell and sat up.

Jensen stepped around the bench and grabbed a blue resistance band from a hook on the wall.

"Here," he said, handing it to Zack. "Stretch yourself out before you seize up."

Zack took the band but was still too weary from his set to move.

Jensen sat down next to him on the bench.

Too close.

"You're up," said Zack, standing. He tossed the blue band onto the floor.

Jensen picked it up. "Let me stretch you out."

Zack shook his head. "Let's keep going. I'll stretch later. I'm fine." His arms felt like twin stones at his side. Definitely, he'd overdone it. But he wasn't sorry. He deserved the pain.

Thérèse: *A great serenity will follow the storm.*

"Hang on," said Jensen, grabbing Zack's forearm.

"What is it, man?"

Without letting go of Zack's arm, Jensen rose to his feet. Sweat still glistened over his face. Zack could see it collected in the crow's feet lining Jensen's eyes.

Jensen clasped Zack's other arm with his free hand, and closed the small gap between their bodies.

Then he lifted his face to Zack's and kissed him on the lips.

Zack shoved the older man's shoulders, hard, and Jensen stumbled backward.

"S-sorry, dude," Jensen stammered.

"What the fuck?" said Zack. His mind flashed to the night in the Porsche; how Jensen kept crossing into his personal space. Zack had hardly given it a thought; gym guys were a touchy bunch, himself included.

Now, he was giving it thought. He eyed the front door of the studio. All he would have to do is bolt through, past the empty reception desk, and onto the street. Never look back.

But he was too stunned to move.

"I just—it seemed," Jensen said. "Like you gave me the green light. Like you were asking for it. The look on your face, during your reps . . ." He trailed off.

"You're out of your mind."

"I am?"

"Abso-fucking-lutely," said Zack. He wiped the back of his hand over his lips, disgust seeping through his body.

"Don't lie to me, Zack. Or to yourself. It's okay. I read your vibe that night, on the drive."

Zack froze. "What?"

"Don't act like you haven't felt it, too. All these months. All our talks . . ."

"It wasn't like that." Zack's hands curled into fists. "You dragged me out on that drive. I didn't even want to go. I was . . . waiting for my girlfriend." He cringed as he spoke the lie, as if Mel could somehow hear him.

Jensen erupted in laughter. "Your *girlfriend*? Puh-lease. When're you gonna give up this boy-toy-to-the-cougars act?"

"Jensen, cut it out. I don't know what you're thinking, but you've got it totally fucking wrong."

"Well," said Jensen, "I guess I misunderstood. Even though you were giving me every clue under the sun. *Beaming* them to me. Hell, our legs even have the same haircut." He laughed and touched one finger to his own smooth-shaven leg. Then he reached and pressed the pad of his finger to Zack's shin.

Zack kicked him away. "Because I shave my legs, Jens? You thought I was a faggot because I shave my legs?"

"That, and about a million other reasons," said Jensen. "If I weren't so sure, I never would've let you get away with it."

"Get away with what?"

Jensen gave a short, bitter laugh. "With stealing from me right under my nose."

Zack felt dizzy. "What . . . what do you mean?"

"Cut the bullshit," said Jensen. "You've been transferring money to Regina Wolfe's business for months. Every other week. Somewhere in the neighborhood of fifty grand. How you planned to weasel the cash out of Regina, I have no idea. By fucking her, I guess. The same way you've gotten every single thing in your life." Jensen thrust his hips forward and back, humping the air.

"I never . . ." Zack faltered. His body began to tremble. Everywhere. He could even feel it in his face. "She . . . It was Regina. It was all her idea."

Jensen barked another laugh. "Regina Wolfe? Embezzling from *me*? A measly fifty grand? Please, Zack. You keep getting dumber. She's as rich as all the other bitches shaking their asses in this gym all day."

"I swear to God," said Zack. "I have proof—"

"Give it up, Doheny. I already talked to Regina. She clearly had no idea. Never even noticed the money was there. Paid me back like—" Jensen snapped his fingers.

"That's not what happened."

"You're lucky I haven't filed criminal charges yet. I've known about this for weeks."

"No." Zack felt an electric current come to life inside him. Hot and buzzing, starting in his legs and shooting up into his chest, into his mind.

"Just admit it," said Jensen, casual now, practically gloating. He twirled the blue resistance band so that it spun a blurred circle in the air. "You're a thief. A thief and a faggot. I can't believe I just offered you a goddamn primo job."

The current in Zack's body sparked and caught fire. He lunged at Jensen, threw him to the ground and pressed his knee into the center of his boss's chest, pinning him down. Jensen groaned and thrashed but could not get away. Zack slid both hands around his neck and squeezed, fingers latched in a vise grip, compressing skin and tendons, muscles and veins. As he squeezed Jensen's neck, Zack heard deep guttural roars rise from his own throat, drowning out the music, the whir of the studio's fan, Jensen's pleas for help. Zack was stronger than Jensen. But his arms were clumsy from the weights he'd just lifted, and his mind was wild with rage, blinding him to the fact that Jensen, despite his flailing limbs and strained yowls of terror, was still clutching the blue rubber strap like a lifeline.

April 17, 2019

SCHOLARSHIP HONORING DECEASED COLOR THEORY COACH TO BENEFIT "DREAMERS"

The death of well-known local fitness coach Zacarias Robert Doheny has been deemed a suicide.

Questions surrounding the circumstances of Doheny's death on March 24 at his place of employment, the Santa Monica location of the Color Theory circuit training franchise, rippled through the tight-knit Westside fitness community.

"It's unfathomable," said Santa Monica business owner Regina Wolfe, who estimated she'd attended more than two hundred workouts led by Doheny. "I had just taken one of [Doheny's] classes at a charity event and marveled over his optimism. It was contagious. It's almost impossible to believe he was actually in a dark place. It breaks my heart to think of him suffering alone with his secrets."

In addition to acting and coaching, Doheny, who was of partial Mexican descent, was an advocate for the rights of Mexican immigrants living the United States.

"He was private about his politics at work," said Jensen Davis, founder and owner of the Color Theory franchise. "But we knew where he stood. That's why I've established a scholarship fund in [Doheny's] name for Mexican children whose futures in the USA are precarious. Zack was a wonderful guy, inside and out, and his goodness deserves a legacy. He will be missed."

Donations to the Doheny Dreamers Project can be made at www.dohenydreamers.com.

Correction: an earlier version of this article linked Zacarias Doheny to the Doheny family who helped establish Los Angeles. Zacarias Robert Doheny is no relation.

MONDAY, JULY 1, 2019

40

REGINA

REGINA CONSIDERED JULY TO BE THE TRUE BEGINNING OF SUMMER IN Santa Monica, since most of June was usually cloudy and overcast. When she'd first moved here from Chicago, fifteen years ago, she'd been incredulous at how the Santa Monicans whined about "June Gloom," as if the lack of sunshine for one measly month deprived them of something critical to their lifeblood, something to which they were deeply entitled at all times.

When, she wondered, as she sipped coffee and nibbled a croissant (after decades of denying herself, she'd begun eating carbs again) in the bright morning light of her backyard, had she become one of them? The on-cue emergence of the sun today, on the first of July, made her feel life had been restored to normal, that all was well with the world. *Yeah, except for global warming and that hateful sociopath in the White House*, she heard Mel say. Even though she was no longer friends with Mel, Regina thought of her—and, okay, *missed her*—often.

Of course, it was not the warm July sun that had restored normalcy to Regina's life. The real reasons were much more complicated. The past year had felt like one long, secret war. She'd fought so many battles—with Mel, with Zack, with Gordon, and most of all, with herself—that to be sitting here, relaxed amid the tranquil beauty of her backyard, the jacaranda trees flaring violet overhead, the tomatoes in her garden (planted by her gardener, Fernando, but whatever) growing fat and heavy on the vines, felt like a gift.

This year, spring was not her time of renewal, but now, the height of summer.

Sometimes, when she woke very early in the morning to take a class at her new gym in Venice, she forgot Zack was gone. Sometimes, in the first flickers of her consciousness, she heard his smooth Florida drawl: *Mornin', sunshine. Let's do this!*

But then she'd blink awake and he'd be gone.

The loss of him gut-punched her out of nowhere, especially if she happened to be anywhere near Main Street (which she avoided at all costs), or when one of the trainers at her new gym, RippedLA, called on her to demonstrate something.

Or when she heard someone use that ridiculous phrase he was so fond of: *hashtag blessed.*

Yes, she missed him. But her sadness dwarfed in comparison to her gratitude for having her family back. In the end, she thought to herself, crossing her lush lawn (Mel: *This is the fucking desert! In the middle of a drought! We should be ashamed of green grass.*) to spray her tomatoes with the hose, family *was* all that mattered.

More than friends. More than money—though, now that she and Gordon had it again, life was much better. Certainly, family meant more than success, or a perfect body.

Regina pinched the new flesh at her abdomen. She'd gained some weight. Not a lot, but enough for Gordon to notice, with appreciation. (*God, I love your little curves*, he'd breathed in bed last night.) Now that she wasn't monitoring every single thing she ate with obsessive precision, she found she had more time for other things. She still worked out, but only three days a week, instead of the seven, or eight, or nine times she'd once held sacred.

There was, it turned out, more to life than exercise. Much more. Like rebuilding Big Rad Wolfe, which currently had a client roster of six and was billing steady retainers each month. Like spending time with Kaden and Mia—lately, they'd been swimming together at the Annenberg House in the afternoons, Regina feeling grateful for the gorgeous public pools Santa Monica offered instead of resentful for not having her own. Currently, the girls were finishing a week of sleepaway camp, due back this evening, and Regina could hardly wait to meet them at the bus.

She was restoring her relationship with her husband. This part had been the slowest-going. Gordon was reluctant to trust her again, but gradually, he was coming around. They were going to couples' therapy every week with an angel of a psychotherapist named Janet—Regina had remembered Mel raving about the woman, and had impulsively booked the first appointment.

Now, with Janet's help, slowly but surely she and Gordon were moving through *healing mode*, as Janet called it, back toward *communion mode*, which, Janet had explained with a meaningful look at Regina, required *authentic transparency*.

Translation: No more hiding. No more lies. Regina wondered whether *authentic transparency* was retroactive; could she and Gordon still have communion even though she would never, *ever*, come clean about the debt they'd carried just four short months ago—and certainly not about the measures she'd taken to hide it—nor about the true nature of her friendship with Zack?

She decided it was okay to let those secrets die. Like Zack, they were gone now. Dead and buried. To unearth them would only bring Gordon more pain than she'd already caused them.

Next week, the Wolfe family would leave on a one-week cruise to the Mexican Riviera, the trip Gordon had booked for his birthday, which was supposed to have happened back in March.

But March had been chaos: their marriage high on the rocks. And then Zack had killed himself, although it was still difficult for Regina to accept that Zack, so full of faith and big dreams, had chosen to end it all so abruptly.

So they'd postponed the cruise. For a better time. Which was *now*, Regina thought gratefully.

"Morning, hon."

Regina looked up from her watering to see Gordon standing on the back patio, coffee in hand, wearing slim black jeans and a T-shirt that showed off his newly trim torso. Since selling *Eighteen Twelve*, he'd been eating healthier, jogging on the beach, even accompanying Regina to classes at Ripped.

"Morning, sweetie," Regina called, shutting off the hose and crossing the yard to kiss him. "You off to the room?" To Gordon's delight, instead of a feature film, *Eighteen Twelve* was being developed into a miniseries for HBO, and he'd been hired to adapt the pilot from his original screenplay. He was currently logging fourteen-hour days in the writers' room and happier with his career than Regina had ever known him to be.

"You smell nice," he said, kissing her again. "And yes, I'm off. But it'll be a short day. I'll be home in time to meet the girls at the bus with you."

"Awesome," Regina said. "I've got a pitch in Playa del Rey at ten. Then I'll be at the office. I think I'll bike over. It's such a beautiful day. Want to pick me up at five thirty and we can go get the girls?"

"Absolutely," said Gordon. "Can't wait. Love you."

"Love you." Regina watched him retreat into the house and down the hall to the front door. As it closed behind him, she picked a lemon from the tree beside the patio and tilted her face to the morning sunshine, bringing the fruit to her nose to breathe in its clean scent.

She could not remember the last time she'd felt so at peace. So calm and contented. She gathered up her coffee mug and empty plate and went inside the house to shower and dress for her pitch.

She was halfway up the staircase when the doorbell rang. She turned and descended toward the front door, trying to remember whether she was expecting a package. Or perhaps Gordon had forgotten his keys again, and rang the doorbell so she'd hear him from the backyard.

Regina peered through the peephole to see a stout, middle-aged

Latina woman she didn't recognize standing on her doorstep. She opened the door.

"Yes?"

"Good morning." The woman carried a canvas briefcase and wore the stern expression of a post office employee. "I'm looking for Regina Prager Wolfe."

"That's me. And you are . . . ?"

The woman reached into her briefcase and extracted a manila envelope, which she extended to Regina. "I'm Camila Rodriguez, process server for Los Angeles County. These are official court documents prepared for you."

"Court documents? For what?" Her heart sped up. Could Gordon be springing a divorce on her? Had he somehow decided, after these months of progress, that she was not to be trusted after all?

"If you do not wish to accept the papers," Camila continued briskly, "they can be left on the ground, but will still be considered valid. Tampering with or destroying the documents also does not affect their validity."

"Please get off my property," said Regina. She scanned the street—were any of her neighbors out to witness? Nosy Susan Bellwether across the street would have a field day recounting Regina's humiliation at the next Alta Avenue Neighborhood Association meeting.

Camila shrugged and set the envelope at the bottom of the steps. "Have a nice day, ma'am." She turned and strode down the Wolfes' flower-lined walkway toward the street. Stunned, Regina watched her climb into a Honda Civic and drive away.

Then she sat down on her front steps, picked up the envelope, and opened it.

This Official Summons orders REGINA PRAGER WOLFE to appear in the Los Angeles County Superior Courts, Santa Monica branch, at the time and date set forth below, to testify

at a hearing pertaining to charges of EMBEZZLEMENT qual-
ifying as GRAND THEFT, as defined by California Penal Code
Section 503 . . .

Regina stopped reading. She ripped the summons in half, then
quarters, until she'd reduced it to ribbons. Then she stuffed the
shredded paper back into the envelope and crushed it between her
palms.

She sat perfectly still on the step, listening to her own breath.

The summer sun had climbed higher in the sky; her cheeks began to burn.

She passed the balled envelope from one hand to the other.

She would not panic. She would stay calm.

She would find a way to fix this.

She always did.

41

MEL

"Bye, Mom!" Sloane called up to the second floor from the front yard as Adam's sleek black Tesla glided up to the curb. "Bye, Lettie!"

"Bye!" Mel and Lettie called back in unison from side-by-side deck chairs on the balcony outside Mel's bedroom.

"Back seat, please!" Mel shouted as she watched Sloane head for the front passenger door of the Tesla. From her vantage point on the second floor, Mel couldn't make out the eye rolls she was sure Sloane was exchanging with Adam right then. Adam let Sloane ride beside him in his beloved electric car, never mind that she was a good twenty pounds below the front seat weight requirement.

But their eye rolls did not upset Mel anymore. Not since she'd made the decision to leave Adam, despite his willingness to start over, work it out, forgive her for the *thing* with Zack, which Adam claimed Zack (*poor Zack*) had confessed to, forcing Mel to confess as well—though she'd dialed the details of their affair *way* back. Once they'd separated, soon after the Burn for Malibu! event, the insular coziness of Adam's relationship with Sloane ceased to make Mel feel threatened. No longer did she feel like the lesser, sloppy, unfocused, ungiving parent: all the things Adam had—unintentionally, but still—made her feel.

Adam was a good man. Mel still believed this. But he was not the man for her. How had it taken her so long to see this? Why had she required so much disaster—his imagined affair, her actual one—in order to realize she'd been wanting to leave Adam for a long time?

Only after she'd finally confessed her affair with Zack to Janet, then sobbed for forty straight minutes on the couch, cat hairs sticking to her cheek, did Janet suggest, ever so gently, that perhaps Mel had *wanted* to believe Adam was having an affair? Perhaps she'd been desperate for a reason to make the terrifying decision to end the marriage? Adam, Mel now saw, was a good man in many ways, but he was terrible at helping her love herself. Because at some point, painful as it was for Mel to admit, Adam had stopped loving her for who she was, right *now*. Instead, he'd become far more interested in the person—Mel 2.0—he hoped she'd become.

Zack, though he hadn't known it, had helped Mel see this. Sometimes, she felt he was not actually gone; that he was still hopping around at the front of a packed class at Color Theory, blasting his country rock, joking over the mic in his easy southern drawl.

Other times, she missed him so much her chest ached. Like when she thought of that day at the soccer game, his eyes shiny with tears as he delivered to her the solution to all her problems—not that she'd been ready to accept it then. *Mel, I love the you—the you that you already are.*

Once, she'd wept so uncontrollably, Lettie—who, bless her, was now sharing Mel's home—had heard her and come upstairs. Had sat on the bed beside her and stroked Mel's back and hair.

She would always be grateful to Zack Doheny. Without him, would Mel have ever found the courage to change her life?

As Adam's Tesla glided away into the summer morning, Mel felt the usual shaky disbelief spread through her body. An almost sickening longing for her daughter, even though Sloane would be back in just forty-eight hours.

Was this really Mel's life now? Sending her daughter off for two nights with "her father"? Just speaking that phrase, which she'd heard so often from the (many) divorced moms of John Wayne Elementary, made her feel ill.

"You okay, Mel?" Lettie laid a warm hand on Mel's forearm.

Mel sighed. "Yes. I'm okay. It's just hard. But I'm getting used to it."

"I know it is hard. But you are so much better now. I see it all over your pretty face."

"Really, Lettie? Because sometimes I still freak out. Adam's a good guy. I mean, he let me have all this." She opened her arms wide. "Do I really deserve to be living in this ridiculous house? When I'm the one who left *him*?"

"He still has a plenty nice house," Lettie said. "With a whole room for his fighting exercises."

Mel gave a small laugh. "Ah, right. He didn't have a jiu-jitsu studio here."

And, she reminded herself, Adam had been the one to insist she remain in the house on Georgina Avenue. *I'm never home*, he said. *And living here would just depress me anyway.*

Mel had agreed to stay. She'd also convinced Lettie and Andres to stay. They'd already moved into the downstairs guest bedroom—temporarily, anyway, back when Lettie was sure she was getting deported. And when, by some miracle that Mel could only explain as a karmic fuck-you to the Big Cheeto, Lettie was granted sudden clemency after a victorious court date, Mel had insisted they move out of their apartment in West LA completely and live with her on Georgina Avenue.

And they had.

"I am picking Andres up now," Lettie said, standing from her chair and stepping toward the sliding door to the bedroom. "His therapy is finished at ten. The therapist says he is doing *much* better!"

"Oh, Lettie, that's wonderful," said Mel. "I'm going for a run soon, then heading to the paper store." Since she and Adam had split, she'd revived Dogwood Designs West, in an edgier, artsier new location in Venice, and had already landed a few small projects—printing a program for the Shakespeare Festival in Topanga, creating the menus for Sukie Reinhardt's niece's wedding. Baby steps, but it felt good to be working again. "Can I take you and Andres to lunch later?"

"Sure." Lettie pulled open the door and stepped inside. Then she turned back to Mel and wagged her finger, smiling. "You are getting too skinny, you know. I will make you eat a real lunch. No kale."

"Never." Mel giggled. "Bye, Lettie."

Somehow, Mel had actually learned to love running. And in the process, she'd shed the twenty pounds she'd regained after quitting Color Theory. And then some.

Alone on the balcony, she pressed her hands against the railing and leaned over the yard. The beauty of it still astonished her—the trees, the flowers, the air tinged with the perfume of gardenias and salt wafting off the dreamy blue Pacific, which she could just glimpse in the distance—but she'd grown accustomed to it, too. Brooklyn was in the past along with Adam, along with Zack. Along with all—okay, *some*—of the reasons she'd once found to hate herself.

Mel knew she was not yet as good as a woman could be. Far from it. But she was on her way. Zack would be proud.

42

LETICIA

Lettie still had nightmares. Andres screaming for help—*Ayúdame! Mama!*—her little boy shaking with fear on the back patio of Mel's house, surrounded by bodies leaping into the air. Bodies forming a wall. Lettie trapped on one side, Andres on the other.

Here! Lettie shouted in the bad dream. *I am here!* She jumped up and down like one of the exercising people, waving an arm. *I am coming to you, my baby—wait for Mama!*

But someone had turned up the volume and pounding dance music crashed out of the speakers.

Get after it, people! the crazy tattooed lady yelled. *Show me them jump squats!*

Tío! Andres howled.

And this was when Lettie always woke, the neck of her pajama shirt heavy with sweat, her son's cries ringing in her ears, her wide eyes searching for Andres, who was, each time, peacefully asleep right next to Lettie in the big bed of Mel's guest bedroom.

Now it was Lettie and Andres's bedroom, although no matter how many times Mel promised Lettie this was true, she could not quite believe it. Found herself waiting for bad news, expecting, any minute, for Mel to ask Lettie and Andres to leave the big and beautiful home on Georgina Avenue.

Lettie wished she could tell Mel the truth of Zacarias's death. Like when she found Mel crying in the sauna Mel had installed by the pool after Adam moved out.

There was only one reason Mel was crying, Lettie knew, for her favorite boss, now a true friend—and roommate—was happy. But for the loss of Zacarias.

Lettie missed him, too. Zacarias the clown. Zacarias the ladies' man. Most, she missed *Tío* Zacarias—the man who kissed Andres's boo-boos and rocked him to sleep when he had a fever. Poor Andres mourned his *tío* with tears Lettie had feared were endless. But the minds of children are changeable, Lettie knew. Two years, maybe less, and Andres's memory of his handsome uncle would be just as hazy as the accident. His *tío* more a hero in a fairy tale than a living, breathing man. Like Lettie's own memories of her and Zack's *abuela*, who had passed away in her sleep just two weeks after Lettie found her brother on the gym floor.

Children were given a gift, Lettie thought, a chance to scrub clean memories of pain and loss and disappointment, like a wash-cloth dragged across a greasy countertop. Good as new.

Lettie too had been given a new beginning. A *re-do* as Mel said to Sloane when the fiery girl fought with her mother, blaming her for the divorce. *Version two*, as Lettie heard Mel call her life after Adam with a bittersweet laugh.

Lettie was taking classes at Santa Monica community college. What a country—America! A free education for any person who wanted to learn, even a poor without-papers woman with a record. Melissa had helped her study for the GED exam, reassuring Lettie when she failed the test not once, but twice. *No biggie*, as Andres liked to say, because here Lettie was, taking classes to earn a certificate in Recycling and Resource Management. Now she was an expert recycler, and hoped to, someday, visit schools, just like the pretty lady in the white doctor's coat at the assembly at Andres's school. She would teach children to save Mother Earth and fight the war against evil climate change.

She had convinced Melissa to stop watering the thirsty front and back lawn, and started a compost pile behind the avocado tree. So what if the rats came at night for a little snack? She was helping save the planet.

Lettie had been saved twice. First by Mr. Jensen, who had put a long and muscled arm around her shaking shoulders as the paramedics lifted Zacarias's still body into the back of the ambulance. She would never forget Mr. Jensen's scent—manly aftershave and mint candies—as he'd whispered close to her ear, shushing her like she was a child. *Everything will be okay, Lucretia.* The snake didn't even know her name. She'd fought the desire to shove him away, kick at his knees with her piss-soaked sneakers, stomp on his face that was so free of lines he seemed to be wearing one of the rubber masks she and Zacarias had worn on Halloween.

But who was *she*? No one. Worse, one of the illegals El Trumpo and his gang blamed for all the problems in America.

She had known staying silent was wrong. That she should go to the police. Tell them something was rotten with Mr. Jensen. Why couldn't the police see it themselves? Were they so stupid they could not see how pale Mr. Jensen was, or how his hands shook, or the bruises on his neck under the turned-up collar of his shirt?

We see what we want to see, she knew that now, and forever. Promised herself it would be one of the many lessons she'd teach Andres so he'd be sure to survive this ugly world.

Everything will be okay, Mr. Jensen had said again and again, like a child waking from a bad dream.

In the back office of the gym, she'd sat with her hands tucked between her legs, not caring if her wet sweatpants made the chair smell like pee, staring past Mr. Jensen's stiff silver hair. She listened, nodding as he talked and talked and talked. She'd learned this quickly in America—how the rich white people used so many words to try to fix their mistakes, as if words had the power of the chemicals she used to clean toilets free of their stinking shit.

We don't want to scare the community, he had said. *So, I'd appreciate it . . . I'd be very appreciative . . .*

She had laughed. Another man using big words that meant nothing to her.

I understand, Mr. Jensen had said. *You're in shock.*

You will give me money. She had surprised herself—was that *her* voice giving commands like a captain?

Yes, of course.

She waited a few long beats, thinking. *I have a small problem with the law. A shoplifting arrest. You will make that problem go away.*

Absolutely. Mr. Jensen pumped his head back and forth. *I'm more than happy. Zack would want—*

Lettie cut in. *Do not use his name.*

She had never interrupted a white man. She had never interrupted any man, knowing it would have brought only pain—openhanded slaps from her uncles and man cousins; worse from Manuel.

The power burned through her—like fire and ice racing through her veins, making her heart beat so fast she lifted a fist to her chest. It had come to her after she had seen her brother flat on the gym floor, neck bent, shit and piss pooled under him. After she'd cleaned up the mess, the chemicals stinging her eyes and numbing her fingertips through the plastic gloves she wore. Most of all, Lettie's power came after Mr. Jensen had appeared from the parking lot behind the studio—had the coward been hiding in the gym's van?—and locked his lizard eyes to hers, pretending to be shocked at the scene.

Knowing she knew the truth.

Now, with her power, Lettie was seeing the world as it truly was for the first time. Knowing people would stop at nothing to get what they needed. Knowing she should be no different.

You will give me all the money I tell you to give, Mr. Jensen. I know you have much money. My brother, Zacarias, he told me. And you will also fix my problems with the law. You will talk to the courts. You will pay.

As Mr. Jensen nodded, his sharp jaw like a saw in the dim light of Color Theory Fitness, Lettie spat on the spongy floor. The foamy wetness landed beside her employer's foot. She would not clean it up. She was finished cleaning up their messes, the fortunate souls of Santa Monica.

ACKNOWLEDGMENTS

Mega-thanks to:

Our Queens in the Machine: Susan Golomb, Maria Massie, Sara Nelson, and Mary Gaule

The Fierro Feinstein and Wolfson Widger families

Kenia, Ita, and Yolanda

The Sackett Writers' Workshop

The city of Santa Monica

Circuit Works

The transcendent power of friendship

ABOUT THE AUTHOR

Cassidy Lucas is the pen name of writing duo Julia Fierro and Caeli Wolfson Widger. Fierro is the author of the novels *Cutting Teeth*, praised by *The New Yorker* as a "comically energetic debut," and *The Gypsy Moth Summer*, called "hugely engaging" by Francine Prose. Widger is the author of the novels *Real Happy Family* and *Mother of Invention*, praised by Margaret Atwood as a "pacey thriller!" and was featured on NPR's *Marketplace*. Both Fierro and Widger live in Santa Monica with their families. This is their first book together.